SKELMERSDALE

SUBJECT TO RECALL
Item on Loan From
QL/P-3 Lancashire

8 DEC 2009

Our Ref:

Your Ref:

SUBJECT TO RECALL
Item on Loan From
QL/P-3 Lancashire

30 DEC 2009
1496945
Out 1496940

FICTION RESERVE STOCK LL 60

1704

AUTHOR	CLASS
SALISBURY, C	F
TITLE	No
Autumn in Araby	WHALLEY
	18349053

Lancashire
County
Council

This book should be returned on or before the
latest date shown above to the library from
which it was borrowed.

LIBRARY HEADQUARTERS
143, CORPORATION ST, PRESTON, PR1 2TB

D1429118

a30118

An Autumn in Araby

By the same author

MALLION'S PRIDE
DARK INHERITANCE

CAROLA SALISBURY

An Autumn in Araby

CENTURY PUBLISHING
LONDON

Copyright © Carola Salisbury 1983

All rights reserved

First published in Great Britain in 1983 by
Century Publishing Co. Ltd,
76 Old Compton Street, London W1V 5PA

ISBN 0 7126 0169 4

WHALLEY

~~CHATBURN~~

18349053

Typeset by Rowland Phototypesetting Ltd
Bury St Edmunds, Suffolk
Printed in Great Britain by
St Edmundsbury Press
Bury St Edmunds, Suffolk

For Rosie

Part One

AT CASTLE DELAMERE,
SUFFOLK, ENGLAND

ONE

Today I stood on the uppermost tower of Castle Delamere and looked out first at the crawling grey North Sea and the great ships passing down towards London river, the Channel, the wild waste of the Atlantic, and the whole wide world beyond. Some of them I imagined to be following the course that I, Suzanna, took in the autumn of 1869, through the Pillars of Hercules to that bluest and most beautiful sea which laps the shores of the ancient world where civilisation was born. And then I was back in the land of the Pharaohs, under the sky of illimitable blue, or in the velvety dusk that lasts only enough time for the evening stars to light up the great canopy of night; then I seemed to catch the perfumes of jasmine and mimosa, the heady aroma of night-scented honeysuckle and that indefinable tang of the desert beyond the palm groves and the white villages where patient donkeys toil round and round the wells all night and day. The desert – garden of Allah.

From the sea, I looked towards the land: to the crumbling cliffs of Suffolk and the slender causeway that connects Castle Delamere, and the fang of rock upon which it stands, to the mainland; a tenuous track that can only be negotiated at low tide and disappears completely in the high tides of the springs which occur every lunar month.

As I stood there, I seemed to see the coming and going of many people who had inhabited the castle from old times: the wild Vikings from across the grey sea who had first fortified the rock against all comers and made it the base for their brutal forays into the hinterland; the black-clad monks who had briefly turned the fortress into an abbey, till the minions of Henry VIII tore down their chapel and dispersed the brotherhood (some claim to have heard the chanting of their plainsong coming from the ruins of the chapel on All Hallows Eve); and then I seemed to see the folk of the later centuries, when the fortress-turned-abbey became a gracious house that has been continuously inhabited ever since. With the waves lapping hungrily at the base of the causeway, they came in their fine coaches and carriages, on horseback, on foot.

On such a day as today, I first came to Castle Delamere, in a hired governess-cart from the village; rattling over the ancient stone paving that the Romans had laid down, swayed by the ruts and runnels, anxious in my heart that I should find everything there as I hoped it might be, but already overawed by the defeating, slab-sided grandeur of the great building that rose, battlement above battlement, tower over tower, pinnacle soaring on pinnacle, the seabirds wheeling and screeching atop of all.

So long ago. Or so it seems . . .

'Will you be wantin' to be fetched back, Miss – or are you a-stayin' at the castle?'

'I'm staying,' I replied. 'My things are being brought from the posting house later today.'

The cart-driver nodded and looked a bit askance, no doubt wondering why he had not been given the extra perquisite of bringing my traps along with me to Castle Delamere.

'I have rather a lot of luggage,' I explained.

He nodded. 'You'll be a-stayin' for quite a while then?'

'Perhaps. I don't know.'

By now, almost within the shadow of the highest tower, we had reached that part of the causeway that rose steeply towards a massive stone archway leading into the vast interior. The driver was obliged to whip up his horse to take the slippery, seaweed-crusted slope, and it was not till we reached the summit that I perceived a drawbridge spanning a wide gap betwixt the end of the causeway and the archway. Moments later, we were rumbling over the huge timbers of the bridge, through whose chinks and on either side of the wooden balustrades one could see the wild green waters seething far below and reaching up pale fingers to claw at the time-worn rocks.

We went under the archway, from whose roof a row of rusty spikes revealed the presence of the barred steel gate that would have been lowered, in days of yore, as a further barrier against the invasion of the castle's dark privacy. Through the arch – and out into the unexpected warmth of a sunlit courtyard.

Our arrival had not gone unnoticed. A woman in black with a long chatelaine of keys suspended from her waist came forward to greet me. About forty-five I put her, with a lived-in sort of face and watchful eyes, her grey-streaked hair drawn back in a severe chignon; she had the remains of what must have been a considerable beauty of face and form.

'Miss Copley?' She took my proffered hand. 'I am Mrs Stittle, housekeeper to Mr Ormerod. The Master is away at Nunwich today, but requests that you join him for dinner in the great hall tonight.'

'And the little boy?'

'Master Rupert is resting, Miss. He sleeps for two hours after luncheon every day. Doctor's orders.' She looked in puzzlement to see me paying off the cart-driver and taking down the small carpet-bag containing my washing gear and a change of linen. 'Is that all the luggage you have, Miss?' she asked, relieving me of the bag.

I explained that the rest of my traps would be following, and added: 'There was so much, you see, that Mr Ormerod wrote requesting me to purchase in London.'

She nodded. 'Ah, yes. He told me about that.'

'Though why it is necessary, I simply don't understand,' I said.

She looked wise; tapped my arm. 'Ah, Miss, when you see Master Rupert – poor little mite – you'll understand,' she said.

The governess-cart was clattering back over the drawbridge as Mrs Stittle led me up a steep flight of stone steps and in through what I took to be the main door of the principal keep, or tower, of the castle. On that October day, though bright and sunny without, my first impression of the building's interior was of a chilling coldness, a graveyard and crypt coldness. This was instantly dispelled by the sight of a vast log fire burning within a grate that must have been all of twelve feet wide and recessed deeply into the stonework of a wall. As I followed my guide, passing close by the fire, I first experienced the bizarre sensation of being chilled on one side of my body and half-roasted on the other.

The hall in which the fire blazed was a quite small apartment furnished only with an oak table in the centre, set upon an oriental rug that gleamed darkly with sombre colours like the skin of an exotic snake. Upon the table was a silver salver and upon that a letter. I could not resist snatching a glance at the latter as I went past on the heels of the housekeeper, and read the legend penned upon its face:

> *Justin Ormerod, Esquire, R.A.*
> *Castle Delamere,*
> *East Suffolk.*

– which is as splendidly exiguous an address as will be found anywhere in the land.

'I will show you first to your suite, Miss,' said my guide, 'for I've no doubt you'll wish to rest a while after your journey. And I'll have a pitcher of hot water brought up to your dressing-room.'

'Thank you,' I replied. The notion of being waited on in my dressing-room – indeed the very notion of *possessing* a dressing-room – was like awakening to a new life.

We came to an archway set in the far wall of the hall, and a spiral of worn stone steps leading up into darkness, through which, with the eye of faith, one could dimly perceive the thin loom of daylight like a good deed in a naughty world.

'Have a care, Miss,' said the housekeeper. 'The steps are very steep, but you'll get used to them. At night, you must always bring a candle, of course.'

The first turn in the spiral staircase brought an increase of daylight; on the second turn, its source was revealed as an arrow slit in the outer wall that broadened out to a wide embrasure on the inner, disclosing the solid stonework to be all of five feet thick. Peering out and down, I could see the North

Sea crawling past below, wave after slow wave; and an open fishing boat bobbing past under sail, with a fine flurry of spray flung high over her bows.

We came to a narrow landing and an oaken, iron-studded door. 'There's nothing here,' said Mrs Stittle, indicating the door. 'This floor's used to store unwanted furniture and stuff. It's directly under yours, which is on the floor above.'

Three more turns in the spiral staircase, two more arrow-slits, and we came to a landing and a door that was a counterfeit of the one below. Mrs Stittle depressed the latch and the door swung open on well-oiled hinges, displaying a soft glow of muted light that, after the sombre gloom of the staircase, was exceedingly pleasant to the eyes.

'This is your sitting-room, Miss,' said Mrs Stittle. 'The bedroom and the dressing-room's beyond. From this window, on a fine day, you can see along the coast to the north as far as Lowestoft, and on a very fine day, I swear you could see as far as Norwich – if 't' were not for the hills in the way.'

I gazed, and was enraptured. It was not beautiful: such an expression fell far short of the majesty and sublimity of the coastal view from my sitting-room window perched atop of Castle Delamere. There I stood watching – with the eye of a wheeling seagull high above the sea and the rocks – a panorama that stretched from the causeway, along the beaches and cliffs to the northward, to the shifting mists that shut out all else beyond. From that wide window, I counted a score of craft of all sizes ploughing the rippled furrows under full sail in the spanking breeze, and some were shaping course so as to pass close to the jutting rock and castle upon which I was perched on high.

My sudden ecstasy was broken by a distant cry. It came from afar, for it was faint, though oddly clear, reverberating up the staircase like a note blown through a hunting horn.

'What was that?' I asked.

'Nothing. A seabird, Miss,' responded the housekeeper. But her eyes avoided mine.

'It sounded like – someone screaming in pain,' I said.

'They do say that the souls of drowned sailors inhabit the bodies of seagulls,' said Mrs Stittle. 'Mayhap it was the sound

15

you heard – a sort of scream – that started the legend in the first place.'

'It sounded to me more like a woman's scream,' I declared. And I cast a sharp look at her. 'Or the scream of a child.'

'Not a child's scream, Miss,' replied the other, and consulted a fob watch that hung from her corsage. 'Master Rupert will now be taking his tea in the nursery with the between-maid who's been acting as nanny since the last one left.'

'Oh, I should like to see him,' I said.

Mrs Stittle shook her head and looked – how to put it? – evasive. 'I wouldn't advise it, Miss,' she said. 'The little feller's not got much of an appetite and has to be coaxed with every mouthful. If you were to appear on the scene, Tweeny would never get so much as another mouthful into him this day.'

'Is he, then, a very – *difficult* child?' I asked her.

But she was not to be drawn. ''Tis not for me to say, Miss,' she replied. 'As I said before, when you see him, you'll understand. And now, Miss, this is your bedroom, with the dressing-room beyond . . .'

Resigning myself to getting nothing further from the woman regarding my new charge, I followed her through a door leading off the sitting-room, to a vaulted, semi-circular chamber whose stone walls were hung, in part, with faded tapestries depicting scenes of the chase, with huntsmen, horse and hounds hallooing through sylvan landscapes. A row of three slender, pointed windows looked out across the sea, filling the chamber with that same soft light through the bottle-glass panes that had so enchanted me upon entering the sitting-room. The bed was sheer delight: a faerie's bed with a high canopy topped with a gilded coronet and hung with swags of stiff silk in a faded gold. As in the sitting-room, the furnishings were of the simple elegance that breathes good taste and riches. There was none of the clutter that characterises our modern interiors; naught but an armchair of gilded wood, upholstered with striped silk of maroon and gold, and a sofa or day-bed in the same manner – which I took to be that of the previous century. A dressing-table and vanity mirror stood by the window wall, a scattering of oriental rugs covered part of the flagged floor like stepping-stones across a cold stream; that was all. The dressing-room that lay off the bedchamber was a narrow compartment containing all the usual offices including an enormous copper hip-bath that was polished to mirror brightness.

'All very nice, Mrs Stittle,' I told the woman. 'Thank you.'

'What time shall you require the hot water, Miss?' she responded. The watchful eyes were searching mine. 'And are you going to take a rest before you meet the master at dinner?'

'I think it might be wise,' I replied.

'Mr Ormerod would like you to join him in the library at seven.'

'Then I had better have the water at six, please. And will whoever brings it wake me if I am not already up?'

She nodded and went out. And I had the distinct impression of someone who was relieved that I was to be asleep and out of the way.

I stripped to my shift and went over to the window. No need for shutters or curtains, for the nearest neighbour in that direction would be the good burghers of Holland, and only the seagulls overlooked my eyrie. Standing there, in the dying afternoon, I thought back over the steps that had brought me to Castle Delamere and the strange charge to which I had been delivered: to look after the ailing, motherless son of one of England's renowned painters – renowned for his work, that is, but unknown in his private life; all my enquiries had evinced nothing about the man whose employment I was to enter, save that he lived in an ancient castle off a desolate part of the East Anglian coast, and in the manner of a recluse.

And the son? What of the child Rupert? What of the strange list of items that I had been instructed to collect and bring from London, which would shortly be arriving – may, indeed, already have arrived – from the posting house in a large cart?

Surely, a child in need of such a plethora of medicaments and outlandish instruments must be very ill indeed, and of an illness that beggared all diagnosis as I understood it.

And why had Mrs Stittle been so evasive about the child?

'When you see the poor little mite, you'll understand . . .'

As I lay myself down upon the faerie bed and drew the coverlet across me, my fingers stole of their own accord to the pearl and garnet ring that I wear round my neck on a fine silver chain, and at its touch, all thoughts of my present circumstance faded to insignificance, and all my mind concentrated upon the great and new tragedy of my life, which had driven me to escape as far as possible from the surroundings that brought the bitter memories rushing back – even to this furthest wild edge of England.

TWO

I was born, the only child of Nathan and Amy Copley, in the parish of Hickleydoek, which is on the southern edge of Dartmoor in the county of Devon, and I was named Suzanna May after my maternal grandmother, who followed her soldier husband to India and died of cholera and is buried there in Cawnpore.

From the top window of our thatched cottage, and on a clear day, one could see the silvery strip of sea beyond the coastal hills to the south that marks the approach to Plymouth Sound; while to the north, the craggy tors of the great moor rise, peak beyond peak, to a horizon of – it seemed to me then – almost continuous mist and rain.

From the top window, also – which was my bedroom window – one could also spy into the grounds of Hickleydoek Manor, seat of the Launey family, squires of the village and its environs since the Middle Ages. Many's the time I have crouched there, in my nightgown, wakeful at some forbidden hour after having been put to bed, read to, and admonished to be a good girl and sleep tight, to see the comings and goings at the Manor: the gentry arriving in their carriages and on horseback for a night of junketing in the great stone-flagged hall that we common folk only saw on one day of the year, on Christmas Eve, when Squire Launey and his family played host to their tenants and workers, together with their families; when we feasted off a whole ram roasted over the vast open fire, together with pasties, thick sausages, blood-puddings, tripe and chitterlings, potatoes baked in their jackets, with rough cider for the grown-ups and blackberry cordial for the children and the religious folks. And after the feasting, we would line up, the grown-ups at the head, and receive our Christmas gifts from the hands of the squire, his lady wife, Giles his son and Felicity his daughter.

The remembrance of Giles Launey, even now, after all that had passed between us, still has the power to make my breath quicken, to remind me of the golden hours of summer and sunshine, the soon-gone days of early youth and all its promises of fair seasons and quiet waters. Giles was a midshipman in the Royal Navy when first I was allowed to accompany my parents to the Christmas Eve party at the Manor: tall and straight he was in his short blue tunic with the three buttons at the cuffs and the white patches at the collar. He was as fair as a Viking, with steely-blue eyes and the complexion of a Devon man and a seaman – ruddy and tanned with the reflection of sun off sea. He was but sixteen, and I only twelve, but I loved him on the instant, and for many years after. And even now, as I have said, the memory of him invokes passions I would rather forget, for a woman never, ever, forgets her first love.

I was wearing my first long frock of blue taffety, and my hair pinned up in a chignon. Feeling tremendously superior to all the other children lined up before and behind me, I waited my turn to be presented with my gift.

Squire and Mrs Launey, Master Giles and Miss Felicity, stood by the bran tub, from which each in their turn took out a present: in the case of the adults, it had been a flitch of bacon or a bottle of porter, a silk scarf or a fairing; for the children, a wooden-top dolly, a bouncing ball, a tin soldier, a picture of the Duke of Wellington at Waterloo – something of that sort.

I had known Master Giles from afar, for had I not seen him riding past on his spirited black hunter many a time, and he never so much as acknowledging my presence by a salute with his whip. Now he stood by the bran tub, and, with the prescience that informs the hearts of all lovers, be they never so young and untried, I *knew* – or, at least, I thought I knew – that he had picked me out from the common ruck of village girls in their gingham and their plaits. Upon that instant, my breath quickened, and I felt my cheeks begin to flame, my palms to moisten.

My turn came . . .

'Why, it's little Suzanna Copley. My, how you've grown, child,' said Mrs Squire Launey, delving into the bran tub and bringing out a wooden-top dolly.

'Mama, I think, I rather fancy . . .'

My glance stole to the speaker. It was Giles Launey. He was looking straight at me as he addressed his mother, and he was smiling: a quirky, appraising sort of smile at the behest of which I would have gathered up a swarm of bees without a qualm.

'What is it, Giles?' demanded his mother, puzzled.

'I rather fancy that Miss Suzanna *(and I who had never been addressed as "Miss Suzanna" before in my whole life!)* is a trifle too old for dollies, Mama. Don't you think that –' he reached down and took from the bran tub a silken Paisley scarf of greens and blues most cunningly interwoven – 'that a grown-up young lady would much prefer – this?'

When I stand at the Bar of Judgement, when all things must be answered for, I shall not forget the thrill of wanting and needing that swept through me when I – a mere child of twelve – had the Paisley scarf gently looped round my shoulders by Mr Midshipman Giles Launey, Royal Navy, and tied there – no doubt with a correct reef knot, sailor-fashion.

All the world may well love a lover, but ill-will in the shape of the British Admiralty had no thought for little Suzanna Copley in her newly-discovered passion, for Giles Launey was dispatched with his ship to the China Station immediately after that memorable Christmas, and I did not see him again for six long years, though scarcely a day passed when I did not think of him with fond regret.

My father's family were Devonian born and bred, and farmers to a man from time immemorial, while on my mother's side, the menfolk had mostly all been of the military persuasion. Uncle Josh, mother's brother, who was a Riding Master in the 17th Lancers and had taken part in the famous charge of the Light Brigade during the terrible Crimean War, had newly retired from the service by the time of my eighteenth birthday and was present at our cottage on that occasion.

It was a happy family gathering, and my mother had baked a

cake and iced it for the event. I blew out eighteen candles and made a wish, the matter of which I would not have divulged to a soul, not if they had pulled out my toenails with red-hot pincers. And, needless to say, the wish concerned Giles Launey in far-off China.

'What's the lass going to do with herself till she's wed?' demanded Uncle Josh, who had commandeered my father's chair on the right-hand side of the fireplace and was smoking a pipe of a most villainous stench.

'Suzanna has helped around the farm since she left school,' responded my mother. 'She has a good hand for the milking, and because her hands are cool, can make cream cheese to perfection.' She reached out and gave my shoulders a fond hug. 'My girl will bide here quite happily till some fine young Dartmoor lad woos and wins her and takes her away from us.'

'*I'm having no Dartmoor hobbledehoy for a husband!*' cried someone, and I realised with a sense of shock that it must have been me, and that the family were all looking at me open-mouthed, all save Uncle Josh, who was grinning.

'Suzanna!' breathed Mother, disapprovingly. 'That's no way to speak of our kind. Your father's people have farmed Dartmoor for longer than the records tell. Hobbledehoy, indeed!'

'I'm sorry, Mama,' I said with contrition, and I really was sorry to have offended them. But how could I tell them, how express, the feeling that was within me? The only person in the whole wide world I wanted to marry was Giles Launey, and he was separated from me by barriers of class, wealth, position, rank, that by no contrivance in our mid-nineteenth-century England could either of us surmount. If I could not be his, I would be nobody's – my mind had been made up on that score for years.

'Well,' said Uncle Josh, exhaling another mouthful of the reeking smoke, 'if the lass isn't for marrying, then she must have a career. Not the marrying sort myself, and in consequence not having had experience o' raising offspring, I would say that I'm badly placed to offer advice. On the other hand, 'tis truly said that he who stands on the boundary may often see the finer points of a game o' cricket.'

'True enough, Josh,' responded my father, who deferred to his brother-in-law in most matters, being a gentle, uncomplicated soul and an ardent admirer of the lean, craggy ex-cavalry-man in the faded lancer's blues who lolled in his favourite chair and who signified for him – a Devon hill-farmer who had never travelled further than Plymouth and Exeter – the whole wide world of adventure beyond the confines of Dartmoor. 'So what would you advise for the lass, eh?'

Uncle Josh looked sagely at me over the bowl of his pipe, as if I might have been a cavalry charger whose wind was sound but whose fetlocks might be a matter of some concern. 'I would say without fear o' contradiction,' declared he, 'that had the lass been a lad, you should have placed him in the Army by now, in the cavalry for preference, and my old regiment the 17th Lancers, the "Death or Glory" boys, 'as first choice. How-somever, she ain't a lad, but a lass.'

'Quite so,' said my father. And no one seemed to have anything to add to that, least of all I.

'Albeit,' continued Uncle Josh, 'sitting as I have been on the boundary o' the game – in a manner of speaking – I have observed a certain quality o' womankind which has extended my regard for the inferior sex far beyond what I would have believed possible in the days afore the Crimea. I speak o' Miss Nightingale and her ladies.'

Florence Nightingale! Of course, Uncle Josh, having been thrice wounded in that war, had regaled us many times, and at length, with the vast changes which the legendary Miss Night-ingale had wrought by her persistent efforts, and against all odds of male military opposition, in the medical and nursing services in Scutari, where wounded soldiers – sometimes not gravely wounded soldiers – were formerly brought in to die unattended, but where later, thanks to the iron determination and infinite compassion of 'the lady with the lamp', even the most gravely hurt stood a chance of life – or at least a decent end, well-tended.

'But how does this touch upon our Suzanna's future?' asked Mother.

'Ah, I had thought you might ask me that,' said Uncle Josh. 'And I have the answer right here, Amy.' He wagged his finger at his sister. 'I have information that Miss Nightingale has opened a training school for nurses at St Thomas's Hospital, London, which is hard by Thames river in the city o' Westminster, and that she is seeking for young women of the right sort to apply.' He fixed me with his shrewd gaze and searched me out, the inner part of me. 'And what do you think o' that for a notion, young Suzanna? Answer me straight.'

It seemed to me then that all my life had been but a preparation for that moment, and the latter years, with the presence of my hopeless love shutting out all other options for happiness, the crowning factor pointing me to a vocation that transcended the calls of the flesh.

'I should be proud and happy, Uncle,' I told him, 'to serve with Miss Nightingale.'

My mother burst into tears, and I think I may have been crying too.

Somehow, it was arranged . . .

Somehow, from the wilds of Devon, my parents managed to obtain the address of the organisation which was administering the training school for nurses at St Thomas's Hospital, London. By return of post there came a note informing Mr and Mrs Copley that Miss Nightingale herself would personally interview Miss Suzanna Copley with a view to admitting her to the training school which would commence studies in the following July. A room was booked in advance at a Paddington boarding-house for Mother and me; and on a February day of high blue skies and sparkling frost, we set off from Exeter in the railway train to the metropolis. The journey, though punctuated by frequent halts caused by snowdrifts on the line and by the locomotive running first out of water and then out of fuel (so we were reliably informed), was completed in less than five hours – a time that has scarcely been bettered to this day.

At noon precisely, we came into Mr Isambard Kingdom Brunel's majestic station hall at Paddington, took ourselves a hansom cab to our boarding-house, spruced ourselves up, and presented ourselves at St Thomas's Hospital at three-thirty sharp. The chimes of the great city, from St Paul's to Bow, from Bow back to St Paul's and on down to St Bride's, St Clement's,

St Martin's, and to the nearby bells of the great Westminster Abbey across the river, were sounding the half-hour as Mother and I tiptoed nervously across the polished parquet of the hospital hallway and addressed ourselves – and, surely, we must have looked like a couple of countrywomen up to the metropolis to sell eggs – to a functionary behind a desk, who, first glowering at us unenthusiastically from behind a pince-nez and afterwards referring to a list set before him on his desk, declared that we were one minute late and that Miss Nightingale would receive Miss Copley immediately; and – this was delivered with a pointed finger directed towards my poor, shrinking mother – Miss Nightingale would receive Miss Copley *alone*!

'Come!'

That was the answer to my knock upon a door covered in green baize to which I had been directed by the functionary.

I came . . .

The room beyond was light and airy, and so near to the river that shifting glances of reflected light from its ever-moving surface were being played out upon the ceiling. The figure seated behind the huge desk in the barely-furnished and size-able room seemed dwarfed by her surroundings. The impression did not remain for long in my mind: Florence Nightingale was not long, or often, dwarfed by anything or anyone.

'You are Suzanna May Copley?'

'Yes, ma'am.' I bobbed her a curtsey.

'Sit down, Suzanna May Copley.'

'Yes, ma'am. Thank you, ma'am.' And I took my place in a straight-backed chair and wondered at the thought that I was almost within touching distance of she who was arguably the most famous woman in the Western world – even though the battle smoke of the Crimea and her triumphs at Scutari had faded four years previously and she had shunned the public eye ever since.

'Mmmm.' Miss Nightingale looked down at a sheaf of papers laid before her, uppermost of which was the letter of application written in my own hand, the outcome of many drafts. Studying the face opposite, I saw the marks of nervous energy that had carried her through her tremendous task, and signs – a tautness about the mouth, a faint shadowing under the eyes – that told of the price she had paid to serve the wounded and abandoned.

'Why do you want to nurse?' The question came like the flick of a whiplash, and she did not look up.

'I – I . . .' My voice tailed off to silence. Faced by the huge and imponderable question, stripped of asides and affectations, I had no answer. Or, rather, I had a score of answers, but none of them matched Miss Nightingale's question in all its starkness.

'Why, surely, you must have a reason.' She looked up, and I quailed before her glance, and knew how it was that she had been able – one small woman in an alien land – to surmount the prejudices of the male military mind and carry all before her.

I could only stare at her; the words would not come.

'Put it this way,' she said. 'You have taken the trouble to make an application to join the training school. You have come, and at some trouble and expense, all the way from Devon to attend this interview. And yet you are unable to answer the perfectly simple question as to why you want to nurse. I find this very odd.'

I swallowed hard. 'There – there are many reasons, ma'am,' I faltered.

Her chin went up. The tired eyes fixed me very firmly. 'I am doubtful,' she said, 'of young ladies who come to me with too many reasons for wanting to follow the discipline of nursing. All too often, in my experience, a plethora of reasons masks a lack of calling, of vocation.'

'Ma'am, I promise you that . . .'

She spoke right through me: 'All too often, with such young ladies, I have found a certain instability of purpose. The will to succeed, to serve, has no permanence. In the face of the rigours of our calling – and they are many – the innumerable reasons that have prompted the probationer to take on the task of nursing show themselves to be no substitute for an iron core of conviction, of dedication, which distinguishes the dilettante from the woman of true vocation.'

'Ma'am, I'm sure that I . . .'

'All too soon,' continued Miss Nightingale, 'such persons

falter in their tasks and search out their minds: "Did I do the right thing in giving myself to this work?" The answer – inevitably, when the question is asked, or else the question never would be asked – is: "No".'

'Ma'am, it's not like that with me. I . . .'

'*Will you not interrupt me, child!*' The tired eyes blazed with the fire that must have stilled the protests of army placemen, swept aside the prejudices of generals and pashas, of titled nabobs in the medical profession.

She resumed: 'The answer to their self-directed question being "No", it only remains for them to invert one of their many reasons for becoming a nurse into equally excellent reasons for quitting the vocation. Hence, a young woman will persuade herself that she, after all, would much prefer to take her place in smart society and do the London Season, hunt with the Quorn, be seen in Brighton, winter in Baden-Baden, yacht in the Solent.'

'Ma'am . . .'

'Equally, she will convince herself that, after all, she is not cut out to act as a second pair of hands and eyes to a fellow creature who cannot fend for himself; but would rather donate sums of money to charity and distance herself from the essential un-pleasantness that lies at the end of charity's long arm. Or, she may very well decide that, after all, her true vocation in life is that of marriage and the rearing of children. In which case, it could only be said that she was following the natural desire of womankind, which is to seek, or to be sought out by, a mate of her own kind, and . . .'

'NEVER!' I cried.

'What did you say, child?' demanded Miss Nightingale in a voice of ice.

'If you will only be quiet for a few moments, ma'am,' I said, 'I will tell you the true and only reason for wanting to be a nurse, which is that I don't ever intend to marry, but to devote my life to the sick. So there!'

It had been said. I had stated my case, which, but for a few moments' confusion of mind, I could have stated from the first.

But the manner of my doing it . . . !

I was aghast at my insolence, my staggering temerity.

I – little country bumpkin Suzanna Copley – had had the effrontery to tell the most famous woman in the Western world to be quiet!

In the long silence that followed, I saw my chances slip away into nothing, like sand between the fingers of an open hand. She neither spoke nor gave any sign; but remained looking at me with cold, reflective eyes, mouth set in a hard, straight line.

Presently, unable to bear any more of her regard, I raised myself awkwardly to my feet, and in doing so caught my heel in the hem of my skirt and all but stumbled and fell across her desk; but I managed to recover myself if not my composure and to back away towards the door, face flaming. The cool regard followed me all the way.

'I – I thank you for receiving me, ma'am,' I faltered, conscious that my bonnet had been tipped askew during my near fall, and realising that I must look like some tipsy fishwife. 'And I bid you a very good day.'

Miss Nightingale picked up the sheaf of papers that lay before her and settled them straight, tapping them edgewise on the desk top and aligning them true. And all the time neither a change of expression, nor the ghost of a change of expression, passed across her impassive countenance.

'Present yourself here on July ninth at eight-thirty in the morning,' she said. 'The bursar outside will give you full details as regards clothing, accommodation, the few and simple rules of the training school, and so forth. Good day to you, Miss Copley.'

The eyes returned to the papers before her.

I joined the Nightingale training school at St Thomas's Hospital the following July, together with fourteen others who had been selected out of many hundred applicants. Why I – a country girl from a peasant family, the recipient of only an elementary village school education – should have been preferred above the daughters of the professional classes, even of titled ladies, will forever remain a mystery to me; though on the few occasions that I came upon Miss Nightingale about the hospital I sometimes chanced to see her giving a wry smile upon our encounter: a secret, turned-in sort of smile meant for herself alone – and it occurred to me then, and still does, that my outspokenness on our first meeting had done me no harm at all.

The Nightingale system of training, as it was afterwards to be enshrined, was in the hands of an experienced matron who had complete and undisputed control over staff and probationers. She it was who directed the course of theoretical and practical training. As to the theory, I managed to hold my own with the others, despite the disparity between my education and that of the majority; and in the practical work, which we carried out in the wards of the hospital, I more than held my own. The training was hard and demanding. Some of us – myself included – had thoughts that we might have chosen the wrong vocation, but of the fifteen probationers, not one abandoned the course of her own free will, though two of our number were weeded out by matron as being not physically strong enough for the work and were quietly invited to leave.

The practical duties in the wards of St Thomas's were often harrowing in the extreme, for through those doors passed the maimed, the ill and the dying of the great metropolis. The toll of the packed, jostling streets was brought to us, many of them dreadfully injured: run over by iron tyres, kicked by horses, crushed under falling loads. I have sat all the long night holding the hand of a dying coster whose cart had been overturned upon him by a runaway stagecoach – only to see him fade away before my very eyes with the dawn, when the soul most easily relinquishes the tabernacle of the flesh. Likewise, I have nursed old folk, tired folk, their life spans ebbing out in peace and quiet, and watched them embrace death with smiles upon their faces – and learned the great lesson that there can be joy in dying. But the experiences that touched me most nearly, prompting doubts as to my ability to carry on, concerned the injury, sickness and death of young children, which I could not abide to witness.

One morning, after having been present at an all-night battle to save the life of a little girl of six with meningitis – a fruitless battle – I went to see matron and asked to be excused duties in the children's wards as a special dispensation – hastening to add that I would gladly do extra duties in the accident wards, which were least favoured by my fellow probationers. Matron listened to me pinched-mouthed and said that she would refer my request to Miss Nightingale.

A week went by. Miss Nightingale, I knew, attended the hospital daily, and though she delegated the running of the training school to matron in matters of detail, nevertheless she kept close supervision upon her charges. I saw her on two occasions during that week, but neither by word nor sign did she refer to my request; though I would swear that her eyes were upon me when I was not looking – particularly on an occasion when she happened to enter a children's ward when I was supervising the midday meal for the little ones.

At the end of that anxious week, matron sent for me. I entered her office in some trepidation and waited to hear my fate. Without any preliminaries, she told me that Miss Nightingale had considered my application and had come to her decision. She pushed a slip of paper across the desk and bade me read it. This I did. It consisted of four lines penned in our mentor's stiff, precise hand:

> As from today's date, Probationer Copley will, subject to the requirements of emergency, carry out *all* of her practical training in the children's wards.   sgd. F. Nightingale (Miss)

Matron gave me the note to keep. I have it still, and will treasure it all my life.

My vocation, as Florence Nightingale had had the prescience to discern, was for the nursing of children, and my revulsion from the sight and sound of their sufferings but the obverse side of my burning desire to help them. Not by any hardening of the heart (a jibe so often directed at nurses, and doctors also), but by a conscious effort to increase my skills and therefore further my great need to bring comfort, ease, contentment, even life itself, to the poor little mites who passed through our hands at St Thomas's, I overcame that revulsion and replaced it with – compassion. And for every small life that slipped through our fingers, for every child who cried with pain through a long

30

night, I took consolation from the ones we had safely brought through the valley of the shadows and sent on their way whole.

In addition to the training of nurses for hospitals and for attending the sick in their homes, Miss Nightingale's intent was also to train the most highly educated among her probationers to became heads of new schools of nursing up and down the country and so pass on the spirit and skills of the original establishment. It was, in fact, a concept that can be said to have been the beginning of modern nursing. Naturally, with my modest background and elementary education, I had no hope of being selected for such an honour, nor, with my mind made up as to the direction which my career should take, did the supervision of a teaching establishment much appeal to me.

It was with some surprise, in my third and final year, that I found myself summoned to the holy of holies, Miss Nightingale's study, one dusky even in late June. I remember it well, walking down the long corridor that smelt of floor polish and the pine disinfectant that our mentor had introduced into the cleansing regime of the school.

I knocked.

'Come!'

As chance had it, I had not seen her for some weeks, and I was appalled at the change in her. Weariness had touched her eyes with its hard fingers and scored lines down each cheek. The mouth, however, bore no traces of defeat as she glanced up at me and waved me to a seat.

'Not that it will be of the slightest interest to you, Copley,' she began, 'but I am compiling a short list of those among the probationers who might be eligible for special training with a view to becoming heads of the new schools.'

'Oh, yes, ma'am,' I commented politely, not seeing why the great woman should wish to take me into her confidence over a matter that so obviously concerned me not at all. 'I wish them all the luck in the world,' I added.

Florence Nightingale's piercing eyes narrowed slightly as if in annoyance. And then, like when a flurry of wind and rain has ruffled the surface of a pool and then passed away leaving it tranquil again, she gave a slight smile. 'You are not interested to hear the names of the three ladies I have chosen?' she asked.

How could I say other than yes? Still puzzled as to why I should be the recipient of her disclosures, I assumed an expression of polite interest, wondering as I did so if I should be obliged to keep the matter a secret from my fellow probationers.

'I will give you the names in reverse order,' said Miss Nightingale, 'commencing with my third choice and ending with my first.' She took up a slip of paper. 'My third choice – Miss Anne-Marie Daventry.'

'Anne-Marie! Oh, how thoroughly deserved!' I cried. Little Anne-Marie, nervous as a kitten when she had begun the training, so frail that one would never have believed she could have survived it, had grown both in stature and in character. She would make an excellent head of a nursing school.

'I'm glad you approve, Copley,' responded the other. 'And for my second choice – Lady Sarah Ilminster.'

'Oh, good!' I could not have been more pleased to hear that she had chosen Sarah – big, strapping, hoydenish Sarah, full of the joy of life, and with the total, radiant, outgoing self-confidence that comes of aristocratic birth, two castles, ten thousand acres in Scotland and a loving heart. I had seen Lady Sarah, whose mother the Countess Ilminster was Lady of the Bedchamber to Her Majesty Queen Victoria, strip and wash an old vagrant from the streets and lift him single-handed into bed, *and* curb his noisesome curses with a few gamey epithets she had learned in the hunting fields of the noble shires.

Florence Nightingale sat back in her chair. Her hand laid lightly against her cheek, she eyed me levelly, and said: 'My *first* choice – not that it will be of the slightest interest to you – is – Miss Suzanna May Copley.'

In the silence that followed her astounding pronouncement, I could only sit and stare, with half my mind assuming a growing conviction that I had somehow misheard her. Finally, I found my voice:

'Did you say, ma'am, that *I* was your first choice?' I whispered.

'I did,' she responded. 'You would do admirably well, and may yet do so, as a head of school. But I am aware that you have other and more driving interests than teaching, Copley.'

'Miss Nightingale,' I began, 'I scarcely know what to say. My thanks for your kindness . . .'

'Kindness does not enter into it,' responded Florence Nightingale. 'Kindness, save in carefully calculated portions, plays no part in my deliberations. I say that you would make a matron of a training school – and, indeed, you may do so one day. Until then . . . ?' The phrase hung in the air, and it was a question awaiting an answer.

'I want to work with children, ma'am,' I said. 'And that is very largely due to your influence.'

She nodded. 'That is what I thought, Copley. And I wish you well in your chosen vocation.' She held out her hand, and I took it in mine. Small-boned, dry and soft, it was like the wing of a bird. 'I will give you the name and address of an excellent agency in Kensington who will certainly have no difficulty in finding you an appointment to suit your needs. After all –' the tired eyes lit up and the chin was raised on high, proudly – 'You are now one of Miss Nightingale's ladies.'

I thanked her and took my leave, never to see her again. Her health, undermined by the privations and mental strains of the Crimea, gave way soon after and she remained, and still remains, an invalid – though as the years passed, her influence, in Government, in the Army, grew ever greater and she is still consulted – as the unchallenged arbiter – on all matters connected with nursing.

A week later, shortly before my departure from the training school, I received a letter from home, written by my mother:

Heather Cottage,
Hickleydoek,
South Devon.
July 8th, 1863

My dearest Suzanna,

We all so look forward to your return. Take the stage to Exeter and then a travelling carriage from the Royal Clarence Hotel in Exeter where they are to be had. Your father says that he will arrange for Farmer Wheatley to bring you in his governess-cart from Buckfastleigh where the carriage will have set you down. On Saturday next is the Hickleydoek Fair as you will remember. Young Master Giles is home from sea and we must now call him Lieutenant Launey. Nothing else in the way of news. We await to see you when you arrive.

      Your ever aff.

      Mother

Giles Launey was home from sea! Long years had passed, and not a day or night when some remembrance of him had not flitted through my mind and warmed my heart. It was impossible that our paths should not cross in the village, where I planned to stay till the Kensington employment agency came forward with a suitable appointment to fit my qualifications. I looked forward to the meeting with none of the trepidation I might have shown three, or even two years earlier; for to have rubbed shoulders with the likes of Anne-Marie Daventry and Lady Sarah Ilminster, not to mention Florence Nightingale, meant that much of their easy assurance had rubbed off on me; and there is nothing so induces self-confidence as to have won a few battles, with one's skills, against the Dark Angel of Death.

I looked forward to meeting Giles again with a very pleasurable anticipation unclouded by doubts as to my own worth. And I supposed that (since the humble Copleys were not on the visiting list at Hickleydoek Manor) our first encounter was likely to be achieved at the annual Fair and Gala that took place – and had done so since time immemorial – on the third Saturday in July.

With images of my life rushing pell-mell through my mind, I must quite soon have fallen asleep, for the weariness of my long journey from Devon to London and from London to the East Anglian coast was quite gone from me and (so essentially stable is the human mind, so capable of self-restoration the human body) I rose refreshed and eager when a timid, pink-cheeked little maid-of-all-work awoke me and told me it was six of the clock. She had with her an enormous pitcher of steaming water that must have taxed her puny strength up the steep spiral staircase; this she took into my dressing-room and, filling the wash-basin, laid the remainder on the marble-topped washstand.

34

'Will there be aught else, Miss?' she asked shyly.

'No thank you,' I replied. 'But – wait – where is the library? I'm sure I'll never find it in all this enormous place.'

'Mrs Stittle, she says she'll be awaiting you in the downstairs hall, Miss, for to show you the way at seven o' the clock,' responded the girl.

'Ah – thank you.'

'Thank you, Miss.' The child bobbed a curtsey and left me. I heard her boots clattering down the perilous spiral staircase with an abandonment that spoke of long usage.

I washed myself, and cleaned my teeth with powder and a stiff brush. There being no sign of my traps, I was perforce obliged to wear again the travelling costume in which I had arrived, but with a clean blouse and jabot, and clean underwear and stockings. My hair – which is black and coarse, but happily very manageable – I simply brushed and combed into a chignon after the manner favoured by Miss Nightingale's ladies. My fingernails I scrubbed and afterwards burnished with a buffer. I neither wore, nor – save for the pearl and garnet ring that I forever kept hidden on a chain at my bosom – possessed any jewellery, so I was soon ready. I had time to do no more than take a more searching look about my splendid quarters when the tiny French clock on the chimneypiece of my sitting-room told me it was time to keep my assignation with my mysterious new employer. A last look in the mirror, a smoothing of my chignon, a minor adjustment to my jabot, and I was ready.

As promised, Mrs Stittle was waiting for me at the foot of the spiral staircase. 'Your things have just arrived from the posting house, Miss,' she informed me. 'Goodness me, but I quite understand why you couldn't bring them with you in Josh Woodley's governess-cart. This way, Miss, the Master and Dr Caldwell are waiting.'

The journey to the library took us the entire length of the castle; through silent corridors lined with frowning, dark por-traits of long-dead dignitaries: cavaliers in love-locks, wigged gentlemen and their ladies of the last century, a host of men in armour from earlier times; up staircases narrow and sump-tuously broad; over a bridge that spanned a dark abyss, till we came at length to the central keep of the castle, the heart of the massive fortress turned stately home. Here, all was warmth and light, with candelabra galore blazing with all the candles of the Milky Way, with vast fireplaces in which whole trees hissed, spluttered and gave out their benison of warmth against the blustery night outside.

We came at length to a long corridor richly panelled in fine woods, at the end of which were double doors. Mrs Stittle opened these, disclosing double doors covered with green baize beyond. Upon these doors, she knocked.

'Enter, please.'

She nodded to me, opened the doors and beckoned that I should precede her. This I did.

'Ah, Miss Copley. What a very great pleasure. I am Justin Ormerod, and this is Dr Caldwell.'

'How do you do, sir.'

My new employer took my hand, and his was cool and dry to the touch. I had the wayward thought that he would be able to make Devon cheeses to perfection. As to appearance: my first impression was of tallness, complexion favouring towards the bronze, deep grey eyes, straight brown hair neatly brushed, very fine teeth. He was clean-shaven.

'So, at last, in the flesh, I regard one of Miss Florence Nightingale's young ladies. One of the praetorian guard of the nursing profession! Your servant, ma'am.' The speaker, Dr Caldwell, I have to say, I disliked on sight, and mostly because, in my three years at St Thomas's, I had seen his archetype come and go, leaving behind them more confusion than had been before, and the last state worse than the first. Short of stature, inclining to gross obesity, with a slimy handshake and a purring, put-on manner, the doctor (and I presumed him immediately to be a doctor of medicine, for he carried with him the very smell of a hospital ward or a consulting room) would have transferred my hand to his lips for a kiss had I not swiftly withdrawn it.

'Did you have a good journey, Miss Copley?' asked Justin Ormerod. And I had the distinct impression that he sensed my sudden revulsion of his companion.

'Very agreeable, sir,' I replied.

'The countryside in East Anglia is very fine.'

'Very fine, sir.'

'And in Devon, also. I know Devon well.'

'Indeed, sir.'

And there the preliminary conversation languished.

During this exchange, Mrs Stittle had remained by the doorway. Allowing for a few moments' silence, the housekeeper said: 'Sir, will it be all right for Tweeny to bring Master Rupert to say goodnight now?'

'Of course, Stittle, of course,' responded Mr Ormerod. He turned to me. 'An excellent first opportunity to see your new charge, Miss Copley. Will you take a glass of sherry wine?'

'Thank you, no, sir.'

'Whisky? It's very smart. Her Majesty and the late Prince Consort – designer and aesthete extraordinary and may his soul rest in peace – picked up the habit of imbibing Scotch whisky at their place in Balmoral, you know. Indeed, I really think that, had poor Prince Albert drunk more of the highland dew and fortified his system, he might not have perished of the fever. What's your opinion on that, Doctor?'

The question, addressed to Caldwell, who was already simulating a paroxysm of sycophantic mirth at his companion's sally, brought forth the answer that he, indeed, was of the same opinion.

The pursuance of the topic was cut short by a tap on the green baize door. Tensed as I was – tensed like a bowstring, I might add – for the first sight of my charge, I could not resist a long glance at Mr Ormerod, who, from the wildness of his last utterance, had distinctly given me the impression that he had been too fervently imbibing (like his companion, where the effect had been immediately obvious) the sherry wine or the whisky, or both. With later knowledge, how wrong I was in my estimation of the man!

'Come on in, Master Rupert. Say goodnight to your papa, to Dr Caldwell, and to Miss Copley, who'll be looking after you.' Mrs Stittle ushered in the heir of Castle Delamere: a frail-looking little fellow of around six years, with a shock of unruly auburn hair, deep grey eyes like his father's, and a strutting, no-nonsense sort of walk. He was wearing a long nightshirt ruffled at the breast, cuffs and hem. And I felt drawn to him on sight.

'Goodnight, Papa.' Rupert Ormerod had a deep and pleasant voice for all the leanness of his years. As he kissed his father's proffered cheek, he coolly swept me from head to foot with those inscrutable grey eyes, and I felt taken apart. 'Dr Caldwell, your servant, sir.' He offered a hand to the physician and shook the other's with no great show of enthusiasm. Finally, he turned his full attention to me.

'I am Rupert Ormerod, ma'am,' he said, and waited for me to present him with my hand.

'I'm delighted to make your acquaintance, Rupert,' I replied. 'And I'm quite sure we shall become the best of friends.'

He took my hand, but made no response; his eyes wandered towards his father.

'Bed, old chap,' said Mr Ormerod. 'No staying up late tonight.'

'Very good, Papa,' was the child's dutiful response. He swept us all with his glance. 'Goodnight, all.'

It was then I noticed the girl standing by the door, and she I decided must be the between-maid who had had charge of the boy since the departure of the late nursemaid. She was a girl not unlike the little maid-of-all-work who had woken me and brought me my hot water: a local lass, no doubt; trained to service by trial and error, nor very good at her job perhaps; she did not look the sort of chit of a thing to whom one would entrust one's only child.

'Come, Master Rupert.' Mrs Stittle held out her hand. Rupert took it. He gave one last, yearning backward glance towards his father. I had the notion that he had a sudden impulse to rush back and throw his arms about Mr Ormerod, and subsequent events did not make me change that opinion – then he was gone.

'What a thoroughly nice little boy,' I declared, when the green baize doors were closed again.

'Oh, well. Oh, well,' commented Dr Caldwell, fishing in his pocket for a snuff-box and tapping the lid before he opened it. He threw a knowing, buttonholing sort of glance at Mr Ormerod. 'We who know, know better, eh, Ormerod?'

My employer ignored this sally and, fixing me with a steady gaze (and how like the gaze of his son's dark grey eyes!), said: 'Is *that* your first impression, ma'am?'

'But of course,' I responded.

'Ah!'

To my right, Dr Caldwell took a gross pinch of snuff, snorting it noisily from the top of his thumb joint – a method of imbibing which I have always found repulsive.

'You would say that my son Rupert is – at your first impression – in all respects – I quote – "a thoroughly nice little boy"? Do I have it right?' asked Mr Ormerod.

'Yes, sir,' I responded vigorously.

Dr Caldwell dabbed his nose with a handkerchief and said: 'My dear Ormerod, we must remember that Miss Copley, for all her new-found expertise as one of Miss Nightingale's young ladies' – he made the qualification sound like an insult – 'can do no more than register her first and entirely subjective view, without a tittle of supportive evidence and in the heat of emotion that one frequently observes in a member of the fair sex when she encounters a personable child – a superficially personable child, I should say.'

Mr Ormerod's comment upon that might have been enlightening, my own would certainly have been heated; but neither of us was given the opportunity to comment, for a stately butler arrived at that moment to announce that dinner was served in the great hall; accordingly, I buttoned up my lip and, seething within, followed my employer out of the library with the odious Dr Caldwell plodding fatly along in the rear.

The route to the great hall took us along an interminable corridor that bent around two sides of the massive building and was hung with trophies of the hunt: horned, scaled and feathered. Whole generations of fish, fowl and beast must have been sacrificed to the guns and rods of Castle Delamere to have provided such a collection. In order to sooth my ruffled temper, I counted a row of stags' heads as we progressed past them, and lost track at something like fifty – for I could not shut out the thought of Dr Caldwell coming up behind me.

The great hall almost beggars description, having clearly been built to feed and accommodate the entire garrison when

Castle Delamere was one of the principal East Anglian fortresses of the medieval age. A long refectory table ran down the centre. It was laid for three at one end and the effect of three neat settings of silverwear and napery stuck out on one limb of that massive, empty sweep of oak and elm was quite risible.

We took our places: I on Mr Ormerod's right, the doctor on his left. It was none too warm in the vast, stone-flagged chamber, and I was glad of the vestigial heat from a huge open fire that was blazing away some twenty paces behind my back.

It was during the first course – which, true to the custom of the very rich, was extravagant as to choice, gross and wasteful as to quantity, over-spiced, over-fancified and in a large part indigestible – that I learned something about my new employer which I had not been able to glean in my previous enquiries. In the midst of slurping his soup, Dr Caldwell, glancing ceilingwards, commented upon the ancient banners that hung in rows on each side of the hall, high up among the massive oak beams; tattered for the most part they were, but all impressively colourful in their own, peculiar faded glory.

'They would tell a fine story of our ancient chivalry, could they but speak, Ormerod,' said Caldwell.

'I don't doubt it, Doctor,' responded the other. 'I cannot, however, enlighten you as to their provenance, except that they bear the badges and coats of arms of my late wife's family who lived here since the Reformation, when Henry VIII gave it to them for faithful service. Well, not actually *gave* – in accordance with the custom of the time, they had it for a peppercorn rent, which was duly paid annually to the crown as late as the beginning of this century.'

'And what was this peppercorn rent, sir?' asked Caldwell.

'A red rose and a white rose on Midsummer's Day.'

'An excellent, cheap rent!' declared Caldwell. He emptied the remaining half of his champagne glass in one draught. 'And a very charming conceit, don't you think, eh, Miss Copley?'

'Very,' I murmured.

This was interesting. So – Justin Ormerod, Royal Academician, had not succeeded to the castle in his own right. Nor had he purchased the same from the proceeds of his practice as a society portrait painter, but had inherited it through the Will of his late wife, including, perhaps, a considerable fortune for its upkeep – which, surely, would be beyond the pocket of even the most financially successful artist. But – what of the wife? She, presumably the mother of Rupert, when and how had she died? I confess to a bump of curiosity. I longed to know more of Justin Ormerod's background: he, seated on my left hand, very cool and slightly sardonic, was answering Dr Caldwell's remarks with a ghost of a smile lingering at the corners of his firm lips . . .

'Do you not think so, Miss Copley?'

He was addressing me; with a start of surprise, I realised that I had been staring at him in an absurdly bemused fashion and not responding at all to his repeated question.

'I – I'm sorry, sir,' I faltered. 'I didn't catch what . . .'

'The issue of young Rupert,' he said. 'I put it to you that one should pursue the disparity between your first, favourable impression of my son, and what Dr Caldwell – and others – have observed about his behaviour.'

My response was delayed by the arrival of the entrées, which comprised a choice of veal and mutton. I took a small chop, and Dr Caldwell a whole rack of them, whilest eyeing the veal for his second assault.

When the servants had withdrawn, I said: 'Sir, I would need to know what Dr Caldwell and others have observed about the boy's behaviour before I could vouchsafe any other opinion than the one I have already formed.'

Mr Ormerod nodded. 'We will say no more on the subject till dinner is finished,' he declared. 'That done, we will summon the between-maid who has had charge of my son since the somewhat precipitate departure of the nursemaid.' He turned to address me directly. 'I propose we leave the encounter till after we have eaten, Miss Copley, for reasons I would not wish to go into at this time.'

'Quite so, my dear Ormerod, quite so,' commented the doctor.

I was left to wonder what revelations were in store.

With the odd detachment which I have primarily observed in

the male, and most particularly in the male of the English upper classes (I would apply no such stricture to Scotsmen or Irishmen, and I have no evidence of Welshmen; we had no Welsh doctors at St Thomas's during my time), Mr Ormerod was able to steer the ensuing conversation quite happily through the topics of the day without touching in the slightest upon the subject which must have been uppermost in his mind; so that we discussed, in the matter of politics and world affairs, the recent British armed expedition into Ethiopia to rescue our envoy and his companions, the impeachment of the United States President Johnson and his subsequent acquittal, a revolution in Spain, and Mr Gladstone's accession to Prime Minister. In matters aesthetic, we – that is to say Mr Ormerod and I – declared that we had both read and enjoyed a new novel called *Little Women* by an American lady named Louisa M. Alcott, and found common ground in the wonder about the discovery of the skeleton of one of our primitive ancestors – dating back, surely, close to Adam and Eve in the Garden – in France. During this time, Dr Caldwell had fallen asleep over the dessert, and the conversation betwixt my employer and me flowed the more freely.

Over the fruit and nuts, Mr Ormerod leaned forward and, gazing at me very fixedly for some moments, much to my embarrassment, said quite dispassionately: 'Miss Copley, you have the most astonishing eyes.'

'Indeed, sir?' I responded, abashed.

'One of them' – he pointed – 'the left one, is discernibly more inclined to the blue than is its companion of the right, which is a very definite green. Did you know that?'

'No, sir, I did not,' I faltered.

'Well, that's the fact of it,' he said. 'I think I may wish to make some portrait drawings of you at some later date, Miss Copley. Would you consent to that, heh?'

'Sir, I would be most flattered,' I replied.

'A full-scale painted portrait might come of it,' he said. 'On the other hand, it might not. One never can tell.' He shifted in his seat and threw aside his napkin. 'If we could but wake the excellent Dr Caldwell,' he said, 'I think we might proceed with the interrogation of that between-maid.'

As if in answer to Mr Ormerod's implied rebuke, the porcine man of medicine shuffled out of his slumber, straightened himself, reached for his glass, and declared himself ready for the encounter with the tweeny.

'You will learn much that you never suspected about your young charge, Miss,' he said, with an expression which was halfway to a wink of complicity.

Mr Ormerod summoned a footman. It was only a matter of minutes before the little chit of a thing who had helped deliver young Rupert to say goodnight to us all was ushered in through the double doors, there to cringe, hungry eyes wide, skinny fingers clutched across her vestigial bosom, waiting to hear her fate.

'What is your name, Tweeny?' asked Mr Ormerod.

(I marvelled that a man would deliver his only child into the care of someone he did not even know by name!)

'Lottie, sir,' whispered the other.

'Louder, child!'

'Lottie, sir.'

'Now, this is Miss Copley, Lottie, who has come to nurse Master Rupert. Will you tell Miss Copley about Master Rupert's habits? We might begin with his eating habits. Does he have a good appetite?'

The wide, hungry eyes, grew shifty – or so it seemed to me.

'He won't eat, sir. Not 'less I persuade him like. "One for Tweeny," I say, "and one for Master Rupert." That way, he'll eat maybe half of his meal.'

'And then what, Lottie?' interposed Dr Caldwell, leaning forward eagerly, with the air of someone who knows and relishes the answer.

'Why, sir, he sicks the whole lot up,' replied the girl. 'All over the table top. All over me, if I should happen to be near enough.'

'Does he do this deliberately?' asked Mr Ormerod.

The shifty eyes grew ever more shifty. The girl looked down at her thin fingers, which were twining and untwining at her waistbelt. 'I – I have seen him putting his finger down his throat for to make hisself sick, sir,' she breathed.

'Why should he do that?' I threw the question at her harshly and

43

loud. She looked up with a flash of fear – and something else – guilt? – in those fugitive eyes.

'Because he's wicked, Miss!' she cried. 'Truly wicked!'

'Show the marks of his wickedness, Lottie,' said Dr Caldwell.

The girl, throwing me a look of defiance, rolled up the sleeve of her dress and bared her left arm. From where I sat, I could clearly see a set of livid marks against the white skin.

'Come closer, Lottie,' said Caldwell coaxingly. 'Don't be afraid. Show Miss Copley your wounds.'

She came near me, holding out her arm in a gesture of self-righteousness. Between wrist and elbow were imprinted the marks of two bites: deep bites, put there by a small mouth possessing a complete set of incisors. All had penetrated well into the tissues.

'And who put those bites there, Lottie?' asked Caldwell. I glanced sidelong at Mr Ormerod; he was sitting with head bowed, his hand pressed against his brow.

'Master Rupert, he done them, sir,' whispered the girl.

'*Why?*' I demanded.

'Because I chided him for throwing up all over the table,' she replied. 'Twice he bit me – see?' Her voice rose in a note of hysteria.

'Can we proceed?' interposed Mr Ormerod. 'I believe you have some difficulty in making Master Rupert settle down to sleep.'

'That I have, sir,' responded the girl. 'Every night's the same, and tonight were no different. He'll not get into bed till I've promised to read to him for half an hour, and when he's there, it's always an hour before he'll close his eyes. And if I stop – if I stop . . .'

'Yes – go on,' prompted Mr Ormerod. 'Miss Copley is waiting to hear. What does Master Rupert do if you stop reading to him before he goes to sleep?'

'Well – he wets the bed, sir. Out of defiance, like.'

Silence.

'I think,' said Mr Ormerod, 'that Miss Copley will have heard sufficient to modulate her first opinion of my son. You may go, Lottie.'

'Yessir. Thank you, sir.' The girl dipped a clumsy curtsey and made herself scarce, with a single, resentful glance in my direction.

The door having closed behind her, Dr Caldwell spread his hands, and I noticed for the first time that his fingernails were filthy and black-edged. 'There you have it, young lady,' he said. 'The child is, in a common manner of speaking, a monster. Three successive nursemaids have managed to do nothing with him. The inept chit of a girl you have just seen has coped better than all of them – but at some cost to her own safety. Those bites on her arm may well turn to evil humours and necessitate the removal of the limb. I do not exaggerate, Miss Copley, I assure you that . . .'

'Mr Ormerod,' I interposed. 'I accepted this appointment on the understanding that I was to be put in charge of a young patient who suffered from a specific disease which required nursing. Upon accepting that appointment, I was charged with bringing from London – from Messrs Tooley, Smirke, Vance and Cadwallader Limited, Medical Suppliers – what amounts to the contents of an entire chemist's shop, together with medical and surgical equipment as would suffice any hospital for a year. Is this to be applied, sir, to a child who has bitten his keeper on the arm and wet the bed – if so, to what end?' I flashed a glance to Dr Caldwell, whose unsteady hand was addressing itself to the port wine decanter.

Having filled his glass and steadied himself somewhat with a deep swallow, the latter responded to my question by addressing our host: 'Mr Ormerod, sir, I take it amiss that I have to defend the disciplines of my profession to a person of the nursing persuasion, even though she may be a former pupil of the egregious Miss Nightingale. However, I will do it. The "entire chemist's shop", as she is pleased to put it, comprises the basic articles of the pharmacy which are necessary to the treatment of childhood ailments, that is to say: antimonial in both wine and powdered forms, calomel, compound extract of colocynth and compound tincture of camphor, Epsom salt, powdered opium and laudanum, myrrh and aloes pills, linseed oil and oil of turpentine, blister compound, blue pill and compound iron pills, carbonate of potash, jalap in powder, sal ammoniac, iron pills.

'Goulard extract, nitre opodeldoc, Turner's cerate, senna leaves. And sweet spirits of nitre.' He paused to draw breath following this astonishing litany. 'As for the medical and surgical equipment: I have ordered Tooley, Smirke, Vance and Cadwallader to provide various measuring glasses, a set of lancets, a probe, various forceps, curved needles, and a set of scales. All of these, I may add, thanks to my excellent professional relationship with the firm of suppliers, have been purchased at fifteen per cent discount.' He took another swallow of his port and, folding his hands across his vast paunch, contrived to look incorruptible.

Determined not to be outfaced by his display of pharmaceutical pyrotechnics, I returned to the attack:

'But what specific disease is the child suffering from, Doctor?'

The mean eyes glinted behind their pouched eyelids.

'Asthma,' he pronounced.

'The boy's suffered from it since birth, Miss Copley,' said Mr Ormerod, 'and I am convinced that this condition is the root cause of his curious misbehaviour. When an attack is upon him, he presents a most distressing sight, with shortness of breath, wheezing, a blueness of the lips.'

'Symptoms which I treat,' said Dr Caldwell, 'by the most modern methods known to medical science, that is: a fever mixture of powdered nitre, carbonate of potash, antimonial wine and sweet spirits of nitre; afterwards applying a very hot bread-and-water poultice to the chest in order to disperse the evil humours; and then I draw off five ounces of blood. At the close of this treatment, the patient invariably relapses into a sound sleep.'

And not to be wondered at, I thought to myself. After such a rigorous regimen, the poor little mite would surely be reduced to a state nearer unconsciousness than healthy sleep. But I made no comment. The dinner ended on that note. Seeing that the men were obviously bent on drinking port and brandy and smoking cigars till the small hours, I took my leave of my employer and the doctor. As the latter bade me goodnight, his pouched eyes twinkled with triumph for having – as he must have imagined – put the little upstart from Miss Nightingale's school in her place.

*

Upon retiring to my eyrie (taking with me a candle to light my way up the spiral staircase, and nearly suffering its extinction from the draught through the arrow slits!), I found the sitting-room piled with a half dozen wooden crates containing the medicaments and equipment that Dr Caldwell had ordered in such enormous quantities and which I had brought with me from London. I opened the uppermost case with the end of my hairbrush and found it to contain the surgical equipment. I took out a box beautifully fashioned with inlaid woods and fine brass fastenings. In it, gleaming potently in the candlelight, lay a battery of lancets – enough lancets to cut the veins of and bleed an entire army. There were three more similar boxes of instruments. The remainder of the items in the case were of similar high quality as to finish and boxing, and wildly absurd as to quantity. As I had stated at dinner, there was enough stuff there to stock a hospital.

It was then I turned over a fold of paper that lay under one of the instrument cases. Sealed with a wafer, it bore no inscription. After a moment's thought, I thumbed open the seal and perused the contents, which proved to be an invoice for the goods that I had collected from Messrs Tooley, Smirke, Vance and Cadwallader Limited; each item carefully recorded by name, quantity and price. The sum total of the transaction amounted to the very high figure of ninety-eight pounds and three pence; but it was the tailpiece of the invoice that commanded my most earnest attention. This read:

On the sum of £98.0.3d, commission on the transaction to Dr Caldwell of Southwold, East Sussex, at 15% – the sum of £15.0.3d – this amt. credited to Dr Caldwell's a/c with us. Sgd. A. A. Armrose, pp T.S.V. & Co., Ltd.

I recalled the signatory Mr Armrose. He it was who had supervised my collecting of the order and had insisted upon my signing a receipt note for the same. A wiry, cunning-looking individual with Dundreary whiskers, he put me in mind – on mature reflection – of a skinny version of Dr Caldwell: the same unctuous manner, the same watchful but shifty eyes.

Well, I thought, Mr Armrose had done badly by his client: by

47

omitting to address the invoice to the good doctor, he had placed into my hands a weapon that I would not hesitate to use if the need arose.

Dr Caldwell had padded out the order to an absurd degree simply to raise the sum total of the transaction for his own ends, and his talk of that 'fifteen per cent discount' – by implication, to the advantage of Mr Ormerod – had been so much humbug; the advantage had gone straight to Caldwell's credit with the suppliers. That the doctor could have risked his reputation for a measly fifteen pounds and threepence was beyond all belief – till I reckoned that half a dozen such transactions around the more lucrative areas of his practice every year might well make the risk very well worth while.

And in such a man had Justin Ormerod reposed the care of his only child! I, who had seen the likes of Dr Caldwell, with their poultices and potions, their eternal blood-letting for every ill known to man, had heard Miss Nightingale fulminating about her experiences of their kind in the Crimea and else-where, could scarcely believe that a man of intelligence would be taken in so easily by a creature like Caldwell, dirty finger-nails and all.

And then I remembered that Justin Ormerod was an artist. And artists are not like the rest of us, or to be judged by the standards by which the common ruck of folk are judged.

THREE

I was awoken by the fluting song of a skylark coming from the edge of the woods beyond the causeway, clear on the still air. Filled with sudden wonder and the realisation of my new surroundings, I leapt from my canopied bed and, running to the window, looked out over the glassy sea and the high blue sky of an Indian summer which had stolen upon us overnight. Instantly, I was seized with the impulse to get out and about. My traps had arrived along with the medical supplies, so I selected a light two-piece ensemble, a straw boater, button boots, a parasol, and lilac gloves. Somewhere not far off, a clock was chiming the hour of eight as I made my way down the spiral stairs and set about looking for someone.

The scent of freshly-roasted coffee and the delicious tang of grilled bacon led me, as soon as I had found my way to the general direction of the great hall where he had eaten the night before, to a flight of stone steps leading down into the castle kitchen, which I found to be presided by a stout lady cook who, greeting me with a curtsey, begged to know my requirements. These I speedily made known, contingent upon which I was soon sitting on a high wall overlooking the shifting sea that surged and gurgled in even the finest weather below the drawbridge, with a mug of steaming coffee beside me on the parapet and a thick rasher of bacon between two pieces of freshly baked bread plastered with farmhouse butter in my hand. Alone in the morning sunlight, with my mouth watering.

Not alone for long . . .

'Good morning, Miss Copley. No – please, I beg you, don't

get up on my account. What a fine picture you make. If I could but recapture it, I should have the sensation of next year's Royal Academy Summer Exhibition.' Giles Ormerod was not newly-risen, not if his Norfolk suit with the mud up to the ankles, the long-barrelled gun, the snuffling Labrador gun-dog, not to mention the three brace of wood pigeons that he threw down upon the stone paving beside him, were any evidence.

'Good morning, sir,' I responded, acutely conscious that I had butter smeared round my mouth – or thought I might have. 'I see you've had a good shoot.'

'A turn around the edge of the woods just after dawn,' he said. The Labrador was poking his nose at the dead pigeons and prodding them with his paw. 'Get back and lie down, Sabu!' he snapped, and the dog cringed away. 'He's very young and untrained,' he said, adding ruefully, 'not so much unlike my poor son. But I hope that you may be of some assistance in that direction, Miss Copley.' The deep grey eyes were turned upon me so fixedly that I looked away. The remainder of my bread, butter and bacon presenting too much of a problem before his close scrutiny, I tossed them down into the sea-washed gully, where, before they were much past the level of the drawbridge, they were set upon by screaming seagulls, who, each stabbing at his importuning brethren with long beak, somehow contrived to snatch a morsel apiece in mid-air.

'I shall do the best I can, sir,' I replied. 'Indeed, I thought to start the day by taking Master Rupert for a drive this lovely morning. What transport do you have?'

'Ample,' he responded. 'A dogcart, governess-cart, a pretty town phaeton which you may find a bit of a handful. Do you drive yourself, Miss Copley?'

'I am a farmer's daughter, sir,' I replied.

'Of course, of course.'

'I will take the governess-cart, if that meets with your approval,' I said.

'Indeed, do,' he replied. 'Drive the lad as far as Nunwich, which is there –' He pointed to the northward, where one could distinguish a smudge of buildings set back from the shore, and a church tower. 'Nunwich is falling into the sea. A hundred years from now, so it's reckoned, more than half of it will be gone, church, churchyard, graves and all.'

'How eerie,' I said.

'This coast is haunted,' said he. 'The blood of countless generations has been spilled here. North of Nunwich there is a stretch of common land where, on one night of the year, folks say that one can hear the din of an ancient battle, with the clash of steel on steel, the screams of wounded and dying men. In the daytime, that stretch of bracken-covered ground is the haunt of many adders, so that it is not much frequented. They say that the adders are guarding the resting place of the dead warriors.

'Yes, we are surrounded by ghosts here, on this remote edge of England.'

His deep grey eyes sought the far horizon and took on a look of melancholy. When he referred to ghosts, I knew with a certainty that brooked of no doubts that he was thinking of his dead wife, the mother of Rupert.

I made no reply. Presently, he seemed to drag himself away from his unquiet thoughts, and said: 'I should tell you, Miss Copley, that I have lately received an invitation to travel out to Egypt at the request of the Khedive Ismail and the Egyptian government, to paint a series of pictures recording the opening of the Suez Canal, which is set for November seventeenth next.'

'Oh, but how wonderful, Mr Ormerod!' I cried. 'What a tremendous honour. And greatly deserved, I'm sure.'

'I have turned down the invitation,' he said.

'Oh, but why? Such an opportunity . . .'

The grey eyes clouded again. 'I couldn't leave Rupert, not in his present state. Not the way he is.'

'Then take him with you!'

'Oh, no, that's out of the question.'

'But it would do him good. The sea voyage. The warm, dry climate of Egypt. What could be better for a child suffering from asthma?'

He shook his head. 'I couldn't risk it, Miss Copley. If he were to be struck down with any one of the pestilences that are rife in the Near East – you are a trained nurse, I do not have to recite an inventory of the hideous and fatal diseases which a young and delicate child might well fall sick and die of out there.'

I knew well enough, for was not Florence Nightingale regarded by the Army and the Foreign Office as one of the greatest authorities on tropical diseases, and had not we, her 'ladies', been rigorously inculcated with that knowledge, since so many of us were likely to be working on the remote shores of our far-flung Empire? I knew of malaria, typhus, cholera, bubonic plague, leprosy, and could recite their symptoms too hideous to contemplate.

So I made no reply. And his eyes were directed once more to the horizon, and his voice was sombre.

'I confess to be not well cut out for the role of a father, Miss Copley, particularly the father of a motherless child. But, having set one's hand to the plough, one must make the best shift of which one is capable. One thing I shall never do, and that is to put the boy's life in the slightest hazard.'

I was to remember that declaration in the months that followed.

Rupert's nursery was on the third floor of the central keep, with a wide and pleasant window that looked down into the sunniest side of the castle courtyard. The girl Lottie was busily coaxing porridge into the child when I entered shortly after leaving Mr Ormerod. Rupert brightened considerably upon seeing me, particularly when I told him that I was taking him for a drive. Three more spoonfuls and the porridge was gone. He scrambled to get into his little Norfolk jacket, cap and boots. Five minutes later, the governess-cart having been ordered by Mr Ormerod, it was ready and waiting for us in the courtyard, with a spanking cob in the shafts.

We set off under the archway, across the drawbridge and out along the cobble-stones. Mr Ormerod watched us go from the battlements. His last shouted instruction to me was to be back before noon, before the tide lapped over the causeway.

Reaching the mainland, I took a right fork that was signposted to Nunwich, and skirted the low wood to our left. I was driving the cob with a light rein, for he seemed to know the rutted road and took the cart, without direction from me, along the smoothest parts. Rupert sat silently at my side, but whenever I looked down and met his eye, he grinned back up at me: a gap-toothed, cheery grin against which one could have warmed one's hands.

If this was a truly wicked child, a monster, I thought, then I never made the right judgement on any child!

We came at length to a small headland, and a hill on whose humped crest I reined-in the cob and, looking back, pointed for Rupert to follow my glance. Away out to sea, a couple of miles distant, the thin line of the causeway joined the massive hump of rock upon which was perched the castle. It looked, in the clear light of that Indian summer's morn, like something out of a fairy tale, the abode of a benevolent giant or a haunted princess.

Rupert nodded eagerly. 'Home!' he said. A small hand reached out and took mine: 'I'm glad you came, Miss Copley, and I hope you'll stay.'

'Of course I will – of *course*!' I promised.

It was downhill, then, till we reached the low cliffs upon which the precarious edge of Nunwich stood. A mile from the village, we could see where the encroaching waters were eating away at the soft sandstone of the cliffs and tumbling them down on to the beach at every low tide. Already there was the masonry of cottages strewn on the shingle; the seaward wall of the churchyard had gone also, and the outer line of gravestones was so near to the crumbling edge as to place the occupants in imminent hazard of having their eternal sleep most rudely disturbed. We drew closer to the village, a pleasant place of flint-faced cottages and fine houses set at the ends of long carriage drives. Near the centre, in a small market square, there was a sign announcing *Refreshments*, where, for a few pence, I bought Rupert a water ice and myself a pot of tea, which we took together at a table in the walled garden of the purveyor's house. The lady of the house seemed to know Rupert by sight and called him 'Little Prince Charming', which made him frown with embarrassment.

Over our refreshments, I decided that we must see the church and the vanishing graveyard, and Rupert was enthusiastic for both – particularly the latter ('Shall we acshewally *see* bones and skelingtons falling into the sea, Miss Copley?' he asked, with all the innocent eagerness of childhood) – but a glance at my watch, prompted by the ring of the village church bell, told me that we had little enough time to cross the causeway on the present tide. Accordingly, we set off back to Castle Delamere, and I taught him a jingle along the way: a rhyming song that Dartmoor children have danced to from time immemorial:

> Blackberry milchard
> Blueberry snail,
> All the dogs in town
> Hang on thy tail.

Beyond the escarpment of Nunwich, with the castle already in sight, we dipped into a lane that was overhung with hawthorn, yew and elder, a place of darkness with a most drear stench of rotting undergrowth which I had noted with some distaste on the way there.

We had not gone far into it, and the castle was already in sight, when from out of the high yew hedge to our right pranced a most outlandish figure clad in rags and tatters bedecked with ribbons, cock feathers, flowers and wheat straw. He was a big fellow, broad as a young bull, with forearms like hams; but his face was as blank as the whitewashed wall of a milking stall, and his eyes – washed-out blue eyes – had the blankness of insanity.

> She 'ad 'er babby on 'er knee, on 'er knee . . .

He sang. And then:

> She 'ad 'er babby on 'er knee,
> Under the walnut tree,
> Under the walnut tree . . .

The cob took some alarm at the appearance of the apparition and I had considerable difficulty in bringing him under control; indeed, I think he might have bolted had not the curious stranger laid a hand on his bridle and whispered something into his ear, whereupon the cob became as quiet as a lamb.

'Don't be afeared o' my grandson Ned, lady,' came a voice from the yew hedge; and out stepped an ancient crone in a mob cap, shawl, and a tatterdemalion frock composed of patches and raggetty furbelows. She looked up at us with eyes of evil wisdom as old as time. 'Ned won't harm you. A fairy's child is Ned.' She tapped her forehead with her finger and nodded knowingly.

'A fairy's child,' repeated the idiot, nodding and grinning inanely, and still – to my discomfiture – holding the cob's head and preventing us from advancing.

The crone held out her hand. 'Cross the palm with silver, lady, and I'll tell you what fate has in store. Seventh child of a seventh child is old Meg, and nothing's hid from her.'

'I'm sorry, but we're in something of a hurry,' I replied, 'and if your grandson will be so kind as to let go of . . .'

The old woman pointed to little Rupert, who had been staring at her throughout the exchange with saucer-wide eyes of awe.

'That child, that lad, is better than they think he is,' she declared. 'And you' – the pointing finger was directed to me – 'would be content in your grief but for a letter. Ain't that so, lady?'

If the former remark had commanded my interest, the latter cryptic comment – which touched upon a subject known only to me and perhaps one other – had me totally beguiled. Rummaging in my reticule, I produced a silver sixpence and presented it to the woman, who sketched a cross above her palm with the coin and then, having disposed of it somewhere among the tatterdemalion, pointed at me again. I quailed before her glance and had the sudden wish to be elsewhere – anywhere – other than in that darkened lane.

'You will travel far, both of you –' and the finger moved briefly to encompass Rupert. 'You will cross three seas. Five will be the number of your perils. And two shall die.'

I reached out and took Rupert's hand to reassure him, but I need not have worried on his account; the little lad was gazing at the crone in rapt fascination.

'If you live, lady, you will marry,' continued the old woman. 'And you will abide in a fine house on a corner. If you live, three

55

sons you will have and one daughter. Do you wish to hear more?'

I nodded, having first confirmed with another sidelong glance that Rupert was still not showing any signs of alarm.

'The palm must be crossed with silver again.'

I gave her another sixpence, and she resumed: 'As to the boy,' again the pointing finger, 'they will soon all know him for what he is. Two of the perils will be for him alone. And if he grows to be a man, he will spend the best part of his manhood in a place of fools who gabble like apes and think they are gods, kings, lords of creation.

'I do not see any more. The rest is darkness.'

With this final, alarming statement, the crone made a sign to her grandson, who straightway released his hold on the cob's bridle and followed his grandmother into the thicket from whence they had come. As I urged the cob forward again, the idiot's voice piped back to us through the shadows:

> *A carvin' knife was in 'er 'and, in 'er 'and,*
> *She ran it through the babby's 'art, babby's 'art,*
> *Under the walnut tree . . .*

The events of the rest of that eventful day might well have driven the details of the old woman's predictions from my mind had I not, immediately upon our arrival back at the castle, committed the general outline of our encounter to paper, together with her words as best I could remember them, with particular attention to the numerals: three, five, two, three, one . . .

Then – as afterwards – I speculated upon those predictions, bearing in mind the quite uncanny insight into my private life with which the old woman had first commanded my attention. The notion of distant travel seemed hardly likely, speculations about my future marriage and the number of my children no more than a shot in the dark; but the threats of danger, of death, of poor little Rupert spending a large part of his adult life in a lunatic asylum, had the power to engender unease. But, as I have said, the remaining events of the day served to dull the edge of my speculations and fears concerning the predictions.

The afternoon was bland. Rupert and I spent most of it in the heavenly little garden that I found tucked away behind the courtyard: a place of whispering cypresses, a tinkling fountain, the scents of honeysuckle, carnation, rose. At his suppertime, I consigned him to the care of Lottie, who had had no difficulties with him at luncheon. And I promised to call in and kiss him goodnight when he had gone to bed at seven.

Alas for the promise . . .

At that time of the evening when Castle Delamere, the austere coast and the wrinkled grey sea took upon themselves a magical enchantment under the dying sun, I went up to what had become my favourite spot on the wall above the draw-bridge, taking with me a favourite book. The book I never opened, being so enchanted by the panorama spread out all round me, by the scent and the sounds of the sea, by the antics of the wheeling gulls, by all Castle Delamere.

As I sat there, with the westward wind plucking at my hair and my scarf, and the gulls screeching above, a dark figure on foot came upon the causeway and slowly approached the castle along its half mile length, coming out of the gloaming of that evening of Indian summer: a tall and gangling figure in a high hat and a cloak that swirled about him like a bat's wings, and who limped heavily upon a stick. As he drew closer, I was able to see little of his face, which was shielded from me by the brim of his hat and the fact that his head was bowed. Upon reaching the steep slope up to the drawbridge, the stranger was compelled to rest and draw breath. It was then I decided that, since it was likely no one else had espied the newcomer, it would be an act of charity to a lame man to go down and welcome him and ask to know his business at the castle.

This I did. By the time I reached the courtyard, the stranger was entering through the archway. At closer quarters he presented himself as a man in his middle fifties, with a drawn, lined face pitted with the scars of smallpox, a shock of white hair descending from his hat to his collar, and a straggly beard.

'Ah, bonsoir, madame,' he said, upon espying me.

'Bonsoir, monsieur,' I responded, and, my French not being equal to the task of protracted dalliance in that language, I continued with: 'Can I help you, sir?'

'I seek Monsieur Ormerod,' replied the stranger. 'You weel please take me to 'eem?'

I indicated that I would do my best, and, motioning him to follow me, I led him into the castle and directed my footsteps as well as I was able (for I had only been there once before) in the direction of the library, where it seemed to me that my employer would most likely be at that hour.

We came to the library doors. I looked to the man whom I had already written into my mind as the 'Limping Frenchman'.

'What name shall I give, sir?' I asked.

'Monsieur weel know me when he sees me,' responded the other.

I had no other option but to tap upon the inner door, which brought the response: 'Come in'. Justin Ormerod was seated at his desk when I entered, a sheaf of drawings before him, a pencil in his hand.

'Yes, Miss Copley, can I help you?' he asked.

'Sir, there's a gentleman who . . .'

I got no further. The Limping Frenchman brushed past me and presented himself to the view of the man behind the desk. Mr Ormerod frowned, narrowed his eyes.

'And who are you, sir?' he demanded.

'I theenk you weel remembair me, monsieur,' responded the other. 'Eeet has been a long time, but there are theengs – peoples – who do not change all that much.' So saying, he doffed his tall hat, presenting a bald pate with long white hair descending from the level of his ears.

The effect upon Mr Ormerod was not immediate, but none the less shocking when it came. For a full half-minute, he stared at the newcomer without any change of expression. And then I saw a shadow pass across his finely-chiselled countenance, and his eyes flared with recognition. He rose to his feet. His voice was strained and harsh:

'Miss Copley, be so good as to withdraw and leave me alone with this – *gentleman!*'

I fearfully obeyed, casting a backward glance at the two men, who stood facing each other. Mr Ormerod had the same expression, but the Limping Frenchman, his back being turned to me, gave me no hint of what might have been written on his face or in his eyes.

I admit to the fault of eavesdropping. Outside the library, I paused for a moment or two, telling myself that my employer might be in some hazard, that the Limping Frenchman (who, surely, from Mr Ormerod's reaction on recognising the man, could be no friend) might be armed and intent to do him mischief; but I could hear very little through the double doors.

Nothing – save one utterance, delivered by the master of Castle Delamere in a hoarse shout:

'By heaven, I thought I was rid of all of you forever!'

Disquieted by that strange and disturbing encounter, I went up to my sitting-room and paced the floor for some time, trying to rid myself of a very keen sense of impending tragedy. It was not till the clock on the chimneypiece declared the hour of eight that I realised I had reneged upon my promise to call and kiss Rupert goodnight. Accordingly, I made my hasty way to the nursery, and arrived outside the door to hear a scream coming from within. At close quarters, it was clearly not only an expression of pain, but also the same sound that Mrs Stittle the housekeeper had dismissed as the cry of a seagull. Appalled, I went in, fully expecting to find that some hideous domestic accident had taken place, and that Rupert, or the tweeny, or both, had fallen, cut themselves, burned themselves.

But, no . . .

The next thing I heard as I crossed Rupert's playroom, with the toys of his evening's games still scattered all over the floor, was the girl Lottie's voice delivering a threat that stopped me in my tracks – coming as it did from the open door of the nursery bedroom beyond:

'Shut yer eyes an' keep quiet, you little bastard – or I'll put the light out an' call the Bogey-man fer to come fer you!'

This was followed by a slap, and a muffled cry of pain.

'Please, Tweeny,' Rupert's whimper, 'please don't put out the light. And don't – don't tell the Bogey-man I've been naughty.'

'Then you go to sleep, damn you! I've no time to waste on you. Isn't my fine fine lad awaitin' me on the end of the

59

causeway, fer to take me to the village dance this night? And I'm a-stuck with *you*!'

Another slap. I pushed wide the nursery door, and saw her deliver it across Rupert's arm.

She heard me. He saw me. Our three pairs of eyes joined across the room. In his eyes: a certain joy. In hers: fear not unmixed with brute cunning and defiance. In mine: surely a blazing fury.

'Get away from him!' I stormed.

'You'll not get him asleep any other way!' she retorted. 'Try what you will, he'll be teasing you till midnight, with his "Give me another tale, do. If you don't, I'll scream and wake everybody".'

'It's not true, it's not true!' cried Rupert. 'I can't go to sleep 'cos she puts out the candle and makes it all dark, an' she says she'll tell the Bogey-man to come if I tell Papa she's been hitting me.'

'Listen to him!' screeched the girl. 'Just you listen to his lying tongue!' Her face was ashen with guilt.

'Give me your arm, Rupert,' I said, and taking the boy's right arm that she had just struck, I rolled up the sleeve of the nightgown and bared it to the shoulder.

From wrist to elbow and beyond, the pink and tender flesh was bruised and blackened in ugly patches. There must have been a dozen such marks upon it, each the size of a five shilling piece.

'The little 'uns – they're allus falling down and hurting themselves, ain't they?' said the girl, haltingly.

I bared his left arm, which told the same story. As upon the other, he had been repeatedly beaten over a long period – some bruises were red and fresh, some dark and angry, some faded to blue or green. Impelled by a nameless fury, I then stripped the boy naked and found other evidence of her savagery: upon the back and the buttocks, the legs, the shoulders; but nothing that could have been seen by anyone when he was fully clothed: and, of course, he appeared fully clothed to everyone but his torturer, who also bathed him.

I could not bring myself to look at the creature, who was by then crouching somewhere over by the wall.

'*Get out!*' I heard someone say in a voice I had never heard before, though it must have been mine.

She fled out of the room. Her way was impeded by a figure at the open door, for I heard a small scuffle. When I looked round, she was gone, but Mrs Stittle was standing there, leaning against the jamb, staring across at the boy in the bed. Having summarily dismissed the evil-doer without a word of reproof (I had not dared to begin, for fear that, in my mounting fury, I might have laid hands on the creature), and feeling cheated of a butt for my anger, I turned upon the housekeeper as a scapegoat.

'I hope that you heard all that!' I blazed. 'So much for Rupert being a difficult child! So much for the screaming seagulls! You must have known what's been going on and have shut your mind to it – if you haven't actually been conniving in the torturing of this innocent, frightened child!'

She came forward into the loom of the candlelight, and it was then I saw, with a sudden lurch of the heart, that the woman's face was streaked with tears.

'I never knew – never guessed for one moment – what was going on,' she whispered brokenly. 'Rupert never spoke of it . . .'

'He was terrified to silence,' I replied, but less harshly than before. 'It's my belief she thought to break him the way they tame the poor dancing bears: by fear and beatings. She forced-fed him to nausea and beyond, and when he was sick she thrashed him. At night – at night, she read to him, though it's to be wondered at that such an ignorant creature is able to read. Aaah . . .' Reaching down, I picked up a book that had fallen from off the bed. Did I say 'book'? The thing I held in my hand could scarcely be said to deserve a term that is applied to some of the noblest creations of man. Dog-eared with long use, cheaply printed on coarse paper with a luridly-coloured cover, it rejoiced in the title of *The Phantom of Hellbrook Hall*, which unlikely creature was depicted on the front, with loving attention as to flowing robes, skull-like head, talons dripping blood, staring eyes – the traditional accoutrements of fairground horror. Thumbing over the grimy pages, I saw that the text matched up to the cover: ill-written and ill-

61

spelt, though largely composed of words of no more than two syllables.

'Is this the sort of thing she read to you, Rupert dear?' I asked.

He nodded. 'She only reads that one to me,' he said. 'And she knows it off by heart. I know if off by heart now,' he added wistfully. He pointed to the creature depicted on the cover. 'That's the Bogey-man,' he said. 'That's the one she promises to tell if I ever tell anyone she hits me.' His little face was suddenly suffused with an unhealthy colour, his breath grew laboured, he began to cough. I immediately discerned the onset of an asthmatic attack.

'Oh, the poor little mite,' said Mrs Stittle. 'Shall I send the kitchen lad for Dr Caldwell, Miss?'

'No, you will not,' I retorted. 'For I've a mind that there has been some complicity between that wretched girl and the doctor. Come, my love –' I gathered up Rupert into my arms, supporting him, feeling, as if in my own body, the agony that was racking that frail form.

It was near midnight before we had Rupert sleeping peacefully. Mrs Stittle, who had shown the most complete devotion during his attack, insisted on remaining with him throughout the night. I decided that, no matter how late the hour, I must seek out Mr Ormerod and apprise him of the true facts about Rupert and the monstrous creature (a creature steeped in cruelty and in the delight of giving pain; we had been lectured upon such persons at Miss Nightingale's school, for they are as sick in the mind as a sufferer from the consumption is sick in the body) to whom he had entrusted the care of his only child. Accordingly, I left the housekeeper with her young charge, confident that her devotion was entirely directed towards the little fellow and that even his own mother could not have cared for him more ardently.

I went down to the library, and was not surprised to see a chink of light seeping from under the green baize, inner door. A tap upon it brought an immediate response for me to enter.

Mr Ormerod was seated in a wing armchair by the fireplace, a brandy glass in his hand. His eyes, when they sought mine,

were as keen as ever, but there was a hint of something like –
what? – *defeat* in his whole demeanour. A brief glance around
the chamber told me that he had got rid of his unwanted visitor.

'This is a late hour for you to come a-calling, Miss Copley,'
he said. 'And I discern from your looks that it is a matter of
some urgency and importance. Will you take a glass of brandy?'

'Thank you no, sir,' I responded. 'What I have to say will not
disaccommodate you for more than a few minutes. In short
terms, you must immediately dismiss the between-maid Lottie
– and without a reference. And you must also dispense with the
services of Dr Caldwell, who, I am persuaded, is a scoundrel.'

'Indeed, must I, Miss?' he replied, raising an eyebrow at me.
'And why must I do these things, if it be not an impertinence to
ask?'

And then I told him all: about Dr Caldwell's sordid fraud
with the medical equipment, about the girl Lottie's cruelties –
everything. When I had done, Mr Ormerod rose, and, pacing
up and down the room for some time, seemed to shut me out
from his thoughts. Presently, he paused, and, fixing me with a
steady glance, said: 'And you think, do you, that Caldwell knew
what was going on all the time?'

I spread my hands. 'How can I prove it, sir? But, yes, I do
think so. The scene that was played out for my benefit – and for
yours, also – on the night that I arrived, in the light of what I
now know, has all the elements of a well-rehearsed charade.
Yes, I believe that Dr Caldwell knew – or guessed – how it was
that this illiterate between-maid appeared to succeed so much
better with a sickly, nervous child than did a regular nanny.'

'What do we do now, Miss Copley?' he asked simply.

It was an opening the like of which I had never hoped to
have; guessing, rather, that I should have to fight and plead
Rupert's case before the bar of his father's conscience. He had
made it all too easy for me – or so I hoped.

'Sir, please may I sit down?' I asked. 'It has been a long
evening.'

'Dear Miss Copley, how very remiss of me,' he cried. 'Pray do
so – and will you not reconsider and accept a brandy?'

'Thank you no, sir, but I should very much like a small sherry
wine,' I replied.

'So you shall. So you shall.' He busied himself in pouring me the wine and laid it at my elbow, at the chair where I had seated myself; he may, or may not, have fortified himself with brandy following the departure of his unbidden caller, but the hand that placed the glass on the side table was as steady as a rock.

'You were about to advise me, I think,' he said, without the remotest trace of irony.

I took a deep breath and steeled myself against my nervousness, and nervous I well might have been to contemplate what amounted to the dressing-down of the master of Castle Delamere, a Royal Academician moreover – not to mention the possessor of a pair of deep grey eyes that bored into my eyes so disconcertingly.

'Sir . . .' I began.

'Yes, Miss Copley? Please continue.'

'Mr Ormerod, what your son needs most of all is what he receives the least of,' I declared.

'And what is that?'

'Love!'

'Love – ah!' Did I notice a slight wavering of that steely-grey glance? Did he but avoid my eyes, if even for an instant. 'And am I to assume, ma'am, that when you say that my son is lacking in love, you refer specifically to *my* love?'

As well to be hung for a sheep as a lamb, I replied: 'Yes, sir, I do!'

'Aaaah! That is very interesting.'

Taking the bit between my teeth, I went on with a recklessness that surprised even myself: 'Sir, the first time I set eyes on Rupert, when he came down to the dining-room to say goodnight, it struck me then – and the impression remains with me – that his only wish was to throw his arms about you and blurt out all his fears, real and imaginary – and heaven knows, for a child of his age, he lived with fears that were real enough. But neither by word nor gesture did you encourage him to be other than a perfectly correct little gentleman. And gentlemen do not betray their feelings, do they, Mr Ormerod?'

'You search me out very closely,' he replied, 'and I think that, in many regards, you find me. I have told you that the role of parent does not well become me. What I must now tell you is that, though I would defend Rupert to the death and beyond, I do not have the natural love that a father should bear for his only child. And for a reason.'

'What is that reason, sir?' I asked, greatly daring.

He took a deep quaff of his brandy before replying. 'Every time I look upon my son, I am reminded of his mother.'

'That is to be expected, sir,' I said. 'And what more natural and desirable?'

'My wife – my beloved wife – died in giving birth to Rupert,' he said.

What could I reply to that? My headstrong nature had pitchforked me into an encounter with this strange and un-accountable man with his mixture of strengths and weaknesses. His simple declaration struck every weapon from my hands. He sat before me, his head bowed, showing the tangle of thick curls behind his ears and in the nape of his neck. I had a sudden and unbidden impulse to reach out and stroke that head for com-fort; instead, I rose to my feet and said: 'Sir, I am sorry if I have overstepped the bounds that a servant should observe between herself and her master. But there it is.'

'You have done well to speak out, Miss Copley,' he replied, 'and I shall abide by your advice. Is there aught else?'

I thought for a moment. 'It might be a good idea, sir,' I said, 'if Rupert had something upon which to lavish the great fund of affection that all children possess. Might I suggest a pet dog?'

He nodded. 'An excellent idea. My friend Squire Rigby of Nunwich Hall, whose daughters' portraits I am at present painting, has an excellent female pug-dog who has recently been delivered of five rumbustious puppies. I will ask for one of them in part payment of my fee for the portraits – and will attend to it tomorrow. Is there aught else, Miss Copley?'

'No more, sir,' I replied. 'Goodnight.'

'Goodnight, Miss Copley.'

I paused at the door, one question still beating in my mind. Again, my headstrong will drove me to pose a question that a more prudent person would have left unasked:

'Sir, your visitor – the Frenchman with the limp – has he departed, or is he staying at the castle?'

'He has gone, Miss Copley,' replied Justin Ormerod, 'and he will not be returning.'

Looking back at him, I saw again the expression of his countenance that had struck me so forcibly upon my entering the library: the look of defeat. And a hint of despair added.

Justin Ormerod, while resident master of Castle Delamere, was never quite the same after that night . . .

The following morning, having met with my friend the cook, and carried my coffee and bread, butter and bacon to my favourite spot on the ramparts, I surprised my employer in the act of scanning the mainland through a telescope. That's to say, I espied him standing on a higher level of the fortification and he did not at first see me. I was able to observe his movements for a full five minutes: first, he searched the cliff road leading to the causeway, then gave his attention to the wood beyond the road, and after that to the cluster of fishermen's cottages to the south. That done, he turned about and scanned a fishing smack that was beating to windward about a mile from the castle rock. Then he returned to the cliff road. It was after he had completed this cycle once more that he saw me looking up at him. Instantly, he snapped close the telescope, gave me a stiff bow of greeting, and disappeared from my view.

I was left with my speculations as to what – or whom – he was seeking for so assiduously.

Notwithstanding whatever problems lay upon his mind, however, he did not forget his promise of the previous night. Rupert, Mrs Stittle and I were having tea in the nursery that afternoon (the girl Lottie had taken her departure, though when and by what means I never did learn) when the master entered with a divine scrap of wrinkled skin, covering an immensely fat little body topped by a countenance of such wrinkled, care-worn lugubriousness as would have touched the hardest heart. This was the pug-dog puppy.

Rupert fell in love with the little fellow on sight – so did the rest of us. Truth to say, the little scrap blotted his copybook by wetting on the carpet as soon as he was put down; but he followed this transgression with a glance of deepest regret to each one of us that had us all in stitches.

He was to be called Clovis: the suggestion came from Mr Ormerod, who said that the little pug put him in mind of a painter of his acquaintance. Rupert, whose ready acceptance of the name, accompanied by an adoring glance towards his sire, revealed only too clearly where his affections lay, was in transports of delight with his new little friend. I exchanged a glance with Mr Ormerod: he nodded and smiled, and it was like the touching of hands, doing much to erase the memory of the awkward moment when I had surprised him with the telescope on the battlements.

The few days that followed the departure of the girl Lottie and the arrival of the puppy passed in an atmosphere of tranquillity which was only marred, for me, by the strange mood that seemed to encompass Mr Ormerod after the visit of the Limping Frenchman.

I took the main meals of the day with him, and sometimes Rupert was allowed to join us at luncheon in the great hall as a special treat. My employer, during this time, seldom did more than exchange the customary courtesies, and spent most of his time pushing his food unenthusiastically round his plate and staring into the middle distance. His working day was spent between the library and his studio on the ground floor of the castle, to which one was only allowed admission on sufferance. I had one occasion to speak to him on a minor domestic matter of some immediate urgency, and found him painting in the studio. He greeted me with some impatience and delivered his decision upon the matter in very short order. I noticed two things whilst I was with him: firstly, the picture he was painting – of a semi-tropical landscape washed by a sea of iridescent hue – was beautiful to the extreme, and, secondly, that his telescope, placed upon a tripod, was trained out of the long window that commanded a view of the causeway and the mainland.

I think it was the day following, or perhaps the day after that, when Rupert was taking his post-prandial nap, that I chanced to go up to my apartment to fetch my sewing. Little Clovis, who had taken to following me everywhere when his little master was not awake and at hand, bounded on ahead of me, corkscrew tail wagging with every step of the spiral staircase, and was quickly out of sight round the next bend. When I came to the first landing, there was no sign of him, but the iron-studded door of the room apartment containing – as Mrs Stittle had put it – 'unwanted furniture' was ajar, and I could hear the little mischief snuffling around inside.

'Come on out with you, Clovis,' I said, pushing wide the door.

No sign of him. The room within was full of furniture covered in dust sheets, pictures and all. From somewhere near at hand, I heard a faint and distinctive snuffle: Master Clovis had taken cover and was defying me to find him.

'Where are you, naughty boy?' I demanded with vastly more severity that I felt. No answer, no response, save a little excited breathing from a dark corner to my right.

Entering into the spirit of the game, I tiptoed towards the sound, which was coming from behind a shrouded sofa. I had no sooner closed with it when my quarry broke cover, and, with an excited bark, sped across the room as fast as his short bowed legs could carry him towards another hide. I followed after, but, moving not so nimbly as he, collided with a piece of furniture and, being obliged to hold on to steady myself, dislodged the dust sheet, causing it to slide to the floor.

I found myself staring at a painting set upon an easel: a half-length portrait of a woman framed in elaborately carved and gilded wood.

And such a woman . . .

Dark, she was, dark as a gipsy, with hair of the special blackness that carries deep blue highlights, and it was worn over her shoulders, unbound. The eyes – dark and lustrous – stared out at me with a hint of mockery. The lips – full and sensuous – were slightly parted to show even teeth of a dazzling whiteness. There was a small mole on her right cheekbone, a minor defect in a perfection of face and form that was in itself a grace note of elegance. The beauty of her form was in no doubt, for she was nude.

There was a name plate set into the lower border of the gilded frame:

Esmée
BY JUSTIN ORMEROD

I had scarcely read this when a tramp of footsteps on the stair outside briefly heralded the appearance of my employer in the open doorway.

'What the devil are you doing here, Miss?' he blazed.

It was on the tip of my tongue to explain that I had come in on the trail of the puppy, that I was up to no harm; but then Clovis, frightened by Mr Ormerod's shout, crept from out of his hide and ran to me to pick him up. This I did, by which time, with the puppy nuzzling against my chin for comfort and rolling his saucer eyes towards the figure in the doorway, my employer augmented his first challenge with a remark that slammed the door on any hope of a conciliatory settlement of the misunderstanding:

'Damn you, woman – how *dare* you spy on me?'

He crossed the room, and, snatching up the fallen dust sheet, threw it hastily over the portrait, hiding the nude Esmée from my view. That was enough for me. Still holding the pug puppy, I swept out of the room, fighting against tears of hurt and resentment, but being determined not to show them.

'Miss Copley, come back here!' he cried.

I did not 'come back'; I kept walking . . .

Running, rather; up the second flight of winding stairs, with the little dog still nestled against my cheek. And when I reached my own door, I opened it and, slamming it behind me, forced home the bolt against intrusion. Which done, I threw myself down upon the sitting-room sofa and, hugging little Clovis close, gave way to tears.

As if from far away, I think I heard his hesitant footsteps ascending the stairway to my door; sensed him raising his hand to knock upon it; imagined how, with a sudden irresolution, the hand and arm fell to his side.

Moments later, I heard his footfalls descending.

I do not cry easily, or often. The crisis being quickly over, I gave little Clovis a saucer of water, then went dolefully to pack my traps for a departure. For how – I asked myself – could I any longer remain under the roof of a man who could think of me as a busybody and – worse – a spy?

I had folded my things upon the bed, ready to pack into the carpet-bag and the two valises that comprised my luggage, and had remembered that, notwithstanding all, I must go and wake Rupert, give him his tea and offer some explanation – any kind of explanation – why the nurse who had consigned him to slumber an hour previously must now be taking her departure from him forever, when there came a peremptory knock upon my door. It was a footman to tell me that the police had arrived, and would I attend upon them immediately in the library?

It is odd to consider that, had the police come but an hour later, and I had quit Castle Delamere forever before that time, the remainder of my life would have taken a totally different course, with different rooms, different places, different people – all the indefinable mishmash of what we call the Future, for me turned upside down and awry.

Part Two

ABOARD THE S.S. *HINDUSTAN*,
BOUND FOR THE NEAR EAST

FOUR

They were three in number: the senior amongst them, a man of middle years and middling height, with watchful eyes and a slight tic in his left cheek, was clad in a caped tweed coat. The others, constables both, were in cloaks and tall hats, uniformed.

Mr Ormerod was seated, as ever, behind his desk in the library when I entered. The others had remained standing. He gestured towards the man in the caped coat, addressing me:

'Miss Copley, this is Sergeant Osworth of the East Suffolk Constabulary. Sergeant, this is Miss Copley, a qualified nurse, who attends my son.'

The sergeant took my hand and bowed over it. At close quarters, his watery blue eyes were altogether more watchful and shrewd than I had at first imagined. The tic in his cheek I found most disconcerting.

'A few questions, ma'am,' he said. 'Just a few questions, that's all. Nothing to alarm.'

'It appears that . . .' began Mr Ormerod.

The sergeant silenced him with a gesture of the hand and a remonstrating glance: 'I will attend to the questioning, if you please, sir,' he said. And to me: 'Miss Copley, I beg you to address your memory to the Wednesday of this week when a visitor called upon the castle. Do you recall the occasion? Do you recall the visitor?'

'The Limping Frenchman!' I exclaimed, involuntarily.

I had the notion that the tic in his cheek was stilled for as long as it took him to digest my declaration. 'Quite so, Miss Copley,' he replied at length. 'The "Limping Frenchman" – yes, that describes him as well as he has been described so far, by those who observed his recent arrival in the district. "Limping Frenchman" – a most economical turn of phrase, if I may say so. But to bring ourselves to his arrival at the castle – can you tell me, please, in your own words, of your part in receiving this – ah – Limping Frenchman?'

I had played little enough part, and told him so; then went on to describe how, upon the Frenchman's request, I had guided him to the library, announced him to Mr Ormerod and left them together. An imp of prudence prompted me – I know not why at that time – to gloss over my firm impression that my employer was not pleased to see his visitor, nor had the latter called to exchange pleasantries. And I made no mention of the remark that I had overheard through the door:

'. . . *I thought I was rid of all of you forever!*'

Sergeant Osworth listened intently to my account, interrupting only once – to ask me by what name the visitor had introduced himself to me.

I cast a quick glance at Mr Ormerod, but receiving no other guidance than a blank stare, replied: 'Why, the gentleman did not give me a name, but said that Mr Ormerod would know him when he saw him.'

'And did Mr Ormerod appear to know his visitor, ma'am?' demanded the sergeant.

'Yes, he did,' I replied.

'At once?'

'After – after a short pause for recognition,' I supplied.

'A short pause – aaaah. As if, would you say, that they had not met for some time, or that the – ah – Limping Frenchman had greatly changed in appearance? Would you say that, ma'am?'

'Something like that,' I replied.

Turning to Mr Ormerod, the sergeant said: 'Sir, you told me you had some difficulty in recalling the man's name, but that you finally remembered it to be Lavache.'

'That is so,' responded the other. 'Jean-Pierre Lavache.'

'Known to you from – how far back?'

'Oh, fifteen – twenty years – when I was a student at the École Jules in Paris.'

'Lavache was a fellow-student?'

74

'He was a friend of a fellow-student. I knew Lavache only very slightly.'

'But it was a cordial relationship you had with this man?'

'Cordial – yes. I would not put it any higher.'

'And in the course of this unexpected visit last Wednesday, how would you describe the tenor of your meeting. Would you call it – the word is mine, not yours – cordial?'

I drew breath sharply. Sergeant Osworth may have heard me. If he did so, he gave no sign.

'Cordial is precisely how I would describe the atmosphere of our meeting,' said my employer. 'But, Sergeant, I simply do not understand the reason for this questioning, and I beg you to explain . . .'

'Jean-Pierre Lavache is dead,' responded the other, flatly.

'Dead?'

'His body was found hanging by the neck from a hawthorn tree in the wood beyond the causeway – *your* causeway, Mr Ormerod. It was found at midday today. As well as can be ascertained, it had been there for about three days – that is to say since about Wednesday.'

'Suicide!' cried Mr Ormerod.

'Or murder,' responded the other. 'He was not a powerful man, nor a man in a good state of physical health. It would have been the simplest thing in the world for a strong and well-nourished man to have overpowered him and strung him up. Did you say something, Miss Copley?'

I pressed a hand to my lips to choke back an exclamation. The police-sergeant gazed impassively at me for a full half minute longer than seemed necessary, the tic working in his cheek, then returned his regard to my employer.

'For what reason did Lavache call upon you, sir?' he asked quietly.

Mr Ormerod said: 'Well, he told me he had fallen upon bad times, and, having come to England to take work as a weaver of fine cloth, which had been his trade, he was without money to set himself up in premises, and begged me for the loan of fifty guineas.'

'And did you lend him fifty guineas, sir?'

'I do not lend, following the dictum that lending and borrowing profit neither the lender nor the borrower. In view of our long, if tenuous, acquaintance, I gave the man fifty guineas as an unencumbered gift.'

'That was mightily generous of you, Mr Ormerod.'

The other shrugged. And then Sergeant Osworth did a surprising thing: taking from the pocket of his caped coat a small paper sack, he emptied out from it on to the desk top before my employer a pile of gold guineas.

'There are fifty, Mr Ormerod,' he said quietly. 'Would you suppose these are the ones you gave Lavache?'

'Undoubtedly,' responded the other. 'That sack, as you see, is printed with the name of my banker's agent in Nunwich, from whom I drew the sum of three hundred guineas the last time I was there – and in that undoubted sack I gave Lavache his fifty.'

'They were found in the dead man's pocket,' said Osworth, eyeing the other man very keenly, the tic pulsating in his cheek.

'Then it would suggest a case of suicide,' said Mr Ormerod. 'Or, at least, not murder for profit.'

'There are other motives for murder than profit, Mr Ormerod,' said the other. 'And even profit itself may take many forms. There is immediate profit, as may come from killing a man and stealing his purse. On the other hand, there may be a long-term profit which cannot be measured in cash. But no more of that, sir. You and the young lady have patiently answered my questions, and I will take my leave with thanks. Your servant, ma'am. Yours also, sir.' He bowed and went towards the door. His pair of matched acolytes, who had stood in their black capes and high hats throughout the encounter without uttering a word between them, for all the world like a couple of crows perched on a fence, fell in line and followed their superior.

Sergeant Osworth paused at the door; turned to regard us.

'It may be of interest that the deceased, unless someone comes forward to pay for a decent interment, will be buried in a pauper's grave tomorrow, since, by law, the money found upon him must be held in trust till claimed by any next-of-kin,' he said.

'I will provide funds for the fellow to have a decent burial,' responded Mr Ormerod.

'I had thought you might, sir,' said Osworth. 'Indeed I did. And very commendable of you, I'm sure. Good day to you both.'

He left us.

Alone with Justin Ormerod, following upon our appalling encounter in the lumber room, I thought to make a quick exit, and then it seemed to me that this was the action of a coward, and quite unworthy of a niece of Riding Master Josh Strick who had fought with the 17th Lancers at Balaclava, so I turned to the master of Castle Delamere (I had not been invited to sit throughout my interrogation by the police-sergeant), and began to blurt out my statement of dismissal:

'Sir, in view of what happened . . .'

Simultaneously, he said: 'Miss Copley, I have been thinking . . .'

I said: 'I'm so sorry. Please go on.'

'No, you shall have your say, Miss Copley.'

'Please – you first.'

'Very well.' He came round the big desk towards me, his deep grey eyes clouded with the presence of some burden, the source of which – to my immediate alarm – I at first thought he was going to confide in me. He did not. Instead, he made a brief and simple statement of his fault in taking me to task with such brutal vehemence. And then, an apology so graceful that I could not do other than accept it:

'Quite unforgivable, Miss Copley, but the more forgivable, I hope, for the hopelessness of the case I plead on my own behalf. I have no excuse to offer, only my deepest regrets, which I trust you will consent to receive.'

'With the greatest of pleasure, sir,' I responded. And what else could I possibly have said?

'You are now no doubt packed to leave?' he asked.

'To a very large degree, sir,' I said. 'It wanted only my carpet-bag to be filled with my overnight things such as I would have used on my journey back home to Dartmoor.'

'Excellent, excellent!' he declared. 'Do not, I beg you, trouble to unpack!'

'*Sir?*' I stared at him, entirely put out of countenance. Was it for this that he had kowtowed and apologised: merely in order, not to accept my resignation, but to *dismiss* me out of hand?

Those deep grey eyes seemed to clear of their burden, and something like a smile of puckish good humour touched the edges of his coldly-chiselled lips. It was gone on the instant, even before he spoke again; and when he spoke, I was astonished beyond belief.

'Miss Copley,' he said, 'I have changed my mind concerning the invitation which I have received from Egypt. In short, I have decided to accept the offer. I may say, Miss Copley, that your arguments regarding the benefits of the sea voyage, the Egyptian climate and so forth, have added great weight to my decision. I shall take Rupert with me. I shall also take Mrs Stittle. And I hope – I dearly hope, Miss Copley – that you will consent to accompany us – for Rupert's sake.'

The tone of the declaration was sincere, the timbre of the voice was free of any overtones that might have suggested that he was being less than honest with me; but, oddly, I had the distinct impression that he was not telling me the entire truth; notwithstanding which I accepted his offer without hesitation.

It was not till evening, when I went up on to my favourite spot on the battlements to enjoy the last of that glorious day of our Indian summer, and saw Justin Ormerod standing up on high, telescope raised to his eye, scanning the causeway, the coastal road, the land beyond and the empty sea, that I gave shape to the random thoughts which had been teeming in my mind ever since he had sprung the surprise upon me: the growing conviction, hardened by what I had just seen, that the master of Castle Delamere's prime reason for suddenly deciding to go to Egypt was not to benefit his little son's health, nor yet for the honour of recording for posterity the opening of the Suez canal – though, perhaps, these issues added the pennyweight which tipped the balance.

No – I became convinced that the events following upon the arrival of the Limping Frenchman – his uneasy searching of causeway, road and sea; even, perhaps, his violent reaction to my accidental unveiling of the nude Esmée – pointed to a deep unease.

Escape . . .

The word forever returned to my mind and took hold of my imagination, colouring the thoughts I had about Justin Ormerod and his unexpected change of heart about the Egyptian journey.

He was going to Egypt *to escape!*
But – from what? Or from whom?

A week later, the five of us – Mr Ormerod, Mrs Stittle, Rupert, myself and Clovis the pug – embarked aboard the steamship *Hindustan* in London river, bound for Port Said by way of Southampton, Lisbon, Gibraltar, Malta and Alexandria.

The last of the Indian summer was dying in the bustle of the busy river and its crowded, narrow-streeted shores. Hand in hand with the excited, wide-eyed Rupert, I stood on the upper deck and saw the baggage being loaded aboard by dark-skinned, unsmiling Lascar seamen, while all about us the arcane and curiously impressive activities of shipboard life – the coiling down of ropes, climbing of rigging, ringing of bells, shouting of incomprehensible orders – went on at full spate.

Of passengers there appeared to be none other than ourselves – at least until the hour before our departure, which was to be at eleven o'clock in the forenoon, to catch the ebb tide downriver. Shortly before then, a carriage arrived on the quay by London Bridge and drew up at the ship's gangplank. A tall, upright, military-looking man alighted and, having paid off the driver, went round to the other side of the vehicle and handed down a statuesque lady in a violet costume, violet hat, feathers and all. By this time, porters who had been standing and idling around had moved to lift down a considerable amount of luggage which was piled high on the rear of the carriage, and proceeded to carry it after the man and woman as they ascended the gangplank.

Rupert and I watched with some interest. It was then that little Clovis insinuated himself into the situation; he also had been regarding the new arrivals, craning his bullet head down towards the deck below. As the gentleman came aboard and was greeted by the purser, the pug gave vent to a riot of staccato barking which is the breed's peculiar method – entirely without malicious intent – of greeting those who enter what they have mapped out as their personal territory.

Upon hearing the challenge, the man looked up with a slight frown, which softened when he saw the three of us – dog, boy and woman – leaning over the rail of the boat deck and gazing down on them. His companion also followed his glance, and revealed her face to us from under the wide brim of her violet bonnet.

It was an unforgettable face: fair to look upon, with wide-set, candid eyes and generous lips that parted in a ready smile. She was about my own age, perhaps a little more.

'What a charming little rascal of a pug-dog,' she said, and waved up to us. Next moment she, her companion and most of their quite considerable luggage passed from our sight.

'Miss Copley, I'm a bit hungry,' announced Rupert, whose appetite – after I had resorted to the well-tried principle of allowing a child to eat when he is hungry and always tempting him with dishes he likes best of all – had arrived at that of a normal, healthy little boy.

'It will be luncheon quite shortly,' I said.

'I don't think I can wait till then,' he responded, and his delicate lower lip trembled; meanwhile he cast a sidelong glance towards the quay, where – and it had not escaped my notice – there was a toffee apple and sweetmeat stall of the most dubious sort. I perceived that the issue called for strategy.

'I have in my cabin,' I told him, 'a pot of Devonshire cream that was sent to me by my mother. You may have what's left of it, Rupert, spread on a biscuit – and there'll be a little left over for Clovis, also.'

The small hand came up and joined mine trustingly. 'That will be nice, Miss Copley,' he said.

The four of us – that's to say Mr Ormerod, Mrs Stittle, Rupert and myself – had been allocated three tiny cabins in the rear of the ship, which were reached by means of a staircase from the boat deck. Passing by the open door of the cabin which she was to share with Rupert, we saw Mrs Stittle unpacking hers and Rupert's traps. She looked round and smiled.

'Is Mr Ormerod back?' she asked. The master of Castle Delamere had taken the opportunity, while he was in London, of calling in at the Royal Academy.

'Not yet,' I said.

'Oh, I hope we don't sail without him!'

'I'm sure we'll not,' I responded.

'How shall we deal with those heathen creatures without Mr Ormerod?' she cried. The good woman, born and bred within sight of Castle Delamere and – like so many peasant folk in my native county of Devon – never having moved further away than the next village, regarded all who lived beyond that compass as heathens. Indeed, Mrs Stittle had no clear concept of where Egypt and its people were, save that they must be situated somewhere beyond London and over the water.

'He will be back,' I reassured her. 'In time for luncheon and in time to sail, never fear.'

In my cabin – which consisted of a small box (with literally not enough room to swing a cat), a writing-desk, a chair, a let-down cot – I provided Rupert with the remainder of the Devonshire cream spread on a biscuit and allowed Clovis to dip his snub nose into the pot and scour out the residue with his questing tongue.

I always aver that one of the delights of children, apart from the joy of watching them recover from illness and spring alive and vibrant, is to observe them eating: to see the unself-conscious manner in which first they regard the object of their pleasure, contemplating as to in which manner they will make their attack: whether to eat the best bits first or leave them till last (the latter method must, surely, must be one of the habits which distinguishes humans from the lesser animals). In the event, Rupert, faced with the problem of a Bath Oliver biscuit thickly plastered with clotted cream the consistency of butter, chose first to lick the cream off precisely half of the biscuit, then eat the remaining half, cream and all.

Leaving him to contemplate the remaining dry half Bath Oliver (watched wistfully by the pug, who had by this time cleaned out the interior of the pot to mirror brightness), I idly turned to the contents of my carpet-bag, which I had piled upon the writing-desk to sort out in order of priorities for the voyage. There was the diary, whose contents I had kept more in the breach than the observance ever since I entered Miss Nightingale's School (and in it, surely, I must faithfully record every

81

day, every hour, of the tremendous adventure ahead of me); an address book containing all the relations and friends to whom I must write; innumerable bits and pieces; a wooden-top doll that had delighted my childhood; the novel that I had not found time to open ever since life at Castle Delamere had turned all topsyturvy . . .

From out of the pages of the novel, as I picked it up, slipped a single half-sheet of writing paper. I turned it over. There, penned in my own hasty hand, was a near-cryptograph which I had composed in a hurry after Rupert and I had returned to the castle following our encounter with the old gipsy woman and her idiot grandson, and which – thanks to the events which had followed – had been washed clean from my mind.

> *. . . the child better than they think . . . you would be content in your grief but for a letter . . .*

And then – alarmingly:

> *. . . You will travel far, both of you . . . cross three seas . . . five perils . . . and two shall die.'*

Very slowly, in a manner of detachment, I felt the hairs of my scalp prickle, every one, and the cold finger of fear trail its way down my spine.

Rupert broke in upon my sudden horror: 'Miss Copley, Miss Copley, I've shared the last half of my biscuit with Clovis, can I go up on deck and look for Papa?'

'Yes, dear,' I heard myself say. 'But ask Mrs Stittle to go with you.'

'Yes, Miss Copley. Come on, Clovis! Race you!'

He clattered out of the cabin, followed by the eager pug. I looked down at the paper in my hand. The enormity of my forgetfulness struck home at me like a dart to the heart. How *could* I, in view of what had happened since, have overlooked the prediction?

It was all there:

> *You will travel far . . . cross three seas . . .*

Very carefully, I pencilled in underneath this declaration:

ENGLISH CHANNEL − ATLANTIC − MEDITERRANEAN.

Of course, the whole burden of the gipsy's declaration had seemed so unlikely that I had largely discounted them – all save one.

All save one . . .

But now – a hardness and roundness of truth was beginning to show itself.

First, the letter: the letter without which – in the gipsy's words – I would have been content in my grief; the letter about which I could not – still can not – bring myself to write, to speak, even to contemplate.

Next, the prediction about our voyage to Egypt, exact in the very particulars of our route.

And what followed . . . ?

Five perils . . .

And:

Two shall die.

The dining saloon of the steamship *Hindustan*, a compartment which occupied the entire width of the ship and almost a quarter of its length, served otherwise as a drawing-room for the passengers and was at night given over to those male voyagers who did not possess cabins but were obliged to sling hammocks – such being the rigours of the shipboard life.

At one o'clock sharp, the tuneful sound of a brass gong summoned us from the upper deck, where we had been watching the passing scenery of London river on our way down to the sea, having left the jetty at precisely the appointed hour. Mr Ormerod, who had arrived aboard in good time, led us in to luncheon. I seemed to detect in him a sense of strain (he had spent the last few minutes before our departure in scanning the jetty below the ship, as if looking for someone).

Someone? His unknown enemy, or enemies, I asked myself.

The seating in the dining saloon comprised two long tables, set side by side and reaching almost the entire length of the compartment. Across the end of these, and forming a hollow square, was a smaller table. All were covered in dazzlingly white napery and very commendable crockery and silverware embellished with the Company's cypher. Mr Ormerod took his place at the head of the right-hand (I have since learned to call it the starboard) table, while I sat on his right hand with Rupert beside me and Mrs Stittle opposite. There were places for at least a dozen others at the same board, but when four other passengers arrived – an obvious man and wife and two grown siblings, male and female – they, in the typical manner of the insular English, sat themselves at the far end away from us, greeting us with no more than the most perfunctory nods, which we returned – perfunctorily.

The arrival of the beautiful lady in violet (for so I had named her in my thoughts when she came aboard) and her escort, the gentleman of military appearance, was heralded by a peal of her laughter on the staircase, followed by a phrase delivered in what, from only one previous example, I had already decided must be her inimitable style.

'Upon my word, Major Woodford, you surely know how to tease a poor gel with your winning, wicked ways!'

She flounced across the dining saloon, pausing only to recognise and wave to Rupert, and to notice Clovis seated at his feet. 'There's that charming boy and his adorable pug-dog!' she cried. Rupert blushed with pure pleasure, and Clovis's tightly curled tail wagged vigorously.

'Who is that lady, Miss Copley?' murmured my employer, in an aside.

'Sir, I've no idea,' I whispered. 'She but spoke a few words to us when she came aboard.'

The lady in violet and he whom she had addressed as Major Woodford took up positions relative to those occupied by Mr Ormerod and me, which is to say that the major sat at the end of the other long table with his companion on his right, so that she had her back to us. They were shortly joined by a clergyman in a twice-about collar, accompanied by a wifely figure of fearsome mien, the both attired all in black, who, abjuring the national inclination to privacy at all costs, took their places on the major's left, so that I had a clear view of them both.

Introductions followed, the clergyman leading: 'Sir,' he said, addressing the major, 'I am Dr Arthur Sommerson, Dean of Archester Cathedral, and this is my lady wife.'

'And I, sir, am Major Jack Woodford of the 18th Bengal Infantry, Indian Army. Your servant, sir. Ma'am. And this lady – my companion . . .'

The lady in violet interposed, announcing herself; to me it seemed perfectly in character that she would not have left the task to any other.

'Petronella Marchcombe. Marchcombe with an "e",' she said. 'Delighted to make your acquaintance. Are you travelling far on this voyage?'

'All the way to Egypt,' replied Dean Sommerson. 'It is my intention to . . .'

The delights of eavesdropping were denied me and I did not learn of the dean's intention at that time, for his announcement coincided with the arrival of the first course, borne to the tables by a veritable army of natives dressed in frock-coats and pantaloons of figured silk, with turbans wrapped around their dusky heads – a sight that made one feel, even in the homely purlieus of the lower Thames dockland, that one was already treading the shores of some remote coral strand.

'Soup or fish, *mem-sahib*?' intoned a dark-complexioned servitor, whose breath was scented with cloves.

From the next table, while I was being helped to an exceedingly fine-looking Dover sole, I heard the dean's lady speak out in a stentorian voice:

'Marchcombe. Ha! Would you be one of the Wiltshire Marchcombes, my dear?'

'Yes, ma'am,' came the response.

'Of the major branch?'

'I am Lord Marchcombe's daughter.'

'I knew your father well when I was a gel. My papa, the Bishop of Southern Uganda, was once chaplain to his lordship's father, your grandfather, and I visited Mountcarey often. Your father was then, of course, a very young man, an ensign in the Guards. Does he keep well, my dear?'

'He hunts three days a week, still. Though, since Mama's death, he has given up the yacht and goes to Deauville only infrequently, and, of course, he has relinquished his appointment as Assistant Aide-de-Camp General to Her Majesty.'

'This was following that unfortunate – er . . .'

'There was no truth in the allegation, ma'am. None whatsoever. The fact is that . . .'

Again, my perverse itch to eavesdrop on other people's conversation was thwarted by the arrival of the next course, which richly comprised a choice of game, curried lamb, steak-and-kidney pudding, or all three. I chanced to glance towards Mr Ormerod, and was amused to observe that he, too, was quite obviously put about at having his luncheon entertainment rudely truncated by the bustling waiters, their noisy plates and serving spoons, their sibilant importunities. That a distinguished Royal Academician should take the same simple delight in listening to other folk's revealing conversation as we of the common ruck (Mrs Stittle, whose back was to the people at the next table, had been unashamedly cocking her head and cupping her hand to the nearest ear throughout) I found most heartening.

'Clovis is asking for a bone,' announced Rupert.

'He shall have mine,' said his father, taking from his plate a leg bone of venison well-festooned with meat, to which the pug addressed himself with tail-wagging delight.

It was as he bent down, and his coat fell apart, that I saw a pistol tucked into my employer's waistbelt.

And why, I asked myself, did Justin Ormerod, R.A. feel the need to go about armed?

Our arrival at the mouth of the River Thames was rudely announced by a sickening lurch, as the great steam vessel rolled over on her bulky side to the accompaniment of broken crockery and glassware in the dining saloon, frenzied and largely fruitless attempts by the Indian waiters to stem the tide of destruction, and a peremptory announcement from Mrs Sommerson that she required to be escorted to her cabin to lie down because she did not in fact feel sick, but felt one of her 'heads' coming on.

The family at the far end of our table also made a hasty departure. We were alone with Major Woodford and his intriguing companion.

'I have scarcely had the opportunity, Major,' said she, 'to thank you for escorting me from Liverpool Street station in such a timely and advantageous manner. We women – alas! – we are nothing on our own.'

(Which was a curious thing to say, for even at such vestigial acquaintance, I would have backed the formidable Petronella Marchcombe against any man – 18th Bengal Infantry and all!)

'It was a pleasure, Miss Marchcombe,' responded the gallant major. 'And such a happy chance that I espied a label on your luggage addressed to the steamship *Hindustan*.'

'Quite so, quite so. Tell me, Major, are you proceeding on to India through the new Canal, when it is opened?'

'It is my earnest hope, ma'am,' replied the other. 'It chanced, you see, that my tri-annual furlough has coincided with the opening of the Canal, and the War Office has commissioned me to attend upon the opening ceremony as representative of the British and Indian Armies, after which I shall aspire to take ship in the first vessel bound for India, to rejoin my regiment in Poona.'

'Poona,' said Petronella Marchcombe, 'sounds so masculine and dashing. Like, for instance, "polo" and "grouse shooting". Are you a married man, Major?'

'Ma'am, I am not,' the major replied.

'Ah!'

I met Justin Ormerod's eye and saw his lips purse with a repressed grin. Mrs Stittle had so far abandoned any pretence of non-involvement in the conversation at the next table that she had pushed aside her plate and half-turned her chair so that she had one ear directed towards the two protagonists. Even little Rupert was gazing across at them, wide-eyed, bemused, puzzled and intrigued. The loud-voiced and unconstrained conversation of the English upper class never fails to charm, as I have reason to know; my friend and lately fellow student Sarah Ilminster, whose mother the Countess had been Lady of the Bedchamber to Her Majesty during five of the sovereign's accouchements, once gave forth to me, in a London teashop, with half a hundred goggle-eyed proletarians looking on, a totally unself-conscious second-hand account of Her Majesty's labours on those five separate occasions. Style is all.

'That, I take it,' said Miss Marchcombe, pointing, 'is the captain's table, and he and his officers are not present at this time because of the navigational complications attendant upon sailing out of the River Thames.' She was referring to the top table.

'I would suppose so, ma'am,' replied the major.

'It is to be hoped that one will be invited to dine with the captain,' said Miss Marchcombe.

'I should think that the captain would deem it an honour if you were to grace his table with your presence, ma'am,' said the major.

And I could not have put it more neatly myself.

The *Hindustan* hugged the Kent coast all that afternoon, and the mist came down so that all we could see from the upper deck were the heights and headlands swathed in grey mystery. Off the tip of Dungeness – pointed out to us by Mr Ormerod – the sharp whistle of bosun's pipes brought sailors on deck and swarming up the rigging to unfurl the sails which (again, Rupert and I were informed by Mr Ormerod) assisted the engine in times of favourable wind. Presently, the white sails were blossoming, filling and reaching above our heads, and the great ship heeled over as the wind took charge. So strong, so advantageous was the wind that the engine was stopped and we were back in the age of sail: with the silence all about us, broken only by the hissing of the white water as it sliced past, the scream of the seagulls wheeling overhead, the thrumming of taut canvas, the creaking of cordage.

'Miss Copley, I should like to make a drawing of you,' said Justin Ormerod, right out of the blue. 'Are you willing?'

'Now, sir?' I asked.

'If you have no other plans,' he replied.

What other plans had I, indeed? Rupert was perfectly happy, walking round the decks with Mrs Stittle, the little pug-dog strutting stiffly behind them, pausing every so often to deliver a libation upon various vertical objects.

'A simple drawing,' he said. 'Head and shoulders or half-length. Over there, by the rail, would be as good a place as any. I will go and fetch my materials. Shall we meet there in, say, a quarter of an hour?'

'A quarter of an hour – yes,' I replied.

'Good.' He turned upon his heel; but almost on the same instant, he pointed away into the distance, away from England.

'Do you see that, Miss Copley?' he cried. 'Do you see the cliffs, over there, the white buildings, the lighthouse? That is France, Miss Copley. Now, what do you think of that?' Before I could reply, he was gone, leaving me to wonder at this, my first sight of foreign parts.

He was back on deck within the quarter hour, with a large sketchbook and a box of materials, a folding stool and an easel. This latter he set up close by the ship's rail and pointed to where he wanted me to stand.

'Leaning against the rail,' he said, 'and looking out across the sea in the direction of England. Yes – like that. Very good. But, Miss Copley, would you be so kind as to remove your hat?'

I was wearing a straw boater with my hair securely pinned underneath it. As one might have expected, the wind immediately teased my long tresses from the pins and they streamed forth. As I fought to bring them in order, he called out:

'No – let your hair be. Let it flow where the wind takes it. That is magnificent. Magnificent!'

He worked away. He did not make the demand that I must stay completely still all the time, but allowed me to move whenever I felt restless, calling me to attention only when he was tackling a particular part – as when he said that I must keep my eyes still.

'Your eyes are very difficult to render,' he told me. 'Apart from being of slightly different colour – which is not of any great moment in this, a black-and-white drawing – they hold a vast quantity of emotions.

'There is sadness there. Have you known great sadness in your life, Miss Copley?'

I did not reply to him; but his question opened a floodgate of memory that autumnal afternoon, midway between England and France, with the wind in my hair . . .

My last night on the ward, Sarah Ilminster and I shared the duty of looking after fifteen gravely ill children. My own special pet was little Amy Forsett, aged eight, who was dying of the consumption. Wasted to a ghost, a strange and unearthly beauty had taken possession of the child in the last few days following a vomiting of the blood that had all but claimed her small life. That evening she had been bled of two ounces by lancet, which should certainly have pacified the evil humours and granted her a peaceful night – one of the last in her pitifully short existence – but such was not the case, for she was fretful, whining, calling for attention, and after a fashion that led me to think that she was not so much in discomfort as requiring the benison of human company, and my own in particular.

'Nurse – are you there?' The small hand stole out towards mine.

'Yes, Amy. What is it?' I took the wasted little scrap of human appendage into mine. 'Can't you sleep?'

'Nurse Suzanna, they say you're goin' away.'

'That's right, Amy. I'm finishing my training, and soon I shall be looking after other boys and girls. That will be my life from now on, you see, Amy.'

The hot, wasted fingers held my hand tightly. 'Ain't you goin' to get married one day, Nurse Suzanna, an' 'ave kids of your own?'

'Oh, I shouldn't wonder, Amy.'

(Giles Launey, does my diploma as trained nurse of the Florence Nightingale School of Nursing bridge the social gap that lies between us?)

'Nurse Suzanna, when I grow up, I want to have lots of kids, lots of girls, and I want for all of 'em to grow up like you.' The small hand clung to mine, the vestige of the young, dying life transmitting itself through to me. And I wept as I had never wept before.

I travelled down to the West Country by stagecoach from the George Inn, Southwark on a morning that promised heat, with rising mist from the river hanging low over the dome of St

Paul's, and the wherries flitting across the limpid water, leaving herringbone traces behind them. From London to Reading, Reading to Castle Cary, Taunton, Tiverton and Exeter, changing horses at posthouses along the way and eating at the exorbitant prices which have made our wayside hostels a byword for chicanery. Imagine being mulcted a shilling for a measly small chop and mashed potatoes, with naught to follow but plum pudding, and a pint of tart cider thrown in for good measure!

From the Royal Clarence Hotel, which stands in the cathedral yard in Exeter and lies within the shade of that most noble of sacred edifices, I departed on the penultimate stage of my journey in a two-horse carriage which I shared with – in addition to the deaf and, I suspected, very drunk driver – a lady from Buckfastleigh who had been to visit her sister in Tiverton, and a gentleman of military cut who spent the whole day-long journey past the southern slopes of Dartmoor taking surreptitious nips from a large silver flask of spirits and gorging himself on meat pasties and various broken pieces of fowl and game.

Under the towering tors of Dartmoor, the heat of the sun was shut out by the fugitive rain clouds that forever flitted in, around and about the deep-cleft valleys of the wild interior. A mile short of Buckfastleigh, our tipsy driver drew rein to allow an adder to wind its sinuous way across the track ahead, for your Devon-bred man will not deliberately kill an adder for fear that its mate, with the special dispensation granted to it by Old Nick, will seek out the killer and bite him.

And so we came to Buckfastleigh, where Farmer Wheatley would be waiting to take me on to my home village. There, in the town square, while I was struggling with my traps, comprising two carpet-bags, a hatbox, and three parcels of presents for my family and friends – with no help at all from either military gentleman or carriage driver – a lean brown hand insinuated itself into my line of vision and taking up a carpet-bag from the luggage rack of the carriage, deposited it at my feet.

'My pleasure, ma'am.' A pair of rich, sea-blue eyes met my gaze. A straw hat was raised to reveal a smooth pelt of butter-yellow hair, and a quirky smile made my heart sing like a lark in the high heavens. It was Giles Launey, and I knew – the way one knows these things – that he had not recognised me as the gawky girl who had been the recipient of his present at the Christmas party all those years previously.

'Sir, you are very kind,' I responded.

'Are you, perhaps, going further?' he asked, and his eyes never left mine.

'To Hickleydoek,' I replied.

He smote one fist into the palm of his other hand. 'Why, that is most astounding,' he declared, and the blue eyes danced. 'I am from Hickleydoek and just about to return there. I would count it an honour, ma'am, to be allowed to transport you there in my own trap.' The blue eyes clouded slightly. 'Unless, ma'am, you have other arrangements,' he added, and he looked for all the world like a little boy who stood in hazard of being denied a second helping of pudding.

'Nothing, sir, that cannot quickly be cancelled,' I told him. And straightway went to Farmer Wheatley's place, which was on the edge of the square, and gave instructions to a maid that I should not have to avail myself of her master's services.

By the time I returned, Giles Launey had stowed my gear in the rear of his trap and was waiting to assist me to mount. A flick of the whip, a click of the tongue, and horse and trap, Giles and I, set off across the steep path over the moor that led to Hickleydoek and a scattering of other remote Dartmoor villages.

'Where are you staying in Hickleydoek, ma'am?' asked Giles, stealing a sidelong glance at me that, to my instant delight, I perceived to be one of earnest appraisal.

'At the Copleys' place,' I replied.

'The Copleys – ah!'

'You know the family, sir?' I ventured.

'Indifferently well, ma'am,' he said. 'They are tenant farmers of my father. Very worthy people. Salt of the earth. I do not know them well because I am mostly away. I am in the Royal Navy.'

'And now *Lieutenant* Launey, so I am led to understand,' I said.

He jerked on the rein and brought the cob to a halt – no difficult task, since the poor brute was labouring up a steep incline and glad of the rest. Turning in his seat, he regarded me with growing realisation of a very visible kind, terminating the process of recognition by pointing a lean brown finger straight at me.

'You are little Miss Copley!' he declared. 'The very same!'

'I'm surprised that you didn't come to that conclusion much earlier, sir. After all, it was not a million years since we last met.'

'That it was not,' he said. 'And I remember it well – the Christmas before I went out to the China Station. Ah, but . . .'

'But what?'

'If I may make so bold, Miss Copley, you have much changed since then.'

'In what respects?' I demanded.

'Ah, in several respects. Now that I perceive you with hindsight, Miss Copley, it is clear that you have not greatly changed in outward appearance. If I may make so bold –' He grinned, his eyes twinkled, and my heart took flight. 'If I may make so bold, you had already, when we last met, taken on the lineaments of womanhood and distanced yourself from the other young ladies of the village on that account. However, there has been added a certain difference. I confess that I do not know how to express it.'

I thought to help him. 'Perhaps,' I suggested, 'I have changed in my manner?'

'One could say that,' he conceded.

'More – how to put it? – assured?'

'Mmmm.'

'Less of the country bumpkin?'

He gave a start of alarm. 'Miss Copley, I never suggested for one moment . . .'

'More – ladylike? Though it's not an expression that I bandy about freely.'

'Miss Copley . . .'

'More the kind of lady to whom you would most readily give your assistance in a small moment of crisis – thought I am sure that, as a perfect officer and gentleman, you would have assisted the oldest, plainest and drabbest woman in Buckfastleigh market-place.'

He spread his hands. 'Miss Copley, you confound me utterly,' he said.

Further discourse on this particular topic was cut short, in very Dartmoor terms, by a sudden effusion of torrential rain, descending from one of the hundred or so clouds which had been scudding overhead since we had left Buckfastleigh for the heights of the moor, and which for no doubt good reasons of its own had chosen to unburden itself upon Miss Suzanna Copley and Lieutenant Giles Launey, spinster and bachelor, respectively, of the parish of Hickleydoek in the fair county of Devon; so that the latter hastily whipped up his cob and induced the animal to pull us to the shelter of a copse of spreading laurels, under which we were able to escape the deluge and enjoy the awfulness of it from afar – which is the best way to contemplate disaster.

The very fury of the downpour so lowered the temperature of the surrounding air that Giles was constrained to produce, from the rear compartment of the trap, a cosy woollen travelling rug, which he proceeded to lay across both our knees and tuck in. During the course of this enterprise, he chanced to catch hold of my hand, which he did not then relinquish, nor did I attempt to persuade him so to do.

It may have been before the squall passed, it may have been after the scudding, moisture-girt cloud had carried its burden to Buckfastleigh and beyond and the sky over Dartmoor had turned to a cerulean blue of the most pellucid kind, that Giles transferring his hand from mine to my cheek, stroked it slowly and with infinite care, and then kissed me so lightly upon the lips that it was like the touch of eyelashes.

'Miss Copley, Miss Copley, you may rest now.'

Justin Ormerod's voice broke in upon my reverie, and I returned to the there and then with a considerable jolt of shock occasioned by the transference.

'It's good,' he declared soberly, nodding and eyeing the work before him. 'I do not have you yet, Miss Copley – not *quite* yet – but I have travelled a very great deal towards you, I think.'

'May I see it?' I asked.

'Of course.'

As I crossed over to where he stood by the easel, the patter of Rupert's feet and the scuffle of the pug-dog following him distracted me. I turned and, as the little boy ran towards my waiting arms, I gathered him up.

'We've been up in the front of the ship,' said he. 'It's called the fore-chains, and we saw a sailor go out there and put a reef on the jib. That's what he called it: "putting a reef on the jib". I want to be a sailor when I grow up, Miss Copley.'

'Your papa has done a drawing of me,' I told him. 'Here it is. I wonder if it's very much like . . .'

I was silenced by the sight of it. It was me – yes. But most absurdly *not* like me, for I lay no claim to beauty, and the creature in the drawing was beautiful, as I have never, shall never, be beautiful. Yet – oddly – in the flow of the hair, the poise of the head, the curve of the cheek, I saw something of what I see every day in my mirror – but transmuted, like base metal to gold, by the hand and skill of the artist.

'You look ever so sad, Miss Copley,' said Rupert, pointing to the drawing. 'You are crying without tears.'

As well I might have been . . .

FIVE

The Hickleydoek Fair, along with other famous Dartmoor celebrations, as at Widecombe and Drewsteignton, has its origins woven into the warp and weft of time and probably dates back to well before the Normans came, well before Julius Caesar and his Romans came; back into the age of the ancient mysteries and the folk who built the stone rings and monoliths that stand in abundance on the great moor. By the mid-nineteenth century, however, the fair had been tamed, thanks to the influence of a series of strong-willed and outspoken parsons incumbent at the village church of St James's, from a pagan festival of anticipation of the crops to be gathered in, to a day of innocent merrymaking, of dancing and singing, of flirtation, partaking of cider and ale from both the front and back doors of the Launey Arms, and ingesting the almost totally indigestible bacon pasty – known locally as 'Lardy Pigs' – which the good matrons of Hickleydoek, my own mother included, baked weeks ahead of the occasion.

That year, as nearly always, it promised rain on the Saturday morning of the fair. By midday, the skies had been swept clear and the sun beat down upon the village square before the church and inn, where the stalls were set out under striped awnings, Lardy Pigs were selling by the score, and cider and beer were flowing from the never-ending libations of the Launey Arms.

The morris-dancers had begun their arcane ritualistic cavorting: bending and circling, white handkerchiefs flirting, bells jingling, ribbons flying. It was then that Giles Launey came to me from out of the watching crowd and laid a hand on my arm.

'I've been looking for you everywhere,' he murmured in my ear.

I experienced a suddenly awakening delight at his touch, at the sound of him, at his scent, which was an amalgam of macassar oil, tweed and well-kept leather. Guiltily, I stole a glance about me; it seemed that everyone must be looking at us and must guess at my feelings, for surely they were writ so plain.

'How are you?' I murmured.

'The better for seeing you,' he replied. 'You are looking divinely pretty today, Suzanna. I could eat you alive!'

'One kiss doesn't give you the right to address me so out-spokenly,' I said. But my breathing quickened for all that.

He ignored my gentle rebuke. 'Tonight,' he said, 'when the dancing starts in the square, we can steal away to a quiet place and talk of this and that.'

'We have already talked of this and that,' I responded. 'You will remember when we drove together over the moor and you complimented me on having turned – like caterpillar into butterfly – from a country bumpkin into a lady. Into the semblance of a lady,' I added.

'There's more that I could say to you, Suzanna,' he whispered, and again he addressed the declaration close to my ear, for the air of *Bean Setting*, the stamp and jingle of the morris men, all but shut out all else.

Before I could frame a suitable response, the portly figure of Squire Launey was upon us; followed by his wife and daughter. Giles's mother was sharp-eyed and overdressed, given to treating the village folk – and that meant me – like lesser beings; though my mother attested that she was a nobody herself before she married the squire, and had used to work in the fields a-haymaking with Mother, in the days when she had been plain Jenny Green.

'Giles,' she said, with scarcely a glance in my direction, 'we are going home for tea. The noise and the heat I find very oppressive. Why the villagers insist upon continuing this rout year after year is quite beyond me.'

She turned to go, but Giles was not for letting me be pushed into the background. 'Mama, this is Miss Suzanna Copley,' he said. 'You'll remember her, of course. Miss Copley's been away in London, studying nursing under Florence Nightingale.'

'Indeed? How very interesting.' Mrs Launey's eyes were green, cold and quite unlike her son's. They swept over me with supreme disinterest. 'Good day to you, Miss Copley. Come, Giles.'

'I don't want any tea, Mama,' he said. 'Full up with cider and Lardy Pigs. I'll stay and join in the fun.'

'As you choose,' responded his mother. Another cold glance in my direction and she was gone.

Giles grinned. 'Mama can be a bit of a bear when she chooses, but her heart's in the right place.'

I said nothing.

Later, when the sun went down and the fiddlers started to re-tune, he took my hand. 'Let's go into the churchyard and dance,' he said.

'In the churchyard?' I said. 'Among the graves?'

'There's none there who sleep so lightly that they'll be disturbed,' he responded. 'None who'll eye us up and down and speculate, make us the subject for gossip – as they would on this side of the churchyard wall. There we shall be – in a manner of speaking – among friends.'

I laughed, following his mood. So we went into the church-yard, and when the musicians struck up, we danced; up and down the cobbled path that led from the lych-gate to the church door, with the gravestones on each side of us, white in the growing moonlight; and as we danced to the wild air of pipe, tambour and fiddle, we circled, bowed to each other, joined hands again and descended down the middle in accordance with the figures, the same that were being danced on the other side of the dark wall in the torchlit square; and I had the thought that we were not unwatched, that my many relations and forebears regarded us from the gloom, awakened briefly from their long sleep: Great Uncle Joss and Aunt Raban, who died on the same day in the year I was born; Grandma and Grandpa Humbert, my mother's people; the twins Amy and Oliver, taken young; and all the rest.

And I thought, as I danced with the man whom I had steadfastly loved during the long years he had been away, he will never marry me, for not only is there the great gulf of birth, wealth and position yawning between us, but he is not the marrying kind, and in any event, his family – Mrs Launey particularly – would move heaven and earth to prevent him from marrying a 'village girl'.

For all that, I was content to be with him, to feel the touch of his hands and bathe in the regard of his admiring, sea-blue eyes; and later, when, breathless and laughing, we collapsed on the oak bench by the lych-gate and he implanted on my lips the tenderest kiss I shall ever know, I half-imagined that my doubting heart was wrong, and that I should one day become Mrs Giles Launey, even if it meant that I would turn into a shrew like his mother, forever guarding the insecurity of my elevation from a nobody to a somebody.

I saw him twice more before he returned to sea. One day, he took me in a two-horse carriage to the heart of the great moor, where we tethered the horses, and, scrambling up the rock-strewn slopes of Brent Tor to its craggy summit, stood arms-entwined and breathed in the ever-shifting glories of the scene about us: the strip of sea behind the scudding mist to the south, the vast mysteries of the ascending tors to the northward. Afterwards, we picnicked off Devon pasties and cider, and cider and kisses. And Giles gave me a ring: a tiny pearl surrounded by a chaplet of garnets, which I took to be half a promise of our engagement, though not a word was spoken.

The last time, he summoned me with a note brought to my door by his groom. It said that he had been recalled to his ship and would I see him at the corner of the lane leading down to the Plymouth road at six that evening?

I was there early, waiting by the milestone on the corner; I heard the carriage coming down the lane, and my heart turned over for yearning. Giles was sitting by his groom, who was driving. For the first time since he had been home, he was wearing naval uniform, and cut a fine figure of romance in the dark boat cloak, the cocked hat, the flash of gilt buttons and gold lace. He alighted and told his groom to move away a pace.

Then he took my hand.

'A sailor's farewell, Suzanna,' he murmured. 'If I had had more time – as I had hoped – I would have made it more memorable.'

A kestrel, flying low over a bank of heather close by, screeched with alarm to see us, and bated away sharply.

'It could never be more memorable, Giles,' I told him. 'Not if we had had all the time in the world.'

'You'll be here when I return?'

'Perhaps not,' I said, 'but I'll leave a message so that you can find me.'

'I'll find you if I have to search the whole world over,' he murmured close to my cheek. 'Goodbye, dearest little Suzanna.'

'Till next we meet,' I responded.

We kissed. One last glance, and he strode swiftly to the waiting carriage, where the groom had been seated with his back discreetly turned to us. I watched him swing himself lithely up and nod to his driver, who whipped up the horses. Down the rutted lane to the Plymouth road he was borne, to the great seaport and the wide oceans that beckoned him beyond.

I watched till he was out of sight, till the distance and my tears shut him out.

I never saw him again: but that was not the worst of it.

Oddly, dusk and sunset brought a lightening of the atmosphere. The mist cleared, so that one could see the vast bulk of Beachy Head, the necklace of lights that described Eastbourne, and the spine of the South Downs beyond and before us. I had all this topographical information from Dean Sommerson, who came upon me when I was taking a pre-prandial stroll around the deck after having changed for dinner and thrown a Paisley shawl round my shoulders against the evening chill. Dr Sommerson (he was very careful to impress upon me again his doctorate in divinity) was an expert in topography and also in the art of photographic representation, he informed me. And his reason for travelling to Egypt with his lady wife (I had the distinct impression that the presence of the formidable Mrs

Sommerson was a matter of some regret to the many-talented divine) was to make a photographic record of the historic opening of the Suez canal, for which reason he had brought with him, so he told me, no less than three camera apparatuses: a Séguier, a Voigtländer and a Von Martins – whatever *they* were. Dr Sommerson's presence I found, notwithstanding the sanctity of his cloth, distinctly unpleasant. He had a habit of touching one's hand or arm when stressing a point, of gazing fixedly into one's eyes for no discernible reason. It was a blessed release when the dinner gong was sounded and the minor, but distasteful, ordeal was over.

His parting gesture – typically – was a touch of the hand, accompanied by: 'You must let me take your photograph quite soon, Miss Copley.'

'That will be very nice,' I responded. And wondered what the formidable Mrs Sommerson would think of *that*.

One could have guessed. Petronella Marchcombe (she was *the Honourable* Petronella Marchcombe – an item of unconsidered trivia I gleaned from the passenger list stuck up outside the purser's office) took her invited place at the captain's right when we sat down to dine that evening at eight. The Hon. Petronella was all in green, looking like a predatory wood nymph, and she made up to the *Hindustan*'s captain in a way that would have shamed a Plymouth dockyard strumpet or put to flight a whole host of Dartmoor shepherds. Captain Bulgin of the *Hindustan* was clearly of a sterner timbre than the average Dartmoor shepherd and bore the Hon. Petronella's shameless blandishments with truly nautical aplomb.

He was a young forty-ish, tall, thick-set as a Dartmoor pony, with a sprinkling of black hair on his high cheekbones, and he looked devastating in his brass-bound tunic. The manifest delights of his well-appointed table were clearly taking second best, on this occasion, to the attentions of the lively young aristocrat on his right.

As at luncheon, when she had been with Major Woodford (who, on this occasion, was picking his disconsolate way through the soup-and-fish in company with Dean and Mrs Sommerson at our opposite table), the Hon. Petronella was notably old-fashioned as regards the relationship between men and women.

For instance, she said – or, rather, trilled or quavered: 'Oh, Captain Bulgin, how could it ever be that a poor, weak woman could ever aspire to sail a fine, tall ship through the perils and exigencies of the deep sea? I so admire you and your brave officers.' The officers in question – those who, like their captain, were not at that time attending to the present perils and exigencies (and they numbered an elderly Scottish gentleman whom I had earlier heard described as the Chief Engineer, two nice-looking junior officers and a wildly-handsome but extremely spotty-faced midshipman) – perked up considerably at this pronouncement.

Captain Bulgin smirked. 'It is the male prerogative, ma'am,' he said, and quoted:

'Men must work, and women must weep . . .
Though the harbour bar be moaning.'

'A very fine sentiment, sir,' replied the Hon. Petronella. And, after a brief pause: 'Are you a married man, Captain?'

Some little time has gone past since that evening, and I would not wish to swear upon an oath in open court as to what immediately followed, but with my hand on my heart and with the best recollection that I have, I would declare that, in all the gathering present – that's to say, the captain's table, our own party, Major Woodford and the Sommersons, the folks at the far end of our table – every soup spoon, every fork containing fish (on this occasion, smoked mackerel) was instantly halted in mid-motion – though little Rupert, who was feeding scraps of mackerel to Clovis, may have been the exception.

'No, ma'am, I am not,' responded Captain Bulgin, hot-eyed.

'Aaah!' commented the Hon. Petronella, with a whole world of feeling.

The small talk at the top table which followed was, for me, somewhat cut off by my employer, who choked upon a spoonful of lobster soup and had to be assisted, with much back-slapping, by one of the Indian waiters; at the end of which he looked shyly at me, like a little boy who had been caught out in the act of laughing in church.

I immediately warmed to him, feeling as I do that good humour – a sense of the ridiculous – outweighs all the minor human failings; and that even if my distinguished employer felt constrained to carry a pistol with him all the time – and for what reason I could only begin to imagine, but it surely had to do with the tragic incident of the Limping Frenchman – he was, nevertheless, to be excused on the score of his sense of the ridiculous.

The dinner – our first aboard the *Hindustan* – progressed its two-hour-long course, refreshed by the Hon. Petronella's outrageous flirting with our gallant captain, who seemed not averse to the blandishments of his beautiful and titled guest. By the end of the third course, Rupert had had enough; his eyes were heavy, so Mrs Stittle took him to bed. I followed soon after and kissed him goodnight. Upon my return, I found that the entertainment from the top table had been curtailed by the fact that the Hon. Petronella and Captain Bulgin were murmuring together, tête-à-tête, while my employer, having renounced the fourth course, was picking moodily at a sliced apple – having apparently exhausted his store of good humour.

I soon made my excuses and left him alone. My cabin porthole giving, as it did, a view of the deck and the lights of the south coast of England in the distance, I spent a few moments before retiring in gazing out at the slowly passing scene.

It was then I saw Justin Ormerod pacing the deck. Head bowed, hands clasped behind his back, he strode to and fro, to and fro; no longer the man of sprightly good humour who had found the antics of the Hon. Petronella so diverting, but a man weighed down by some intolerable inner burden.

I shut the curtain, not wishing to intrude upon him, and lay me down to sleep.

Sleep came to me easily after the rigours of the day. When I awoke, the motion of the vessel had ceased and we were lying beside the dock wall in Southampton.

At least a score of fresh passengers came aboard that morning, most of them travelling in the hardship of the lower classes and many of them persons of colour, some with the tiniest of babies – and all bearing what appeared to be their entire possessions, including cooking pots, chairs, tables, even folding beds. At luncheon that day (we were due to resume the voyage on the afternoon tide, so the notices said), the saloon tables were entirely filled, and we made the acquaintance of the two persons sitting immediately adjacent to us: one, a Russian gentleman placed on Rupert's right, who introduced himself as Kiprenski, tucked his napkin firmly under his heavily-bearded chin, settled the folds carefully over the generous slopes of his flowered waistcoat, and proceeded to address himself to and remove every course, together with all the available wines.

The gentleman opposite, seated beside Mrs Stittle, hailed from America and announced himself as Henry J. Marius. He was tall, well-made, with a fine shock of curly hair, and an alert, humorous look – and he announced that he was a journalist setting out to report on the Suez canal opening for a syndicate of newspapers in his native country. Upon hearing my employer's name, he expressed great interest and animation and insisted upon shaking hands with Mr Ormerod for the second time, saying that he had long been an admirer of his work, which he had seen in public and private collections in both America and Europe. Mr Marius then, by cautious stages, transferred his attentions to me, and by the entrées had elicited my occupation, place of birth, background, taste in music and literature, whether I was affianced, and whether I would care for a stroll around the upper deck after luncheon was over? To the latter, I had no option but to agree, for Rupert announced that he wanted to walk Clovis round the deck also, and would I go with him?

In the event, the three of us went for a stroll around the deck, with the little pug-dog bounding on ahead, taking steep ladders with reckless abandonment, flinging himself round corners, winning himself amused glances and comments from the sailors who were engaged upon taking aboard stores – great crates and sacks – from a crane on the dockside.

When Clovis had traversed three circuits of the *Hindustan*'s deck and the rest of us only two, Rupert decided he must keep up with his pet and set off after him at a run, with me calling to him to have a care on the ladders and not to get in the sailors' way, nor go near the rails and fall overboard.

In the dark hours of the night, when the spirit is lowest, when death seems very near and mortality as cheap as the lowest coin of the realm, I sometimes relive the horror of the few minutes that followed.

Relieved of the burden of Rupert's chattering company ('Do you know any Redskins in America, Mr Marius? I bet you'd have to be jolly brave to fight a Redskin, Mr Marius'), my companion continued to press what one could only describe as a gentle suit, gleaning from me the knowledge that I had never been abroad before (Mr Marius had been abroad widely and frequently and would be delighted to show me the sights of Lisbon, Gibraltar and all ports to the East), always taking hold of my arm to assist me up and down ladders – and always being slow to relinquish his grip.

We had been, perhaps, four more times in promenade – and Clovis had overtaken us once, closely followed by his panting young master – when we came upon the widest part of the deck, in the middle of the ship, where the sailors were loading the crates and sacks into the dark maw of an open hold.

And then – suddenly – alarmingly – *it happened* . . . !

The little boy and the pug were ahead of us. On high, a crane was swinging a huge wooden crate over the ship's side and towards the hold. I was engaged in conversation with Mr Marius, trying to explain that it would be quite out of the question for me to go ashore alone with him at our next port of call – Lisbon – and take dinner with him, and meeting his very gentle but puzzled queries as to why with no very good explanations.

Suddenly, he looked up.

'Holy Moses!' he cried. And bounded forward.

I saw it then. It happened quite slowly, really. The big wooden crate on the end of the long gallimaufry of ropes and hooks began, during its progress above the deck, inexorably to slip out of the cradle of rope that had been gathered about it.

'Run, young feller – run for your life!' shouted Mr Marius. And Rupert glanced round in sudden alarm to see the tall

American striding, pell-mell, towards him. He may have thought that the other meant him harm. The pug-dog certainly thought that Mr Marius meant his young master harm, for he flew at the former's ankles with a loud yap of fury.

It was at that instant that the huge crate slipped out of its cat's cradle and fell. Mr Marius, reaching Rupert, gave the boy a shove that sent him flying across the deck, to land – fortuitously – in a pile of ropes. The American himself, with a small pug-dog attached to his ankle, continued to dive forward, and landed on the deck at the same moment that the crate descended with a rending, splintering, searing crash upon the very spot so lately occupied by boy, man and dog.

I rushed forward to give help. Rupert was already on his feet, pale-faced with shock. I picked him up, and joined the group of sailors who had gathered about the American.

'That was a brave thing you did, Mister,' said one. 'That kid would sure as hell have been killed outright if it hadn't been for you.'

'Damned bravest thing I ever saw,' said another.

We all looked round at the wrecked crate, from out of whose shattered staves poked what appeared to be a considerable part of a steam engine, brass boiler, pistons, furnace and all. I shuddered.

Mr Marius was watching me very closely. There was something about the intensity of his gaze that held my eyes longer than I would normally have dared. He then smiled up at Rupert.

'Sorry about that, young feller,' he said.

Rupert, over-wrought, buried his face against my shoulder.

'He's only very young, you see, Mr Marius,' I said. 'But one day, he'll appreciate that you saved his life just now.'

At that juncture, there came the sounds of a scuffle and a squabble on the quayside. A group of the *Hindustan*'s sailors, clearly distinguishable by their smartly beribboned straw hats, were angrily jostling a roughly dressed fellow who, from what one could gather, was in charge of the crane ashore which had so nearly been the source of a tragic accident.

Words and phrases came drifting over to us.

'Keep out the alehouse when you've a job like that to do!'

'By heaven, if you were a navy man, that'd cost you twenty lashes, you drunken sot!'

It appeared, then, that the crane man had been inebriated. And that explained a lot.

My hand, then, in the act of stroking Rupert's smooth hair, suddenly grown terribly rare and precious, paused in the act – as I recalled the gipsy's words:

'Five will be the number of your perils. And two shall die.'

I shuddered: it was as if someone had walked over my grave.

We left Southampton soon after, skirting the bulk of the Isle of Wight and heading down-channel to the wide waste of the Atlantic. Naturally, I swiftly apprised Mr Ormerod of the near-tragedy, and he betook himself to thank the gallant man who had snatched his small son's life from the very brink of eternity. As to Mr Marius's gentle importunities concerning myself, I decided that, if and when he might next invite me to dine ashore with him, I would accept without hesitation – for how could a woman hesitate to place herself in the escort of such a gallant gentleman?

Poor Rupert, possibly on account of the strain and shock involved in his dreadful experience, suffered a bad asthma attack that evening, the first that he had had since the departure of the odious Lottie. Mrs Stittle and I attended him till he was recovered, and the good woman volunteered to sit up with him throughout the night in case there was a recurrence, in which event she would summon me.

Dinner that evening was notable for the (in my opinion) quite scandalous behaviour of the Hon. Petronella March-combe. Nor was I willing, at that time, entirely to excuse the behaviour of my employer . . .

Picture my arrival at table for dinner – a little late, for I had stayed to read a story to Rupert (NOT *The Phantom of Hellbrook Hall!*). There sits, in the place usually occupied by Mrs Stittle on our employer's left, the Hon. Petronella, and dressed in an evening frock of such outrageous *décolletage* as would have shamed a Plymouth dockyard strumpet. And she, with no more than a nod in my direction as I take my place, returns her attentions – that's to say her fluttering eyelashes, her pursing of rosebud lips, her enticing voice – to Mr Ormerod.

'Sir, I had no *idea*, no idea at *all*, not till the purser told me, that you were *the* Mr Justin Ormerod of the Royal Academy, the same as painted my mother and father, the Lord and Lady Marchcombe, together with my two small brothers, at Mountcarey Towers. I, myself, was at finishing school in Switzerland at the time, or I would have been included in the group portrait. Such a pity.' Much fluttering of eyelashes.

'I recall the painting well, Miss Marchcombe,' is the response. And he is positively writhing with pleasure. If he were a puppy dog, he would be rolling on his back to have his tummy tickled! 'The picture gave me great pleasure, as much from the éclat it earned for itself at the Royal Academy Summer Exhibition as from the very great kindness and hospitality extended towards me by Lord and Lady Marchcombe.'

Silence, and then:

'Are you married, Mr Ormerod?'

'Alas, Miss Marchcombe, I am a widower.' And not a flicker of an eyelash, nor the suppression of a smile, to hear the gambit that he has already heard the minx direct at two gentlemen in succession!

A voice at my elbow: Mr Henry J. Marius, taking advantage of Rupert's absence, has occupied the vacant seat on my right that lies between me and the Russian gentleman Mr Kiprenski; Mr Kiprenski, who is enthusiastically addressing himself to the soup and fish, can scarcely have noticed the change of neighbour.

'How's the boy, Miss Copley?'

'He's had an asthmatic attack.'

'So I heard. I'm very sorry.'

'But he's much better now.'

'Oh, I'm very glad to hear that, Miss Copley, I really am.'

The four-part conversation continues in counterpart, and I am paying as much attention to the other as to my own – perhaps more so . . .

'I should greatly like you to paint my portrait, Mr Ormerod.'

'I should be delighted, ma'am.'

'Miss Copley – er – Miss Copley . . .'

'I'm sorry. Yes . . .'

'The sea air, you know, and the dry lands of the south, will greatly benefit the little fellow's condition.'

'I'm sure you're right, Mr Marius.'

'I should like you to paint me in the character of Diana, goddess of the chase, Mr Ormerod. Zoffany – you have heard of Zoffany, the painter of the last century who greatly excelled in theatrical subjects – painted my great-grandmother, and she then a young gel of my own age, in the character of Diana. Though in rather scandalous costume, ha-ha!' A glance down at her scandalous *décolletage*.

'You would suit well as Diana, Miss Marchcombe.'

(Oh, would she not? Diana, goddess of the chase – how aptly named!)

'Miss Copley, may I have your attention for a moment, please?'

'Yes?'

'As regards our call in at Lisbon, I should like to renew my offer of yesterday, which was that I should much like to take you on a tour of the city and then dine you at a very nice little restaurant known to me for many years. Very friendly, with an excellent table.'

'Mr Ormerod – I *declare* that you must paint me as Diana!'

'Very well, Miss Marchcombe.'

'Full length, I think. Bearing a bow and arrow. Perhaps about to let fly at a passing stag – rather like the version that Mr Zoffany painted of my great-grandmama. We would make an admirable pair in the long gallery at Mountcarey.'

'Quite so, Miss Marchcombe. I remember the Zoffany well.'

'Do you, now?'

'Lisbon is a charming and interesting city, Miss Copley.'

'So I have heard, Mr Marius.'

'You will consent to let me show you round – and afterwards to dine you?'

'Mr Marius' – and this in a very loud voice, so that my employer and his ogling companion shall have no doubt but that of the pursuer and the pursued, one pair, at least, has arrived at a swift and satisfactory conclusion – 'that will be a great pleasure.'

The Hon. Petronella casts me a swift sidelong glance, which I affect not to notice; my employer is so engaged upon gazing upon his fair companion that I think he has not heard my declaration.

So much for the dinner after Southampton. During the early hours of the following morning the *Hindustan* ran into the most appalling storm off the Devon coast, which struck out of the darkness in one wave and a gust of wind that laid the great ship on her side. I immediately clambered from my cot (I had nearly been *thrown* from it!), and rushed to see how Rupert and Mrs Stittle had fared next door. The latter was up and awake like myself, having been shockingly summoned by the arrival of the tempest. Rupert, happily, was still sleeping like a babe, rocked in his tight cot, eyes closed, a thumb tucked into his mouth, peaceful. Nor had Mr Ormerod stirred from his cabin next door.

The gale continued unabated. Mrs Stittle and I retired to my cabin and made a pot of tea upon a spirit stove which I had brought with me. Holding on to the edge of my cot with one hand whilest sipping the heavenly brew and noting from the alarming angle of the contents of the cup a counterfeit of what must be happening outside, I was presently summoned by the excited voice of the steward who looked after the first-class passengers. Knocking upon my door and calling upon me by name as 'Nurse Copley', he begged me to come and assist with a child who had suffered an injury at the first onset of the tempest. Leaving Mrs Stittle to keep watch and ward over our own precious charge, I put on a coat over my night shift, picked up my bag containing essential medicaments, and followed the steward, through cavernous passageways and down steep ladders, to what seemed the very bowels of the vessel, while constantly obliged to pause with every passing wave and hold on for grim death, lest I should be hurled sideways or downwards. And all the time the great force of the English Channel, mingling with the eastern edge of the Atlantic Ocean, hurled and bucketed massive gouts of its tremendous self upon the decks above.

The scene in the lower deck compartment containing the most humble of the *Hindustan*'s passengers was like one of the inner circles of Hell as described by Dante. In the light of two or three tallow dips like those which had dimly illuminated the death of Nelson in the bowels of H.M.S. *Victory* were half a hundred frightened, nay, panic-stricken men, women and children, and a priest whom I took to be of some obscure faith. He it was who guided me to the centre of the compartment where, lying in a hammock, whose obedience to the wild movements of the ship was being kept somewhat in check by two coloured women, was a little girl of about Rupert's age. She was unconscious; her light coffee-coloured brow was marred by a livid contusion that explained why.

'Zena, she fell down the steps when the first big wave came, Missie,' said the priest. 'And done broke her leg.'

One of the women drew back the blanket that covered the child, revealing the left leg which was fractured above the knee, as I swiftly established by the deformity of the part, the unnatural looseness, the shortening of the limb. While considerably more concerned about the injury to the head, I set about treating the leg: pulling the two portions of the bone in opposite directions until the limb had the same length as its partner, then applying a makeshift splint and binding it firmly. There being a certain amount of swelling, I made a cold lotion of Goulard's extract in a pint of water and applied it to the parts. Throughout all this, the women steadying the hammock, the priest, the ring of faces surrounding me, never wavered in their attention. When I had finished, there was a concerted exhalation of breaths and a murmur of approval. Half a hundred faces split in smiles of appreciation.

'Thank you, Missie,' said the priest. One of the women by the hammock, who was clearly the mother of the little girl, kissed my hand.

'Zena, she wake up pretty soon, you think, Missie?'

'I don't know,' I replied. There being nothing else I could say. It was possible that the child's skull was fractured; I had neither the knowledge nor the means to deal with that. One could only hope.

Little Zena died without recovering consciousness in the early morning, and was buried at sea in the customary manner. As a British subject, she was accorded the covering of her national flag, which was afterwards carefully folded up and put away for the next obsequies after the slight form had slid from off the plank jutting from the *Hindustan*'s stern.

I watched the ceremony at close hand. Captain Bulgin, magnificent in his brass-bound uniform, recited the last rites; and the Hon. Petronella Marchcombe watched, along with a sprinkling of the first-class passengers who had chanced to hear of the mid-morning diversion, from the after end of the boat deck above. I did not see my employer up there, nor Major Woodford, nor the Russian gentleman.

Zena, having been dispatched to her last resting place with surely more pomp and ceremony than would ever have been predicted for one of her humble birth and station, and her small corpse, wrapped in a sailor's coffin, which is a tube of coarse sailcloth weighted with scrap lead, having been consigned to the deep, there arose a keening from the steerage passengers who were grouped about me, and the mother of the dead child reached out and took my hand.

It was at that moment that the sound of a gong from above announced to the first-class passengers that a serving of mid-morning *bouillon* and coffee was about to take place. The sea having considerably reduced its fury, they swiftly departed to refresh their sharpened appetites.

Out of the mist I discerned, far off, a jutting tongue of land. Pointing, one of Captain Bulgin's young officers provided me with the information that this was Cap Finisterre, the western-most tip of France and the entrance to the Bay of Biscay.

The following day, the *Hindustan* arrived in Lisbon.

SIX

'*Five will be the number of your perils . . . two shall die.*'

The prediction never left me; I spoke of it, however, to no one.

Our arrival in the busy, bustling, noisy, devastatingly attractive port of Lisbon, with its scents of spices, its redolence of colour, the swaggering walk of its darkly handsome people, the blue sky and sea commanding all, served as a startling contrast to the storms of the grey English Channel and the Bay of Biscay. Their Indian summer, greatly protracted into autumn, caused most of the lady passengers, myself included, to walk abroad with a parasol against the ruinous rays of the sun (though, truth be told, my early years as a child on Dartmoor have forever given me the doubtful benison of ruddy apple cheeks that neither paint nor hope will ever fade to the fashionable pallor of our times).

The gipsy's prediction was already beginning, as I have suggested, to haunt me. The morning of the little girl's death, I had taken a sheet of writing paper and penned upon it the following:

FIVE PERILS
One – the falling crate.
Two – the storm.
TWO DEATHS
One – the child Zena . . .

Immediately upon writing the missive, I screwed it up and threw it aside. In no time, I recovered it, straightened it out, and locked it away amongst my most private belongings, feeling as I did so an unaccountable sense of self-guilt.

The Hon. Petronella's pursuit of my employer, following what might be termed her preliminary skirmishes with the two palpably less promising males on shipboard at the time (what, after all, is a mere major of the Indian Army, or, indeed, the captain of an ocean liner, compared to a Royal Academician of international fame, who only had to stay alive long enough, and continue painting well enough, to ensure himself a knighthood and attendant honours?), continued with unabated intensity. On the morning of our arrival in Lisbon, there was obtained by her a handsome small sailing cutter, together with a handsome large Portuguese helmsman. She must take darling little Rupert for a sail round the harbour and environs of the port, and his papa must come too. I was not included in the invitation.

I watched them go off: a white bird flaunting its wide wings against the limpid blueness of the harbour, where the very pebbles on the sea bed were visible, together with the shoals of fish that darted back and forth with every passing shade and movement; and Rupert in his sailor's hat waving back at me, whilst the Hon. Petronella, very girlish in a wide straw and a pink pinafore dress, was already addressing herself to the enchantment of Justin Ormerod, R.A.

'Miss Copley, I gather that we leave on the afternoon's tide, so I shall not have the inestimable pleasure of escorting you ashore tonight. However, there is Gibraltar, there is Malta, not to mention Alexandria, Port Said . . .'

Mr Henry J. Marius was a balm to my ruffled feathers, though why the Hon. Petronella's pursuit of my employer should in any way ruffle my feathers was to me – at that time – a matter of puzzlement.

'Such a pity,' I replied. 'But I shall greatly look forward to Gibraltar, not to mention Malta, Alexandria and Port Said.' As well be in for a pound as for a penny, I told myself.

The entire remainder of the morning was, for me, totally eclipsed as to events by the arrival aboard of another passenger. I was on the upper deck at the time, and walking Clovis (who had elected – and with some display of temper quite unusual in a pug – *not* to be lifted into the Hon. Petronella's sailboat for a trip round the harbour), when all at once there was a disturbance down on the quayside below: a clattering of hooves, cracking of whips, sharp cries in Portuguese; and the crowd of loafers who seemed forever to hang about down there in the hope of a coin in exchange for a small service rendered to a rich foreign passenger was rudely scattered by a trio of covered one-horse carriages not unlike our hansom cabs, which drew up at the foot of the *Hindustan*'s gangway. The rear two vehicles were piled high with luggage inside and on top; the leader contained the solitary figure of a lady in a feathered toque, all in white, and a white gown. The obvious splendour of the small cavalcade silenced the growling loafers who had at first objected to the cavalier treatment they had received from the cab drivers; they crowded nearer to watch with awe the apparition who was handed down from the leading vehicle.

An imperious stare about her. Her white parasol she put up with a sharp *thruckk*.

'Is this the ship which is to convey me to the opening of the Suez canal?' she demanded in a high, clear voice.

Her driver seemed to intimate that this was so.

'It appears, to me, to be very small for the task,' was her comment. 'Tell someone to escort me aboard.'

From somewhere, a very young ship's officer was produced, and he escorted the lady up to the deck. I paused in my perambulations, pretending to be engaged upon looking and listening to the charivari on the quay below, but all the time sliding sly glances towards the newcomer and listening with ears standing out on stalks for her next outrageous comment.

'And where,' she asked, when they had reached the deck, 'is your captain, young man?'

'He – he's ashore, ma'am,' replied the unhappy, pink-cheeked youth.

'A-*shore*?' In a note of high affront.

'At the harbourmaster's office, ma'am. He – he'll be back aboard pretty soon.'

'Will he then?' The lady picked a lorgnette hanging from a gold chain at her generous bust, eyed the other through it, up and down, head to foot; nor did she appear to be much impressed with what she saw. 'What is your name, young man?' she demanded.

'Thu-third Officer Timms, ma'am,' replied the other in the dying voice of someone who knows that he has fallen short.

'Well, Third Officer Timms, you will wish to inform your captain – *when* he returns – that Mrs Wayne Barlowe is here – Barlowe with an "e". He can then escort me to my stateroom. Meanwhile, I shall take a short rest and a some light refreshment. You may go.'

'Th-thank you, ma'am.' The youth saluted clumsily, and departed.

Smothering a smile, I turned to continue my walking of Clovis. It was not to be.

'*My dear young lady!*' The honeyed tones of the address did not permit of anything other than instant obedience. It was a summary command, strong as those she had directed to the young officer – though wrapped up a little.

'Yes?' I turned.

She was at me in three swift paces. *Thruckk* – the parasol was down. Her gloved right hand reached out and touched my cheek, gently as gossamer.

'Charming,' she murmured. 'So pretty. What is your name, my dear?'

'Suzanna Copley. And you are Mrs Wayne Barlowe – with an "e".'

We both laughed.

And then, oddly, we were friends on the instant. She took my arm and steered me towards a line of deckchairs that stood, unoccupied, under the awning of the boat deck, out of the sun.

'I must take a short rest,' she declared. 'The voyage from New York was insufferable beyond all belief. A short rest and a small glass of sherry wine, which I always take at this hour. Do you suppose there is a steward on duty hereabouts? What a very charming dog. I adore pug-dogs. My father, the Admiral, had a pug-dog named Girlie who lived to be fifteen and then fell down a well, would you believe?'

She could have been any age from forty to seventy. The perfectly-formed countenance, the slightly aquiline, commanding nose, the dark eyes, the satin complexion under the sheer silk veil told only of a lifetime of impeccable care, and nothing of the years that had passed in the process. Her figure, likewise, was of a sort that makes heads turn in envy or admiration – depending upon proclivity. When we seated ourselves, and she had arranged her stark white, flounced skirts, even Clovis, who, if he had any faults at all, was given to jumping up at strangers, did no such thing to Mrs Wayne Barlowe, but settling himself back on his plump haunches, stared up at her with his large-eyed, sad-faced expression of utter adoration.

'You are a very beautiful boy,' Mrs Wayne Barlowe told him, 'but you will not swiftly advance the arrival of my sherry wine, I fancy. Upon my word, the service aboard this ship leaves much to be desired I find – and I have only been here so short a while.

'Ah, who is this personable young man with the adorable profile, my dear? He looks in your direction as if you were acquainted. Call him over here, I beg you.'

Amused, I gestured to Mr Marius, who was pacing the deck towards us, and effected introductions.

'Of the Boston Mariuses?' demanded my new friend, offering her elegant hand.

'Yes, ma'am,' replied the other.

'I knew Oscar Marius,' she said. 'He was once briefly engaged to my niece Darleen Mae. The severance of the engagement was rather abrupt, but carried out with a discretion that speaks well of both families' civility. The wedding presents were all returned.'

'Ma'am, I think you must be Admiral Barlowe's daughter,' declared Mr Marius, who had been studying my companion closely and with a speculative expression. 'And we have met before, have we not? Your face is familiar. Could it have been at that same, doomed engagement party of my cousin Oscar and your niece Darleen Mae?'

'Where else?' said Mrs Wayne Barlowe. 'Where else indeed. But you would have been only a little boy at that time.'

'Ma'am, I was nine.'

'I remember you,' declared Mrs Wayne Barlowe, wagging a finger at him. 'A most charming boy. And now, you will perform a small service for my friend and me.'

'Of course, ma'am. Anything. Anything!'

'Pray find a steward, I beg you. Have him bring me a small glass of sherry, dry. Very dry. Come to think of it, two small glasses, for I am sure that Miss Copley will indulge. Off you go, you sweet boy.' She patted his cheek.

When he had departed, this astonishing woman turned to me and said, astonishingly: 'That young man is in love with you, my dear.'

I distinctly felt my jaw sag open of its own volition, and swiftly closed it. 'Oh, I think you – you must be mistaken, Mrs Wayne Barlowe,' I protested. 'I only made Mr Marius's acquaintance in Southampton, and . . .'

She lightly tapped my wrist with the crook of her parasol. 'Mark my words, my dear,' she said. 'You will receive a proposal of marriage from that quarter before this voyage is ended. I know about these things. I have been married thrice. Twice widowed, once divorced.

'Shall you accept him if he proposes? Will you give him your heart? He really is a most attractive male, and I tell you, my dear, I have known males! Will you accept him, heh?'

The effrontery of the question disarmed me completely. Only frankness remained to combat such an approach. I was frank.

'My heart is not mine to give, ma'am,' I whispered.

'Ah – you are already affianced!' she said. 'Well, these things can be adjusted to suit changing circumstances – as was demonstrated in the case of my niece Darleen Mae and Mr Oscar Marius. She married a poor Texas rancher and lived to rejoice the day: their few paltry acres were found to be lying upon a sea of oil. I beg you, please continue, my dear. I sometimes think that I do go on rather.'

'It is – it is not as simple as that, ma'am,' I whispered, and the tears began to well.

'Then tell me, my dear,' said Mrs Wayne Barlowe. 'Tell me all. In the telling, you may gain much release.'

And so, to this totally outrageous woman of uncertain years, whom I had known for all of ten minutes, and whose confidences I had not the slightest reason to trust, though my vocation had taught me much about human nature, I told all.

Well, not *quite* all . . .

*

As I told my story my fingers strayed impulsively towards the pearl and garnet ring that Giles Launey had given me – the way that I held it as a pathetic talisman of might-have-been every night when I closed my eyes to await sleep.

To Mrs Wayne Barlowe, I skirted briefly over my background and nursing training; told her of my early love for Giles, how, when we met again after the passing of years, he had not recognised me.

(*'Ah, what romance, my dear. The very fabric of true romance,'* was her comment.)

At my account of our final parting, I detected a tear fall from the corner of her lustrous eye that was directed towards me and descend behind the almost invisible veil that sheathed her splendid countenance.

(*'What sadness! The young sea-warrior and the sorrowing maiden!'*)

After Giles's departure to sea, I soon received a letter from the Nursing Employment Agency to which Miss Nightingale had recommended me, informing me of two appointments which might suit: the first, a Children's Home in Bath, the other a similar establishment in Peebles, Scotland. Naturally, I plumped for the former, on account of its relative proximity to Devon, to Hickleydoek and home – to the ever present, always possible return of Giles . . .

Bath was, is, ever will be, a delight to the eye, the heart of elegance. The Children's Home was a well-found establishment for young orphaned cripples set on the edge of the great basin that looks down upon the city of squares, crescents, quiet streets, which lights up like fairyland in strings of pearls with every dusk.

The children were well cared-for, loving, lovable, and obedient. The Director, Dr Hardcastle, was a tall, dark-avised gentleman seldom seen without a very tall hat and with a cigar stuck from the corner of his mouth, and was adored by all his small charges, though I seldom saw him unbend so much as to remove his cigar to kiss one of them on the brow. He delighted himself – and the children – with his tricks of sleight-of-hand, one or other of which he would perform in every ward before 'lights-out'. There was the Disappearing Handkerchief, which was always greatly applauded. A hushed silence fell over his small audience when he produced strings of flags from his right ear. I grew very fond of him.

Then came – the cholera.

For those who have never nursed this hideous disease, I will draw a veil over the details. For those who have, no more need be stated, save that the onset was sudden, widespread, and devastatingly fatal in many cases. Three children produced symptoms on the same evening. By the following day, two of the lay nurses, a visiting physician and a dozen more children succumbed to the scourge. Dr Hardcastle was an inspiration. He adhered to the copious use of salt as a never-failing specific. I still have his prescription which I daily administered to our patients, together with his instructions as regards diet: diet was to be of a light and soothing nature, composed of veal or chicken broth, rice, batter and bread puddings. He made much of what he reviled as the absurd use of prescribing tincture of rhubarb (as we had been advised, let it be said, at the Florence Nightingale School).

However, notwithstanding Dr Hardcastle's inspiration, and despite the efforts of the medical and nursing staff of the home, we lost eight children and one lay nurse to the cholera. It was upon my return from one of the seemingly endless obsequies at the churchyard of St Stephens – the last, as it turned out to be – when I had flung myself into a chair in the nurses' rest-room, that my eye fell upon a copy of *The Times* lying open upon a side table nearby my elbow.

The headline incited my attention:

GALLANT SELF-SACRIFICE
OF YOUNG NAVAL OFFICER

Which was sufficient to persuade me to take up the newspaper and scan through the contents of what lay beneath the – for me – most poignant announcement.

I read through it with the numb sensation of having been led into some charade, some kind of party game, that must, in the end, be declared to be a matter of pretence. I mean, it was not possible that the name I read was the name I adored. It could not be so that at that time and in that place, this thing should have been fortuitously delivered into my hands by the mocking Fates.

But it was. It had been.

GALLANT SELF-SACRIFICE
OF YOUNG NAVAL OFFICER

Gives Life in fruitless attempt to save Tar

BY OUR NAVAL CORRESPONDENT

In Plymouth, on the 4th of last month, as H.M.S. *Dauntless* was preparing to attach herself to the buoy in the Sound below the Hoe, a naval rating, charged with the task of alighting upon the huge metal buoy from a whaleboat, with the object of attaching a line from his ship to the ring of the buoy – an extremely hazardous task in rough seas – toppled and fell into the turbulent water and was carried away. His Officer of Quarters, LIEUTENANT GILES LAUNEY, R.N., aged 25, of Hickleydoek, Devon, immediately dived from the high bows of the battleship in an attempt to rescue the man, one ABLE SEAMAN THOMAS FINN, of Tavistock, Devon, aged 35.

'Don't do it, Giles!'
Disregarding this call of his brother officer, LT. PIERS POPPER, who was present at the scene, the gallant officer plunged into the torrent, and in rising seas and failing light struck out after the doomed Jack Tar. More boats were lowered, and an extensive search made of the area, but neither man was ever found alive. The sea delivered up the bodies of both on Thursday last, and a full Court of Enquiry has been ordered by THEIR LORDS OF THE ADMIRALTY into the tragedy, particularly as regards the hazard of requiring men to perform such feats as clambering on to slippery, sea-washed buoys in storm conditions . . .

There was more, but not much more. Her Majesty the Queen herself had instructed her Private Secretary to send a letter of condolence to the dead officer's parents, Squire and Mrs Launey of Hickleydoek Manor, Devon. There was talk of the

Patriotic Fund presenting a posthumous Sword of Honour to the self-sacrificing hero.

I gave the newspaper cutting to Mrs Wayne Barlowe, and she read it through with the aid of her lorgnette, mouthing silently on every word. And when she had done, she placed her hands in mine.

'What you must have suffered, my dear,' she said. 'And to have lost such a fine young man. But you are young, child. The world opens up before you. Grief is not sufficient. One must count the memories. Think of it – you have briefly enjoyed the love that was not fated to last. Set it in your storehouse of memories. Build upon it. Make your future life a rock founded upon a rock.'

My storehouse of memories! A bitter thought!

I replaced the newspaper cutting – flimsy, now, with much folding and unfolding, and already yellowing with age – into my reticule, along with the letter that I had received, by a tragic chance, from Giles within a few days of his death.

But I did not show my new friend the letter; I had never shown anyone that letter.

The Hon. Petronella's boating party arrived back at the ship at noon, all of them pink-cheeked and windswept by their experience. Rupert, who had struck up a friendship with the big, handsome Portuguese boatman, again declared that he was going to be a sailor when he grew up. I kept my own counsel on that remark, and consigned him to the care of Mrs Stittle, to wash and change him for luncheon.

Mr Ormerod seemed very animated, stimulated – as I thought sourly – by the Hon. Petronella's lively company. When we took our usual places at table, he asked me how I had spent my morning, and did I not think that Lisbon harbour and the surrounding countryside looked very fine, and was it not a great pity that the sailing plans had been changed and one would not be able to go ashore that evening? To all this I replied with a certain brevity, conscious as I was that my employer's eyes were tending to stray towards the Hon. Petronella, who, not yet having taken her place at the luncheon table, was bending her considerable charms towards Mr Kiprenski. The

Russian and she were standing by a large porthole – which was more of a window – at the end of the saloon. The aristocratic charmer was pointing out to Mr Kiprenski various places of interest that fringed the harbour, and which she and her sailboat party had viewed at closer quarters. Her manner of address, her habit of moistening her lips at the commencement of every comment, the way in which she occasionally touched her companion's sleeve when making a point, afforded me an inexplicable irritation.

And then – in came Mrs Wayne Barlowe . . .

She came as a bird of paradise will descend upon a flock of bedraggled crows. All conversation ceased immediately. Her imperious presence, the feathered toque, the parasol which she handed to a gaping steward, her manner of handling her skirts, every look, every gesture, was perfection.

'Sir, I should like to sit at your left hand.' This to Mr Ormerod, who was gaping with the rest. And without waiting for his acquiescence, she took her seat there, and no less than three stewards stepped forward to place her chair.

A swift glance told me that the Hon. Petronella had seen this move and was to a very obvious degree put out by it, for she had established herself in the place now occupied by the newcomer. I observed the process by which she at first decided to challenge the usurper and claim back her seat; then, how she resolved to take the next best place nearest to Mr Ormerod, which was on my right, three seats down, beside Rupert; finally, how she very sensibly (or slyly) took the course of putting a bold and cheerful face on it.

'How do you do, ma'am,' she said, addressing the newcomer.

'How do you do, my dear,' responded the older woman with a considerable amount of grace.

Introductions followed, directed by Mr Ormerod, during which the Hon. Petronella conducted herself admirably, taking into consideration the fact that she had, so to speak, graduated by way of Major Woodford and the ship's captain to proximity with the most eligible gentleman aboard – only to find herself ousted from his side by a lady who, though discernibly older than she, far eclipsed her weight of years by sheer style and charm – plus a certain outrageousness.

Both had clear, high-pitched voices. The fact that they were not immediately adjacent meant that they had to speak loudly to address each other. The conversation that followed was listened to by, surely, everyone in the saloon: I saw Dr and Mrs Sommerson at the next table pause with forks halfway to their lips; Major Woodford blinked slowly and made a great play of looking into his wine glass while cocking an attentive ear.

'You are from Boston?' said the Hon. Petronella. 'That is in Lincolnshire, is it not?'

'I refer to Boston, Massachusetts.'

'Oh, you are an American lady. I have never been to America, but my father, Lord Marchcombe, has been there on two occasions.'

'I met him on both occasions,' was the reply.

This appeared to set the Hon. Petronella back a pace. It was several minutes before Mrs Wayne Barlowe returned to the attack, and everyone, or nearly everyone, had resumed eating.

'Were you at the Paris Exhibition the other year, my dear?' asked Mrs Wayne Barlowe of her adversary.

'Yes, I was.'

'Delightful, was it not?'

'We scarcely saw a thing, for the crowds were so great. Mama fainted in the crush and Papa was very cross.'

'I had no such problems.'

'Indeed – and why not?'

'*I* was there at the invitation of the Emperor Napoleon the Third. He and I have been close friends for years. I accompanied his party at the Exhibition and saw simply *everything*, my dear.'

There was a sudden explosion of hastily controlled mirth. Or it may have been that Mr Marius was choking on a mouthful of soup. In any event, he dabbed his lips with his napkin and went very red.

Pink-cheeked also, the Hon. Petronella returned her opponent's fire. 'The Paris Exhibition was not to be compared with the panoply that attended the marriage of the Prince of Wales,' she said. 'Mama and Papa were present, of course – in robes and coronets,' she added, for good measure.

'I was there also,' responded the implacable American lady. She lifted the lower part of her veil and took a sip of Muscadet wine. 'I remarked to your father afterwards that his coronet was awry.'

By then, the Hon. Petronella's lower lip was visibly trembling.

'Papa never mentioned meeting you,' she said, with a clear note of challenge and disbelief.

Mrs Wayne Barlowe shrugged, picked up a bread roll, broke it with devastating expertise, plastered upon one morsel a sliver of butter.

'Well, he wouldn't, *would* he, my dear?' she replied in her loud, clear voice.

The Hon. Petronella's response to that – avidly awaited, surely, by everyone present – was never delivered, for at that moment a sailor burst into the dining saloon, taking off his cap respectfully as he did so.

'Who's the lady or gentleman what owns the little pug-dog?' he asked.

'Clovis!' cried Rupert in anguish.

Mr Ormerod leapt to his feet. 'What's happened, fellow?' he demanded.

'He's been in a fight with a dog on the jetty, sir,' replied the sailor. 'We parted the two varmints, but the little feller's had a bit of a bite, like.'

'Oh, Clovis, you were so foolhardy to go down the gangplank on your own and get into a fight with a horrid, rough foreign dog!'

We made such a fuss of him, and he rolled his great, sad, saucer eyes in appreciation. The bite was in his neck, but the puggish rolls of skin and fat had protected the jugular and other veins and arteries. We bandaged him up and added a fancy bow to round off the effect, making him look so sweetly comical that we were constrained to hug him all over again, Rupert, Mrs Stittle, and I.

'I think it would be a good idea to keep him on a lead when we're in port,' I said. 'For if he's a tendency to rove, we very well might have to leave him behind when the ship sails, and that would be awful.'

'I'd stay behind and look for him if that happened,' declared Rupert stoutly.

'It won't be necessary, dear,' said Mrs Stittle, 'for we'll do as Miss Copley suggests. Put his lead on him right away, dear, and we'll take the little feller for a walk round the deck and leave Miss Copley in peace.' And to me: 'I 'spect you've got some letters to write, Miss. And they say that the last collection for mail will be at six o'clock, just afore we sail.'

'Thanks for reminding me,' I said.

I wrote a short letter home, and another to Sarah Ilminster. Truth to tell, I was out of kilter for letter-writing, being oppressed with an inexplicable sense that something was wrong – terribly, terribly *wrong* – with the circumstances of this voyage to the Suez canal. Nor could I put my finger on the exact point at which the wrongness betrayed itself to me, though I sought hard to find it.

Was it the circumstances of my employer . . . ?

Here was a relatively young and successful Academician, who nevertheless carried a gun for his protection, who had had an extremely dubious visit from a strange foreigner who had been found dead soon after; a man, furthermore, who, in my opinion, was sailing to Egypt not so much to fulfil an extremely prestigious commission as to escape from someone – or something; a man who, though the soul of civility, had blazed up at me when I had entered a forbidden room and gazed upon a forbidden portrait – the nude 'Esmée'.

Who was Esmée? Was she Rupert's dead mother?

I had been feeling myself curiously attracted to Justin Ormerod, which was not surprising on the face of it since he had many of the attributes that attract a woman: he was famous in his own field, handsome, presumably rich, possessing a masterly manner overlaid with a certain – how to put it? – melancholy, which the great Lord Byron must have possessed and which had made him also irresistible to our sex.

I did not see in the naked rivalry between the Hon. Petronella and Mrs Wayne Barlowe any cause for concern, since the former was so obviously a flirt of the first water and the latter a piece too old – at least ten years too old, though, as I have observed, it was difficult to pinpoint her age – for my employer.

Perhaps, I told myself, it was the incident of the dog-fight and little Clovis's injury that had put me out of kilter – and instantly dismissed the thought as being too trivial.

No – there was a nagging feeling of wrongness, and it kept returning. Nor till after that fateful night that followed, was I able to resolve it.

The *Hindustan* sailed shortly after six on the evening ebb tide, and we stole out of Lisbon harbour, past a long line of anchored warships bearing the British ensign, past a flotilla of Portuguese fiishing boats on their way out to the sardine swarms, under the cold grey eyes of a fortress, and out into the grey Atlantic.

Mrs Wayne Barlowe did not appear for dinner, and Mrs Stittle told me that she had ordered a light collation to be taken to her cabin. The Hon. Petronella, somewhat quenched in spirits I thought, sat opposite me and carried on a brave attempt at a conversation with Mr Ormerod; but my employer seemed preoccupied and answered only in monosyllables, so that she finally gave up and directed her charms towards Mr Kiprenski, who had taken the place on her left. I distinctly gained the notion that the Russian was something of a ladies' man, notwithstanding his unaccommodating appearance. From their conversation, I learned something about him.

'And what takes you to the Suez canal, sir?' asked she.

'Madame, I was requested by my embassy to attend and report upon the proceedings.'

'You are a diplomat?'

'A diplomat – yes.'

'And you reside in London?'

'At Imperial Russian Embassy – yes.'

'I have attended many functions at the Imperial Russian Embassy, Mr Kiprenski, but I do not seem to recall you being introduced to me.'

'Ah – but you see, madame, I have been at Russian Embassy for only one night, and most of my luggage is there, still unpacked. I joined ship at Southampton in a very great hurry, having received instructions only the night before.' The explanation, delivered with an oily smile upon that Slavonic countenance, and a narrowing of the eyes, struck me as a thoroughgoing lie.

But why should Mr Kiprenski, diplomat, baldly lie about such a perfectly straightforward thing as having joined the ship in Southampton when he could so much more easily have joined it in London?

I retired early that night. The ship's smooth passage through a glassy sea promised a sound night's sleep. Having bidden goodnight to my companions, I took a brief turn round the deck. The coastline of Portugal was close at hand on the left side and I could clearly see clusters of white houses high on the hilly shores, where even at that hour the lights were twinkling like strings of diamonds. Ahead lay a jutting promontory, which, so a sailor informed me when I enquired, was Cape St Vincent, which we were due to pass about midnight.

The Reverend Dr Sommerson was on the boat deck above me, struggling with a photographic contraption that stood in an ungainly manner on three legs. His lady wife waved to me, and I called out 'goodnight'.

Alas for a good night!

It was like a scream that came from out of a deep, dark tunnel, and I awoke with it ringing in my ears, sitting upright, stark and instantly alert, the way a trained nurse will immediately react to the cry of a patient in the night.

Had I heard aright – or had I dreamed it?

The cry was repeated, then. And now it was more of a groan – the groan of a man in near-mortal pain. I knew the exact timbre, the nicest nuance of the sound, for I had heard it often at St Thomas's Hospital: such a cry had the costermonger made who had been crushed in the overturned dray. And it came from the direction of Mr Ormerod's cabin!

Flinging on my peignoir, I rushed out, and almost into the arms of Mrs Stittle, who had emerged from her cabin at the same moment. The woman was wild-eyed, frightened. Her hair stuck out in curling rags, giving her the appearance of a scarecrow.

'It was the Master!' she cried. 'It was Mr Ormerod!'

I did not reply, but burst open the door of Mr Ormerod's

cabin without the finesse of knocking. What I saw there steeled my trained mind to instant reaction. I barred Mrs Stittle's entrance.

'Make sure that Rupert's asleep,' I ordered. 'And on no account allow him into this cabin. Then have a steward bring me water. Fresh water and plenty of it. And then I shall need the medicine chest from out of my cabin. Hurry, do!'

'Oh, Miss – what could have happened?' she wailed, having seen some of it.

'Go, now. Quickly!' I breathed. And she went.

Justin Ormerod lay on the floor beside his bunk. Naked to the waist and sprawled upon his face in a widening pool of blood. He was half-conscious and moaning quietly.

I went on my knees beside him and carefully turning him over (and he was some weight, being powerfully built), quickly located the seat of the bleeding as being a deep slash that extended from the shoulder, across the deltoid muscle and thence across the breast almost to the left nipple. The cut was deep, clean, vicious, and, given no attention, likely to be fatal.

Applying pressure to the main source of the bleeding, I managed to bring the worst of it under control, and was glad of the arrival of a steward, who came with the ship's doctor – a portly man in his night attire, upon whose wheezing breath I instantly detected the smell of strong spirits, notwithstanding which he made a commendable task of sewing a row of sutures along the ugly wound (though, I have to say that I could have done it better, faster and neater!), after which I assisted him in laying across the affected area a piece of lint wetted with extract of lead, covering the whole with a length of greased lint to prevent the dressing from sticking, and afterwards bandaging shoulder and chest.

'This will need to be renewed every day,' said the surgeon.

'I will attend to it, sir,' I told him.

He nodded with approval, for he had seen me at work with the dressing, and knew I was well capable.

'Who did this thing?' he asked. 'It was no accident, nor would any man but a lunatic inflict such a hurt upon himself.'

'I – I don't know,' I breathed.

Justin Ormerod, at that moment, stirred and gave a small moan of pain.

'Let us lift him back into the bunk,' said my companion.

It took our united strengths and skills in handling the hurt to get him back into his bed without further increasing his agony. When this was done, the surgeon left me, after prescribing tincture of opium in sufficient doses to relieve the pain and induce a peaceful sleep upon the patient fully recovering consciousness.

After busying myself by mopping up the congealing blood that lay in considerable quantities on the floor (and which might so nearly have become, literally, the victim's life blood), I brought a chair and sat with him, looking down into that finely-chiselled face and reluctantly bringing myself to the awful realisation that my assumption concerning Justin Ormerod's reason for quitting Castle Delamere and England had been correct. He was going to Egypt to evade an enemy.

But – *the enemy had come with him!*

I took turns with Mrs Stittle to sit with him for the rest of that night. While she watched, I locked myself in her cabin with the sleeping Rupert – for, if the father moved in danger of his life aboard the *Hindustan*, might not also the son?

Towards dawn, when the thin grey light seeped in through the curtained porthole and I extinguished the lamp, the shift of shadows must have registered behind the closed eyelids of the man in the bunk, for he stirred, moved his body, winced with sudden pain, and without waking, uttered one word, one name: *'Esmée!'*

(Again the enigma of Esmée – who *was* Esmée?)

He had recovered consciousness shortly before midnight, when the worst effects of shock and a massive loss of blood had been to some degree mended by the beneficent hand of Nature. Though he was still drowsy, and in great agony, I had managed to get down him a dosage of the opium, which would keep him drugged and free of the worst of the pain for some hours.

At eight o'clock, when the discreet sound of a muted gong distantly informed the first-class passengers that breakfast was being served in the saloon, I pulled the bell-cord for the steward and asked for coffee and bread rolls to be brought to our cabins. Nor did I admit the fellow with the tray till he had properly announced himself and his errand; only then did I unlock the door.

The ship's surgeon came soon after and examined the patient. We were both of the opinion that Mr Ormerod should be kept in a drugged state till his constitution had sufficiently mended as to allow him to accept the pain and shock. My only fear was for the evil humours that might be set up within the wound, but my colleague was of the opinion that the extract of lead would have an inhibiting effect upon the formation of the humours. Nevertheless, he added, we would have to watch for any signs of a feverish condition.

He left me, pausing at the open door and turning to address me.

'You realise, Miss Copley, that I have had to report the exact circumstances of this incident to the captain, who will be required by British Mercantile Law to hold a full and free enquiry into the matter as soon as our patient is in a fit condition to make a statement and be questioned upon it. No matter how embarrassing to the parties concerned.

'I will call again at noon, Miss Copley.' And he left.

'No matter how embarrassing to the parties concerned' . . .

He had delivered that particular declaration to the accompaniment of a most searching glance. Did he think – despite all my efforts to save Mr Ormerod – that I had been responsible for his ghastly injury? Did he, perhaps, suspect that we had had a lovers' quarrel and that I had taken a knife to him after being scorned? (I had seen plenty of such cases during my hard apprenticeship at St Thomas's!) The very notion was grotesque. I almost laughed aloud.

When Rupert woke, I gave him milk and buttered bread rolls while Mrs Stittle sat with the patient. To his enquiries about the absence of his father and why we were not having breakfast with the other passengers in the saloon, I answered that his papa was not feeling well and was resting, and when he had finished up his nice bread and butter I would take him and Clovis for a stroll round the boat deck. To this he agreed with much pleasure, and the pug responded to the key word 'walk' with a frenzied wagging of his curled-up tail.

Though the sea was calm, it was quite blustery up on deck, and there were few passengers about, for which I was most grateful, since it was beyond belief that the story of my employer's wounding had not spread like a bush fire throughout the close confines of the ship. Nor was I wrong. On the second circuit of the boat deck, I espied the formidable Mrs Wayne Barlowe ascending the stairs, who waved to me and called out that she must speak with me. Dressed in a tweed two-piece, tweed cloak, Tyrolean hat with jaunty feather, she looked for all the world like one of those intrepid women who climb mountains and ride on camels across Africa. And, as ever, her hairdressing and *maquillage* were impeccable.

'My dear, I have heard all!' she announced. 'The news at breakfast was sketchy, rumour-tainted, and quite inadequate. I had no thought to disturb you, who must have had a most appalling night, so I summoned the captain to my cabin and demanded to be told everything. He was not tremedously willing: made some feeble excuse that he was required on the bridge for some arcane and undoubtedly spurious reason connected with navigation. But I am a close friend of the shipping company's chairman, as I speedily made him aware, and that young man – who knows which side his bread is buttered, if I ever saw one such – told me all. How appalling, my dear. And how is Mr . . . ?'

Finger on lips, I signalled her to silence, indicating Rupert, who was staring up at her in open-mouthed awe.

She nodded. '*Ah, oui! Pas devant l'enfant!*' Beaming down at the little boy, she said: 'Can you beat your dog in a foot-race to the end of the boat deck and right back here?'

'Sometimes,' said Rupert gravely, 'but sometimes he cheats and gets under my legs.'

'There is a small prize for the one who wins right now,' said Mrs Wayne Barlowe.

'Come on, Clovis!' piped Rupert. And they were off.

We watched them go. 'I take it that the boy knows nothing, then?' she asked me.

'No.'

'Nor have you any idea who could have attacked Mr Ormerod – a sleeping man – in such a brutal and cowardly manner?'

'No,' I replied, adding: 'It's a complete mystery.' Since I had no intention – at that stage at any rate – of taking Mrs Wayne Barlowe, or anyone, into my confidence regarding my fears.

One hand pressed to her handsome bosom, the other holding my arm, she said in tones of tremulous sincerity: 'I am your friend, my dear. If there is anything – any way in which I can use the levers of my influence and my connections, any help or service I can perform – you have only to ask.'

'Thank you, ma'am,' I whispered, embarrassed, but rather touched.

Any further discourse was cut short by the return of Rupert, pink-faced with exertion, followed by his little dog. Mrs Wayne Barlowe took from her reticule a jujube and gave it to the winner of the foot-race, and another to the runner-up. She winked conspiratorially at me.

'We will settle this affair together, you and I,' she assured me, *sotto voce*.

When Rupert and I arrived back below deck, Dr Sommerson was waiting for me in the lobby outside my cabin door. The good dean was alone and in a highly excitable state.

'Miss Copley, Miss Copley!' he cried. 'I have something most disturbingly *significant* to show you, and I wish to do so before I pass on the evidence to the ship's authorities.'

Puzzled, I handed Rupert over to Mrs Stittle's care and, receiving her assurances that Mr Ormerod was sleeping comfortably, I followed the dean.

Their cabin was on the deck below ours and not so well appointed. Of Mrs Sommerson there was no sign, but almost the entire space not taken up by the twin bunks was occupied by the paraphernalia which I loosely connect with the art of photography: there were glass dishes and other containers filled with sharp-smelling liquids, there were optical devices galore scattered on tabletops and chairs, and looming over them all like a praying mantis on three legs was the device I saw him tinkering with on the boat deck the previous evening when I was taking my postprandial stroll.

'Well, sir?' asked I.

He took up a sheet of glass upon which was imprinted a photographic image. 'Look at that, ma'am!' he announced, with the air of a conjuror producing a rabbit from a hat. 'Do you not think *that* is significant – in view of what happened last night?'

Taking the glass over to the light, I examined it. With the eye of faith, one could dimly discern that the scene represented there was the rear end of the upper deck, as seen from the angle of the boat deck above, where I had observed the dean with his photographic device the previous evening. That being said, the thing was so dark and smudged as to be all but indecipherable as to detail. One could pick out the lightness of the holystoned deck against the darkness of sea and sky, and – most puzzling to me – the horizon was streaked with lines of lights in a confused horizontal pattern.

'Do you mean – that?' I asked, pointing to the lights.

He clucked his tongue and shook his head. 'No, no, no, my dear young lady. Those are the lights on the shore as registered on the plate during our passing. The plate was exposed for half an hour, you see. This is necessary when one is taking an experimental photograph in bad light conditions. No, the lights are of no significance at all, save to indicate the protracted length of the exposure. No, what is significant – and disturbing – is – *this* . . .'

He pointed with his finger along a row of circular shapes, dark against the shadowed superstructure.

'Ah, they are our cabin portholes,' I said, peering closer. 'That must be mine, with Mrs Stittle's and Rupert's next to it. And there's – Oh!' I drew a sharp breath.

'Allow me,' said the dean, and he placed a large magnifying glass over the spot at which I was staring.

'There's a – a man standing by Mr Ormerod's porthole!' I cried. 'He seems to be peering in, or listening.'

'A Lascar seaman, if I am not mistaken,' said the dean. 'Observe the light-coloured turban, the black jacket and the white pantaloons which those fellows affect. But what, dear Miss Copley, is the most significant factor of all?' He paused. Eyed me. 'Remembering what I have told you about

134

the length of exposure, and the explanation for the lines of lights.'

I thought for a moment, then it came to me.

'Why!' I cried. 'He must have been standing there for a long time, otherwise . . .'

'Otherwise his image would not have impressed itself upon the photographic plate!' continued the dean, eyeing me with the admiration of a man who has unexpectedly found himself in possession of a talking horse. 'I estimate that he must have been there for most of the half hour, as you say listening or peering in at Mr Ormerod, to have registered such an image in the shadows.'

'And his coming and going – would they not also be registered, sir?' I asked.

The dean looked disappointed in his pupil, thrust out his lower lip in the semblance of a pout. 'A movement so swift, and in such a bad light, would not register,' he replied. 'And it is likely that his departure was particularly swift, coinciding with my return to the boat deck above him, to cover the camera's lens on the completion of the half-hour exposure.

'For you see, my dear Miss Copley, I was not present during all that time. The sole witness – one may say the mute witness, were it not for the fact that it spoke to us loud and clear – was my camera!'

After the ship's surgeon had been to examine the patient at noon, I found time to be alone for a short while and, retiring to my cabin, took out the sheet of paper upon which, in Lisbon, I had made some essay into recording the outcome, be it true or false, of the gipsy's prediction.

FIVE PERILS
One – the falling crate.
Two – the storm.
TWO DEATHS
One – the child Zena . . .

To the first paragraph I added:

Three – the attack upon Justin Ormerod.

After some minutes of reflection, I added an observation at the bottom of the page:

(1) *Does Zena's death come into the
      reckoning, or was the gipsy referring
      only to our party?*

And then, after much heart-searching:

(2) *Was the falling crate an accident after all???*

SEVEN

We were due to dock at the famous British naval base of Gibraltar at six o'clock that evening. By mid-afternoon, with the mountainous coast of southern Spain half-hidden in drifting rain squalls which had fallen upon us with alarming swiftness, and a perilously mounting sea, I was alarmed to see the onset of fever appear in our patient, and by his high colour, sweating, laboured breath and the angry pinkness surrounding his wound when I dressed it, that the evil humours had already formed within the tissues.

I sent for the surgeon, meanwhile making up a fever mixture to administer. This consisted of a drachm of powdered nitre, two drachms carbonate of potash, two teaspoonfuls of antimonial wine, and a tablespoonful of sweet spirits of nitre – all in a half pint of water. The surgeon arrived as I was completing the mixture, and upon enquiring its ingredients gave his approval, averring that this was the finest specific known and would certainly never be bettered.

After administering a dose of the fever mixture, I next proposed the application of cold water, to be sponged upon the entire body. The surgeon seemed puzzled by this treatment, till I informed him that, in my experience, the cold water excites an increased circulation on the skin, and by its benumbing and astringent effect forces the excess blood to recede, then, by contracting the vessels, causes any excess of it to return. Somewhat baffled (for he was clearly a member of the medical profession – and there are so many! – who have not benefited from the enlightenment of modern teaching), he agreed to the treatment; accordingly, Mrs Stittle and I stripped the patient and sponged him from head to foot with cold fresh water.

And so we came to Gibraltar, which, alas, I saw no more of than a sweep of stubble-covered rock rising up into the mist of the decidedly autumnal evening; nor did I find either the time or the inclination to give any thought to Mr Marius's kind invitation to show me the sights: by nine o'clock that evening, my employer's condition had so deteriorated that the surgeon – conscious, no doubt, of his own shortcomings – was for putting the patient ashore to the military hospital there. I had heard enough about military hospitals which, notwithstanding the great work of Miss Nightingale, still left much to be desired, that I would not countenance the idea.

'If you are not willing to take on the responsibility for the patient, sir,' I told the surgeon, 'then I am!' To which he hunched his shoulders in resignation and proposed that we draw off a few ounces of blood to relieve the pressure of the humours; a course which – since I have never been a strong advocate of blood-letting, and I was feeling the ascendancy of my victory on the issue of the military hospital – I strongly opposed. And with success.

There followed another night of vigil, in which I had plenty to occupy my mind during the long watches . . .

Following upon Dr Sommerson's report to the captain concerning his photographic revelation, I had heard that the Lascar seamen had been summoned on deck immediately upon our arrival in Gibraltar and had been closely questioned as to their doings on the previous night. From the steward who brought me a supper tray to Mr Ormerod's cabin that eve, I learned that the examination of the Lascars had been at best inconclusive, at worst negative. It appeared that each and every one of the men had at least two fellow-Lascars who could vouch that he was otherwise engaged in either work or leisure during the whole time that the camera was recording the scene on the upper deck.

'Mind you, Miss, them fellers was taught the art o' lying at their mothers' breasts, if you'll pardon the expression,' was the steward's opinion.

In the dark hours of my vigil, it did not seem to me that a

Lascar seaman could have been responsible for my employer's hideous wound, since it contradicted my notion that Mr Ormerod's secret enemy was with us, had followed us, aboard the *Hindustan*. And whoever that enemy might be, it flew against the face of likelihood and abused the simplest canons of coincidence to accept that he was, quite by chance, a seaman aboard the ship that was carrying his intended victim to Egypt.

Then who, I asked myself over and over again, was the turbaned figure who had crouched by Justin Ormerod's porthole, watching and listening, for something like half an hour? And why had he done so?

I longed to confide my fears in someone, but loyalty to my employer forbade it. A man who kept his secret so closely, whilst carrying a pistol for protection (and much good had that done him in an emergency! I had found it under his pillow and had hidden it in a drawer), would scarcely thank an interfering employee for blundering into his affairs and spreading them around.

All in all, I decided in the watches of that night in Gibraltar that I would keep quiet. Keep my eyes and ears open. Help the stricken man with all the skills at my disposal. Care for his child.

With the utterance of this resolve, my fingers stole to the ring that I wore always on a chain round my neck. Thank goodness that my unresolved and unresolvable love for Giles Launey had given me the fortitude to accept my vocation and not be led astray by the devices of the flesh. Given all else, I might have fallen in love with the man by whose side I was sitting, whose talents were manifest, whose worldly possessions might have turned the head of any woman, whose Adonis-like body I now cared for with the chaste devotion of my calling. But it could never be.

As I had truly said on another, recent, occasion, my heart was not mine to give. After Giles Launey, there stretched before me a lifetime of celibacy, and the sad speculation of what might have been.

We resumed our voyage on the following morning, and I never

saw our leaving, for Justin Ormerod, after a night of fever, was too weak to sit up and sip his broth, and I had to feed him from a spoon, with his head raised on a pillow, a tiny sip at a time. By the time I had tended to him, washed him and changed his dressing, and Mrs Stittle had taken over from me so that I could go on deck for some fresh air, the Rock of Gibraltar was no more than a dramatic hump rising out of the mist astern of the *Hindustan*'s mackerel-patterned wake.

There were several other passengers on deck, and many came up to enquire about the patient's progress. To all of them I gave the formula reply: 'As well as can be expected'. Truth to tell, with the ship shifting out to sea again, I had a pang of unease about my bold decision to take the responsibility for Mr Ormerod's welfare. What if he should die? I asked myself. How to face Rupert and tell him that, because of my stubborn pride, my overweening self-confidence, I had dismissed his father's last and only hope of survival?

My doleful reverie was interrupted by the arrival by my side of Major Woodford, who, after enquiring about Mr Ormerod's condition, asked permission to walk with me a while.

'How is the youngster bearing up under all this?' he asked, as we set off down the main deck towards the bows.

'He knows only that his father is ill,' I replied. 'At his age, to tell him more would be an intolerable burden.'

'You must have your hands full, Miss Copley,' he said.

I shrugged. 'I have Mrs Stittle, and she and I do turn-and-turn-about with looking after Rupert and his father. Fortunately, I've managed to persuade the purser to release one of his cabin-maids to relieve us from time to time. She's with Rupert now, reading to him in his cabin.'

'Thereby leaving you free to have a stroll,' said Major Woodford, 'for which I should be very grateful – indeed I *am* very grateful – to her.'

The oddness of his remark and the tone in which it was delivered caused me to glance sidelong at him, to see what I might see in his countenance. What I saw was a bland, brick-red face enlivened by a black moustache of military cut, a pair of deep blue eyes that gazed steadily back at me unwaveringly and entirely without subtlety.

'Children are a blessing, ma'am,' he said. 'And a family is a blessing, each to each.'

'Indeed, you are right, sir,' I responded, feeling somewhat out of my depth.

My attention was then taken by a small cluster of folk who were standing right up in the bows of the ship. They were pointing down into the water and calling aloud. And there, close by the ship's stem as it cleaved its way through the water, a pair of dolphins plunged and leapt in a manner that reminded me of the joyful Dartmoor ponies that were raced at the Hickleydoek Fair in the evenings with the laughing boys upon their backs. So taken was I by their antics, by the manner in which they playfully dived under the racing stem of the ship, reappearing moments later with a leap right out of the water to a merry wriggle and a flourish of their taut, smooth bodies, that I lost track of the fact that Major Woodford, after a brief comment upon the delight of the dolphins, had resumed his discourse and was now posing me a question.

'I'm sorry, sir,' I faltered. 'You must think me very rude, but what was that you asked me?'

'I asked if you thought that India would suit you, ma'am,' he replied.

'I scarcely know, for I have never been,' I said. 'Miss Florence Nightingale, who is frequently consulted by the War Office on medical and other matters in the tropics, and who receives many reports on the conditions there, once told me that there was important nursing to be done in India.'

He shook his head. 'I could never countenance the idea of my wife pursuing a career,' he said.

'Indeed, sir?' What else to say?

He nodded. 'To put it briefly, ma'am, I am in receipt of an adequate income apart from my Indian Army pay.'

'That is – very convenient for you, sir,' I replied.

'As to promotion: I have every hope of gaining my lieutenant-colonelcy in five years' time when I shall then be thirty-seven years of age, which is young for one's own command of a regiment of native infantry.'

'*Very* young, I should have thought,' I replied, glancing for a means of escape. 'You are to be congratulated upon your prospects, sir.'

'It may be the 7th Bengal, or the 1st Madras.'

'Indeed, sir. And which would you prefer?' Another swift glance to see if there was any chance of someone coming to my rescue.

'Well, the 7th is very smart, and had the distinction of remaining loyal during the Mutiny of 'Fifty-seven.'

'That's not to be sneezed at, Major.'

'Indeed not. On the other hand, the 1st has excellent head-quarters outside Poonah, with most commodious married quarters built in the days of the British East Indian Company, when style was everything, regardless of expense.'

I saw Mrs Wayne Barlowe emerge on deck. She was alone.

'That is certainly a consideration, Major,' I said. 'You are married, then?'

The bland face seemed to take on a different shape. 'Indeed I am not, ma'am,' he replied. 'Indeed, a bare five minutes ago it was that I asked you . . .'

'I must fly!' I cried, squeezing his hand. 'Mrs Wayne Bar-lowe is looking for me on a matter of great urgency. Goodbye, Major. I so enjoyed our little stroll.'

'But – ma'am – Miss Copley . . .'

I fled.

Mrs Wayne Barlowe was promenading slowly in the direc-tion of the stern; she turned at the sound of my footsteps.

'My dear, good morning to you. And how is . . . ?'

I tucked my arm into hers. 'Walk a little quicker,' I whis-pered, 'and continue to engage me in earnest and continuous conversation.'

'Why, what has happened?'

'Major Woodford . . .'

'Ha! – and what has the gallant major been up to?'

'Was just about to propose to me, I think!'

'Then you must be right, for a gel's instinct is never wrong in these matters, save in cases where she desires a proposal most earnestly, then she is frequently disappointed.'

'Or – he may have proposed to me already – only – I wasn't listening.'

142

'Indeed? Then I hope, my dear, that you did not similarly *accept* his proposal – while you were not listening.'

'Oh, I'm sure I didn't.'

Mrs Wayne Barlowe laughed. 'Let us hope not! That would have been extremely careless.'

We sipped *bouillon* on the boat deck, seated in reclining chairs, both well wrapped in cosseting rugs, with stewards hovering about, obedient to my companion's every whim. At her behest, they went down to the cabin and returned with the news that Mr Ormerod was sleeping peacefully in the charge of Mrs Stittle and that Rupert was taking Clovis for a walk under the supervision of Amy, the cabin-maid.

'Of course, Mrs Wayne Barlowe,' I said, 'there are two patients in my charge, for I still have daily to dress the bite that Clovis received in Lisbon.'

'Poor little mite,' said my companion, dabbing her lips with a lace handkerchief. 'Is he making a good recovery?'

'As a matter of fact, I'm rather afraid he's not,' I replied. 'At least, he seems to be all right in himself, but the bite persistently refuses to show signs of healing up.'

She laid her cup of *bouillon* aside, adjusted the veil about her smooth, perfect countenance, leaned back in the chair and closed her eyes. 'And how is the egregious Petronella?' she asked. 'Does she still seek to pursue Mr Ormerod?'

'Very much so,' I said, 'but, as she carefully explained to me this morning in a note that she sent down to my cabin, she cannot abide a sickroom, and apologised for not calling to visit the patient. However, she continues to send down various gifts: flowers and chocolate that she obtained in Gibraltar. Several light novels.'

'There is much in that young woman that reminds me of her father Lord Marchcombe,' declared my companion. 'A very personable gentleman in all superficial respects, but at bottom – a cad.'

'Indeed?' I scented gossip, and was mildly interested. Mrs Wayne Barlowe was happy to oblige me.

'The matter of Lord Marchcombe's resignation from the post of Assistant Aide-de-Camp to your Queen has never been thoroughly aired,' she said, 'but I am privy to the details.'

'I remember that Mrs Sommerson touched upon the affair,' I said, 'but Petronella denied it all.'

'As well she might. The matter was within an ace of becoming an open scandal. It is one thing, my dear, to make advances to the Extra Lady of the Bedchamber, but it is simply not done to chase the poor woman round and round the royal bed at Windsor Castle!'

'How awful!'

'But worse followed!'

'Indeed? What?'

'Queen Victoria entered the bedchamber at *le moment critique*, just as milord had caught his victim and was about to embrace her.'

'No-o-o-o!'

'And for that, he was required to resign from his post and from all his public appointments, surrender a very handsome *pied-à-terre* in a royal grace-and-favour apartment at St James's Palace, London, and retire to the family seat in Leicestershire – which is draughty, and has a plumbing system that was radically modernised during the reign of the first Elizabeth – and content himself with chasing parlourmaids.'

I was thoroughly enjoying her scandalous drollery, but she seemed inclined to want to take a nap. I had to change my patients' – *both* my patients' – dressings, so I took my leave of Mrs Wayne Barlowe.

As I got up from my chair, she opened one eye and said: 'So, you have had one proposal on this expedition. Be assured that you will receive at least one more. My countryman Mr Marius is quite besotted with you, my dear, and will certainly put the question sooner or later. I had the notion that it would be sooner, but one – even I – cannot be right all the time.'

Amused, I retorted: 'I fancy Mr Marius isn't very pleased with me because I stayed aboard to do my duty instead of going ashore with him in Gibraltar last evening. Leastways, he's been avoiding me since then.'

'He'll be back, my dear,' said Mrs Wayne Barlowe. 'A

dyed-in-the-wool, four-square, copper-bottomed, go-getting Yankee he – if ever I saw one. He'll be back, never fear.'

I shook my head and laughed, and had gone no more than a few paces when something occurred to me. Turning, I asked: 'Mrs Wayne Barlowe, whatever happened to the poor lady whom the Queen caught in Lord Marchcombe's embrace in her bedchamber?'

'She fared badly,' responded my informant. 'As you might imagine, the Queen having caught her in Lord Marchcombe's arms, and rejecting her protestations of innocence, dismissed her from her post. The poor gel, cut off without a penny by her noble family and ostracised by smart society, sought consolation in religion, became a convert of the Catholic Church and is now, I believe, the Reverend Mother of a convent school in Nigeria, Africa, that devotes itself to the spiritual and educational needs of piccaninnies, and is probably well on her way to beatification. All because she was chased round a royal bed by a peer of the realm.

'And now, will you leave me, my dear? I must have my half-hour's beauty sleep before luncheon.'

I left her and went on my way, curiously lightened in heart by what could only be described as her performance.

I sensed as soon as I entered the cabin that something was badly amiss. The very odour of a sickroom, to a trained nurse, gives her a foretaste of how she might find her patient. The sweat of fear, the sweet stench of gangrene, the miasma of approaching death – these are only some of the portents which one can apprehend. Perceiving something alien, to which I could not give a name, I crossed swiftly to the bunk where my patient lay sprawled, his arms thrown out, the coverings disturbed by his feverish movements, so that he was half-nude, save for the bandage that swagged his chest and arm. He was in a profound fever. And he was alone; of Mrs Stittle, who was supposed to be watching over him, there was no sign!

I settled him as best I was able, and was removing the outer bandages from the wound preparative to putting on a fresh dressing, when the cabin door burst open and Mrs Stittle stood there, her face chalk white, eyes staring.

'Oh, Miss!' she cried. 'Thank heavens all's well. I had such a terrible turn when I got your note.'

'Note?' I asked. 'What note?'

'Why, the one that was put under the door here, Miss. I 'spect you gave it to a steward to deliver by hand, but the feller simply stuck it under the door. Why, I might have missed it. I searched for you everywhere. Thank heavens, to find you alive and well!'

'Mrs Stittle, do you still have this note?' I asked, trying to keep the note of rising alarm out of my voice.

'Why, yes, Miss.' She fumbled in the pocket of her pinafore, produced a folded scrap of paper, and gave it to me.

I read the lines which were inscribed there in pencil, in hasty, impersonal capital letters:

MY LIFE IS IN DANGER. MEET ME ON THE UPPER
DECK AT ELEVEN O'CLOCK. SUZANNA COPLEY

'What's it all about, Miss?' demanded the woman. 'What do you mean by scaring me like that?'

'I didn't write this note, Mrs Stittle,' I replied.

'Then who did, Miss?' she breathed.

'I don't know.'

'Was it someone who wanted to – to frighten us, maybe?'

'I don't know.'

'Or maybe –' I saw her struggle with an explanation which I myself had with reluctance accepted moments before. 'Or maybe whoever it was wanted to get me out of the way, so that they could – could . . .'

She pointed to the helpless, less than half-conscious man on his bed of fever.

'I think it was no more than a stupid, cruel joke, played upon us by a person with a retarded sense of humour!' I declared in a high-pitched, strained voice that did not sound like my own. And then, brusquely: 'Oh, come, Mrs Stittle, let's not waste time on a silly joke. Mr Ormerod has decidedly taken a turn for the worse. Let's change his dressing, and if I don't like the look of the wound, you must go and fetch the surgeon – not that he'll be of any great assistance!'

Removing the dressings revealed what my senses had told me: the wound was further gone in mortification and pus had formed, while the surrounding skin was inflamed to a dangerous redness. I could as yet detect no odour of the dreaded gangrene – but it could well have been present in its early stages.

The discomfort of our handling him in his fevered state somewhat raised Mr Ormerod from his drug-induced semi-consciousness. He groaned and mouthed something.

And mouthed it again: '*Esmée . . . Esmée . . .*'

'He's been saying that all morning, Miss,' whispered Mrs Stittle. 'Over and over again. Whenever the ship gave a bit of a lurch, whenever I shifted his pillow to make him more comfortable, he'd come out with this foreign word. A name, is it? Sounds like a name.'

'Be off with you, Mrs Stittle, and fetch the surgeon,' I said.

'Yes, Miss.'

'And mark you, I shall lock the cabin door behind you, so you will have to knock and announce yourself before I let you in. From now on, we'll do it not only during the night, but also in daytime.'

Her eyes flared with sudden fear. 'Miss, so you think that . . . ?'

'I think nothing!' I snapped in reply. 'I am merely being prudent. Now, be off with you.'

'Yes, Miss.'

As she opened the door, I was constrained by a sudden impulse to pose a question: 'Mrs Stittle, what was the given name of Rupert's mother?'

'Why, I don't remember offhand, Miss, for she was afore the time when I went to work at the castle. But it were something like Doris, or Daisy. No, I've got it wrong, it were – ah – Diana.'

'Diana. And what was she like – was she dark?'

'I never did meet her, Miss, but I heard tell as she was fair. Fair and delicate as a babe. Died in giving birth to little Rupert, poor motherless mite. I'll be off, Miss.'

I locked the door behind her. Returning to my patient, I gazed down at him, meanwhile cleaning his wound with a piece of lint, gently, so as not to rouse him again.

So, I thought, the enigmatic Esmée was not the wife and the mother of the child. Who then was she?

And why, in the extremes of his agony, did he forever call out to her?

The surgeon was of the opinion that the evil humours had won over our ministrations and that gangrene was setting in. He further added that, had such a condition as he now saw in the wound been confined to a limb, he would seriously have considered amputating the same. In other words, he consigned our patient to the prospect of an almost certain death!

I was not of that opinion, and told him so in round terms. We agreed to differ, but from that time there was no amity between us. He restated his opinion that Mr Ormerod should have been put ashore at Gibraltar; I stuck by my guns and reiterated that having taken upon myself the responsibility for my employer's well-being, I would continue to discharge that responsibility. A weak man, he seemed grateful for my declaration, since it absolved him completely. He even conceded that he would continue to visit the patient twice daily and any time I summoned him in a crisis. But it was gesture from afar: from then on, he was no more than a vulture perched up in a tree, waiting for something to die.

Alone, I addressed myself to the copious notebooks which I had filled during my training, and devised a regime of treatment which entailed the constant cleansing of the wound by hot and cold fomentations and a dosage of the fever mixture three times a day and three times a night. The rest was a matter of constant attention and continuous nursing. This I devolved upon myself while the patient's crisis lasted, which, from training and experience, I took to be two days, or three at the most. The *Hindustan* was due to call at Malta on the fourth day; I had to force myself to accept that, by then, Justin Ormerod would either be on the way to recovery – or dead.

Under the circumstances, it was necessary that I remained with my patient day and night; accordingly I had Mrs Stittle bring in some bedding from my cabin and I made up an arrangement with an armchair and a footstool that would serve me well enough for a few hours' sleep when it was absolutely vital not only for my own well-being but for that of the patient. At St Thomas's we were always warned against impairing will and judgement with extended all-night vigils. A nurse, to be of any use, must retain a cool head and her bodily strength. To this end, while remaining constantly with Mr Ormerod, I permitted myself the necessary luxury of six hours sleep in twenty-four, taken in penny packets of an hour or two whenever I felt my eyelids growing heavy; at which times, I summoned Mrs Stittle to keep watch and ward over the patient and to rouse me if he showed the slightest change.

I was woken often in the days and nights that followed.

The course of the fever, as is so often the case, ran erratically: in the morning, after a disturbed night, he would sleep quietly and peacefully for a short while. All too soon, the evil humours in the wound would begin to plague his brain and the turning and the threshing, the insufferable body heat, the frenzied mutterings would begin again.

And that name was forever on his lips when the delirium struck at him: '*Esmée . . . Esmée . . .*'

On the third night, but for my aversion to him and all his works, I would have sent for the surgeon, so grave was the patient's condition. Indeed, though it was against my beliefs, I myself drew off three ounces of blood from a vein in the arm, and, surprisingly, it seemed to bring relief. The following morning – blessedly – the inflammation of the wound had lessened, there was not the slightest odour that would have betrayed the presence of gangrene, and Justin Ormerod was tranquilly asleep. The crisis had passed. He lived.

It was then I retired to my own cabin, leaving Mrs Stittle in charge, and slept for twelve hours. When I woke, all motion had ceased in the ship and the distant rumble and slight vibration of the great steam engine were still. I looked out of my cabin porthole to see that we were alongside a jetty, and that by the light of flaming torches, a small army of coal-blackened men were carrying dark sacks up the gangplank. On high, ancient stone ramparts that had stood the test of time and siege soared, battlement upon battlement, to the night sky all dressed with stars.

We were in the Grand Harbour of Valletta, Malta. The

personable Captain Bulgin had brought his ship safely to port for refuelling; in much the like manner and greatly to my joy and delight, I had steered Justin Ormerod back to life.

Early next morning, a note was brought to me by a steward:

> Miss Copley, ma'am,
>   I have not troubled you with my importunities because I know that you have been driving yourself unconscionably hard these past days. However, I am now told that Mr Ormerod is getting better, but that his nurse is sorely in need of some fresh air and a change of scenery. To this end, I should be happy to take you on a conducted tour of the island, which I know well. I will attend you at 9-30 am and I have to warn you that I am not taking 'no' for an answer.
>   Yours ever,
>   Hal J. Marius

I was there on time. He had hired a one-horse, open carriage with a fringed cover against sun and rain. The driver was young and exceedingly beautiful: he wore a scarlet hibiscus flower over one ear and regarded me with smouldering admiration.

From out of the harbour, we rose up a steep street till all below was a great void and the rock-walled canyon of Valletta's Grand Harbour was laid out, with its floor of shifting turquoise and emerald, and the white decks of anchored ships.

The outskirts of the city quickly gave way to a countryside of dry stone walls and plateaux set with whirring windmills. We rounded a rocky crest – and then all Malta was spread before us: hill succeeding hill, to an horizon of shifting blue-grey, upon which the compact shapes of small towns stood like pieces of cut-out scenery in a child's toy theatre, all crowned with proud basilicas topped with domes and stately towers.

First, he said, we would pass Mdina, which was called in the Maltese language the Città Notabile, the notable city. It took a long drive through a dark countryside of low hills and stone walls overhung with prickly pear, through streets of stately villages, until all at once we saw a mass of palaces, churches and fortresses soaring above us: this was Mdina.

From Mdina to Mosta. Mosta, as my guide informed me,

though only a village posing as a town, possessed a church that boasted the third largest unsupported dome in the world, as I was able to see and gauge for myself when we had negotiated the labyrinth of winding streets packed with vehicles of all kinds and the slow-moving, silent, smiling, black-clad Maltese women with their shopping baskets.

We spoke little, and then only about the unfolding of our surroundings, upon which Mr Marius was a fount of deep knowledge and unconsidered trifles. When we were through Mosta, he bade our driver to turn about and, taking a different road, convey us to the other end of the island in time for luncheon.

'The small restaurant I have in mind,' he explained to me, 'is kept by a widow lady who is arguably the best cook in Malta. It overlooks Marsaxlokk Bay.' He spelt out the word for me.

'Marsaxlokk,' I repeated.

'I am very worried for you,' he said.

Surprised, I retorted: 'Why so?'

'Need you ask?' he countered. 'Someone's after Ormerod, that's plain to see. As I understand, nothing was stolen from his cabin and Dr Sommerson photographed a Lascar seaman standing at the cabin porthole for around half an hour. To me that spells an attempted murder for reasons other than gain.'

I took a deep breath and said: 'It's possible that the would-be murderer had in mind yet another attempt after we left Gibraltar.'

'Why – what happened?'

Taking from my reticule the mysterious note that had been delivered to Mrs Stittle under the cabin door, I gave it to him and explained the circumstances surrounding its receipt.

'Have you shown this to anyone else?' asked my companion.

'No,' I replied. 'What would come of it? The Lascars would be questioned again, and to no avail. Hideous suspicion would fly around the ship, of which I would swiftly become the principal recipient.'

'Why do you say that?' he asked.

I hesitated before replying. And then: 'The ship's surgeon implied in so many words that I might have wounded Mr Ormerod during a lovers' quarrel.'

151

'The devil he did!'

'So you see, people who think as he does – and there may be many – would only regard this note as further proof against me. As a clumsy attempt on my part to divert suspicion from myself to an unknown party. But – it's not only for that reason, nor even principally for that reason, that I don't want to stir up any more mud.'

'Then for what reason are you really concealing this evidence – from everyone but me?'

I had an impulse, there and then, to tell him all: about the Limping Frenchman, Justin Ormerod's behaviour following the Frenchman's death, my conviction that he was running away from someone, the growing certainty that he had only succeeded in drawing his mysterious enemy along with him, as a predator will follow its prey through the darkest thicket and in the most secret places of refuge. But I said nothing. And Mr Marius, respecting my silence, did not press the question, but drew my attention to the hooked fingers of a wide bay in the distance, beyond the bare, autumnal fields, where the masts of anchored ships stood up as thick as a pine forest in the glassy calm.

'Marsaxlokk,' he said. 'Are you getting hungry?'

The restaurant was a rambling, paint-flaked building at the end of a quiet road. Inside, there was a tall room with whitewashed walls and scrubbed tiled floor. The room smelt deliciously of newly-baked bread and spices. Beyond a french window and balcony, the smooth surface of the bay reached out beyond the headlands to the horizon of sea that stretched as far as the African shore just over the curve of the earth.

'Good day, lady and gentleman.' A stout little woman in black bombasine and a startlingly white apron bustled into the room. 'Are you wanting to eat perhaps?'

She showed us to a table on the glass-covered balcony overlooking the bay. We were the only customers. The menu was short and simple, and I left the choice to my companion. I remember that meal well, both as regards the food we ate and the disastrous turn which the conversation took.

We began with young, small mussels in the shell, cooked in a delicately-flavoured clear soup.

'How long have you been working for Ormerod?' asked my companion.

'Since the summer,' I replied.

'Do you find him – er – an easy man to work for?'

'Mr Ormerod is an artist,' I said. 'And they are not like other folk. I wouldn't call him an easy man, but he's very generous, and though he desperately feels his own inadequacy as the father of a motherless child, he nevertheless tries very hard to do the best he can for Rupert.'

Mr Marius had no comment to make on that, and indeed said nothing more till we had been served with the next course: a freshly-made omelette, light as thistledown and subtly flavoured with chopped herbs.

'Why, since Ormerod feels his inadequacy to bring up the boy alone, has he never remarried, I wonder?' said my companion, pouring me a glass of wine.

'I really have no idea,' I countered.

'I mean, here's a fellow who's young – can't be a day over thirty-two or three – distinguished, presumably wealthy. He's what some folks would describe as "a good catch", wouldn't you say? Why has no bright woman snapped him up?'

In answer to this question I merely shrugged, having become uneasily conscious of the fact that I was being interrogated – and uncomfortably aware of the possible motive that lay behind my companion's questions. I resolved to change the subject, which I did. After all, he was my host at what purported to be a civilised luncheon.

'What are your interests and pursuits, Mr Marius,' I asked, 'apart from your journalism?'

'Golf,' he replied. 'In fact, golf is the reason for my coming to Egypt. The assignment to report on the opening of the canal for the Jessup Press Syndicate is merely a pretext with which I provided myself, to salve my conscience over what would otherwise have been an extraordinarily expensive fulfilment of a lifelong ambition.'

'And what is this lifelong ambition?' I asked.

He grinned. He really did have a most devastating grin that crinkled the corners of his eyes. 'To drive a golf ball from the top of the Great Pyramid of Cheops so that it clears the base,' he said. 'After that, I can die happy.'

'Is such a thing possible?' I asked.

'Theoretically – *just*,' he replied. 'But tell me, Miss Copley – and by the way, my name's Henry, but my friends call me Hal – why did Ormerod require the services of a highly-trained hospital nurse to accompany his party to Egypt, when, surely, any competent nanny could very well look after the boy, who seems perfectly healthy to me?'

I took a deep breath, and began: 'Mr Marius . . .'

'Hal – call me Hal,' he interjected.

'*Mister* Marius, your implied question . . .'

'You'll excuse me, Miss Copley, but it's the newspaperman in me. As regards Ormerod, I scent a story. And for reasons I've stated.'

The motherly proprietress of the restaurant had come to gather up our plates. She was somewhat put out when I brushed aside my unfinished and excellent omelette, and was the dismayed witness to the humiliating scene that followed.

'Mr Marius,' I said, deliberately trying to keep my voice – and my temper – as even as possible, whilst being hideously conscious that the former was becoming ever more shrill at the edges and the latter was rapidly slipping out of my control, 'your interest in my employer concerns me not in the slightest, save that, as a matter of principle, I find it odious to be questioned about the person who pays my salary. For your information, I have no idea why Mr Ormerod has never remarried, nor have I any observations about who may, or may not, have attempted to murder him.

'Finally, sir, in answer to your unspoken question, I have not been, am not now, nor ever shall be Mr Ormerod's lover.

'And now will you please take me back to the ship?' I concluded, rising.

He paid the bill and from somewhere procured another carriage. By then, the overcast which had lightly threatened the island had given way to rain, covering the bay of Marsaxlokk and the forest of ships in its drifting curtains of mist, and rattling down upon the roof of the carriage in which Henry J.

Marius and I sat in a mutually embarrassed and – at least, on my part – resentful silence; while out on the stark hillsides, water streamed over pitted rocks and into shallow valleys; and when we passed through one village, I saw in a drenched graveyard, huddled round a naked grave under a grove of cypresses, a party of mourners standing like silent black crows while a soaked priest intoned.

We came at length to the harbour wall in Valletta, where we parted company at the foot of the gangplank, and I briefly thanked him for my outing before he had a chance to pay off the cab-driver. I then turned, ran up the gangplank and left him standing.

Mrs Stittle greeted me at the head of the staircase leading down to the stern cabins with the good news that Mr Ormerod was sitting up, fully conscious, and taking a little broth as nourishment.

Justin Ormerod, in my opinion, made a most remarkable recovery from the malignancy of his grave wound. He spent a comfortable day – though too weak and exhausted to do other but sip broth from a cup – and slept well that night. We sailed for Alexandria at dawn (a voyage, so we were informed, of three and a half days), and he awoke as bright as a trivet next morning. Moreover, he sent a message by Mrs Stittle to ask me to come and see him.

He was not alone; the Hon. Petronella was with him. And she in a two-piece in navy blue and braided white (*very* nautical!), with the most exaggerated bustle I have ever set eyes upon.

'Well, hello, Miss Copley,' she said. 'Had a nice tour of the island with the American gentleman?'

She was perched on the edge of Mr Ormerod's bunk, holding a cup of broth and a spoon, poised in the act of placing the latter against the patient's – *my* patient's – lips. Her whole demeanour was that of possessiveness, of being in charge; by the very lilt of her voice, by her manner of addressing me, by her gestures, the raising of her eyebrows upon my entrance, by the very outrageously fashionable habit she had on, she was telling me that the day of the nurse was over and the day of the chatelaine had dawned.

'Miss Marchcombe has been most kind to me,' said my employer in the weak voice of a man who has not spoken properly for days.

'It was nothing,' said she, her wide-set, candid eyes flickering from him to me. 'When I learned that Miss Copley had gone ashore, I deemed it my duty to take my place by your side. She has striven so hard for you, Mr Ormerod, and she deserved her well-earned change of scenery.'

'You ladies,' breathed Justin Ormerod, relaxing back against his pillows, 'have been most kind and attentive to me. I am aware that, but for your sakes, I should not now be alive.'

I had no reply to that, but turning on my heel I went out of the cabin (being extremely careful not to slam the door), and went up on deck.

The kiss of the wind, which still carried with it the fingertip touch of rain, was balm to my heated brow and to my ruffled temper. Looking back along the spreading wake of the ship, I saw St Paul's, Malta fading into the soft drapes of enfolding mist. A whistling sailor went to the rail and threw over a bucket of garbage. Instantly, from nowhere, a trio of wheeling, screaming gulls descended upon the flotsam and fought over every piece.

I wept a little, mostly out of tiredness, partly out of pique and self-pity. Mrs Wayne Barlowe had predicted that the American would propose to me; and show me the woman who is not flattered by a proposal of marriage, however unwanted. Alas for flattery! It was clear to me that Mr Marius had regarded me as no more than a mouthpiece from which he could extract a newspaper story about the life and loves of an internationally famous painter.

The intrusion of the Hon. Petronella, who had not been able to bring herself to visit the sickroom during the crisis, but who, in the eyes of my employer, was jointly responsible for his recovery – that was the last straw.

So I wept a little – and saw the last of Malta disappear in the mist, which cleared a little to the southward as I was standing there, so that I perceived a bare tract of sandy coastline backed by distant hills: my first sight of Africa.

*

The Hon. Petronella having taken on the role of chatelaine, I confined myself to changing the patient's dressing daily and watching his condition – which continued to improve. She it was who brought his meal trays (the food chosen by them jointly, after no doubt protracted deliberations!). Freed of the major part of nursing duties, I was able to give more attention to Rupert and take my meals with him and Mrs Stittle in the saloon. Already the sea air and the warmer climate were having a beneficial effect upon the little boy, who had not suffered an attack of asthma since leaving Southampton, and who daily grew more robust as his appetite for wholesome food (as opposed to jujubes, sweetmeats, sticky buns and the like) was sharpened by the fresh air and the exercise which he took around the deck with his beloved Clovis, whose bite wound, though partly healed, was still giving me some cause for concern.

My best companion in the last days of the voyage was Mrs Wayne Barlowe, who lightened my spirits considerably with her amusingly scandalous tales of high life in Boston and New York, London, Windsor Castle and Balmoral (at both which royal residences she had been a guest of the Queen), Deauville, Cannes, Monte Carlo and Nice. In strictest confidence, she informed me that she had been the lover of two royal dukes, the king of a middle European country, a prime minister, and several millionaires. And all told with the greatest candour, totally unaffected, and with no pretence of lowering her clear, high voice against the ears of eavesdroppers. I grew quite to adore her.

My twin banes in those last three days aboard the *Hindustan* were (discounting the egregious Petronella!) Mr Marius and Major Woodford, both of which gentlemen I took the utmost trouble to avoid, for they constantly sought my company at table and on the deck when promenading. The major, particularly, was most persistent in his attentions. One afternoon he cornered me on the boat deck and I was quite certain that he was going to resume his protracted and unwieldy offer of marriage. I escaped with the pretext that I had to change Mr Ormerod's dressing and give him his medicine. The last I saw of the good major was him standing there with his hat raised in polite valediction, an expression of deep hurt on his bland, handsome countenance.

With every day, every watch of which was signalled by the ringing of the ship's bell, the magic of Africa came closer to me, and I spent most of my spare hours either on deck or peering out through the porthole of my cabin to see the ever-changing coastline of desert, mountains and strange white towns slide slowly past. The desert having always had a poignant fascination for me, I peopled the misty distances with veiled Touregs, romantic sheiks on plunging white steeds, the call of the *muezzin*, the scents of spices and exotic blooms in the teeming bazaars. On a balmy night when the *Hindustan* was steaming past a jutting headland and so close inshore that I could hear the cheerful shouts from a group of white-garbed natives watching us from a pier, I smelt the tangy scent of sage coming from the desert beyond and felt at one with the great continent.

At the dawn of the fourth day, the towers, domes, breakwaters and bristling masts of Alexandria came in sight. Native sailing craft had been swarming round us all day. It was now with difficulty, surely, that Captain Bulgin managed to steer his ship through the packed masses of boats that jostled and jockeyed for the harbour entrance.

Rupert was with me. He danced with delight to see the great, strange city spread before us, with winking lights still displayed like necklaces of diamonds.

The pulse of the engine ceased. There was a sharp order called out from the bridge, and the anchor plashed into the still waters of the harbour. We had come to our journey's end.

The passengers crowded the rails and were importuned by the native pedlars in the boats that immediately massed against the ship's side: in fractured English we were offered silks and fine linens of Araby, rare carpets, straw hats, woven basketware, brass trays and knick-knacks of the same material (no doubt all produced in Birmingham); sprays of frangipani, hibiscus flower, mimosa and jasmine; while vendors of food and drink plied eggs and bread, spiced pancakes, sherbet, tea, Turkish coffee from tall brass urns, lemonade, and – unexpectedly – Scotch whisky.

'Miss Copley, Miss Copley!' cried Rupert at my side, 'see

that chap in the nightgown holding up a little snake? Can we buy it, Miss Copley, please? Please, Miss Copley!'

'I don't think Clovis would approve of a snake, dear,' I answered.

'Mmmm, I s'pose you're right, Miss Copley.'

'Time for breakfast,' I said. And turning found myself face to face with Henry Marius. The expression on his face – grim earnestness – immediately drove from my mind any thought of resentment at his indelicacy (considering our then relationship) in waylaying me.

'Miss Copley,' he began. 'I'm afraid for . . .'

'Not Mr Ormerod!' I cried.

'No, it's Major Woodford,' he replied. 'When did you last see him?'

'Why at dinner last night. He was sitting next to you at table. But – what . . . ?'

'And you haven't seen him since?'

'Why, no . . .'

'Then he's been missing from this ship for the last twelve hours! He hasn't been seen since dinner last night, for he shares a cabin with a Dutch pastor from Haarlem who suffers from seasickness even in the calm weather we've been having and has spent all the time from Gibraltar in bed. Pastor de Jong says that the major hasn't shown up since last night. I checked around. No one's seen him all day. He's nowhere to be found. There aren't many places one can hide out on a ship – and why should he wish to hide out?'

'What – what are you trying to tell me?' I demanded, guessing what was to come. Remembering the gipsy's prediction . . .

'If he's not aboard,' said Henry Marius, 'and I'm pretty certain in my mind that he's not aboard and hasn't been aboard since the last time I saw him and talked to him – and we'd arranged to meet up today to discuss the situation on the North-West Indian frontier *vis-à-vis* Russia and the Afghanistan issue – then there's only one answer.'

'He – he fell overboard!' I breathed, appalled.

'Or was *pushed!*' replied the American.

EIGHT

Within the hour, the Royal Navy having been alerted, three frigates put to sea to search for Major Woodford. It was a forlorn hope, but a brave one. The three slender ships, under both steam and sail, raced past the anchored *Hindustan* with pennants snapping in the evening breeze. My heart went out to that gallant, inarticulate soldier who had thought enough of me to want to make me his wife, and I prayed that contrary to all likelihood and probability the Navy might find him.

Immediately upon our arrival, also, there appeared aboard three Egyptian dignitaries bearing an invitation from the Khedive Ismail Pasha to all those first-class passengers who had come to Egypt to view the opening of the canal. As an official guest of the khedive, Justin Ormerod was honoured with an invitation of his own, and the information that a carriage would await him and his party on the quay at nine of the clock to convey them to the reception.

'You will come with me, of course, Miss Copley,' he said.

'Why – yes, I should be most delighted,' I replied, astonished that he should have asked me.

'I have also asked Miss Marchcombe and Mr Marius to join our party,' he said.

(No surprise that he had invited the Honourable Petronella, but an embarrassment for me that Hal Marius would be with us.)

The question of what to wear at a reception in a near-royal palace in Araby did not greatly vex my imagination, for I had only one evening gown, a hand-me-down which I had been given by dear Sarah Ilminster and which she had worn at innumerable hunt balls: a smooth black velvet with a bustle that rivalled Petronella's most outstanding creation, but with a quite scandalous *décolletage* into which I prudently decided to pin a lace handkerchief for modesty's sake. Attired and with my best bonnet and a light cloak against the night air, I was on deck shortly before nine, and was handed into a waiting boat by Mr Marius.

'You look most charming tonight, Miss Copley,' he said.

'Thank you so much,' I replied coolly.

Mr Ormerod was conveyed down to the boat by two sailors, weak as he still was and with his wound still not perfectly healed. He looked incredibly romantic in the moonlight: pale of visage, dressed in his formal black, lineaments unmistakably distinguished, and bearing a strange air of melancholy.

And then – of course – we had to wait for the Hon. Petronella.

'Did she get my message, I wonder?' asked Justin Ormerod.

'Sir, I took it to her myself,' replied Hal Marius. 'I'm sure she won't be long.'

She will be long, I thought. There will be no artifice of the toilette, no subtle device of *maquillage* that she won't try and try again. If she has ten evening gowns to my one, she will try on all ten, with *maquillage* to match. And she will keep us waiting here till Doomsday till she gets it right.

I was not far wrong. A quarter of an hour elasped before the Hon. Petronella treated us to her presence, and she had to be conveyed down to the boat by the two sailors who had similarly conveyed Mr Ormerod (and they performed the latter task with an infinitely better grace, let it be said, than that with which they had performed the former.)

'Oh, I am in such a mess tonight!' she declared, settling herself comfortably upon the most comfortable seat in sight. She smiled at me. 'All my clothes are so old and tatty, and my waist has grown so thin that they hang around me like a washerwoman's aprons. You will be quite ashamed to be seen around with me tonight, my dear.'

She was wearing, as well as I could discern under the cloak that was thrown casually over her shoulders, a formal gown of *tissu d'or* that fitted her like a glove, with a bustle aback as would have supported two cats in comfort or a fair-sized dog. Her *décolletage*, which was plainly on view, outstripped the bounds of propriety as I knew it by at least an inch. Even as she spoke to me, my hands slid covertly under my cloak to unfasten the safety-pins that held in place my improvised modesty bodice and remove it.

We were swiftly closing with the shore. 'As a journalist, Mr Marius,' said Justin Ormerod, 'you are doubtless well briefed on our host for tonight. Perhaps for the sake of the ladies, and indeed of myself, you will be so kind as to inform us on the background of the khedive.'

'With pleasure, sir,' responded the American. 'Ismail Pasha is the hereditary viceroy of Egypt under the Turkish rule, and as such enjoys near-royal sovereignty. He was educated in Paris . . .'

'Paris I adore!' interjected the Hon. Petronella. 'If he was educated in Paris, the khedive must have tremendous style. Er – how *old* is Ismail Pasha, Mr Marius?'

'Er, he must be shy of forty by a couple of years, Miss Marchcombe,' was the reply.

'Forty is a lovely age for a man,' declared the outrageous Petronella. 'Don't you think so, Miss Copley?' Without waiting for any reply I might have mustered, she went on: 'My papa, Lord Marchcombe, always says that a man's triumph is to reach the climax of his career by the time he is forty, for that is the age at which he can most effectively exercise his abilities. Needless to say, by forty, Papa had achieved all he had set out to do.'

(Including catching the Extra Lady of the Bedchamber after chasing her round and round the royal mattress, I thought uncharitably. And much good *that* did him!)

She prattled on gaily till we reached the quay where our carriage was waiting, and a fair-sized crowd of picturesquely-clad Alexandrians assembled to see us mount the fine crested carriage with its four spanking greys with nodding white ostrich plumes on their proud heads and coachmen, postillions and outriders to the number of eight, all dressed in a livery of purple and gold with the national headdress, the red tarboosh, set atop of all. And we never did hear the remainder of Hal Marius's peroration upon the life and career of the Khedive Ismail Pasha.

A squad of soldiers armed with sticks parted the crowd – none too gently – to let us pass through to the carriage, and we were subjected to wide-eyed scrutiny from the people, most of whom, on closer examination, proved to be less picturesque than half-starved and miserably poor. Something like a sigh went up when they beheld the Hon. Petronella in her *tissu d'or*, which she displayed by throwing a wing of her cloak over one shoulder in a most theatrical manner – presumably for the enlightenment of the populace.

A crack of the whip and we were off. The short drive from the quay took us along a broad and rather fine avenue that skirted the harbour and which, so Mr Marius informed us, was called the Corniche. The houses facing it were large and imposing, of marble and sandstone, with impressive, high, wrought-iron gates leading to well-kept carriage drives shaded by palm trees and exotically-flowered bushes. But I was shocked beyond all belief to see whenever we passed the end of a side street the decay and squalor that existed just beyond those proud stone façades: veritable rookeries of dilapidated tenements (some of which had actually fallen down and were blocking the narrow rabbit-warrens of streets), where ragged people picked their ways, uncaring.

And so came at last to the palace of the khedive. A military band was playing 'Rule Britannia' in our honour as we drove in through gilded gates and came to a halt before an impressive portico and a wide sweep of steps where uniformed and tarbooshed dignitaries were assembled to welcome us. Introductions followed, and I was put in the care of a charming young Egyptian in diplomatic uniform, who introduced himself to me in perfectly accented English as Sheikh Mansour el Abbes and accompanied me up the steps and into the palace.

'The palace, alas, has seen better days, Miss Copley,' he said. 'His Excellency, unfortunately, finds the miasmas and humidity of the coast and the delta unbearable and prefers the dry heat of inland. He caused the Abdin Palace in Cairo to be built. You will see it, ma'am, when you travel by the royal train to the capital.'

'Oh, I should very much doubt if I shall be invited aboard the royal train,' I said. There seemed no point in being other than candid with this extremely personable and obviously well-connected aristocrat. 'I am merely a hireling,' I explained. 'An appendage of Mr Ormerod's household. But,' I added staunchly, 'a graduate of Miss Nightingale's School of Nursing.'

'You will be invited,' he responded. Under his trim black moustache, his firm lips parted to show white, even teeth. 'I am not without influence, Miss Copley.'

'Thank you, sir,' I faltered.

'In Cairo, also, you will see the new opera house,' said my self-appointed but very welcome mentor, 'which has been built to coincide with the opening of the canal, as has a specially commissioned opera from Signor Verdi. Unfortunately, the opera house is quite a way from completion, so we are hoping either that the workmen will manage to get the roof on in time, or that the gods of the old pharaohs will be merciful and determine that the very small amount of rain that we can expect in Egypt at this time of the year will hold off on the opening night.'

We both laughed.

'And this, ma'am,' he continued, 'is the reception hall of the palace. We will take our place in the queue and I will personally present you to the khedive.'

'Thank you,' I whispered, by then quite overawed by my surroundings.

The reception hall would have taken the great hall of Castle Delamere in one corner, there to be almost entirely unnoticed. The centre of the ceiling was occupied by a vast, lofty dome faced with blue and white tiles in formalised floral patterns. The walls were hung with oriental carpets of undoubted pricelessness. The marble floor of black and white lozenges was similarly spread with rugs of incredible design and colouring, the heart of which display was one long carpet of blue and gold which stretched the entire length of the chamber, past a water fountain which coolly plashed into an alabaster basin in the centre of the hall, to the far wall, ornate with gold and silver work and inlays of the most flamboyant convolutions, where upon a gilded throne there sat the khedive of Egypt, receiving, one by one or pair by pair, the long line of guests who queued the entire length of the great hall on the great strip of priceless carpet, whispering quietly to themselves, some in awe like myself, some wearing a casual air, as if a chamber which resembled something out of *The Arabian Nights* was a common-place to them. Ahead of us in the queue I saw the Hon. Petronella, who had closely attached herself to Justin Ormerod, and Mrs Wayne Barlowe, wearing a stunning evening gown in leaf green that only she could have got away with, thanks to her figure and her poise. At the moment of our joining the reception queue, she was just being presented to the khedive, who was so taken by her presence that he signalled a lackey to bring a chair for her and place it alongside his own. There then ensued a space of some ten minutes or so while the queue fretted and fidgeted, as the ruler of Egypt and my flamboyant friend were engaged upon a most – or so it seemed – intimate and button-holing conversation.

'Who is the most charming English lady whose presence promises entirely to throw out the Court Chamberlain's care-fully timed programme for the evening?' murmured Sheikh Mansour in my ear.

'She is not English, but American, and a very determined lady,' I explained. 'Indeed, I'm sure that if the khedive were willing she would happily command his attention for the entire evening, so that we would wait here and shuffle our feet, snatch glances at our timepieces and mutter complaints under our breaths – all to no avail.'

He smiled – again that broad, disarming smile. 'You sound as if you would bear her no resentment on that score, Miss Copley,' he observed.

'I would not, sir,' I replied, 'for I regard her as one of the most engaging and enchanting creatures of my acquaintance, and I should not be surprised if the khedive finds her the same.'

'She looks charming, your friend,' said my companion, adding gallantly, 'but I think that I have the advantage of the khedive in my choice of conversation partner. Now – about what shall we converse while we wait? The choice is entirely yours.'

'Tell me, please, about the canal,' I asked him.

He nodded. 'With pleasure, Miss Copley. The canal has taken ten years to build, against an estimated six years, and my country provided four-fifths of the work-force. A matter of 25,000 forced labourers.'

'Forced – *forced* labourers?' I asked, bemused. 'You mean . . . ?'

'Slaves,' he responded. 'In all but name. The great pyramid of Cheops was built by similar means in the 4th Dynasty. That took twenty years and no less than 100,000 men. But at least they had the consolations of religion – as well as the lash – to urge them on. My wretched countrymen who dug out the canal in order that the British, the French, the Portuguese should be able to move more quickly from their empires in the Far East had only the lash – and the threat of starvation – to inspire their efforts.'

I looked at him evenly; he met my gaze. 'You are angry, Sheikh Mansour, I think,' I said.

He shrugged. 'Not angry. Weary, rather,' he said. 'As a result of the canal, Egypt is on the verge of bankruptcy. Though she has paid more than fifty per cent of the construction expenses, she has been obliged to sell her shares in the canal company to the British government and her forthcoming profits to French bankers. And the rights to that waterway which tears a furrow through our land will not revert to the Egyptians for ninety-nine years, in 1968.'

'But – how *a*wful!'

He shrugged his broad shoulders. 'It is the will of Allah. But sometimes I think that Allah would have willed differently if our rulers had been more prudent.'

'But,' I said, and indicated the dark blue diplomatic uniform he had on, with its festoons of gold lace across the breast, from cuff to elbow, and banding the high collar, '*you* are surely of the ruling class in this country. Is there nothing you could have done, or could still do?' I could have bitten off my tongue as soon as the words were spoken, horrified as I was by my indiscretion. But he merely smiled and said:

'I have no power here, Miss Copley – save that of being able to ensure that you are invited on the royal train to Cairo. That far my influence reaches and not much further. This ridiculous uniform that I wear is simply the trappings of a courtier.'

'But – you are a sheikh . . .'

'Nominal ruler of a small tribe in the Western Desert, Miss Copley. Leader of a few hundred nomads and sometime warriors. I can exert no influence here.'

'Then why are you here,' I asked sharply, 'and not back there with your people, improving their lot, perhaps?' Again I had stepped beyond the bounds of tact, propriety, good manners.

Again he merely smiled and said: 'I am here, Miss Copley, because my late father, who raised a revolt against His Excellency's predecessor, Mohammed Said Pasha, and who was defeated by the Turkish cavalry, was obliged to send me to the khedive's court as a surety for our tribe's good behaviour. And here I must remain – a desert Bedouin playing the role of flunkey – till the khedive graciously frees me of my sworn parole and permits me to return to my people.

'Ah, I see that your charming friend has at last released His Excellency from her fascinating thralldom, and we shall at last move forward again.'

This I was relieved to see, for I was worried for my employer. Someone had thought to provide the obviously ill-looking man with a chair, but I was convinced that the event was too much for him.

There was one last check on our advance to the throne, and one I could have forseen: when the Hon. Petronella and Justin Ormerod were presented, and the khedive had made much of his official artist to record the opening of the canal, he was seized upon by the indomitable, never tiring Petronella, who gave of her all – her bewitching eyes, her trilling voice, her never-failing repartee, the scandal of her *décolletage* – to outstrip the performance of Mrs Wayne Barlowe; and indeed might well have done so, had a bearded dignitary bearing a tall white stick not leaned forward and murmured something in the khedive's ear. He was, as my companion similarly whispered in my ear, the Grand Chamberlain, who was concerned about the supper rapidly getting cold, the entertainers becoming bored and out of kilter with their art. Contingent in any event upon this interjection, the khedive dismissed the pouting Petronella in very short order.

The remainder of us (Sheikh Mansour and I were almost at the end of the queue) were given very short commons.

When my turn came, it was – from my mentor: 'Your Excellency, I present Miss Copley from England, who is a graduate of Miss Nightingale's School of Nursing.'

I dipped a curtsey and received a nod from the man on the throne. The Khedive Ismail Pasha was a thick-set fortyish man with a beard, dark, searching eyes and a sensuous mouth.

'Mees Nightingale, she do great work in Crimea,' he growled. 'When next you seeing her, pray convey my felicitations.'

'Yes, Your Excellency,' I whispered.

Another nod. I was dismissed.

My great concern was for Justin Ormerod; and Sheikh Mansour was most helpful: at his command my employer was conveyed to a sumptuous sofa in a quiet alcove, where he immediately fell asleep. The sheikh then guided me gently by the elbow to a chamber scarcely less splendid than the great hall. It was there that the guests were congregated and chattering like magpies.

'Remain here, Miss Copley, and I will fetch you a drink,' he said, adding with a smile: 'There is only coffee or sherbet, I'm afraid.'

'Coffee, please.'

He left me, but I was not alone for long. 'You must introduce me to your handsome new friend.' It was Hal Marius.

Something was nagging at a corner of my mind. Despite my new-found aversion to the American, I had a notion that he, better than most, could supply the answer I sought.

'Do you think the Navy will find Major Woodford alive?' I asked.

He hunched his shoulders and made a lip. 'The outlook isn't good,' he replied. 'I checked with the navigator's chart as soon as we'd discovered the major had gone missing. At no time during the night did the ship pass closer than five miles from the shore, and there was no moon to speak of. Assuming that he went overboard between dusk and dawn – for if he'd gone in daylight, the chances are that he'd have been spotted from the deck – Woodford will have been in the water by now – er – from between twelve to twenty-four hours, which is a long time for even a strong man to survive in the Mediterranean at this by no means clement time of the year. On the other hand, he may have swum ashore, a matter of five miles in the pitch dark with no compass. No, listen, I'm not being facetious – just facing up to the facts.

'All in all, Miss Copley, no, I don't think the major had a chance in hell once he went over the side in the dark. And that's the truth of what I think, God help me.'

'Thank you, Mr Marius,' I said. 'You've answered my question, and in the way I had feared.'

'I'm sorry,' he said. 'But that's the way it all adds up in my mind, and I'd be fooling you, Miss Copley, if I told you otherwise.'

Sheikh Mansour returned with a servant bearing two minute cups of coffee upon a silver salver, and I introduced the American to the Bedouin chief. The two men seemed to hit it off as the saying is, and immediately went in to what promised to be a protracted dialogue on the subject of driving a golf ball from the top of the Great Pyramid to clear its base. I left them to it, and took my coffee and sought out Mrs Wayne Barlowe. Predictably, she was surrounded by admiring menfolk, Europeans and Egyptian gentlemen, with a smattering of her own countrymen. Upon my approach, she dismissed them all with an imperious wave of her hand and bade me sit down beside her.

'I have made a great éclat,' she announced to me, *sotto voce* and even shielding her mouth with her fan to exclude eavesdroppers – a most unusual thing for her to do.

'Indeed, ma'am, and what is that?' I asked.

'The khedive, I am convinced, wants to take me as his lover.'

I gazed at her, astonished at her declaration, which outscandalised even Mrs Wayne Barlowe's most scandalous comments.

'But, surely, ma'am,' I said in all my innocence, 'the gentleman is already married.'

'He has the permissible four wives allowed to a gentleman of his faith,' she replied blandly. 'And in addition to them, I am reliably informed that he has no less than five hundred –' she leaned closer to me: in truth, she had never been so discreet, '*concubines*, my dear! *In this very building!*'

I looked about us, and registered a fact that had thus far missed my notice. 'But there is not a single Egyptian lady present, ma'am,' I said.

'Nor will you see them tonight, my dear,' she responded. 'Though for a very great treat you may be permitted to visit the *Haremlek* or harem and be introduced to the wives and nod to some of the concubines. You will be given mint tea or sherbet, sweetmeats and dried fruit, and you will gossip about the latest fashions of Paris and London.'

'You are very well informed,' I said. 'Have you visited a harem, ma'am?'

She waved her shapely, velvet-gloved hand. 'Oh, my dear, many times. Casablanca, Fez, Tripoli, Algiers. The Bey of Algiers was madly in love with me and offered to settle ten thousand English pounds on me if I would accede to his desires.'

I forbore to ask if she had so acceded.

'I did not,' she replied to my unspoken question. 'He was thirty years older than I, and the liaison could only have brought him unhappiness.' She pressed her hand to her splendid bosom. 'With me, love must always go hand-in-hand with true happiness. You, my dear, who have known both happiness and grief in love, will appreciate my sentiments, for it is truly said that in matters of the heart, experience is all. Ah, they are serving supper. And high time too, for I am quite famished.'

A host of servants served supper upon a vast oriental rug laid in the centre of the chamber in what I took to be Arab fashion. We were bidden to sit upon silk cushions bordering the carpet, and by observation and precept, one was soon to discover from the examples of our host and his court that cross-legged was the most comfortable, though it posed some problems with the disposal of one's bustle. The food was served in dishes of bright brass and copper and smelt most appetising. I found myself next to Dean Sommerson, the photographic cleric. He was able to instruct me that one ate from out of the nearest communal bowl, using one's left hand only. This proved to be difficult, but the meats and their sauces, the vegetables and sliced fruits, the various types of unleavened breads, were all of a consistency to aid the method. And there were ample fingerbowls of scented rosewater in which to freshen one's self from time to time.

An Egyptian gentleman in a military-style uniform sat on my left; he never addressed a word or glance to me throughout the meal, but dipped constantly and doggedly into our communal pot and only paid me the slightest attention – one of envy – when I contrived to pick up a particularly succulent morsel of meat.

'This is very good, Dean,' I commented. 'What is it, pray?'

'It may very well be lamb, Miss Copley,' responded the divine.

'Aah.'

'On the other hand, it might well be goatling.'

'Oh!' My hand, stretched out towards the pot, halted half-way. My Egyptian neighbour, overtaking it with his, dipped in and brought out what, to my imagination, could only have been part of the hind leg of a very small goat. I resigned myself to a slice of candied fruit, which was excellent and of reassuring provenance.

'I am extremely sorry to hear about Major Woodford,' said the dean, dabbing his fingers in the scented water. 'I have prayed for his safe rescue, but I have great fears.'

'And I,' was all I could say.

'I am of the opinion, Miss Copley,' and here the dean lowered his voice and stole a glance around the seated guests, 'that there is mischief among us.'

I distinctly felt the hairs at the back of my neck rise and prickle in sudden alarm.

'Indeed, sir, and why do you say that?' I asked.

'I can only say that I wish I had set up my camera on the boat deck last night,' was his reply. 'There was no moon, of course, but the last of the sunset. If that was when Major Woodford made what I pray was not his demise, the camera could well have recorded the means by which he went.'

'And by – by what means do you think he went, sir?' I asked.

'The Lascar did it. My Lascar.'

171

'But it has been disproved that what appeared on your photograph was a Lascar of the ship's crew,' I breathed.

'A disguise, ma'am. And what more simple or more easy to pass muster aboard a ship which is teeming with the fellows, and, to our eyes, all looking alike? I tell you that if I were to wrap a turban around my head, put on a pair of white pantaloons and a dark jacket such as they all affect, I could shuffle past you on the deck of the *Hindustan* at dusk or later without your giving me a second glance – the more particularly so if I had thought to darken my face with a little kohl.'

The enormity of his declaration was bursting in upon my mind, sharpening my terrors, shedding light upon my own private knowledge concerning my employer. But I must tread warily. A man of God my companion might be, but I was in no way placed to confide in him any more than, say, Hal Marius or Mrs Wayne Barlowe, both of whom I knew much better.

'You think then, sir, that this mischief of which you speak is being caused, not by a member of the ship's crew, but by –' with a discreet gesture of my hand I encompassed the people about us, who included all the first-class passengers of the *Hindustan*, with most of whom I was on speaking or nodding terms – and they numbered about thirty-five or forty – 'by one of these here present?'

The clergyman nodded. 'I do, Miss Copley!' And he sounded very confident.

'How can you be so sure of this, sir?' I asked.

His glance wavered for a moment; then returned to meet mine again. 'Miss Copley, I am persuaded to confide in you to some degree,' he said. 'And this because you are of the nursing profession. A lady called to a vocation. Almost like a deaconess or a nun. And this I have not confided in my own wife.' His eyes drifted away again. 'My wife, my beloved Mary, is not given to retaining confidences or secrets.'

'What are you going to tell me, Dr Sommerson,' I breathed. 'Are you going to name the person you suspect of . . .'

'That I am not, Miss Copley,' he interjected, 'for I am of the opinion that such knowledge might well redound to your disadvantage, to say the least. What I will give you is a general caution to observe, both now, or in circumstances which might follow.'

'Sir, you mystify me,' I said. 'Do you know or do you not know who assaulted my employer, or who might have brought Major Woodford to his present state – whatever that may be?'

He dipped his fingers and dabbed his lips with a napkin, for during our discourse he had not paused in the act of enjoying for himself a right good supper.

'I think I do, Miss Copley,' he replied.

'Then – for pity's sake – who . . . ?'

'Pity,' he said, 'is at the heart of it. This very night, or perhaps tomorrow, I shall confront the person concerned with my evidence – evidence which, I hasten to add, is totally ambiguous and would not stand a jot or a tittle of a chance of even being admissible in a court of law.'

'And then?' I asked, wonderingly.

'And then,' said the divine, 'I shall get down on my knees and pray for that person to be forgiven, if forgiveness is called for. And I shall hope that that person – if guilty – will join me.'

'And then?'

'And then, insofar as is permitted by the canon of my church, I shall give absolution.'

'And *then?*'

'And then, the absolved sinner will wish me to be present at the authorities when the full civil confession is made.'

I stared at him in alarm. 'Dr Sommerson, you will be taking a terrible, a most appalling risk,' I said.

'What other course is there for me, Miss Copley?' he replied. 'I could not possibly denounce this person – who may be perfectly innocent – to the authorities on the wholly circumstantial evidence I have. Even if I were not a man of the cloth, my conscience would demand that I confront this person and seek the truth.'

Even while he spoke, in a quiet voice yet firm, I seemed to see this man of God looking up at me from out of a grave. His grave.

And then he said: 'A warning, Miss Copley – *Beware of someone who is not what that person might appear to be!* I can say no more.'

*

173

The remains of the meal having been cleared away, the guests retired to sumptuous divans set around the walls of the chamber, where, reclining upon silk cushions and sipping exquisite Turkish coffee, they awaited the entertainers. I took the opportunity to call upon Justin Ormerod in his quiet alcove. He was awake, and had a better colour. I asked him if there was anything he needed. He smiled and shook his head, his eyelids already drooping again. It angered me to think that following upon her presentation to the khedive, the Hon. Petronella had totally neglected the man to whom she had been paying the most obvious of attentions. The reason was not hard to find: she had rushed to take her place at the khedive's left side during supper and had – as well as I was able to observe, for I had other things on my mind – vied with Mrs Wayne Barlowe, seated on his right hand, for the ruler's attention.

The entertainment had the virtue of novelty. First came a line of shuffling figures. Clad from head to foot in voluminous robes and heavily veiled, they only declared themselves to be females by the sinuousness of their movements and by the only part of their bodies which was visible – the hands: small and shapely, with excessively long nails, moving with liquid grace. They danced a very simple repetitive figure to the music of reed pipes and tambour, at the end of which they shuffled out in line. The item was very well received and applauded.

Who . . . ?

Who? I asked myself, watching that circle of the khedive's guests: the men in uniform or formal evening wear, many of them glistening with orders and decorations; the women in fine gowns and sprinkled with jewels, their *coiffures* and *maquillages* for the most part of perfection. Who among them was not what he – or she, for the dean had been careful not to reveal the gender of the person he suspected – might appear to be? . . .

Next there came a short man carrying a basket and a pipe. I had a notion that he might be a snake-charmer and I was not wrong. Squatting on his hunkers, he took off the lid of the basket and played upon the pipe, swaying from side to side the while. Almost instantly, a small, evil head emerged from its container and proceeded to sway in time to its master's movements. Yet another of the creatures appeared, but this one was not so

174

tractable as its consort but quickly slithered out of the basket and made a swift, rippling move across the carpet towards the wall. Screams of alarm rose from the women in its intended path; but the charmer, laying down his pipe, reached out and seizing the reptile by the tail deposited it, hissing and lunging at him, back into the basket.

Sickened, I fled, for I have a detestation of snakes and could never abide to walk on Dartmoor in the hot summer without wearing stout boots. No one appeared to see me leave. In the corridor outside I took a deep breath of the night air, which, cool as it was and scented with mimosa, honeysuckle and a host of other nameless perfumes, made a delicious contrast to the crowded, heated chamber I had left.

There was a garden beyond a colonnaded courtyard: a place of palm trees, fountains and fairy lights strung from flame-headed hibiscus and bougainvillea, and, beyond, a hint of the sea with the lights of the port reflected upon it in long pendants of silver and gold. Newly-watered grass lovingly scissor-cut to perfection suavely yielded to my stockinged feet, as having taken off my shoes I walked the length of the night-kissed garden and rounded the long, low, white palace, enjoying the sensation of being alone and curiously cosseted by the night.

Alas for being alone . . . !

Rounding the corner of the palace, I was assaulted by shouts and the sounds of a struggle. In the gloom ahead I perceived three figures fighting together, though it almost immediately became clear to me that the odds were set at two against one. The central figure, whom the other two were trying without any discernible success to pinion, was clad in the flowing robes of a native; his opponents, as I then swiftly became aware, were dressed in the uniform of the khedive's guard.

'Let me go, damn you! I am a guest here!'

I knew the voice as soon as the imprecation was uttered.

'Major Woodford!' I cried out. 'Can that be you?'

'Miss Copley! By George, tell these fellows who I am, I beg you!'

I might well have persuaded two Egyptian soldiers who spoke no English that the person whom they had apprehended in the act of trying to attend the khedive's reception in what I took to be the garb of a native was in fact a British officer and known to me, but the notion somewhat strains credulity. As it was, my advocacy was not put to the test, for help was at hand in the person of Sheikh Mansour, who, having no doubt seen me leave the reception, came after me to discover if I was well.

'Miss Copley, what is the matter?' he asked.

'Please tell your men to release Major Woodford,' I pleaded. 'I can vouch for him.'

'What's more, sir,' interposed the gallant major, 'I have an invitation to this reception, but having only just arrived in Alexandria by somewhat curious means, and not having had time to bath and change, I deemed it more civil to hurry here dressed as I am.'

A quick exchange of Arabic secured the release of the prisoner, and the guards departed, shaking their heads, no doubt in puzzlement at the ways of the British. I effected introductions.

'Delighted to make your acquaintance, Major,' said the sheikh. 'But what –' indicating the other's raiment, 'brings you to Ras-el-Tin palace in the guise of a Western Desert bedouin?'

'It is not a long story, sir, and I will dispose of it swiftly,' replied the other. 'Briefly, as I say, I have arrived here part by swimming the sea, part by native fishing craft and part by camel. The guise was given to me by the excellent fellows, your countrymen, who rescued me from the waters. I had need of them, for I was only wearing a nightshirt and a dressing gown when I was impelled into the sea at about eleven-thirty of the clock last night whilst taking a cigar and a stroll on deck before retiring.'

'Impelled – you say *impelled*, Major?' queried Sheikh Mansour.

'That I do, sir,' responded the other. 'I was tossed overboard as if I had been no more than a rag doll. A rag doll, I tell you!'

Sheikh Mansour looked at the major's tall, well-muscled build, and so did I.

'I find that very difficult to believe, sir,' said the sheikh.

'And I also, sir,' echoed the other. 'I am light heavyweight boxing champion of the Indian Army, at Sandhurst Military

Academy I carried off all the cups and medals for gymnastics, and I have in my time run down a deer and swum the English Channel. Nor was my last night's enforced swim any mean feat, for having seen the light of the fishing boat far off, I made towards it and must have covered at least two miles. But I tell you, sir, and I tell you, Miss Copley, ma'am, the fellow who tossed me overboard was my match and more.'

'How did it come about?' I asked, breathless.

'It happened this way, ma'am,' said the major. 'I had paced to the end of the main deck near to the stern when I perceived someone moving in the shadows by the taffrail. Mindful of the attack upon Mr Ormerod, I challenged whoever it was to come forward and declare himself.'

'And he did?' interposed the sheikh.

'That he did, sir!' said the major. 'In truth it can be said that I called down a hurricane upon myself. The attack was like lightning, impossible of defence, brutal in its execution. In a trice, my arm was taken in a grip that for me to have resisted would have caused it to be broken. Helpless, my leg was then similarly seized, and I was then as defenceless as a trussed chicken. Whereupon my assailant had but to bend his back and, still holding me by a leg and a wing, tip me over the side as neatly as you please.'

'Did you see his face?'

'Did you recognise him?' The sheikh and I posed the questions simultaneously.

'No, it was too dark for that,' replied the major. 'But one thing's for sure.'

'And what's that?' I asked.

'The fellow was a Lascar seaman,' responded Major Woodford. 'Dressed like the rest of 'em aboard the *Hindustan*!'

Before we all departed back to the *Hindustan* to spend the night, the khedive's Grand Chamberlain announced in most excellent English that the royal train to Cairo would depart at noon the following day, that those specially designated would travel aboard that train and the remainder follow in another luxury express. Luncheon, he said, would be taken aboard the train, and carriages awaiting in Cairo station to convey us to specially prepared suites in Abdin Palace, the khedive's new residence in the capital.

As we took our leave, Sheikh Mansour buttonholed me and drew me on one side.

'You will travel in the royal train,' he said. 'Did I not tell you that I had some small influence in court, albeit that I am merely a desert nomad dressed up?'

'You are remarkable,' I replied.

He looked at me with his dark, brooding yet curiously humorous eyes: 'I am pleased that the good major has returned safely,' he said.

'Oh, yes, it was wonderful – wonderful!' I replied. 'Such a nice man, a fine, gallant officer. It would have been a tragedy if he had been lost.'

'You are perhaps – greatly attached to him?' he asked.

I drew breath sharply. 'Oh, no, nothing like that,' I replied. 'We met on the boat. I greatly respect him and he – he esteems me. That is all.'

Sheikh Mansour nodded. 'Friendship is a wonderful thing. I should greatly aspire to be your friend, Miss Copley. Do you think that would be possible?'

'I – I cannot see how it could be otherwise,' I replied. 'You have been so kind, so helpful.'

'In Cairo,' he said, 'I will take you for a ride out of the city and into the desert, to the place of my people, which is called by us the Garden of Allah, the great sea of sand. Do you ride?'

'Why, yes.'

'*Bismillah!* It shall be so!' Taking my proffered hand, he lightly kissed it.

I shared the carriage back to the quayside with Mr Ormerod, Hal Marius, the Hon. Petronella – as before. The latter prattled all the way. My employer, wearied after his efforts following his grave wound, fell asleep with his head on my shoulder. As we drove through the silent streets – silent save for the howl of a dog and the sound of a pipe wailing from behind a shuttered window – I tried to shut out Petronella's prattle and concentrate my mind upon a strange feeling which had settled upon me that evening, which had seemed to begin at the beginning of it and grown more intense as the night progressed.

It was a feeling of – curious lightness. It was the feeling I had experienced on that far-off Christmas occasion when Giles Launey had given me the present in Hickleydoek Manor, and the more so when some years later I had met him – and had not been immediately recognised – on my return from London. It was – a sort of awakening, once known never forgotten. I touched my talisman: the ring – *his* ring – that I secretly wore always around my neck, and tried to conjure up what had done this thing to me.

Was it remotely possible that time had healed the hurt of Giles Launey, and that someone, somewhere, had awakened my sleeping heart again?

I looked to my male companions: to Justin Ormerod, whose head was upon my shoulder. The man who kept a nude portrait of a woman not his wife hidden away, the man whose body, thanks to my having nursed him, no longer had any secrets from me. Was it he who, all unaware by me, had stirred the quiet recesses of my heart?

There was Hal Marius, who, according to Mrs Wayne Barlowe, was intent on asking me to marry him. Well, he had done no such thing, and I had not gone a long way towards forgiving him for probing into my relationship with my employer. He sat opposite me now, his top hat perched jauntily on one side and a private, lop-sided grin upon his lips, as listening to Petronella with the minimum of interest he made occasional polite interjections. Our eyes met, and he gave me the faintest sketch of a conspiratorial wink. I looked away.

Had Sheikh Mansour el Abbes lit the tiny flame within me that night? His charm and attraction were obvious enough, and to be courted by a handsome desert aristocrat was enough to turn any woman's head.

(*'I should greatly aspire to be your friend, Miss Copley . . .'*)

I had come to this point in my speculations when the carriage arrived by the quay, where the *Hindustan* had by then been brought alongside. Waking Mr Ormerod, I assisted him up the gangplank with Hal Marius taking his other arm.

We parted company in the passageway outside my employer's cabin, and it was the Hon. Petronella who, I think, spoke for all of us at the end of that memorable day.

179

'*I* shall make very sure that my cabin door is locked. Indeed, I shall also put the heaviest piece of furniture against it for good measure,' she declared. 'I think it's little short of a scandal that first-class passengers should be subjected to a man with murder on his mind. And I shall be very glad to leave this ship tomorrow.'

Before retiring, I took out the sheet of paper upon which I had been keeping the reckoning of the gipsy's forecast. And to the first paragraph under *Five Perils*, I added:

Four – Major Woodford thrown overboard.

Part Three

IN EGYPT,
ON THE OCCASION
OF THE INAUGURATION OF THE
SUEZ CANAL IN THE
AUTUMN OF 1869

NINE

The autumn weather of Alexandria was most pleasant to the eye and to one's well-being, for there was a brisk maritime breeze that put me in mind of the wind coming over Plymouth Hoe on an April morning, with the touch of ozone in its scent and the tang of iced sorbet to the nostrils. I was up and about early, assisting Mrs Stittle to pack Rupert's things and afterwards Mr Ormerod's. Before breakfast, Rupert and I took Clovis for a walk along the Corniche. The little dog's wound showed signs of healing at last, but he was far from his usual perky, strutting self, and his habitually tightly-curled tail hung limply; notwithstanding which, we had an offer to sell him – this from an itinerant street pedlar-cum-entertainer, of the sort I learned was called a 'gully-gully man'. He was a shrewd, sharp-eyed old fox of a man in a striped nightgown-like robe, who drove Rupert almost to a distraction of delight by producing tiny, cheeping live yellow chicks from his ears – that's to say from Rupert's ears. In fractured English, he offered me two English pounds for Clovis – which I of course declined.

He then offered to tell my fortune by reading my palm. He was very insistent, though pleasant, and Rupert urged me on. And so for the expenditure of an English florin (which the gully-gully man carefully rang upon the balustrade of the Corniche to make sure that it was good silver), he took my hand in his bony, brown, dry and paper-thin grasp and gazed down upon the lines exposed there.

'Well?' I said. 'What do you see?'

To my sudden horror, the change in his expression, which

was from mildly cynical amiability to wide-eyed alarm, was then exacerbated by the way he let go of my hand as if it had turned red-hot. Next instant he was fleeing from me, yellow chicks and all, nightgown flying.

'I think you've frightened him, Miss Copley,' piped Rupert.

The incident, though of no consequence in itself, left me with a decided sense of unease.

At eleven-thirty of the clock, carriages awaited at the gangplank to convey us and our baggage to the viceregal train. In fact, Rupert and Mrs Stittle, along with the pug, were following in the later train with all the luggage. Thanks to Sheikh Mansour, *I* was travelling in high style!

We left the towering bulk of the *Hindustan* for the last time, and I for one was not sorry to see the back of her.

The opening of the Suez canal was set for 17 November, which was only days away. I drove in a carriage with Mr Ormerod, the Hon. Petronella and Mr Kiprenski. I sat side by side with the latter, who almost immediately engaged me in the most earnest and gushing conversation.

'Why, good Miss Copley, I have not seen you for so long a time. You have been busy with your patient. I, alas, have been consigned to my bed with *mal de mer*.'

'I'm sorry to hear that, Mr Kiprenski,' I said. 'But surely the Mediterranean was as calm as a lake all the way from Malta.'

The man's clever, darting eyes narrowed with amusement. 'Miss Copley,' he said, 'I am a Muscovite, and to live in Moscow is to live as far away from sea, ships, waves, the threat of *mal de mer* as almost any place on earth. A good Muscovite (and I am a good Muscovite, for I never saw the sea till I was thirty years of age, and it made me feel queasy even to look upon it from the dockside at St Petersburg) will enjoy *mal de mer* once out of sight of land.' He lowered his voice, glancing at my employer. 'Mr Ormerod is still looking very pale and weak,' he murmured. 'Has it been established who was responsible for the dastardly crime?'

'No, it has not,' I replied. 'Though all the evidence points to one of the Lascar crew.' I was not in business to confide in the Russian diplomat about my fears that, far from it being a

184

member of the *Hindustan*'s crew, I was of the opinion that Justin Ormerod's secret enemy was a passenger – who was still among us now that we had left the ship.

The railway station in Alexandria and the handsome boulevard that led up to it (but, still, every side street revealed the slum misery that lay only just beyond the marbled finery of the main thoroughfares) were lined with cheering people held back by blue-coated troops. From every lamp post across the boulevard were strung slogans written in Arabic (a pretty script, like butterflies wandering across the banner), in French, which I understand but imperfectly, and in English:

LONG LIVE EGYPT, THE KHEDIVE, THE CANAL OF SUEZ.

And:

LONG LIVE ENGLAND AND MR BENJAMIN DISRAELI.

And others.

The railway station was new-looking and raw, but impressive. A whole cohort of tarbooshed troops were gathered there, together with no less than three military brass bands all essaying to play together. We dismounted from our carriages and were informed by fussy functionaries that His Excellency was due to arrive imminently and would we bunch ourselves together on the station steps to bow and curtsey when he alighted with his entourage. The clock over the station façade stood at midday precisely. Oriental near-despots are not ruled by the clock, and railway trains, as well as people, must wait upon their whims and fancies. A whole half hour ticked slowly past while the three brass bands struggled hard if not to keep to the same key and tempo, at least to maintain the same tune.

Dean Sommerson sought me out. He had set up his camera on a tripod at the top of the steps, to record the historic occasion of the khedive's arrival. He seemed cheerful, like a man from whom a great burden of trouble had been sloughed.

'Miss Copley,' he said quietly, 'I have been greatly wrong in one sense, and yet not in another.'

185

'Indeed, sir?' I responded, bewildered.

'I have confronted the personage whom I suspected of having committed the dastardly attacks,' he whispered. 'The accusation was denied, and I am quite sure, I totally accept, that I have been wrong in this matter.'

'Oh, well, that's a relief,' I replied, 'to know that at least one member of our party is innocent. Would you be so kind as to tell me in confidence, Dr Sommerson, who that person might be? So that with one, at least, I can feel at ease.'

The old pouched eyes clouded. 'That I can not, Miss Copley,' he said, 'for reasons which, if I were able to confide in you, would be immediately apparent to you.'

A stir in the crowd, some sporadic cheering, the shouted orders from the officers of the guard of honour predicated the arrival of the viceregal party. My informant tipped his hat to me and fled back up the steps to his camera, leaving me to puzzle out his closing remark.

The khedive's procession comprised no less than three open landaus and six closed berlins. His Excellency travelled in the leading landau, with a squadron of cavalry riding escort. In the two following open coaches were dignitaries of his court, amongst whom – and I have to admit with a sudden quickening of the heartbeat – I discerned Sheikh Mansour. These carriages were emptied and, the khedive leading, the menfolk ascended the steps to the rousing, if dissonant strains of what I took to be the Turkish national anthem. As His Excellency passed, we bowed and curtsied according to our persuasions. I caught Sheikh Mansour's eyes and he smiled at me. There came a flash of bright light and the crowd gasped in awe and some alarm. The source of the eruption emanated from Mrs Sommerson, who was holding on high a contraption which, so I later learned, contained the metal magnesium, which upon ignition further lit the scene and permitted her husband to produce a better picture with his camera.

(In fact, I have a print of the very picture that Dr Sommerson took that day. Now greatly yellowed and faded, it shows the khedive in his sumptuous uniform and tarboosh mounting the steps. It depicts Mansour, not in his diplomatic uniform but in a black frock coat, with his tarboosh tipped ever so slightly jauntily to one side. He is acknowledging my curtsey with what is halfway to a salute. I curtsey low, and it is as if I am making the salutation to him alone. In truth, the photograph, comprising the life and death ruler of Africa's most important nation, with three brass bands and a cohort of troops, not to mention the entire population of Alexandria crowding the background, is really about Mansour and me. I treasure that photograph greatly and shall do so all my life.)

The khedive and his male entourage having entered the station, the open carriages drew away and the six closed berlins were brought forward to the steps. The bands ceased playing. The crowd was still and silent. A dignitary with a tall white stick went forward, lowered the steps of the first berlin and opened the door. He then stood well back.

From out of the coach there stepped a figure sheathed all in black from head to foot, as with a tent. She (and only by her gait was she discernibly a female) was followed out of the conveyance by three identical figures. They scurried up the steps together in the total silence and stillness. These I took to be the khedive's four wives.

More was to follow. The same procedure was employed with the second berlin, and with the rest; but from out of each of these there emerged not four, but eight similarly garbed females all in black from head to toe. I counted forty in all.

These were the khedive's concubines – a mere handful of the legendary five hundred.

The viceregal train comprised six sumptuously liveried carriages, the last four of which had their windows discreetly curtained. As we made our way to the front two coaches, one was aware of much twitching of curtains, much regarding of dark, kohl-painted eyes, as the wives and women of the harem searched out the menfolk – and womenfolk – who were accompanying their lord and master to Cairo.

The two remaining coaches were, respectively, a lounge or boudoir and a dining saloon. And all of the newest and most luxurious design, with engraved glass, most subtle carving and gilding, comfortable button-back chairs, suave oriental rugs. There were only twenty or so persons in the viceregal suite, of whom I knew Sheikh Mansour, Messrs Marius, Woodford and Sommerson, Mrs Sommerson, the Hon. Petronella and Mrs Wayne Barlow. Having settled my employer comfortably in a seat, I approached Mrs Wayne Barlowe, who was addressing one of the Egyptian courtiers. As ever, she dismissed her companion at my approach and patted the seat beside her, for me to take.

'My dear,' she said, 'have you observed the Marchcombe gel this morning?'

'Why, no, ma'am,' I replied. 'Not particularly, that is, though I did drive to the station in the same carriage.'

'There is a gel, if I know one,' said my friend, 'who has spent the night in tears. And no paint nor powder, nor will nor good intent can mask it. I, who have known sorrow (Oh, God, have I not known sorrow!), discerned it immediately I set eyes upon her this morning. You must speak with her, my dear. Make sure that she is seated at your table for luncheon. Be kind to her. Draw her out of her sorrow, if you can. It almost certainly concerns an *affaire* of the heart. Do you know to whom she has currently given her heart? I must confess that I lose track of her many and diverse plunges in the direction of romance. Would you like a drink of cognac?'

'Ma'am, I seldom if ever touch spirits,' I replied.

'Well, knowing the abstemious habits dictated upon the Egyptians by their religion,' said she, 'I came provided.' Before her on the table was a glass of sherbet. In one swift move she took from her reticule a silver flask from which she poured into the sherbet a libation of glistening brown spirit, and winked at me.

'Ma'am, you look so elegant this morning,' I was constrained to comment. And indeed she was: in a pale lemon costume of raw silk, with the simplicity of decoration that announces perfection of *couture*. I, in my one and only travelling dress of drab seersucker, felt in the searing light of her elegance like some farmer's daughter up from the country – which, I suppose, I always am.

'It must surely be from Paris,' I added.

'Not so, my dear,' she responded. 'I designed it myself, and it was run up for me by a clever little dressmaker in Boston.'

'And I love your bonnet,' I said.

She touched it: a confection of feathers that must have consumed a whole aviary of exotic birds. Her perfect features assumed an expression of self-regarding, of serene contentment, under the diaphanous veiling. 'This is from Paris,' she said. 'I went there specially to order it from Lavalle – to my own design, *naturellement*.'

At that moment, the discreet notes of a gong announced that luncheon was being served in the forward coach. Preceded by the khedive, we filed into the dining saloon. Mindful of Mr Wayne Barlowe's injunction, I aligned myself with the Hon. Petronella.

'Do come and sit with me,' I said. 'We so seldom have the opportunity to chat.'

Her eyes met mine. Yes, she had been crying. There was a touch of misery in every line of her face – though it was a lovely young face without many lines to speak of.

'How kind of you,' she responded. And she took my hand in hers.

In the event, the two of us were guided by Sheikh Mansour to a table for four in the centre of the carriage. Petronella and I sat facing. Somewhat slightly to my dismay, Hal Marius joined us and sat beside Petronella. To my entire satisfaction, however, the Sheikh, when he had finished his courtly duties, came and took his place by me.

With a gushing of steam, much clanking of metallic parts, the sound of the tripartite brass band playing heaven knows what and the plaudits of such of the populace of the ancient city of Alexandria as could be crammed into the station yard, the viceregal train drew out of the station, clattering over the complex of rails, out of the shade and into the blinding sunshine of the Egyptian autumn, and headed out, through unbelievable shanty townships and squalor indescribable, past smallholdings where women and children down to the very smallest laboured, backs bent, in pocket handkerchief-sized patches, and where patient donkeys patiently went round and round hauling endless pannikins of water.

And then, suddenly, we were out of the squalor of greenness and into the bare, basic, arid, clean desert.

'The menu,' said Sheikh Mansour, 'is of the French persuasion and the more excellent for that.' He smiled and passed me a menu card. I have it still, along with the photographs and other souvenirs of my Egyptian venture.

LE TRAIN VICERÉGALE

Le 10-ième Novembre, 1869

Frivolité

Caviar · Jambon Epicure · Terrine de Foie Gras
Primeurs à la Greque · Lyon Sausage · Cèpes Marinés
Sardines de Nantes · Olives de Lucque · Canapés Rillette

Potage
Consommé Réjane · Bisque de lobster Americaine
Velouté Lafayette · St Germain au Tapioca

Poissons
Pompano Sauté Amandine · Sole Bonne Femme

Entrées
Vol-au-vent à l'Emperatrice · Terrine de Dindon Rouennaise
Grenouille Figaro · York Ham à la Gelée
Noisette d'agneau Tourangelle · Minute steak Valoise

Desserts
Pears Miss Suzanna Copley · Savarin aux Fruits
Profiteroles au Chocolat the Honourable Petronella Marchcombe
Petit Fours Mrs Wayne Barlowe

I was enchanted to see that I had been given the accolade of a title to a dish of pears, and I passed the card over the Petronella, so that she would see that she had been similarly honoured.

'I suppose that this graceful gesture was your doing, Sheikh?' I asked of my neighbour.

Mansour shrugged his shoulders and grinned. 'Though I carry very little weight in this court,' he said, 'I am frequently permitted to add odd grace notes of elegance in matters of protocol – like, for instance, paying homage to beautiful women.'

His eyes – those dark, romantic, desert warrior's eyes – burned at me with an intensity that made me look away.

'What a singular honour,' said the Hon. Petronella. 'I must send this menu to Mama and Papa, they will be most awfully bucked.'

'I would go a long way,' said Hal Marius, 'indeed, I would walk that extra mile and more, to have a dish named after me. Do you think you could fix it, Sheikh?'

Mansour grinned. 'You are not of that sort, my friend,' he responded. 'I would name a horse after you, maybe. Or perhaps a sword.'

'I do so adore caviar,' said Petronella. 'At Mountcarey, which is our family seat in Leicestershire, my papa has a weekly consignment of Ikra caviar sent from St Petersburg by the diplomatic bag.'

'That is tremendously smart,' said Sheikh Mansour. 'Would you like me to tell you about the arrangements which await you in Cairo and beyond?'

'That would be of aid,' said Hal Marius.

'Simply ripping,' said Petronella.

I nodded.

The train clattered over a junction in the rails and swung through a wretched village full of mud huts and shanties built of scrap, where naked children stood and stared, to a barren wilderness of sand and scrub. Negro waiters in startlingly white garments and the ubiquitous red fez began to serve us. I took caviar.

'Abdin Palace,' said the sheikh, 'has had two entire wings turned over to housing the distinguished guests and their entourages. In addition to those present on the train today, there is the Empress Eugénie of France, the playwright Henrik Ibsen, the novelist Théophile Gautier, together with a large party of journalists, military and naval officers, and members of the Jockey Club of Paris. A little more of the caviar, if you please, waiter.'

'And the opening ceremony next week, Sheikh?' asked Hal Marius. 'How will that be arranged?'

'You will all travel to Port Said at the head of the canal on the day prior to the ceremony,' replied the sheikh. 'At a suitable time on the 17th, possibly before luncheon, the procession of ships, perhaps headed by the Egyptian viceregal yacht *Mahroussa*, but more likely, out of courtesy to the Empress Eugénie, by the French imperial yacht *L'Aigle*, will pass down through the canal as far as Lake Timsah, where the fleet will anchor for the night for a grand reception aboard the *Mahroussa* and a discharge of fireworks from gunboats of the Egyptian navy. On the following morning, we shall proceed to the end of the canal. And, my friends, for the first time in the history of the world, the great continent of Africa will have been divided from the continent of Asia.'

'Oh, it's all so thrilling,' said Petronella, who seemed somewhat to have recovered her spirits, or possibly she was enjoying the effects of the champagne which had been served – though I noted that Sheikh Mansour turned his empty glass upside-down when the waiter approached him. 'And what happens after the passage down the canal, Sheikh?' she asked, taking a sip of her champagne and flashing her eyes at him over the rim of the glass.

'Celebrations of all kinds will take place in Alexandria and Cairo,' replied the other. 'We are running out of hope that the opera commissioned from Signor Verdi will be performed this year, although the *maestro* has delivered certain key arias and choruses which the cast has learned to perfection. But, alas, the main body of the work still rests in the mind of Signor Verdi.'

'What is the subject of the opera, Sheikh?' asked Hal Marius.

'It is set in the ancient Egypt of the Pharaohs,' replied Mansour. 'I have been told the title, but I cannot recall it.'

We had proceeded to the second course when the train slowed to crawling pace and finally to a halt close by another village of mud huts thatched with grass that straggled along the banks of a narrow canal. At a signal from the khedive, Sheikh Mansour went to see what had occasioned the delay. He returned from the front of the train, bowed and quietly addressed the khedive, who was seated at table with Mrs Wayne Barlowe (oh, and how, on reflection she had so neatly excluded Petronella from the viceregal table by hoisting her upon me!). The khedive seemed amused by the sheikh's explanation of the delay and patted his shoulder in an indulgent manner.

'What is it?' asked Petronella as soon as the sheikh had sat down again.

'A bullock has fallen asleep on the line ahead,' replied he.

'Well, can't they ask it to move?' she demanded.

'It belongs to the village headman,' he explained. 'Apparently it is an animal of some value and the villagers are somewhat concerned that it might break a leg and have to be destroyed if it were precipitately awakened, hauled to its feet and dragged across the line and down the embankment into the village. So they are doing it by gentle degrees. By persuasion. By mutual consultation. It is the way of the Arab.' He shrugged his broad shoulders and grinned.

'Why, look at all those people!' trilled Petronella, pointing out of the window. 'Are they going to attack us, do you think, Sheikh?'

A fairly large gaggle of men, women and children: the men in the eternal Egyptian nightgown, the women all in black and veiled, the children for the most part naked, both girls and boys, were clustering at the window and gaping at us and at the rich fare laid out on our table. The children, the babies even, had eyes that were swarming with flies and not even their mothers troubled to brush them off, presumably because it was a task that they had long since learned to be fruitless.

'Oh, my God, look at them!' exclaimed Hal Marius. 'They're telling us they're starving.'

'They almost certainly are,' replied Sheikh Mansour. 'See how they point to the scraps on our tables and then point to their empty mouths. They, my dear friends, are the *fellahin* of the Nile valley. They have slaved in Nile mud since time immemorial. Built pyramids to the glory of our ancient gods. In the recent past, they have carved a canal between Africa and Asia when many declared that it could not be done.' His voice was rising in a bitter intensity, and I glanced towards the khedive and saw a deep frown of disapproval appear on his brow. 'And today, by Allah, *some* of them shall eat!'

A blank-faced waiter, innocent of what was going on, brought a whole rack of lamb on an enormous dish for us to inspect and approve. Rising to his feet, Sheikh Mansour reached out and, lowering the carriage window, called out something in Arabic

193

to the people clustered below, whereupon, seizing the rack of lamb, he tossed it out to them.

'They live like dogs!' he declared. 'They are perfectly happy to fight like dogs over scraps, and be grateful to Allah for small mercies!' He then said something in Arabic which appeared to have been directed to the khedive, for the latter half-rose in fury and signalled to a uniformed military aide to attend him.

The sheikh then dabbed his lips with his napkin, and, bowing to Petronella and myself, and slightly more perfunctorily to Hal Marius, walked out of the dining car.

At a nod from the khedive, the military aide followed after the sheik.

The wretched villagers were still fighting over the scraps of lamb: men wrestling with children, women with their own offspring, clawing with fingernails, snapping with teeth, screaming imprecations, fumbling, scrabbling, falling. I hid my eyes. And the train moved forward, unregarded by them, gathered speed, flashed past the wretched village and was soon out again into the desert.

'I fancy that our friend Sheikh Mansour has gotten himself into a spot of trouble,' murmured Hal Marius. 'It's one thing for an Arab to dispense alms to the poor – even joints of lamb – indeed he tots up credits in heaven for so doing. But to declare his ruler to be a tyrant – and that in public, before the latter's honoured guests – now that's a horse of a different colour.'

I stared at him in some alarm. 'Is *that* what the sheikh said just now?' I asked.

'I have only a little Arabic,' he replied, 'and I wouldn't take the stand and give evidence on oath as to the precise wording of the declaration. But, yes, that's substantially what he said.'

'He'll never be released from his parole while he carries on like that,' I said.

'What parole's this?' asked Hal Marius. And I told him the sheikh's story.

By this time we were passing through the lush and fertile fields of the Nile valley. Luncheon had been cleared away. Petronella had succumbed to the heat – which, despite the constant movement of huge fans in the ceiling worked by a little black boy with a length of cord, was considerable in the carriage – and had fallen asleep with her carefully-arranged ringlets resting back against the lace-covered headrest. Others, too, were asleep. I saw the back of Dean Sommerson's bald head similarly resting.

'And there,' said Hal Marius, pointing, 'is Cairo!'

I followed his pointing finger. 'Cairo!' I murmured in wonder.

They came in sight over the palm trees set at the edge of all the tiny fields where peasants laboured, bent-backed in the searing sunlight: a row of domes and tall pinnacles, sand and ochre-coloured, with flashes of shining green and gold.

'There you see the mosque of Sultan Hasan,' said my companion. 'And there, high up, the Cairo Citadel, built by the great Saladin.'

'The Pyramids?' I queried.

'Are way out of town. You won't see them from the train. But we'll go there. The Egyptians have built a road to Giza, where the great pyramids and the Sphinx stand, especially for the French Empress to travel there in comfort.'

'The khedive has certainly spared no expense for the inauguration,' I said.

'Maybe it could have been better spent on improving the lot of his people,' said Hal Marius.

I thought of the wretched people back at that village, fighting each other and their children for scraps of the rich man's meat, and I nodded.

And so we came to Cairo, the most important and most ancient city of the African continent. The outer environs, having seen the glories of the towers and domes from afar, were distressing in the extreme. More squalor: narrow streets bisected by muddy streams where black-clad women washed clothes and naked children pranced and splashed; back yards fenced-in to the size of hearthrugs and containing a few spavined chickens that pecked around in hope of a blade of weed.

And then – all unexpectedly – we steamed into a great, new, busy station and our train journey was over. A long red carpet swam into view. A military band struck up the air that I had come to realise was the National Anthem. The train drew smoothly to a halt, with the door of our carriage precisely aligned with the end of the long red carpet, on which anxious dignitaries in sumptuous robes and bright uniforms waited to greet their ruler.

'Oh, heavens, Miss Marchcombe's still asleep!' I whispered, as the viceregal party at the top table rose in a gaggle, nodded thanks to their host, and prepared to follow His Excellency out on to the red carpet. I reached out and shook Petronella, who came out of her slumber with lovely eyes misted with deep dreams.

'Oh, is it five o'clock already and time to get up?' she asked, bemused.

'No, it's only barely four, but we're in Cairo,' I replied.

'I suggest we hold back and let most of the others go,' said Hal Marius. 'I fancy Mrs Wayne Barlowe and her ilk will be closest to the khedive and won't thank the likes of us for treading on their heels and trying to get into the limelight.' To which advice I readily agreed.

The Hon. Petronella, complaining under her breath that she was 'not prepared to show herself publicly and why had I not been woken earlier?', produced from her reticule a mirror and a vanity box, by the aid of which she proceeded to dust rice powder on her nose. She then ran her fingers through her marginally tousled hair and – lo! – it was immaculate again (another attribute which I envied our aristocratic travelling companion!).

The khedive alighted from the carriage, with Mrs Wayne Barlowe immediately behind him, looking particularly stunning in her pale lemon silk and the confection of millinery that had depleted an aviary. She met my eye and treated me to a smile and something approaching a wink as she was handed down to the platform by the khedive himself.

The military band played another verse of the National Anthem.

'Let's go, ladies,' said Hal Marius, rising.

We filed down the carriage, the American leading, with Petronella behind me. Most of the passengers had by then alighted, save for the Sommersons and another couple. As we drew abreast of the former, Mrs Sommerson was chiding her husband, who still sat with his head lolled back against the rest, his eyes closed.

'My dear Arthur,' she said, 'you simply cannot sleep the whole afternoon away! Rouse yourself, do! I am strongly of the opinion that that second glass of champagne was not a good idea for you, and in future I shall forbid it!'

She gave him a quite vigorous push. Hal Marius turned to me and grinned.

'Arthur!'

It happened! Slowly, and with a curious dignity, the Reverend Dr Sommerson swayed to one side in his seat and rolled to the carpeted floor at my very feet, where he lay – and continued to lie – face downwards.

'*Arthur!* Get up this instant. You are making a total spectacle of yourself. Wait till I get you alone in our room!'

With a prickling feeling of premonition, I knelt beside the dean and with some difficulty turned him over. I felt for his pulse: there was none. I layed my hand over his heart: there was neither heartbeat nor respiration. I opened one of his eyes – and his wife screamed to see the pupil and iris turned upwards almost out of sight in the socket of the skull.

'What – what's the matter with him?' she cried.

'I'm afraid that he's dead, your husband's dead, ma'am,' I replied.

The drive through Cairo to the Abdin Palace was a nightmare that has mercifully faded from my memory. I have vague recollections of masses, cheering crowds, of sunlit streets and palm-shaded avenues. Mrs Sommerson sat beside me – or, rather, half-lay in my arms, her head pressed against my shoulder, weeping continuously in a high, keening sound. She had with difficulty been persuaded against bringing her husband's body with her in the coach (it had been taken away discreetly upon a stretcher to, as I ascertained, the mortuary of a local hospital).

Abdin Palace I found to be a vast edifice of grey stone with two wings jutting out each side, approached through wrought iron gates of tall and gilded magnificence. The coach containing Mrs Sommerson and myself was brought to the right-hand wing, and it was Sheikh Mansour who handed the two of us down.

'You ladies have apartments in the *Haremlek*,' he said. 'These maids will attend upon your needs.'

Two black-clad and veiled women appeared and, taking the weeping widow by the arms, helped her up the steps into the palace.

'Miss Copley, shall I summon a doctor for Mrs Sommerson?' asked the sheikh.

'No, it won't be necessary. I have a sleeping draught in my baggage, and that will calm her and give her a good night's rest,' I said. 'But what of the dean?'

'He is dead, Miss Copley.' He looked surprised. 'What more to say, save that I have sent a message to the rector of the Anglican church? Obsequies and burial cannot greatly be postponed in Egypt, even at this time of the year, and will almost certainly take place tomorrow. Is there aught else, Miss Copley? I seem to detect another question trembling on your lips. What is it, pray?'

'Sheikh Mansour,' I said quietly, glancing first over my shoulder, though heaven knows why, 'is there a competent doctor at the hospital to which Dean Sommerson's body has been taken?'

He raised an eyebrow at that. 'Why, of course, Miss Copley. Just because we have lived a little longer in the sun, you must not think that we are barbarians. The science of medicine was practically invented in the valley of the Nile.'

'I'm very sorry,' I said contritely, 'and I meant no offence. It's just that – well, Sheikh, would you please see to it that they establish the cause of the dean's death?'

He looked puzzled. 'I think, dear Miss Copley, that even I could establish that. Surely, at his age and – though I met him and spoke with him only briefly – what I considered to be his somewhat infirm condition, he died of a stroke or a heart attack.'

A crane flew overhead, quite low. I saw it distinctly and marvelled at its motion. I waited till it was out of sight before I replied.

'I think – it may be possible – that he was murdered.'

Sheikh Mansour did not look as alarmed and surprised as I had expected. As a desert warrior, I suppose he was familiar with rude and violent death. He merely raised an eyebrow again and murmured: 'Why should you think so, Miss Copley?'

So, I told him everything – or nearly everything: about the attack upon Justin Ormerod, Dean Sommerson's conviction that he had identified the would-be assassin, and the rest. When I had done, he nodded gravely. 'I take your point, Miss Copley. But, as you said, the dean told you only just before mounting the train that he had confronted this mysterious personage and had been assured that he was mistaken.'

I drew a deep breath. 'But supposing,' I said, 'that he was *mistaken* in believing this personage's assurances?'

'Aah!' He nodded. 'Now you have a case, Miss Copley,' he said. 'You are a shrewd lady. I will certainly see to it that a post-mortem is made upon the body of the dean. And will inform you of the result. After that – we must decide what to do. Or not to do. Is that agreed?'

I gave him my hand. As on another occasion, he transferred it to his finely-sculptured lips and implanted on my fingertips a kiss so light as to be discernible only to the eye.

'I will go now,' he said. 'The little boy Rupert and your maid will be here soon. They also have an apartment in the *Haremlek*. Till we meet again, Miss Copley.' A flash of those brooding yet humorous, berry-black eyes and he turned to leave me.

'Sheikh Mansour . . .' I began.

He turned. 'Yes, Miss Copley?'

'Was it wise of you to rile the khedive?'

He shrugged. 'It was not. But it will scarcely make any difference. Short of a miracle, I shall not get free of my parole. All that has happened is that I shall from henceforth be under closer surveillance. Goodbye, Miss Copley. *Bismillah!*'

'*Bismillah!*' I responded.

Rupert and Mrs Stittle arrived half an hour later. They had had, said he, a most scrumptious high tea aboard the train, with iced cakes, strawberries and cream, ice sorbet, and his favourite – sardines!

The long day had wearied him, and I prescribed a nap before

supper. We put him to bed and left him in the shadowed gloom of the lofty, shuttered chamber.

When we had closed the door, Mrs Stittle said: 'I heard about his reverence, Miss. Isn't it awful? Poor Mrs Sommerson. How's she taking it?'

'As badly as could be expected,' I replied. 'And the worse for being so far from home. I've given her a sleeping draught and she's quiet now. Have you seen anything of Mr Ormerod?'

'No, Miss,' she said, 'but one of the maids – she speaks the Queen's English as well as you and me – told me that all the menfolk are over in the other wing of the palace, it not being considered proper in these parts for ladies and gentlemen to mix. It's ladies and young children at one end of the house, gentlemen at the other. Do you fancy a nice cup of tea, miss? The maid makes a good one. Not like we're used to back home, of course, but I might get around to showing her how to do it proper like.'

'No thanks, Mrs Stittle,' I replied. 'I think . . .'

'Yes, Miss? Are you all right? You look a bit peaky to me. Like Rupert, you'd probably be better for a little lie down.'

'It's only the heat in here,' I said. 'What I need is some fresh air. I think – I think I'll go for a walk.'

The sentries guarding the gates of the palace sprang to attention and smacked the butts of their guns when I went out past them, to which salutations I felt constrained to respond by waving my parasol. The street outside, shaded with palms, was cool. A water-cart drawn by a slow moving pair of buffaloes driven by a small boy carrying a long stick was sending a fine spray into the thin tilth of sand that covered the surface of roadway and pavement, settling the dust, freshening the air. I followed it a short distance, strolling in the early evening sunlight and shadow.

Two things were obsessing my mind: firstly, I was concerned – indeed, terrified – that the gipsy's prophecy appeared to be coming to pass, and I had no way of stopping the relentless march of Fate. One had died, two more might well have died.

Who was to be next . . . ?

And then, in a lighter yet no less puzzling vein, there was the strange feeling that had come upon me during the khedive's reception in Alexandria: the feeling which I compared with my experiences with Giles Launey, the first and only love of my life. A whole day and a night had passed, yet still the feeling persisted, and I was able to seek it out by then and give it some shape and coherence – even though it brought me no nearer to its cause.

It was as if – as if there was a distant melody just outside the range of my hearing, a beautiful and most exquisite song whose echoes and overtones were nevertheless within the compass of my senses, so that I could feel the vibrations. Or, again, it was as if I had only to turn the next corner of my life and I should stumble into someone coming towards me, and he – it was a man, though he had no name, no face in my mind – would reach out and take me in his arms to prevent me from falling. I was disturbed yet curiously elated by these sensations.

I had walked some distance from the palace along this shaded avenue when I passed the end of a narrow street that promised interest. It was the entrance to a bazaar, or *suq*, of which I had read. Bursting from every narrow doorway as far as the eye could reach were goods of all description and some that defied description: there were rugs and carpets of colourful and most intricate design, copper and brassware piled high, gewgaws and knick-knacks galore, Aladdin's lamps, scarves, shawls, slippers, tall glasses and small coloured birds in cages. It was a delight to look upon.

Though alone, I felt perfectly safe to enter this place of enchantment, for, as I told myself, it was broad daylight and I was simply going to walk up the narrow street till I reached the end and then retrace my steps.

Alas for good intentions . . . !

There was scarcely room for two people to pass abreast, and I was obliged to press myself back against the wall to allow the passage of a donkey piled impossibly high with woven yellow baskets. A hand plucked at my sleeve, and a toothless old fellow with a most engaging manner rattled off something to me in Arabic, pointed to his display of wares, which comprised highly-coloured foodstuffs from which a small boy constantly waved away the questing flies with a whisk. I thanked the old gentleman, shook my head and went on my way. Next I was accosted by a cheerful young man who carried upon a sling an enormous brass container, like a portable tea-urn, curiously engraved and embellished. Without waiting for me to say yea or nay, he tipped up the receptacle and poured from it a long, thin stream of amber liquid into a glass, which he then proffered to me. I had no course but to take it, masking my distaste as I speculated upon the origins and composition of the beverage, not to mention the thought of how many people's lips had touched the glass that day. In the event it was some kind of citrus drink, though heavily flavoured with sugar to sickliness. I drank a little of it and handed the glass back. I then gave him an English sixpence for his pains, which seemed to please him mightily.

I went on. The *suq*, which had begun as a medley of shops and stalls selling everything that could be imagined, very soon sorted itself out into particular areas of trade. For a considerable stretch of the narrow street as it mounted a low hill crowned by a mosque, whose towers and domes could be discerned against the limpid blue sky that was already fading to violet, the trade was that of the shoemaker. At every doorway there squatted craftsmen with their needles and thread, sewing sandals of the most exquisitely soft leather, tall riding boots with high heels and turned-up toes, slippers sewn with gold lace and semi-precious stones for the ladies of the *Haremlek*. Beyond that was the abode of the carpet-makers, where through every doorway I saw young girls weaving at looms of the most primitive sort the most delicious patterns in wool and silk, while their employers – mostly stout and prosperous-looking – lolled in the shade outside and sucked mouthfuls of smoke from what my reading had informed me to be hookah pipes, only briefly regarding me as I went past and then returning to their dreams of affluence.

Beyond the carpet-makers the craftsmen in inlaid gold, which is called damascene: each pattern being beaten by a sharp point into dishes, goblets, sword blades and suchlike metal objects, and then filled with the precious metal.

And beyond the gold-workers the hatters, makers of the ubiquitous tarboosh. Next the sweetmeat vendors, and then the woodworkers, the leatherworkers, basket-weavers, purveyors of coloured birds and exotic fishes, sellers of paper flowers that defied the eye to detect their artifice, merchants in subtly carved furniture, glassblowers who were able to draw out the molten material into fantastical complexities of shape and colour.

Then I decided that I had better retrace my steps to the palace. It was simply a matter of turning round and walking back the way I had come: past the furniture-sellers, the basket-weavers, leatherworkers, and so on.

But – no . . .

I first became aware of my mistake when I came upon a crowded part of the *suq* where small animals, rabbits, rats, mice, and suchlike rodents, and even brightly-coloured snakes and lizards were being offered for sale. Immediately I knew that I had not passed that way before. It was then that, examining the composition of the street more sharply, I realised that I had set foot not in a street but in a labyrinth of streets, each blending into the other by almost imperceptible turns and junctions, so that the unwary stranger, by taking a single wrong turn out of the hundreds of turns offered him in the course of his walk would become irretrievably lost.

And I was lost!

To ask the way seemed out of the question, having no command of the language; notwithstanding which, I made the attempt, requesting of a passing woman the way to the Abdin Palace. All I could see of her was a pair of kohl-smeared eyes peering out at me from a thin slit between veil and headdress; they instantly widened with terror, she turned and scurried away like a black spider.

This is ridiculous, I told myself. All I had to do was to determine upon which direction I intended to take and then proceed along it in as straight a line as the lie of the labyrinth permitted me. Sooner or later, I should be out of the *suq* and into the broad boulevards, where I should certainly find a cab to take me back to the palace. This resolve having been made, I oriented myself by the setting sun and, keeping it broadly behind me, made off down the street in a roughly easterly direction. So far, so good.

Five minutes later, the demands of the twisting, narrow streets had brought the sun abreast of me. A little while, a very little while after that, and I was back where they were selling the small rodents and reptiles. I could have wept.

I then bethought me of the mosque, whose dome and towers I occasionally saw appearing above the narrow rooftops. If I made for the mosque, there would certainly be someone there – a priest, a person of scholarship – who could speak English and direct me. Fixing my eye upon the beckoning fingers of the towers, I turned off into a steep alley that promised to lead me straight up to my goal, and immediately found myself out of the cheerful hustle and bustle of the *suq* and in a place of frowning, eyeless walls and dark doorways, while the alley grew ever steeper underfoot and narrower with every twist and bend. And no sign of the mosque above the rooftops.

I decided to retrace my steps to the *suq*, and was almost immediately brought face to face with the fact that I had again miscalculated. At the next bend in the alley, descending, I was presented with a choice of *two* directions – one to left, one to right – and had no means of telling from which direction I had come up, for both were indistinguishable!

Being thoroughly determined not to panic, I again took stock of my position. I was presented now with three choices: to take one of the two paths that certainly led back to the *suq*, or to retrace my steps back up the narrow alley. The latter being abhorrent, I made a random choice between the first two.

I had not been going for very long before I knew that I had again made the wrong choice.

And then the children came. There must have been a dozen of them, perhaps more, little creatures with ragged nightgowns and shaven heads. They clustered about me; the biggest and most audacious pranced in front of me, making as if to block my path but always moving away. The smallest and most timid followed behind, sometimes plucking at my sleeve and my skirts, always dancing back when I turned to snatch myself free.

Through them, through the ministrations of the children, I quickly passed from alarm to fear, and from fear to near-panic. They laughed and jeered when I broke into a stumbling run on the steep, rutted cobblestones. My bonnet fell off and was only restrained by its strings about my neck. I lost a shower of hairpins and my chignon fell in scallops about my neck. One clumsy foot caught up against the hem of my skirt and tore it. I nearly fell. In the act of reaching out to support myself against a wall and regain my balance, I dropped my reticule. Instantly it was scooped up by one of the screaming children. I made a snatch to recover it, but the little thief fled and his companions with him, bare feet pattering. Their cries of triumph faded away up a narrow, dark entry up which I would not have followed for all I possessed in the world. I leaned back against the flaking plaster of the wall, halfway to being defeated.

And the light was fading. Soon it would be night.

Then there came a blind man, a beggar with a tin of rattling coins. He hobbled slowly up the narrow street towards me, questing the sides of the walls with his stick. He passed quite close, so close that I saw the hollow, sightless eyes and was almost touched by his probing stick.

And then – *they* came . . .

I knew at once that they were looking for me, having been given word of my presence in the district, possibly by the fiendish little wretches who had stolen my reticule. There were two of them: young, powerfully built fellows, both. They came running up the street like hounds on the scent, and stopped when they saw me. One of them pointed at me and muttered something to his companion. They both grinned, and then made their way towards me at a sauntering pace, confident, assured, hell-bent – I sensed it.

I could have run. But to where? And to seek protection from whom? Had I my reticule, I might have bargained with them for my safety, for it had contained over ten English pounds. I had nothing, not even a common language with which to plead for their mercy upon my helplessness. Nevertheless I was determined to show them my mettle. In that dire strait, I thought of Miss Nightingale and what she might have done in like circumstances, and was on the instant inspired. The hands that straightened my bonnet and set it atop my head again and tucked the worst of the wayward locks beneath it may have been trembling, but the task was done nevertheless. Taking a firm hold upon my furled parasol, I drew myself up to my full height and met them with a challenging stare. They halted a couple of paces from me.

'Now, see here,' I said in a voice that sounded not one bit like my own, but bore distinct overtones of Miss Nightingale's when she used to reprimand a pupil for some minor offence, or some doctor for a piece of blundering incompetence. 'See here, I am an Englishwoman. Do you understand?'

'Eengleesh – aaah!' They understood that part well enough.

'I want you to guide me to the Abdin Palace. You will be rewarded.'

'Abdin.' They both nodded and grinned at each other.

'I may as well tell you that I am a friend of Sheikh Mansour el Abbes. Sheikh Mansour – you have heard of him?'

'Sheikh Mansour – aaaah!' More grins and nods.

I became aware that the situation was slipping from my grasp. For one thing, my declarations, my tone of voice, my assumption of authority easily worn, did not seem to be putting the two men in any awe of me; indeed, their amusement increased, they nudged and jostled each other, muttering comments about me in their harsh-sounding tongue. And then one of them – the bigger and coarser-featured of the pair – took a pace nearer and addressed a remark to me in Arabic for which, by his looks, by the baring of his yellowed teeth in a bestial grin, I needed no translation. I raised my furled parasol to strike at the hand which advanced towards me; he brushed it aside with ease. Next instant the hand was at my throat, scrabbling to take a hold of the neck of my dress with the clear intent of ripping it away.

I fought him, then. Till a brutal blow with his clenched fist jolted my head back against the wall. My senses reeled. Everything, their mocking laughter, the sense of touch in my fingers as I slid down the wall and on to the ground, became very far away. As unconsciousness overcame me, they were stooping over me and reaching down . . .

The sound of a scream aroused me from a senselessness that could not have lasted for more than a few seconds, for when I opened my eyes, I was still lying there unharmed, and three – not two – shadowy figures were struggling in the gloom some distance away. The scream still echoing in my mind I at first thought to have issued from my own lips. This was not so. It came from a man who, having been picked up by an arm and a leg, was being thrown bodily to the ground. He lay there, writhing.

With a pattering of bare feet and a wail of terror, one of the other figures broke away and fled. As he momentarily slipped out of shadow into moonlight, I recognised him as the slighter of my two would-be assailants.

Who, then, was the third man?

I raised myself up on one elbow and stared across at him, but could make nothing out but his silhouette. It was clear that he was a native, for his head was banded about with a turban cloth. As I watched, I clearly saw him crook a beckoning finger at me, and one word came out across the gloom.

'*Follow!*'

Then he was gone from me, silently. By the time I had gained my feet and recovered my parasol, he was no more than a dark shape at the next corner, waiting there, waiting for me to follow him.

'*Have no fear!*' The whisper came loudly in the narrow alley.

I stumbled forward. By the time I reached the corner, he had slipped away, but not far. There was a declivity in the alleyway ahead, and a tunnel that pierced right through the lower floor of a rickety tenement building of such decrepitude that it appeared to be standing up only by the aid of a cat's cradle of wooden props. My guide was clearly silhouetted against the moonlight at the far end of the tunnel. Again, the beckoning finger, and the injunction:

'*Come!*'

I followed him through the tunnel and out the other side. There was no sign of habitation in the mean area in which we moved, no sound but the distant howl of a dog. It was now night, and the moon was full.

The transition from despair to hope, from terror to relief, from death to life, suddenly came upon me. Instead of the odours of decay, I quite clearly smelt the heady scent of night-flowering honeysuckle. All at once, instead of gloom, there was light. Instead of silence, sound – the sound of carriage wheels rattling over cobblestones, the homely clip-clop of hooves. I ran with joy and anticipation spurring me on, round a corner, under an archway, and into a broad, well-lit boulevard full of people – some of them, by their garb, Europeans and quite a few of them discernibly English – taking their evening stroll or drive. My nightmare was over.

But where was my guide?

I looked behind me. He was standing in the shadows, and I must have passed by him very closely. In the loom of the street lamps, I could now see him more clearly, though not his face. He was wearing the light-coloured turban cloth, the black jacket and white pantaloons of a Lascar seaman from the *Hindustan*!

'Who – who *are* you?' I breathed. 'And why did you save me tonight?'

He gave me no answer, but with a barely perceptible wave of his hand slipped back into the darkness – back the way we had come.

The first persons I accosted – an English couple from Manchester, so they informed me, and in Egypt for the inauguration ceremony – were able to point the way to Abdin Palace: in fact, it was only five minutes' walk down the boulevard and then turn left.

My mysterious rescuer and guide had brought me nearly 'home'.

TEN

Mrs Stittle greeted me upon my arrival back at the *Haremlek*. I did not tell her about my alarming adventure, though she seemed to look a mite askance at my dishevelled appearance. Sheikh Mansour had been searching all over the place for me, she said; for the khedive had ordained that the pick of his honoured guests should dine together – both men and women, but only European women – in the presence of the French Empress. The sheikh had secured an invitation for me, and I had just three-quarters of an hour to bath and change!

Mrs Stittle had a hot bath already drawn for me. None of your hip baths, either, nor even the fine copper tub that I had had back at Castle Delamere, that took three scullery maids four journeys each to fill with buckets of hot water from the scullery. The bath room to our apartment in the *Haremlek* was tiled, floor, walls and ceiling, in blue and white – and the bath was a rectangular pool let into the floor, with running hot and cold water to the touch!

I stripped and lowered myself into the soapy, scented water. Mrs Stittle did not seem averse to remaining. She gathered up my discarded clothes and gave me the latest news. Mr Ormerod, it seemed, had had a fine completely equipped studio placed at his disposal in the palace and had agreed, as the first part of his commission, to paint a full-length, life-sized portrait of the ruler in his full ceremonials. And *that* Mr Marius (she had a way of saying '*that* Mr Marius' which led me to suppose that she did not entirely approve of Hal Marius, notwithstanding the fact that he had unquestionably saved Rupert's life in Southampton) claimed that his golf clubs had been stolen somewhere between Alexandria and Cairo, and was disgracing us all by making a tremendous fuss about the palace. ('But, Miss, he can't be blamed, I s'pose. I mean, well, they're not like us, them *Colonials*, are they? Don't know how to behave proper in fine company!')

The best news of all was that, despite the rigours of the train journey, Rupert had had his nap, his supper, and had gone to bed as right as a trivet half an hour since, and hadn't coughed once or been fretful.

'And isn't that lovely, Miss?' she said. 'Well worth coming all this way among heathen folks, for to make little Master Rupert better.'

Well worth it . . . ?

I supposed so. One small boy's health against the gipsy's prophecy – so much of which had already come true – was it too hard a bargain?

Lying there in the cosseting warmth of my scented bath, I thought back to the dark, stinking alleyways above the *suq*, to the peril in which I had terrifyingly stood from the two brutes who had assaulted me. And I shuddered, as if someone had just walked over my grave, as well they might have.

As if to echo my thoughts, Mrs Stittle said: 'The funeral for the Reverend is at three in the afternoon tomorrow. Gentlemen only attending. I've put out your white taffeta, Miss. Will that suit, do you think?'

My exiguous wardrobe being what it was, the white taffeta (another bequest from darling Sarah Ilminster) simply had to suit the occasion. I put it on, assisted by Mrs Stittle, and viewing myself in a pier glass was of the opinion that I didn't look too bad, and would have looked better if only my skin had been of the fashionable waxen pallor, instead of my confounded Devon countrywoman's russet that no device – neither the application of vinegar, nor saltpetre, nor even scrubbing with pumice – would eradicate. With a sigh I picked up my fan and my evening reticule (and what, I thought, had been the fate of my other one up in the alleyways above the *suq*?), and went to dinner.

A cheerful, tarbooshed manservant was waiting for me at the door of the *Haremlek* and guided me to the central block of the palace, to the state apartments where the function was to be held.

Upon entering a vast hall blazing with chandeliers and glittering with the jewels of a hundred women, not to mention the dazzling orders and decorations of many of the menfolk, I was immediately approached by Sheikh Mansour, who was wearing his diplomatic blue and gold.

'They told me you had arrived back,' he said. 'I have placed you with your friends at table. Regrettably, I must be dancing attendance on the Empress's two ladies-in-waiting tonight. But there is something I must hastily tell you before the imperial party arrives to lead us all into dinner.'

'About – Dean Sommerson?' I prompted.

He nodded. 'I sent my aide-de-camp to the hospital with strict orders not to return till he had elicited the truth. Well, the truth we may still not have.'

'I don't understand,' I faltered.

He cast a sidelong glance, as if to make sure we were not overheard. 'No less than three distinguished physicians were present at the autopsy,' he said, 'and all three were of the opinion that the dean died of natural causes, either a failure of the heart or a massive stroke.'

Greatly relieved, I said: 'Poor Dr Sommerson. Still, he had the mercy of a quick end.' Then I looked keenly at my companion, who was looking keenly back at me. 'But you imply that it may not be the truth?'

He nodded. 'There was one other physician present. A young fellow newly qualified, assistant to the most senior of the three. He was of the opinion that certain unaccountable peculiarities suggested – poison!'

'*Poison?*' I echoed the word so loudly that several people turned round to regard me with surprise.

'That was the young man's opinion,' said Sheikh Mansour. 'However, as so often when the young contradict the opinions of their elders and betters, his suggestion was treated with scorn, notwithstanding which it was with reluctance allowed to be included in the report – as a footnote.'

'And where is the report?' I breathed.

'Thanks to my aide-de-camp's persistence, it was sent by special messenger to the Ministry of the Interior.'

'Then – something will be done? The truth may come out?'

Sheikh Mansour cocked an eyebrow in the way he had. 'The report will arrive upon the desk of a minor functionary of the ministry in the morning,' he said. 'If it does not get lost among his papers, he may, in due course, refer the matter to his superior, who, if there is sufficient baksheesh involved . . .'

'Baksheesh – what is that?' I asked.

'The word means "gift", but has come to embrace the larger area of bribery and corruption,' he said. 'When submitting an application to various ministries in Egypt, it is customary to indicate in pencil the amount of baksheesh forthcoming in the event of a successful outcome. And the amount is usually paid over in advance.'

'I have a little money,' I whispered. 'And to get to the truth, I'd gladly bribe . . .'

'Too late,' said Sheikh Mansour. 'Too late, dear Miss Copley. Even supposing that the minor functionary passes on the report to his superior, and even supposing that the latter is not so deeply involved in the details of the ceremonial connected with the inauguration of the canal as not to spare a few moments on, say, next Tuesday or Wednesday in perusing an autopsy report on an insignificant foreign priest, and even if he espies the brief footnote, it will still be too late. Dean Sommerson will be buried in the Christian cemetery tomorrow and that will be the end of it.'

'But surely,' I pleaded, 'enquiries can be made!'

He shook his head. 'Furthermore, Miss Copley, that report, if read, will become conveniently lost. Consider: one is asking the khedive to accept that one of his guests was poisoned at luncheon in his own viceregal train and within touching distance of where he himself sat. Would he allow this to be whispered in the chancelleries of Europe, not to mention the back streets of his own capital – and in *this* week of all weeks?'

'But something should be done!' I breathed. *'Something!'*

'Nothing will be done,' he said. 'And all your tears will not make it done.' He reached and touched my cheek, damming the wayward tear that I had not been able to suppress. He frowned. 'How came about this bruise on your cheek, Miss Copley?'

I winced with the slight pain of his fingertip on the spot where my assailant's brutal fist had taken me, and I determined in that moment to tell him what had happened – but my resolve was thwarted by a sudden blast of trumpets in a fanfare of brilliant sound. This was immediately followed by a roll of drums, then by the stirring opening bars of what I recognised as the French national anthem, the *Marseillaise*.

'The empress comes,' whispered Sheikh Mansour in my ear. 'Don't forget to curtsey.'

At the close of the French anthem, the band struck up the Egyptian, and when that was done, the assembled guests formed in two lines each side of the inevitable red carpet that stretched from a glittering staircase at one end of the vast chamber to an arched doorway at the other. It was down this honorific pathway that the viceregal party passed: the khedive leading, with she who could only have been the Empress of the French by his side.

I had heard much of Eugénie, consort of the very opportunistic Emperor Napoleon III, who had won himself the throne of his famous forebear by rather dubious stratagems. The husband may or may not have been an adventurer, but the wife was all empress: auburn hair slightly steaked with grey and worn in a most elaborate coiffure supporting a diamond and emerald tiara that flashed a thousand lights with every slight movement of her head; deep blue eyes and a complexion of the most fashionable ivory pallor; the looks of an intelligent, courageous woman to whom one warmed immediately – till one noticed the imperious tilt of the head, the touch of arrogance about the eyes, and one remembered that she had been born a Spanish princess and had never known what it was to be crossed in anything.

Rippling curtseys – my own included – followed the progress of empress and khedive down the chamber.

'Now I will hand you over to Mr Marius, who will take you in to dinner. I must join my ladies-in-waiting.' The sheikh kissed my hand. 'Will you ride out with me tomorrow? I will show you the desert and the pyramids. Unhappily we shall be

213

chaperoned by two members of the khedive's Turkish guard, who have accompanied me everywhere since my indiscreet outburst on the train. You will come?'

'Of course,' I said. 'Thank you so much.'

'At twelve noon tomorrow.'

'Twelve noon.'

He led me to Hal Marius, who looked hot and uncomfortable in his evening tail coat and stiff shirtfront and high collar, and also rather pink and cross, which I instantly attributed to the loss of his – presumably – precious golf clubs. He had the grace to brighten slightly when the sheikh placed me in his care and departed.

'I like your frock,' he said.

'Thank you,' I responded.

'You'll be glad to hear,' he said, 'that we won't be squatting on our hunkers and dipping out of a communal pot tonight. Presumably in deference to the empress, we're eating civilised.'

'What a relief,' I said.

We both laughed.

He took my arm and we followed the drift of guests entering the vast dining-room that lay beyond the archway. I saw the Hon. Petronella being escorted in by a tremendously distinguished-looking gentleman with a grey beard and a host of decorations on his evening dress coat that made him look like a Christmas tree. She flashed a glad smile at me and sketched the suggestion of a wave.

'The Prussian ambassador,' murmured Hal Marius, answering the question I was asking myself. 'A widower, a prince of the nobility and owner of the second largest iron foundry on the Ruhr. Do you think dear Petronella will manage to land this, her newest and most prestigious of fish?'

'She will not fail from want of trying,' I replied. 'One really has to give her full marks for perseverance.'

'Indeed, yes.'

The light banter, the brilliant surroundings, the air of grandeur, the sheer unreality of it all but muffled the memory of the horror that I had experienced that evening. It was only when I reached my place at table and the chair was drawn back for me by a tall, well-made native servant in robes of cloth-of-gold and

214

a high plumed turban that I was jolted back in time and place. His eyes met mine for an instant, and he was the same brute who had assaulted me and struck me. I backed away from him and gave an involuntary cry. The mild surprise with which he greeted my action, the look of sudden concern that flitted across his – surely – bland and honest face, broke the spell. He was nothing like the creature of my living nightmare.

'Is something the matter?' asked Hal Marius when he had taken his seat on my right. 'I thought I heard you exclaim just now.'

I took a deep breath. 'I've had a most appalling experience this evening,' I replied. 'I'm not so sure that I want to talk about it just now, but unless I talk about it very soon, and confide in someone, I shall never sleep tonight, and if I do I shall have nightmares.'

'That sounds bad,' he said. 'May I make the suggestion that you leave the confidences till we come to the coffee at the end of what promises to be a most excellent meal, which you won't want to spoil by dredging up bad memories?'

He passed me the printed menu, which was part-French and part-English, in deference to the khedive's distinguished guests. I have it still.

Le Diner à l'honneur de
S.I.M. L'EMPERATRICE EUGÉNIE DE FRANCE
at Abdin Palace, le 14 Novembre, 1869

FIRST COURSE
Julienne soup Henrik Ibsen · Velouté Jockey Club de Paris
Turbot and Lobster Sauce · Pompano Sauté Armandine
Mulligatawny Soup Justin Ormerod, R.A.

ENTRÉES
Vol-au-Vent Guiseppe Verdi · Fricasseed Rabbit
Filets de Boeuf Théophile Gautier · Canards à la Rouennaise
Filets de Poulets aux Coucombres Disraeli

SECOND COURSE
Veneson Roti S.I.M. L'EMPERATRICE EUGÉNIE
Sirloin of Beef and Horseradish Sauce H.M. QUEEN VICTORIA
Wiener Schnitzel H.E. THE KHEDIVE ISMAIL PASHA

Charlotte à la Parisienne LE CANAL DE SUEZ
Gâteau de Riz Ferdinand de Lesseps
Cheesecakes · Blancmange · Cabinet Pudding
Eggs à la Neige
Partridges

DESSERT

I was pleased to see that my employer was honoured by the
accolade of a dish named after him, along with other distinguished artists and writers and de Lesseps, the genius who had
created the canal against advice of his friends and the scorn of
his detractors (the latter were of the opinion that to carve a
canal connecting the Mediterranean with the Red Sea would
mean that half Europe would be inundated by the joining of the
two waters which God had decreed to be kept apart by the giant
continent of Africa. What they had overlooked was the ancient
simple rule that water always finds its own level, and that the
Mediterranean and the Red Sea had been at substantially the
same level since the Creation). I thought I espied M. de Lesseps
at the top table two places down from the empress and deep in
conversation with Justin Ormerod. The former's lineaments I
recognised from the many newspaper illustrations that had
been made of him in recent years. The latter, my employer,
looked devastatingly handsome and distinguished in his evening dress suit with the badge of some order or other suspended
about his neck on a watered silk ribbon. He looked pale and his
face had become drawn with his suffering. He looked like –
what? – a martyred saint, and incredibly romantic. As I
watched him, he glanced up, caught my eye and nodded and
smiled. I smiled in return.

'Ormerod seems to be getting on fine with de Lesseps,' said
Hal Marius. 'But then it's not to be wondered at. The artist and
the visionary, they're really cut out of the same bolt of cloth.'

I looked at him, conscious that I had been neglecting my
dinner partner. 'And out of what bolt of cloth are you cut, Mr
Marius?' I asked him.

'Hal – call me Hal, for heaven's sake call me Hal. Well, I'm neither artist nor visionary. I suppose I'm an idealist – oh, yes, I'll have the mulligatawny soup . . .'

Our conversation had been disrupted by the descent of a line of waiters bearing the dishes of the soup and fish course. I addressed myself to the turbot in a lobster sauce, but had not stabbed the first mouthful with my fork before the neighbour on my left, who proved to be Major Woodford (and how that egregious soldier had secreted his presence from me for even so short a time was beyond all belief), murmured in my ear:

'Ma'am, I must have words with you.'

Not a proposal of marriage! The intolerable pressures of the day with which, I told myself, I had coped with remarkable fortitude, should surely absolve me from such an assault.

'The mulligatawny is very good,' said the neighbour of my right. 'How is the turbot, Miss Copley?'

'Very nice,' I replied.

'I think,' said the neighbour of my left, 'that I have unmasked the scoundrel who is behind all the devilry that's been going on – the attack upon Ormerod, my own brief encounter with the Angel of Death, and all that.'

I glanced at him sharply: there was something about the major's appearance – a certain touch of the casual in the tying of his bow tie, a drooping of the eyelids, a quite definable slurring of the speech – which immediately suggested to me that the gallant major had been at the bottle and was in a well-advanced state of inebriation.

'Indeed?' I murmured.

'Kiprenski!' he hissed, nodding towards the Russian, who was sitting at the table opposite, deeply engaged in a mono-logue with a uniformed functionary of the khedive's court who quite clearly was more concerned with his soup than with his neighbour's rhetoric. 'Kiprenski is behind it all!'

'You asked me,' said Hal Marius, brushing my hand with his to attract my attention, 'what sort of person I am.'

'And you said that you were an idealist,' I replied.

'Kiprenski – he's behind it all!' declared Major Woodford. 'For him I swam three miles and damned nearly fed the fishes. Not that he was primarily engaged, of course. The swine who tossed me overboard would only have been a mere hireling. But the Russkie's behind it all, you mark my words.' His voice grew louder and more bellicose. There was champagne and claret provided on the table, and he poured himself a large bumper of the latter and quaffed it deeply.

'What is that fellow going on about?' murmured Hal Marius.

'Nothing – it's nothing,' I replied.

'Well, as to being an idealist,' he said, 'it goes no further, I'm afraid, than a certain cynicism about other people's motives. F'rinstance, I ask myself why Britain and France are the senior partners in the canal enterprise, and the answer comes up straight and true: the canal gives them more direct access to the Far East and the opportunity to extend their empires.'

'I would like the fricasseed rabbit,' said Major Woodford to the waiter who hovered by him, and to me he whispered: 'The Russkies, you know, are hell bent to get into India. They're forever stirring up trouble on the Afghan border. Ma'am, I have done long service on the north-west frontier and know the Khyber Pass like the palm of my hand. I can tell you that the hostile tribesmen could not survive and fight us as they do were it not for Tsarist gold from St Petersburg and Russian guns.'

One of the waiters paused by my elbow and presented me with a silver salver upon which lay a card engraved with the name *Justin Ormerod, R.A.*

I picked it up and turned it over. On the reverse was inscribed in my employer's dashingly elegant hand:

> *Will you pose for me tomorrow morning at*
> *10 of the clock? My manservant will call*
> *upon you and direct you to the studio.*
> *Yours ever, J.O.*

When I looked up, he was watching me. I smiled and nodded. His expression was washed with a sudden pleasure and the tiredness seemed to forsake him. No longer the martyred saint, he was as I had first known him: strong, masterful, full of the creative vitality which I have always associated with the artistic temperament. I rejoiced to see the change from the poor, half-dead creature whom I had nursed back from the edge of the grave.

'Ormerod's made a sparkling recovery from his wound,' said Hal Marius, mirroring my thoughts. 'I like the fellow, and that's a nice kid he has.'

'Yes.'

'I guess he'll remarry one day soon.'

'I shouldn't wonder.'

'It's no life for a widower bringing up a motherless kid, particularly if it's a boy. I should know. My mother died when I was little. When I look back – God, I must have run my old man ragged. I wonder he didn't smother me.'

I made no reply. We had had this conversation before, in Malta, and no good had come of it. Why he was tempting me to speculate about my employer's future marital plans was quite beyond me, unless one attributed it, as he claimed, to his newspaperman's 'nose' for a story. And then I remembered Mrs Wayne Barlowe's declaration that the American would certainly propose to me. In which case, he might well want to know if I had any kind of romantic attachment to Justin Ormerod. However, Mrs Wayne Barlowe's prognostication had not come true: Hal Marius and I had – apart from the unfortunate incident in Malta – a friendly relationship, nothing more.

In the second course (out of sheer patriotism, I plumped for the sirloin of beef and horseradish sauce H.M. Queen Victoria!), I met the eye of Mrs Wayne Barlowe, who was – predictably – at the top table and only three places away from the khedive. She was in a most sumptuous gown of sequinned silk, silver on gold, with a plume of three black ostrich feathers perched atop of her elaborate coiffure. She nodded and smiled at me, raising one eyebrow. The message came as clearly as if she had spoken it: relating to the man on my right, she asked, *'Has he proposed to you yet?'* An imp of mischief prompted me to shake my head. She received the message, made a moue, shrugged her elegant shoulders and flashed me a devastating smile.

'The beef,' said Major Woodford, 'is tough, but that's the way of it once one has left Dover. The Indians, now they have the measure of their damnable tough beef. They chop it up into small pieces, boil it to death and curry it. Do you like curry, ma'am?'

'I have never tasted curry, sir,' I replied.

He nodded. He was far gone in his cups. 'Take my word for it, ma'am, the Russkies are behind all this. I shouldn't wonder – I shouldn't wonder if that rascally Kiprenski ain't planning to sink the vessel in which he's going to travel through the canal next week. They're great ones with the infernal devices, the Russkies. Think of it, ma'am – to block the canal on the day of the inauguration! There'd be many a joyful heart in the Kremlin if that were brought about.' His voice, growing ever louder and more belligerent, was attracting some notice from those about us. Hal Marius was frowning. The people sitting opposite were similarly displaying their displeasure. The major, seemingly impervious to the atmosphere he was creating, poured himself another glassful of claret and tossed it back.

Happily, he behaved through the third course, picking away at his savoury and only mumbling quietly to himself under his breath. At the close of the dessert, the Khedive Ismail Pasha rose to his feet and proposed the health of the Empress Eugénie. There then followed a succession of toasts: an Egyptian dignitary proposed the distinguished guests; he who had been pointed out to me as the Prussian ambassador, dinner partner of the Hon. Petronella, rose to pledge the khedive and the Egyptian state; a gentleman announced to be the writer Théophile Gautier addressed us in what I am sure must have been the most elegant French, which, regrettably, was entirely lost on me.

My left-hand neighbour roundly applauded all the toasts and pledged them in bumper glasses – all downed in one long gulp. At the end of it, he swayed unsteadily to his feet and, swaying still, proposed the toast:

'To Her Majesty's dominions, on which the sun never sets!' Upon the conclusion of which declaration, the gallant major slipped, slowly, by degrees, and with a certain majestic dignity, to the floor.

Major Woodford having been quietly and discreetly carried out of the chamber by soft-footed menservants, the gala dinner drew towards its close with Turkish coffee and the buzz of general conversation. Fortunately bereft of my left-hand neighbour, I was left with the one on my right hand.

'You were going to recount your appalling experience of this evening,' said he, 'so that you will be able to sleep without nightmares.'

Even as he spoke, the brilliance of the gathering, the parakeet chattering of the diners, stark white napery and glittering silverware, dazzling chandeliers, seemed to give way to the dark alleyways above the *suq*, and I was reliving my terror.

'I met the Lascar this evening,' I said. 'The Lascar from the *Hindustan*, the same one who almost certainly wounded Mr Ormerod and threw the major overboard.'

'You *met* him?'

'Encountered, rather. There were no formal introductions.'

'And he attacked you?'

'No. I think he may have saved my life!'

'Your *life*?'

And then I told him everything: of my folly in wandering so far into the labyrinth and getting myself lost; how I was set upon by the two ruffians – and of my rescue. He listened to me in silence till I had done.

'And you believe your rescuer – the Lascar – was one and the same as the would-be assassin from the *Hindustan*?' he asked.

'I have thought it over from every possible angle,' I said, 'and can only arrive at one conclusion that fits every point. In order to have been on hand when I was attacked, that man must have followed me from the Abdin Palace to the *suq*. It strains coincidence beyond all belief to suppose that he should have stumbled upon my plight entirely by accident.'

He nodded. 'I take your point,' he said. 'But that begs another question: why did he follow you from the palace? To do you harm?'

'Why else?' I asked.

'Then why did he then save you from others who were similarly bent on doing you harm?'

I shook my head. 'I – I can't answer that,' I said, 'though I've asked myself a score of times this evening. Can it be – can it be that he had a particular fate planned for me, and that he will now bide his time till another opportunity occurs?'

'That is a fanciful explanation,' said Hal Marius. 'There is another, simpler reason why he could have followed you into the *suq*.'

'And what is that?' I asked.

'To protect you and keep you from harm,' he replied blandly. 'You, a lone woman in a notoriously perilous district.'

Rupert was asleep when I looked in at him before going to bed. The pug lay on the coverlet by his young master's feet; he stirred at my entering and gave a wag of his convoluted tail.

The window of Rupert's bedchamber looked out on the inner enclosed courtyard of the *Haremlek*, where a single jet of pure water plashed coolly down into a tiled pool and a spreading magnolia tree displayed its velvety leaves in the moonlight. I clasped my ring – Giles's ring that I wore forever round my neck – and thought of what the day had brought: beginning with the tragic, unexplained and perhaps inexplicable death of Dean Sommerson, and ending with the strange surmise that Hal Marius had implanted in my mind.

Could it be so – that the would-be assassin had sought to protect me? And, if so, why?

Retiring to my own room which was separated from Rupert's by Mrs Stittle's, I took out the much-folded sheet of writing paper containing my attempt at recording the results of the gipsy's predictions.

To the number of deaths, I then added:

Either First or Second – The Reverend Dr Sommerson, Dean of Archester Cathedral

And to the five perils:

Four – Major Woodford is thrown overboard.
Five – I am attacked in the streets.

And then I appended the following note:

If the death of the child Zena is to be counted, the prophecy concerning the two deaths is complete. IF NOT . . .

and:

Similarly, if the storm in the Bay of Biscay is to be counted among the five perils, the prophecy concerning the five perils is complete. BUT, AGAIN, IF NOT . . .

I lay down upon the bed, but had no inclination to extinguish the light. Staring up at the highly-patterned ceiling, I pondered on the grim arithmetic that I had produced. Accepting the absurdity of believing in the gipsy's predictions (and surely they *were* absurd, weren't they?), it could be said, on one count, that the dangers and deaths had ended and that the nightmare was over. On another count, there remained one more peril, one more death.

It was not a thought that was conducive to slumber; however, while still considering my grim arithmetic, I fell asleep, and slept soundly till I was awakened by the sounds of small coloured birds singing from the branches of the magnolia tree in the shady courtyard.

Breakfast in the *Haremlek* was served in one's bedchamber by black Sudanese girls, plump as butterballs and bubbling over with irrepressible good humour. They brought mint tea in tiny crucibles, buttered oatcakes, dates and fresh figs, all of which I tasted with a certain guarded relish.

Mindful that I had agreed to pose for Justin Ormerod at ten and had also promised to ride out with Sheikh Mansour at noon (and I hoped that the two arrangements would not clash), I chose my attire with some care. It seemed to me that my two-piece of white linen trimmed with dark blue braid would suit both occasions, the more so if I put on my riding boots to keep the earlier appointment, so that I should not have to come back and change. After some thought, a simple straw boater with a veil commended itself as headgear.

It was while I was pinning the boater in place atop my chignon and fixing my veil that I met my eye in the mirror and saw reflected there the sudden and awful thought that had struck me all unawares: remembering the portrait of the mysterious Esmée, it came to me that I had not questioned for an

223

instant but that Mr Ormerod would expect me to pose fully clad.

But supposing – *supposing* he was assuming, unquestioningly, that he would be painting me in the same state as that of Esmée! Artists being what they are, untrammelled by the conventions of polite society and granted sweeping freedoms in matters of propriety, might he not indeed assume it? At the very thought, I saw my eyes widen with alarm and the colour rush to my cheeks. And yet why should it be so? I had nursed him through a near-fatal wound. There was nothing about his finely-wrought body that held any secrets from me any longer. If the nurse had the licence of knowledge, why not the artist? That stated to myself, it was with no great trepidation that I received the news from one of the Sudanese girls that a manservant was awaiting at the door of the *Haremlek* to escort me to Mr Ormerod's studio.

I joined my guide and followed him into the central block of the palace, where he led me through stately courts and coolly shuttered halls to a glass-walled conservatory at the rear of the palace, which looked out on to a formal garden set with spreading trees and lawns of startlingly bright green, criss-crossed by narrow water courses where white swans preened their beauty. In the centre of the conservatory, standing by an easel bearing a blank canvas, was my employer.

He looked up from a painting table upon which lay a palette, paints and brushes.

'Ah, good morning, Miss Copley!' He smiled, and it was the Justin Ormerod I had first known, with his health and strength, his good colouring restored. And yet – and yet – there still lurked in his fine eyes that fugitive, haunted look that had appeared there on the day that the Limping Frenchman had come to Castle Delamere.

'Good morning, Mr Ormerod. I'm so glad to see you looking well,' I replied.

'I have been most uncommonly well nursed,' he declared. 'The khedive's personal physician has examined my wound and pronounced it to be well on the way to mending. He left me with no doubt but that I owe my present recovery – even my life – to you.'

'That is my vocation, sir,' I replied, as ever at a loss to know how to accept praise for simply doing my duty.

'Quite so, quite so,' he said, 'and you are a credit, a shining example to that vocation, Miss Copley.' He paused, as if he would say more, but was hesitant to do so.

It was I who broke the awkward silence that followed.

'You wish to paint me, then, sir?'

'That is so,' he said. 'Though I will come right out and confess to you, Miss Copley, that my main intent was to meet you in a privacy that is not normally accorded to men and women in the surroundings of an oriental palace. But Art excuses everything. In short, Miss Copley, I am drawing upon my artistic licence in order to speak with you on a purely personal matter of some great importance to me, and, I trust, to you also.'

My heartbeats quickened. 'Indeed, sir?'

'But first,' he said, 'let us begin, and I will talk as I paint. Will you please assume a pose? And, if you don't mind, I should like you to take off your hat and veil.'

'Of course.' Did my fingers, anticipating further requests, tremble slightly as I obeyed him?

He regarded me, his head on one side, forefinger tapping his cheek. 'Yes, that will do excellently well, Miss Copley. Just remain as you are – but turning your head ever so slightly to your right.'

My relief in finding that, after all, he had no intention of asking me to pose undraped momentarily drove out my puzzlement concerning his reason for contriving our meeting other than to paint me. In the few minutes that followed, while he mixed colours on his palette, addressed himself to his easel, eyed me narrowly and made a few bold strokes upon the pristine canvas, my puzzlement returned.

Presently, he said: 'Miss Copley, I am going to tell you a story which will both amaze and disturb you. It concerns a part of my life which, though I have achieved a certain public fame with my Art, I have so far been able to keep private to myself alone. However, in view of what I have in mind, it becomes necessary that I reveal all – or most – of the burden that I carry. Do you want me to continue?'

'If you wish it, sir,' I whispered.

'Picture, then,' he said, 'a young English student of painting in Paris. Ignorant of the ways of the world. Supported only by a grudging, lean remittance from a stepfather, eked out with what he was able to make from portrait drawings of people in the cafés and bars of the Latin quarter where, in the traditional style of *la vie Bohème*, he lived in a one-room attic studio with a view of the Luxembourg gardens.

'Turn your head very slightly more to the right, Miss Copley, please.

'The one thing that informed his life, giving it colour and direction, was his devotion to painting. For painting he would cheerfully have begged in the streets to gain a crust, for painting he would – and on occasions nearly did – starve. Nothing else mattered: neither love nor friendship, health, wealth, ambition; nothing mattered but to seize upon the appearance of things and encapsulate them forever upon the yielding surface of canvas with brush and paints.

'Do not move your eyes, Miss Copley, please: I am working on them now.

'One day, into this dedicated, almost monastic life, there appeared a woman: a model for the figure who came occasionally to pose at the atelier where the young student took instruction. Something – I have never been able to fathom what – attracted this woman, this young, clever, witty and indescribably beautiful woman, to the poor, gauche, shy student. She took him in hand, insinuated herself into his life. Visiting his attic studio, she immediately took it over and turned a dusty attic into a place of light, colour and flowers. For him alone, she posed for nothing, far into the night. When he tired, she did not tire, but spurred him to greater efforts. Her energy, her inspiration, bore fruit. Within six months, he had assembled a score of canvases with her as the central subject. The first gallery owner who set eyes upon them snapped them up. The pictures were exhibited in the rue de la Paix to the éclat of the entire Parisian art world. The smart critics of the prestigious dailies and intellectual weeklies raved over the new "discovery".

'He returned to England with his model. That autumn, the couple were married in a quiet country church: a modest ceremony that suited his temperament, for, though largely under her domination, he had his way in some matters.

'If you would like to rest for a few minutes, Miss Copley, I am quite able to complete this passage without your help.'

'Thank you,' I breathed.

I sauntered quietly round to watch him at work, and was astonished by what I saw: what I saw was a fleeting image of myself as in a double mirror, head turned slightly away, the face and figure still only suggested, as in the light of a shadowy room – but quite unmistakable. As I watched, he boldly sketched in the dark background beyond the head and shoulders, and made my costume into a thing of white linen and dark blue braid. I marvelled that, from out of a blank white canvas and in so short a time, he could have created an image that was so truly myself, as I knew myself.

'So we have our young student risen to instant eminence,' said Justin Ormerod, stabbing with his brush. 'He exhibited at the Royal Academy in London and was soon informed that he would in very short order be proposed for an associate membership of that august body.

'It was then he discovered the truth about the woman he had married: she, of mixed French and English birth, was betraying him with at least half-a-dozen men, and with a complete disregard for the sanctity of their home, or even of the marriage bed. Will you now resume the pose, please, Miss Copley?'

I obeyed.

Presently, he resumed his tale, his voice balanced at the flat, matter-of-fact level with which he had begun the narrative; though by now it was quite obvious that he was recounting his own life with the woman whom I knew to be the Esmée of the forbidden portrait. Indeed, he then dropped the slender subterfuge of the second person and slipped into the first.

'My wife had a brother,' he said. 'A charming ne'er-do-well, a failed actor – that was how she represented him to me. I never met the fellow. She joked about what she called his "naughtiness" and asked me to provide the money to send him abroad – away from France and the bad company he was keeping – to make a fresh start. She had newly promised to mend her ways and dismiss her many lovers. Besotted with her still, and grateful to her for my newly-won success, I gladly parted with five hundred pounds for the brother. This I paid over to an associate of his who travelled to London for the occasion. This man's name was – Jean-Pierre Lavache.'

(Jean-Pierre Lavache! The Limping Frenchman, who had died in a wood beyond the causeway of Castle Delamere! My mind fled back to the day when the sergeant of police had interrogated us both on this man's fatal visit . . .)

'Raise your head slightly, Miss Copley,' said Justin Ormerod evenly. 'To resume: the convenient disposal of the erring brother in no way mended our relationship. My wife rid herself of her current lovers, but made small shift to conceal the fact that she had taken to herself a fresh assemblage of like-inclined gentlemen. Furthermore, I was peremptorily summoned to attend my bank, where the irate manager informed me that I was grossly overdrawn on the account that I held jointly with my wife Esmée. When I taxed her with the discrepancy, she brazenly admitted that she had been sending regular large sums of money to her brother Marcel. She explained that Marcel was addicted to gambling and women, and that he seldom had any luck with either. And then she laughed in my face.'

'Mr Ormerod, why are you telling me all this?' I asked. 'It must be so distressing for you, and . . .'

'As to why I am telling you, Miss Copley,' he interposed, 'that will come later. As to the distress – well, I have become hardened to that over the years, and I have been happy in the blessing of many consolations.

'Head up again, please. But perhaps you are getting tired. Perhaps we should finish for the day.'

'No, no, I can continue,' I said in haste. Anything – anything but to have him tell his harrowing story to me face-to-face. The act of his creating a painting with me as model distanced us to some degree, each from each.

'I spoke of consolations,' he said. 'A year after our marriage, my wife left me for one of her lovers. I became a celibate, dedicating myself entirely to my work, just as it had been when I was a student in Paris. And then I met – Diana . . .'

'The mother of Rupert!' I blurted out, and instantly wished that I had kept my peace.

'Indeed, the mother of Rupert,' he replied. 'But the path to our marriage and Rupert's birth was stony all the way, and culminated, as you already know, in Diana's death.

'She was the daughter, the only child, of a rich East Anglian landowner, the master of Castle Delamere. I met her when her father commissioned me to paint her portrait for the occasion of her twenty-first birthday. She came to my studio for the sittings – properly chaperoned, of course. I depicted her seated in a white dress and a straw hat trimmed with red roses, with a bouquet of red roses on her lap. I have the picture still. In the course of painting Diana, I fell in love with her and she with me. It was very difficult, in the circumstances, to express our love: the lingering touch of hands, the unspoken words, the unfinished remarks, the charm of looks. But love will always find a way. One chaste kiss, only, was sufficient to seal the compact between us.

'I think you should rest now, Miss Copley. I can continue without you for a while.'

Again I stole round the back of him and marvelled at the advancement he had made in so short a time. The head was in a much more finished state, the figure also, and he was now dashing in, with sure and practised strokes, an impression of the oriental garden beyond the glass-walled conservatory in the background.

'It's wonderful – *wonderful!*' I breathed.

'Somehow, by some means,' he said, ignoring my comment, 'Esmée discovered about Diana and me – though heaven knows there was little enough to discover – and she returned to me, having drained her lover of his cash and driven him half out of his mind, I shouldn't wonder. I remember her words very clearly: "If you think you are going to divorce me and marry that whey-faced little English bitch for her money, you are much mistaken, my dear," she said.

'And then there was the brother. The image of him that she had presented to me – that of a charming ne'er-do-well – was entirely shattered by a *cause célèbre*, a murder trial in France which was widely reported in the London papers. Marcel

Mayol was no charming ne'er-do-well, but an adventurer, a swindler, and – finally – a cold-blooded killer. Returning to France after his brief exile at my expense, he rejoined his former accomplice Lavache in a wild welter of crime that ended in the slaughter of an entire family – man, wife and two children – by this dastardly pair. They escaped the guillotine on a technicality, but were sentenced to the penal colony in French Guiana known as Devil's Island for life.

'Do you think you could take up the pose for just five minutes more, Miss Copley? There is a small statement I must make to the face. And my sad tale is also drawing to a close.'

'Of course,' I said. And took my place again.

'Esmée was killed!' he said brutally. 'She fell from her horse whilst riding out in Rotten Row. The girth snapped and unseated her at the gallop; this much emerged during the coroner's inquest, which delivered a verdict of "Accidental Death", together with a general admonition against horse-riding with faulty tack. Diana and I were free to marry, which we did as soon as propriety permitted. Her father settled half a million pounds upon us both and the deeds of Castle Delamere. We were happy together for only a brief spell. You know the rest, Miss Copley. My wife died in giving birth to our son.

'You may rest now, Miss Copley. I have done with this rather summary study of you. One day, I should like to develop it into a finished, formal painting.' He wheeled round the easel on its castors for me to see the picture. The last few minutes' work had wrought miracles, with pinpoints of reflected light in the eyes, in the hair, on the cheek, on the curve of the lips.

'It's very flattering,' I murmured. 'And yet, in a sense it's not. You have painted my faults as well.' I paused and regarded him: he was looking steadily at me. 'Mr Ormerod, why have you confided the secrets of your life to me?'

'Because you should know,' he replied, 'before I have the temerity to ask you to become my wife and the stepmother to my son.'

ELEVEN

A pretty French ormolu clock on an elaborate ironwork table flanked by spreading ferns told the hour of eleven. In one brief hour, Justin Ormerod had painted what was surely a minor masterpiece, had admitted me into the hidden workings of his two marriages, and had made a declaration that left me speechless and bemused.

He walked over to the glass wall that looked out on to the garden. Arms folded, his back turned to me, he was silent for a while, then he said: 'I do not ask for an immediate answer, for I appreciate that this has come as a complete surprise to you. Add to that, there are – complications – which will certainly influence your decision. With your leave, I will now tell you of these complications. Would you care for a glass of sherry wine?'

'No thank you,' I replied.

'You won't mind if I partake? Will you not sit down?'

I took my place on an ironwork seat which had an exceedingly comfortable cushion. After he had poured himself a drink, my employer seated himself on a similar chair opposite me, but not close, not within touching distance, nothing like. And surely I detected a slight tremor of his hand as he raised the glass to his lips and took a sip of the straw-coloured wine.

'I spoke of complications,' he said. 'You were privy to the first manifestation of these complications at Castle Delamere, shortly after you arrived.'

'The day that Jean-Pierre Lavache came,' I said.

He nodded. 'Lavache brought a message from Marcel

Mayol. Both men had escaped from Devil's Island, and Mayol's criminal mind was entirely directed to me. In short terms, he accused me of engineering the death of his sister by tampering with the saddle girth in order to free myself to marry Diana Lumley and gain a fortune. The message was quite frank, open, direct, utterly brutal: I had killed his sister to win a fortune; now that he was free, nine-tenths of that fortune – he was quite precise on that point, nine-tenths – should revert to him as the injured, bereaved party in the transaction. In default of which he would kill my son.'

'Oh, no!' I cried.

'As if to underscore his threat, I think that he then murdered his accomplice Lavache, who, having carried out his errand, had possibly become a useless impediment to him. In any event, the lesson was not lost on me: Mayol was no further away than the end of the castle causeway – *and he would carry out his threat!*'

'And so?' I whispered, awed, horrified.

'And so, as you know, I accepted the commission to come to Egypt for the inauguration,' he said. 'You will recall that we departed from the castle after dark, that we changed coaches several times along the way, and, eschewing the public railway, travelled through the night to London docks. What you do *not* know is that I laid a false trail over our movements. To the Royal Academy, I made it known that I had turned down the Egyptian commission, but was taking my son and two ladies of my household for an autumn vacation to either Scotland or Ireland. And the servants of the castle were given the same story immediately prior to our departure. In short, I entirely deceived Marcel Mayol as to my intentions. I have given that scoundrel the slip, and now he will never harm my son – for we shall never return to England and to Castle Delamere!'

I stared at him for a long time, unable to frame the words that must surely jolt him out of his complacency; it was he who, in the event, mouthed them for me.

'You are about to declare, Miss Copley,' he said, smiling and wagging a finger at me, 'that I have not, after all, given Mayol the slip, that somehow he has outwitted me and in fact accompanied us on the voyage out here. You will point to the assault upon my person as proof of this.'

'If the assault was not made by Marcel Mayol, then by whom, sir?' I asked.

'As was established by poor old Sommerson's photographic apparatus,' he replied, 'the culprit was one of the Lascar seamen.'

'And the reason for the attack?' I countered.

'Robbery. What else? But I cried out, and the fellow panicked and fled.'

I thought for a moment and said: 'And what of the attack upon Major Woodford?'

'That attack is contributory proof to my theory,' he replied. 'The Lascar was lurking there, awaiting his chance to break into another first-class cabin as soon as the occupant was asleep. He was spotted by Woodford, and took the violent course of throwing him overboard. It is all of a piece with the scoundrel's treatment of me: if caught out in his nefarious intent, he does not hesitate to maim or kill without compunction. Happily, we are now rid of him, for we shall never set foot aboard the *Hindustan* again – thank God!'

I drew in a deep breath and slowly exhaled it to the count of five, an exercise which I had found to be most useful in my student days when dealing with difficult patients and even more difficult doctors. And then, having calmed myself, I resumed my argument.

'What of Dr Sommerson's death?' I demanded.

He stared at me with wide-eyed astonishment and truly genuine shock. 'You are not suggesting,' he said, 'that the poor old fellow died of anything other than a heart attack, or similar? What possible connection could the natural death of an ailing septuagenarian cleric have with an escaped prisoner from Devil's Island?'

I did not reply. It was on the tip of my tongue to tell him about my experience with the ubiquitous Lascar, but it seemed useless and possibly cruel to rid him of his illusions. He was convinced that he had outwitted Marcel Mayol, and this was possibly so. After all, the greater part of my case – that he had not – was prompted not so much by the chance hazards, death

233

and near-deaths which had dogged our passage from England to Egypt as by their relevance to the gipsy's prophecies. Was I to say to him: 'Mr Ormerod, a gipsy warned me that all these things would happen, and they have'? He would think me out of my mind. So I said no more.

He was on his feet again, and staring out of the glass wall.

'Do not think for a minute that I have been complacent,' he said. 'I have carried a pistol all this time. But I am now convinced that I have given Mayol the slip and that young Rupert is safe, and his inheritance also. For myself, I care nothing. I am perfectly willing, for my son's sake, to quit England and seek anonymity in a foreign land. To this end, before we left, I instructed my lawyer to make an offer for the Villa Cimbrone in Rapallo, Italy, whose lease has come up for sale. There, on the southern end of the Salerno peninsula, high above the wine-dark sea, one will find peace – and safety.'

He turned to me; the sunlight behind his head cast his face in shadow, and I could not see the message in his eyes.

'Will you come with us to the Villa Cimbrone, Suzanna Copley?' he asked gently. 'I know that you feel nothing for me but a certain esteem, but that esteem may grow with usage. I, on my part, confess to a feeling stronger than esteem for you. I think it happened when I perceived that one of your eyes is more blue than the other, and that you wrinkle your nose when you laugh.'

'I do no such thing as wrinkle my nose!' I declared.

'That you do,' he replied. 'And it is most engaging. Come now, I don't ask for an answer today, but here's my formal declaration. I, Justin Ormerod, a widower of the parish of Nunwich in the County of Suffolk, beg the hand in marriage of Suzanna Copley, a spinster of the parish of . . .'

'Of Hickleydoek, in the County of Devon,' I whispered.

'Of Hickleydoek, in the County of Devon,' he repeated. 'And I will make this declaration again in one week, at the termination of the celebrations connected with the opening of the Suez canal, at which time I shall wish to proceed to Italy, and, if the negotiations for the lease of the Villa Cimbrone are brought to a successful conclusion, to take up residence there.

234

'Suzanna, you will love southern Italy,' he said in a quite different tone of voice. 'Your warm heart will flower like an exotic bloom under those illimitable blue skies. The Villa Cimbrone, its elegant courts, its breathtaking gardens, the balustraded terraces that look out over the Gulf of Salerno so far below that the fishing boats are mere specks on the brilliant sea – all this will be enriched by your presence.'

'Mr Ormerod, you . . .' I began.

'Say nothing,' he commanded me. 'Wait. Think of it. Search your heart. Consider. I ask nothing but that you consider. A week – so short a while, though it can determine the pattern of a lifetime. Answer me then, but not before, I beg you. Do you agree to that?'

I nodded. 'I agree, but . . .'

'No "buts",' he admonished me. 'The word "but", like "if only", should be banned from our language as the terminology of half-life. Life should be concerned not with "let's not", but with "why not?", with the unequivocal "yes" instead of the "yes, but". Let us leave it there, Suzanna. And now, as I understand from the palace grapevine that you are riding out with our excellent friend Sheik Mansour at noon, I think I must release my delightful model, confidante and – may I say it? – possible bride-to-be.'

I gave him my hand. He kissed it, and my heart gave a treacherous lurch to see the intensity of the gaze he directed to me.

'*Au revoir,*' he said. 'Enjoy your ride.'

When I reached the door and turned to look back, he pointed to the portrait. 'I will sign and date it,' he said. 'When it is dry, I will varnish it and have it framed in carved and richly-gilded fruit wood, as befits such a model. And it will be yours.' He smiled. 'Notwithstanding your answer in one week's time, it will be yours to keep.'

I still have that portrait.

At noontide, the clatter of hooves on the drive outside the *Haremlek* announced the arrival of Sheikh Mansour, and this was confirmed by one of the Sudanese girls, who, wide-eyed and obviously intrigued by my connection with the madly handsome desert aristocrat, informed me that he was awaiting my pleasure.

Mansour dismounted at my appearance and bowed his head in salutation, though he did not take my hand. He was wearing what I understood to be the traditional dress of the desert Arab: a simple headdress banded by a circle of woven silk, a loose-fitting tunic over a linen shirt, baggy pantaloons tucked into high boots of soft suede leather.

'To the desert!' he exclaimed, and flashing me a brilliant smile assisted me to mount an extremely fine-looking little grey mare. 'She is called Bit-o-Musk,' he said, 'and I think she will give you no trouble.' He himself had a rather worn-looking bay who had obviously seen better days. There were others with us: two scowling, brutish fellows in the trappings of the khedive's Turkish bodyguard. Both were superbly mounted on jet-black stallions which were wild of eye and restless to be off. I thought I discerned the reason for the disparity between Sheikh Mansour's horse and those of his escorts; it transpired that I was not far wrong.

We clattered out of the palace gates, the sheikh and I side by side, our Turkomen following. The sentries saluted and Mansour acknowledged the same with a flourish of his whip. Our progress through the city attracted a considerable amount of interest from the promenaders, the smart folk at the outside café tables, the small children who ran alongside us, barefoot, calling for baksheesh. Before very long, however, we came to the seedy outskirts which mercifully soon gave way to an open plain. Beyond all that, as far as the eye could see, stretched a grey and gold wilderness of mountain and sand.

'The Garden of Allah!' said Sheikh Mansour, pointing with his whip. 'Let's go, Miss Suzanna! *Bismillah!*'

He set his mount into a gallop, and I followed after. The little mare responded beautifully, but she had more looks than speed, though she had no difficulty in keeping up with my companion's bay. I was interested to see that our escorts – with whom Mansour had so far exchanged neither a word nor a glance – easily pulled out and, taking station to left and right, reined in their mounts to keep pace with us.

For a while we followed a narrow canal which snaked its way

through smallholdings. We galloped through a tiny village of mud huts, where naked children and veiled women came out to watch our passing. Presently the hard-baked ground gave way to yielding white sand. Our mounts' pace slackened as the going became more difficult. We were in the desert, the Garden of Allah.

We proceeded for about an hour, alternately galloping and walking, saying nothing to each other though we continued to ride stirrup to stirrup. At the end of that time, Mansour urged his horse at the full gallop up a steep hillock of sand and I followed after, joining him when he halted at the summit. He pointed away to the northward.

'Behold!' he said. 'The largest man-made objects upon this earth!'

'The pyramids!' I breathed.

They were, perhaps, ten miles distant, and etched against the horizon: three perfect pyramidal shapes, one notably larger than its consorts: the Great Pyramid of the Pharaoh Cheops, as I had been told at school in Hickleydoek; and how could I have guessed, in those far-off days in the little village schoolhouse in the shadow of the parish church, that I should one day look upon the great pyramid and its companions – and in the company of a handsome desert sheikh withal?

'And now we will eat, Miss Suzanna,' said Mansour. 'Come, my people have it already prepared.' He led the way down the other side of the sand dune to where, in a gully at the foot of it, there stood a long black tent, a dozen horses and camels tethered there, and a group of Arabs, men and women, who greeted our approach with welcoming cries and waves.

We dismounted by the tent, one side of which had been raised to reveal a shaded interior set with rich carpets, silk cushions, and the trappings of a feast.

'Here stands my right hand,' declared Mansour, introducing a fiercely bearded desert warrior who was hung about with a long curved sword, cartridge bandoliers, and daggers galore; yet his hand, when it took mine, was as gentle as could be. 'He is called Achmed ben Yussuf, and in my absence he rules our tribe at my command. And this is his brother Abdullah.'

A younger edition of Achmed gave me a brief nod. I pre-

237

sumed that Abdullah clove to the more conservative Arab attitude which regards women as mere chattels. There were four heavily veiled females present, but Sheikh Mansour made no move to introduce them to me; having observed my arrival, they retired, chattering like magpies, to a trio of cooking fires some distance from the tent, but not so far that their culinary preparations were not borne on the still, hot air in the most appetizing galaxy of aromas.

Achmed ben Yussuf scowled to see our two Turkish escorts, and growled something to Mansour, who replied with a careless shrug of the shoulders and a brief response – a response that seemed not to please his second-in-command overmuch.

'Come into the shade of the tent, Miss Suzanna,' said my host. 'We'll drink sherbet while the women complete the luncheon. My Achmed, I should explain, is for excluding the Turks from our culinary arrangements, but I have pointed out to him that the customary hospitality of the Bedouin extends even to one's enemies, provided they come in peace with their scimitars sheathed, and that this concession even extends to one's enemies' dogs. The Turks will be fed, but the food will be thrown at them – as one would throw food to dogs!' He laughed, baring his white, even teeth.

'The Turks, I take it, are with you to prevent you from escaping to your tribe in the desert?' I ventured.

'Of course,' he replied. 'The khedive, in spite of his high pretensions, does not have a great deal of style. Because of my angry outburst on the train he is of the opinion that I may break my oath.'

'But you would not?' I suggested.

He smiled brilliantly, shrugged his shoulders, flicked away a fly that teased his cheek. 'I will tell you, Miss Suzanna,' he said, 'that Achmed has brought with him to this lunchtime rendez-vous the swiftest steed in my late father's stable. She is out there now, in the horse lines. Astride her, I could swiftly and safely be out of range before the damned Turks could unsling their carbines and open fire.'

'Then why don't you do so?' I asked.

'On the other hand,' he said, 'the contrivance of giving me a broken-down old hack, whilst my gaolers (there is no other word) are mounted on thoroughbreds is extremely risible. If I so willed it, mounted as I am and with my gaolers on two of the best steeds in the khedive's stables, I could still, by the ways known to the Bedouin, outride them.'

'How would you do that?' I asked, intrigued.

'By taking to the soft sand, where one horse is no better than another and only the rider counts. By plunging down precipitous slopes where the rider's courage is everything and is instantly communicated to his mount.'

'So why do you not do it?' I pleaded.

Again that smile. 'Because I have given my parole,' he replied. 'The Khedive Ismail may hold my oath in some disregard, but I do not. There is no need for him to send his Turkish louts to watch over me. Were there a red carpet stretched from here to the remote oasis where my people presently have pitched their tents, I would not take it.

'A Bedouin owns very little, Miss Suzanna.' The dark eyes were intensely fixed upon mine. 'He has, firstly and most importantly, his horse or his camel. Then he has his sword, his knife and his gun. Perhaps he may own a couple of slaves or more. A wife – or four wives. But above all these material things is that which he prizes most: his word, his honour.

'I would as lief break my hated parole with the khedive Ismail as plunge my hand into a basket of horned sand vipers.'

The women brought luncheon to us then: aromatic morsels of meat and vegetables pierced on skewers and freshly roasted; long rice, dry and hot like the desert itself; strange sauces bubbling in the bottom of clay crucibles, into which Mansour showed me how to dip pieces of unleavened bread. We ate with our fingers, Arab fashion, drank sweet sherbet and pure spring water.

'I think,' said Mansour, 'that you are in love, Miss Suzanna, but I have not yet assembled in my mind with *whom* you are in love.'

I paused in the act of transferring a portion of deliciously tender lamb to my lips.

'Sir, you have the advantage of me,' I whispered. It was the only reply I could frame on the spur of the moment.

'Whether it is your distinguished employer, or some other gentleman, I cannot at this remove discern,' he said. 'I have, however, two very distinct impressions. Firstly, that you yourself are not clear in your mind as to who this gentleman is. Secondly, I have the unequivocal feeling that it is not myself who is so singularly honoured. And that is a pity.

'Will you not try some of these candied yams? They are quite excellent.'

'Thank you,' I murmured. 'They look – very nice.'

Mansour clapped his hands and brought all four dark-clothed women running to his summons. At a brief exchange of Arabic, two of them squatted at one end of the richly-patterned silk carpet that covered the floor of the tent. One of them had a small hand-drum, the other a flute, and with these instruments they proceeded to sketch out an irregular rhythm, to which the other pair – discernibly younger and more attractive, even under the voluminous gowns and the heavy veiling – danced in a singularly serpentine manner.

'Miss Suzanna,' said Mansour at length, 'may I proffer some advice to you?'

'Please do,' I replied, beginning to become accustomed to his wayward turns of thought.

'Mr Ormerod,' he said, 'now he is a very worthy man, but I would liken him to a finely-tempered sword blade that may contain a tiny crack. I should think that, with the prescience I have detected in you, Miss Suzanna, you have discovered this. Yes?'

'Mr Ormerod has had – a lot of troubles in his life,' I said.

'Indeed? Is that so? I am not surprised to hear it,' responded my host. 'May I pose the thought that the distinguished Mr Ormerod's troubles may possibly have been largely of his own making?'

'I don't know what you mean,' I responded.

He clapped his hands, and the players and dancers backed away out of the tent, bowing deeply as they departed. A silence fell. Away upon the horizon, the largest man-made objects on earth stood out as sharp and angular as the harsh desert sunlight could make them.

'I have said that I think you are in love,' said Mansour. 'In support of this declaration, I offer the explanation that I am the seventh child of a seventh child, and all my siblings having been slaughtered in the rising against the Turks, I speak as a solitary voice, alone. But I am seldom mistaken when I am inspired to speak of what I see with my third eye, which is in the mind.'

'Who will I marry?' I asked upon a wayward impulse that I could not deny.

His dark eyes flared. He was obviously put out by the directness of my question. He hunched his shoulders and tapped his cheeck. He breathed heavily, dipped his long, tapered fingers into the candied yams, and, renouncing them, washed in the fingerbowl in which a single, perfect flower floated.

'You are, after all, the seventh child of a seventh child,' I said, half taunting, half teasing him.

He sighed, raised his hands, and, taking off the Arab head-dress, threw it to a far corner of the tent, then ran his fingers through the thick black thatch of his close-cropped hair.

'I see it quite clearly,' he said. 'I saw it in you from the very beginning, and this is my despair, Miss Suzanna.

'You love this man, and you will eventually marry him. Unlike Mr Ormerod, he is like a properly-tempered sword, that though pressed upon and fought about will not break.' He paused.

'Yes,' I asked. 'There is more?'

'There is more,' he said. 'You will live in a place that stands on a corner.'

It came back to me then: the gipsy's prophecy:

You will marry . . . and abide in a fine house on a corner . . .

We rode back to the city in the cool of the late afternoon, cantering and walking by turns, the sour-faced Turks follow-ing; nor did we address a word to each other all along the way, being each occupied with their own thoughts.

I was overwhelmed with Mansour's prediction, echoing as it did the gipsy's words with such precision.

So I was to marry. So the vow of celibacy that I had made to myself after Giles's death, a vow that I reinforced every time I touched the pearl and garnet ring that I wore forever round my throat, was due to be broken.

But married – to whom . . . ?

The speculation absorbed my mind all the way to the Abdin Palace. Upon our arrival there, it was immediately apparent that something was amiss. At the entrance to the *Haremlek*, a trio of the palace guards were in an excited exchange with the Sudanese girls who were shouting and gesticulating towards the building.

'Leave this to me,' said Mansour, slipping from his saddle.

The guards salaamed and the girls fell almost to their knees at his approach. He posed a sharp question in Arabic, which brought a passionate response from the girls. This he silenced with a gesture, and repeated his question to the guards. What they then told him caused him to frown and nod. Turning on his heel, he came back to me. I saw tragedy written on his face, and was afraid.

'What is it?' I whispered.

'The little dog – the young boy's dog – has gone mad and bitten someone,' he said.

'Not – not Rupert! He hasn't bitten Rupert?'

'No. A woman. The woman who is travelling with you.'

'Mrs Stittle.'

'That would be she.'

I closed my eyes and had a vision of horror. Miss Nightingale, with her experience of the Near East, had included in our syllabus a study of the dread disease of hydrophobia, commonly called 'rabies', which is traded from one living creature to an other by a bite, is almost impossible – on account of the length of time it takes for the symptoms to emerge – to diagnose at an early stage, is impossible to cure, and is invariably fatal. And little Clovis had been bitten in a dog-fight in Lisbon. I should have guessed that the hazard of contagion was there and taken steps to prevent the tragedy that was now almost certain to unfold.

'Where is he now – where is the dog?' I said.

'In the garden court, so they tell me,' said Mansour. 'No one else will go near him, never fear. I suggest you attend the poor woman who was bitten. I will go and fetch my pistol.'

'Your pistol?'

'To shoot the dog,' he said, surprised. 'Surely you must know that he cannot be allowed to live.' He assisted me down from my side-saddle, nodded briefly to me, and walked swiftly away.

The *Haremlek* was in a turmoil. Surely all the khedive's legendary wives and concubines must have gathered at the windows which looked on to the inner court where the fountain plashed and the magnolia spread its waxy leaves to the dying sun.

'Miss Copley, Miss Copley!' It was Rupert, his face streaked with tears, his voice choked with sobs. 'They say that Clovis has gone mad and'll have to be killed. Don't let them kill him, Miss Copley. He's only a little dog, and he only gave Mrs Stittle a bit of a nip, and she's not really mad at him at all, are you, Mrs Stittle?'

'It's nothing really, Miss,' said the good woman, displaying her right hand, where a small set of punctures on the heel of the palm oozed a few spots of blood. 'I don't know what came over the little feller. We took him out for a walk in the garden, and then when he didn't want to come back in, I argued with him for a bit and then I stooped to pick him up – and he bit me.'

The women about us were in a high state of hysterics, and I knew the reason why, for rabies was endemic in their country and they were very well aware of the perils – as Mrs Stittle was not, for because we are an island, the scourge is really quite rare, and I had never seen a case in all my nursing training. Again I cursed myself for not having forseen that the dog-fight in Lisbon would lead to this: with the poor woman condemned to die in a most appalling fashion, after protracted agonies.

The women were pointing out into the garden court, which was half in shade and half in sunlight. At the shadowed end, I espied the cobby, squared-off shape of the little pug-dog. He was sitting on his hunkers and looking about him, saucer-eyed, tongue lolling. A dog less resembling a mad dog I had never seen. And then he stood up and took a few paces further into the shade.

'I'll go and talk to him,' I said.

'Miss Copley, he's in a right nasty frame of mind,' said Mrs Stittle. 'These folks say he's gone mad and must be killed.'

'We'll see,' I said. And pushing my way through the jabbering women of the *Haremlek*, I opened the french window that let out into the garden, an action which brought a renewed and more frantic response from the dark-clad wives and concubines. It was a blessed relief to close the door behind me.

'Hello, Clovis,' I called loudly. 'How are you?'

Normally this salutation would have resulted in a frenzied wagging of the convoluted tail; not on this occasion: he merely looked at me with his great sad eyes. I measured the distance between me and the water fountain. Remembering the symptoms of rabies, the most significant of which is the fear of water – giving the disease its name hydrophobia – I reckoned that in the last resort, if he came to attack me, I had only to leap in the ankle-deep water of the fountain bowl and I should be safe.

'Poor Clovis,' I said. And advanced towards him.

He remained seated, but at my approach shifted his posture slightly and gave a throaty bark that could have signified anything, good or ill.

'Shall we go for a walk?' I said.

The world 'walk' was one of the words to which he habitually reacted with animation; but not on this occasion. The folded ears did not prick up, nor did the curly tail give the accustomed flurry of pleasure.

I took another pace forward. He growled.

'Miss Suzanna! Stand aside! I am going to shoot!' This was Sheikh Mansour. He was standing at the open french window, a pistol in his hand, aimed.

'Miss Copley, Miss Copley, don't let them kill Clovis!' wailed Rupert.

Taking in both hands all the measure of courage that I possessed, and a loan on that which I did not possess, I advanced upon the pug-dog and, disregarding his warning growl, gathered him up in my arms as if he had been a baby. He did not bite me, but only gave a piteous whine. I carried him back to the french window.

'Put away your pistol, Sheikh,' I said. 'This is not a mad dog, but merely a frightened little dog in pain. I saw him limp when he walked. Do you see his trouble?' And I showed them the left front paw, with a cruel thorn driven deeply into the soft pad. I plucked the thorn out quickly. Clovis gave a yelp of pain, but almost immediately after he licked his paw, and then my hand.

'Miss Suzanna,' said Sheikh Mansour, 'you are the bravest lady it has been my honour to meet, and it is a matter of great regret that my dwelling place does not stand on a corner.'

They made such a fuss of me at the Abdin Palace. I suppose it was the women who passed the news around. There was a kind of Tom Tiddler's ground betwixt the *Haremlek* and the male end of the palace: a shady courtyard set about with fig trees and magnolias, where it was possible for the women to watch the proceedings through the heavily barred windows of the *Harem-lek*. An *ad hoc* reception was held there that evening in my honour – and in honour of Clovis, who was sporting a bandaged paw by courtesy of the khedive's personal physician, no less. And the palace band played selections from light operettas.

Justin Ormerod sought me out. 'I am most grateful to you, as ever, Miss Copley,' he said. 'I think that it would have broken young Rupert's heart to see his beloved dog shot before his very eyes.'

'Thank you,' I replied. There was nothing else to say.

My employer was buttonholed by one of the khedive's aides about arranging sittings for the state portrait. Hal Marius sauntered up to me. He had a glass of sherbet in his hand, that being the only drink on offer, but I had the clear impression that he had been refreshing himself at more potent wells.

'Well done,' he said. 'You are the heroine of the hour.'

'You have a button missing off your coat,' I said.

'So I have, so I have,' he said.

'Well, if you'll send it round to my room, I'll see if I have one to match it in my workbox and sew it on for you.'

'I'll do that, and thanks,' he said. 'You know, you took an awful risk with that dog. He was bitten in Lisbon and it was an even bet that he'd taken rabies. What did they teach you at the Florence Nightingale school – apart from being tremendously British and keeping a stiff upper lip?'

'Sir, I think you are drunk,' I said, without any severity.

'Yes, ma'am, and you are beautiful,' he responded. 'Tomorrow, however, I shall be sober, but you will still be beautiful.'

'Mr Marius . . .' I began, the germ of a most absurd notion having just come to me.

'Hal – call me Hal,' he said.

'Hal,' I said, 'where do you live?'

'Why I live in a suitcase, or wherever I hang up my hat,' he replied. 'A roving newspaper reporter can't do much else.'

'But you must have a family home. You must have been brought up *somewhere*.'

'Why, yes, in Indiana.'

'Is Indiana a town – a city?'

'It's a state.'

'And your family home. Tell me – where is it situated?'

'Why it's situated in the middle of nowhere, at the front of a low hill, by a meandering stream.'

'Not in a street?'

'There is no street, as you'd define a street, in fifty miles, ma'am,' he said.

'So if not in a street, certainly not on a corner?'

'Ma'am, there isn't a corner nearer than Indianapolis,' he said. 'But why do you ask?'

'It was just an idle thought,' I said.

Little Clovis came limping up to me on his lame leg, twisted tail wagging enthusiastically. I picked him up and held him against my cheek, rejoicing in the small pleasure of feeling his eager tongue licking my ear.

TWELVE

The inaugural opening of the Suez canal was informed by the most elaborate ceremonial, surely, since the Ancient Egyptians celebrated the completion of Cheops's Great Pyramid. We travelled back to the port of Alexandria by train to join the viceregal yacht *Mahroussa*. It was an entirely uneventful journey, which I passed in the company of the Hon. Petronella, who seemed disinclined to conversation, and spent most of the time gazing out of the window at the passing scene. I had a brief word with Mrs Sommerson, who said that after some thought she had decided to continue with the tour because her husband would have wished it so. She also informed me that she had arranged for the dean's last photographic plates to be developed in Cairo and that she would send me one as a souvenir. For this I thanked her. She seemed, no doubt through the consolations of her religion, to have accepted her husband's passing with a calm serenity, and surely had not the slightest suspicion that his death might have been the result of foul play.

The *Mahroussa* was moored at the dockside at the place recently occupied by the *Hindustan*, which had returned to England and was not to be privileged to pass through the canal to India till her next voyage. With the viceregal yacht was the famous imperial French yacht *L'Aigle*, and she, we had been told, was to have the honour of leading the inaugural procession of ships from Port Said to Suez, along the longest single man-made waterway on earth.

Our own party was established in adjacent cabins on the boat deck. Mine was luxuriously appointed in Saxe blue and gold, and had its own bathroom with running hot and cold water, together with a small kitchen fitted out with – of all things! – an ice-box for cooling drinks, with which I found my cabin to be plentifully supplied, from the eternal Egyptian sherbet to the finest champagnes. Mrs Stittle and Rupert were established on one side of me, Justin Ormerod a few doors down. The voyage from Alexandria to Port Said, in which one rounds the maze of islands and lagoons of the Nile delta, would take about sixteen hours and was to be made largely at night. It was about five o'clock in the afternoon, and I had taken tea with Rupert and Mrs Stittle when I decided to go out on deck for a breath of fresh air. The weather was distinctly autumnal, with a stiff breeze blowing off the land that whipped up the waters of the harbour and sent the ever-circling seagulls skeetering on their wing ends. Hugging my pelisse more closely about my shoulders, I set off for a brisk walk round the boat deck. And who should I bump into at the first corner but Hal Marius, similarly engaged.

'They've turned up!' he declared, eyes dancing.

'What have turned up?' I not unnaturally demanded.

'My golf clubs,' he replied. 'It seems that they were left aboard the *Hindustan*, but were fortunately found before she left for England and were put aboard here. Isn't that great?'

'I am so happy for you,' I said, amused.

'Now I shall be able to carry out my ambition to drive a ball clear of the pyramid's base,' he said, falling into step beside me as I resumed my perambulation. 'After the inauguration, there'll be another whole fortnight of junketings in Alex and Cairo, so we'll have plenty of opportunity.'

'We?' I repeated. 'Who is "we"?'

'Why, you and me,' he said. 'Didn't I ask you to accompany me? I thought I had. Do you have a good head for heights? It's a long way up.'

'I suppose I have,' I replied. 'But I'm not sure that I . . .'

'It's fixed then,' he said cheerfully. 'First chance we get to play hookey from receptions and gala performances at the opera, we'll drive out to Gizeh and you'll watch me hit that ball clear of the base.'

I did not comment further. Nor did we speak till we had

made another complete circuit of the deck, and then my companion addressed me in a very different, a serious, tone of voice.

'Any further developments regarding the mystery of the Lascar?' he asked.

'I . . .'

'Yes?'

I made a fresh start: 'Mr Marius, I . . .'

'Hal – call me Hal.'

'Hal, I feel inclined – though I shouldn't – to confide in you.'

'Feel free. I'm known to many damsels in distress as a good shoulder to cry on.'

'It goes without saying that I expect your complete discretion.'

'It will go in one ear and out of the other.'

'Very well,' I said. And during the course of three more circuits, I told him everything that Justin Ormerod had told me in his Cairo studio: about his first wife Esmée, her scoundrelly brother and his escape from Devil's Island, the threat to Rupert's life – everything.

When I had finished, my companion looked grimly at me and said: 'So Ormerod thinks he's shaken off this Marcel Mayol character, but you don't think so – right?'

'Well, what do you think?' I countered. 'You have all the evidence.'

We paused by the ship's rail. From a porthole of a deck below, a pair of hands and arms emerged with a bucket of scraps and tipped them into the waters of the harbour. Instantly a flock of screeching seagulls descended upon them and fought over every morsel.

'I think you're right, Suzanna,' said Hal Marius. 'On the evidence that Ormerod has, he's got some justification for thinking that he's given Mayol the slip. What he doesn't know is that the Lascar followed us – indeed, may have accompanied us – to Cairo. And that's a piece of evidence that simply won't go away.'

'Do you think I should tell him, after all?' I asked.

'It would put him on his guard.'

'He's already on his guard. He carries a pistol, always.

Following the attack upon him, and by his orders, we lock ourselves in our quarters at night.'

'Then leave things as they are. You've got an ally now. You've got me. I'll watch over you, Rupert, and the rest.'

I felt better for that.

We sailed an hour later, and I was standing with Rupert and Clovis by the rail as the *Mahroussa*'s great side-paddle wheels churned the surface of the harbour to a wild froth and we slid out of the breakwater and into the open sea.

'A fine vessel, ma'am. A fine vessel.'

I turned to see the speaker, and my heart lurched. I was looking into my past, at my lost love. He was not Giles Launey, but his near counterfeit: eyes of steely blue, face heavily bronzed and hair bleached almost to whiteness by tropic sun and salt spray. And he was wearing the uniform of a Royal Navy officer.

'Lieutenant Conigsby, at your service, ma'am. Neville Conigsby. I am seconded to the *Mahroussa* as liaison officer.'

Haltingly, I introduced myself and Rupert. He must have thought me very odd, for I could not keep a tremor from my voice and had a fevered compulsion to run away from him and hide. And cry my eyes out.

'Well I'll tell you a few things about the *Mahroussa*, young fellow,' said Conigsby, picking up Rupert and setting him on the rail above the great paddle box. 'For a start, she's British built, and at 478 feet long and 3762 tons, the biggest steam yacht afloat.'

'Gosh!' exclaimed Rupert, eyes dancing.

'If you're not otherwise engaged, I should be most honoured if I might take you into dinner tonight, Miss Copley,' murmured Lieutenant Conigsby.

Searching frantically for a pretext to refuse him and miraculously finding one, I blurted out: 'I'm afraid I can't. I – I've rather a headache, and I shall retire quite soon.'

'Luncheon tomorrow, then?' He cocked his head on one side and gave me a quirky grin. He was Giles Launey all over again. I felt my throat tighten and the treacherous tears prickle my eyes.

'Excuse me, Lieutenant,' I said, brushing past him. 'I've suddenly remembered something I should have done. Would you mind keeping an eye on Rupert till someone comes up to fetch him?'

'With pleasure, Miss Copley.'

I reached the corridor leading to my cabin before I broke down. Blinded by tears, I did not at first see Mrs Wayne Barlowe emerge from her door and confront me. She laid a hand on my arm.

'My dear, what's amiss?' she cried. 'Ah, but you are so upset. Come into my cabin. Come. I will give you a little pick-me-up, and then you shall tell me all your troubles. A trouble shared is a trouble halved, you know.'

As might be expected, my flamboyant friend's cabin was about twice the size of mine and regally appointed. She settled me in a comfortable button-back chair and, opening her dressing case, took out a bottle of amber-coloured liquid which she proceeded to pour into a glass till the latter was half-full. She then passed it to me.

'Please, what is it, ma'am?' I whispered.

'It is Scotch whisky, my dear,' she replied. 'Scotch whisky was first introduced to me by your dear Queen Victoria when I was staying at Balmoral. She herself takes a dram every evening after dinner without fail, and swears by its efficaciousness as a remedy for ailments both mental and physical. I confess myself quite charmed with the stuff. There – sip it up, my dear.'

I took a tentative sip and gagged on the neat spirit, though its fiery progress down my throat certainly dispersed the choking sobs that had been racking me.

'And now,' said Mrs Wayne Barlowe. 'Tell me all, my dear.'

'I – I have just been brutally reminded – by a young English naval officer on this boat – of the man I told you about. The man I once loved,' I said.

'The gallant fellow who gave his life in trying to save another!' she said. 'Ah, yes, that story affected me greatly. But you speak of the man you *once* loved. Death does not part us from our loved ones, my dear. The love remains – though one must not live with the past, but journey on through life finding new loves along the way, and still treasuring the old.'

I looked down into the glass of amber-coloured liquid in my hands and thought I saw there the maelstrom of water that had swallowed up Giles Launey. And then I said: 'My love for him died with him – or a very few days after.'

Mrs Wayne Barlowe drew in a sharp breath, and her hand went to her throat. 'Oh, my dear,' she said. 'You disturb me greatly. But I sense there is even worse to follow!'

I nodded, took from my reticule the letter – his letter – which, like the newspaper cutting had been folded and unfolded, read and re-read so many times that it resembled a piece of antique lace, and passed it to my companion.

'He wrote two letters on the day he died, when his ship was approaching Plymouth,' I said. 'One to me, the other to a brother officer in another ship. Having written the letters, he sealed them up and addressed them.

'Only – only he put the wrong names and addresses on the wrong letters. The letter you have there, addressed to me, is the one he penned to his friend. As you will see.'

She read it slowly, mouthing the words quietly, her lorgnette moving at a snail's pace along the lines. I could have read it aloud with her, every word. All burnt on my heart and my soul in a bitter canker.

H.M.S. *Dauntless*
At sea, off Plymouth.

My dear Jack,
Splendid to receive your note with news of *les filles jolies* in Chatham town. I myself have a pretty little thing in Plymouth, wife of an itinerant salesman who is away more often than he is at home, at which times his little spouse is not averse to entertaining gentlemen – for a small consideration. I shall hope to see her tonight if only this gale permits us to enter harbour.

I have told you of the winsome Dartmoor filly I have been quietly bringing towards 'the starting post' these few years since she blossomed into maidenhood – a state in which I do not intend she remains for much longer. No itinerant salesman's wife she, for tho only the brat of a common yeoman farmer, she has aspirations towards marriage, if I'm not mistaken. It may be that I shall have to coax her a little way along this primrose path in order to achieve my object with little Suzanna. *Cum finis est licitus, etiam media sunt licita* – which, since you did not have the benefit of my classical education, I translate for you as 'The end justifies the means'.

Keep me posted with all your latest news.
      Ever yours,
      Giles L.–

When she had finished, Mrs Wayne Barlowe without a word reached out her hand and took hold of mine. We sat for a while in silence, then carefully folding up the tattered letter, she gave it back to me and I replaced it within my reticule.

'He must have been dead before the letters were even posted from the ship,' I said. 'I often wonder on the nature of the one that he addressed to his friend; it must have puzzled Mr Jack very much. With the advantages of his classical education, he was able to compose most affecting love letters, with quotations from Shakespeare, Robert Burns, Robert Herrick. I remember some lines he once penned to me from Herrick:

> Gather ye rosebuds while ye may,
> Old Time is still a-flying:
> And this same flower that smiles today,
> Tomorrow will be dying.

'I suppose Herrick's poem "To Virgins, to Make Much of Time" echoed Giles's philosophy. He certainly ran out of Time most unseasonably.' I bowed my head and the tears came again.

'You must go and lie down, my dear,' said Mrs Wayne Barlowe. 'The excellent Scotch whisky will render you drowsy in a very short while and you will sleep. When you awake, you will feel better, and the ghost that this young man aboard the ship caused to rise before you will appear for what it is: not even a ghost, but a scarecrow in tatters with a pumpkin for a head. Off with you, now. No, I'll not brook any argument.' She kissed me on both cheeks, squeezed my hands and bundled me out of the door.

But I did not sleep. When darkness came, and I could hear

the strains of a string orchestra coming from the great dining saloon than ran almost the entire length of the deck below me, the clattering of dishes and the hum of conversation, I was tempted to put on a dinner dress and join the throng, to be with people, to be part of the world and away from aching memories. Instead, throwing on my pelisse, I went out on to the boat deck.

It was a chill November night, with a touch of frost in the air and a hazy ring around the moon. Away to our right, a few fitful pinpoints of light low down on the sandy shore of the great delta. Behind us, the red, white and green lights of the imperial yacht which the *Mahroussa* was guiding to Port Said. Above the muffled sound of music coming from our own orchestra below, came the strident rhythm of a galop from the French yacht.

I looked down into the tumbling wake with its winking lights of fluorescence and thought of life and of extinction. The experience of meeting Lt Conigsby had awaked in me dark thoughts that I had believed myself to have put aside long since, and then I thought of my friend Mrs Wayne Barlowe's words: that the ghost which had been raised was really no more than a scarecrow with a pumpkin for a head. One day, I told myself then, I would rid myself of the last of his memory, of what might have been, but never would have been.

It may have been the jaunty music of the galop, it may have been the delayed effects of the Scotch whisky, but it was with a curiously lightened heart that, after trying the door of Rupert's cabin to assure myself that Mrs Stittle had remembered to lock them in after they had had their early supper, I went back to bed, and – oddly enough – slept like a babe till breakfast time.

By nine o'clock we were already in sight of the canal entrance, and passengers and crew lined the rails to catch the first glimpse of one of the latter-day Wonders of the World. Rupert was there with Mrs Stittle and the dog. I saw my employer, who was standing on the yacht's bridge with the gold-braided captain and his officers: he waved to me and smiled. Hal Marius was lounging near the front of the ship: a solitary figure in his tweed suit, puffing on a curly pipe.

Moments later, Lt Conigsby was at my elbow. 'Captain's

compliments, and would Miss Copley and Master Rupert care to join him up on the bridge for entering harbour?'

Rupert jumped for joy. Leaving Clovis with Mrs Stittle, we followed Lt Conigsby up the steps to the bridge, where we were introduced to Captain Leclerc, who, like most of the officers aboard the *Mahroussa*, was French. Justin Ormerod greeted me warmly, and there was an unspoken question in his eyes: had I yet come to a decision about his proposal? I affected not to notice what was plainly obvious, wished him a very good morning, and was it not all so exciting?

Presently, the captain having given an order, the ship swung to the right, towards Port Said and the canal entrance, meanwhile emitting a raucous blast of her steam horn, no doubt to inform her consort *L'Aigle*, who was following close behind. As we drew nearer the entrance, a continuous splash of black and white along the shoreline – which I had taken to be rocks – revealed themselves as *people*: thousands and thousands of people in native dress – the men in white 'nightgowns', the women in their universal black – watching and waiting our arrival. The sound of their cheering came to us across the glassy, grey water.

I gave a start – I think we must all have given a start – when a thunderous crash of gunfire shattered the air and a cloud of white smoke wafted slowly across the entrance. Lt Conigsby permitted me to look through his telescope, supporting it upon his own shoulder, and I saw a line of cannons stretched, wheel to wheel, along a breakwater. Again a detonation made me half jump out of my skin, then another, and another, as the whole line of guns fired from one end to the other in succession. We counted a salute of twenty-one.

But it was when the gunsmoke had cleared away that I beheld the most awesome sight of all: beyond the breakwater lay the town of Port Said, its towers and minarets etched against a grey skyline. And in the harbour were ships, hundreds of ships, all at anchor – and all ablaze with flags; flags that streamed from every masthead, strung in streamers from masthead to masthead, from ship to ship, as they lined the path which the *Mahroussa* and *L'Aigle* must take.

As we drew abreast of the first ship in the nearest line, every vessel present began to blow long blasts on its steam horn, while upon every deck there suddenly appeared white-clad sailors, who, running from nowhere, as it were, quickly took up position along the rails, facing outward. And as we passed each ship, they waved their hats in unison and gave three concerted cheers. It was a most affecting display of welcome and must have taken hours to rehearse to the peak of perfection it achieved.

The *Mahroussa* dropped her anchor opposite an imposing domed building on the quay, while *L'Aigle* anchored slightly ahead of us. There then followed a colourful and exciting coming and going of small boats to and from *L'Aigle*. With much shrilling of bosun's pipes the khedive, in magnificent naval uniform with a tarboosh, a long curved sword at his side, his chest a-glitter with diamond-studded orders and banded with a broad sash of watered pink silk, descended to a waiting boat from whose stern fluttered a white star and crescent upon a green background. He had been preceded into the boat (as Lt Conigsby informed me, the custom always is for the most senior officer, or the most distinguished person, to be last into a boat) by the party of especially eminent dignitaries who were to voyage through the canal in the place of honour aboard *L'Aigle* as guests of the French Empress. Justin Ormerod was there in the boat, among princes and potentates, diplomats and admirals.

And there, also, was Mrs Wayne Barlowe – of course!

She waved to me.

By midday, when the ships raised anchor for the passage to Suez, the sun, belying the grey morning's dull promise, came out in tropical brilliance, and sailors raised white canvas awnings above every deck.

With much hooting, cheering, and yet another salute of guns from the shore, the imperial French yacht nosed her way slowly into the first length of the canal, which stretched as straight as an arrow and as far as the eye could see across the desert for fifty miles, to the new town of Ismailia, which was approximately halfway to our destination, and where the fleet was to spend the night in a riot of feasting and balls on shipboard.

As soon as the *Mahroussa* had entered the canal, a buffet luncheon was served on the quarter deck, so that passengers would be able to watch the passing scene. It was there I was buttonholed by Major Woodford, who looked extremely dashing in his regimentals and confided in me that he was carrying a pistol.

'That feller Kiprenski,' he murmured close by my ear. 'Haven't let the Russkie scoundrel out of my sight since breakfast. There he is now, chatting to the Marchcombe gel, as if for all the world it wasn't gall and wormwood for him to see these ships passing through the canal, bringing the Indian Empire nearer and confounding the Tsar's dastardly plans to conquer the sub-continent by stealth.'

'You don't *really* think, Major, that Mr Kiprenski is going to blow a hole in the ship's bottom and sink her in the canal?'

'He may or may not have that intent, ma'am,' responded the gallant major, 'but he'll not carry it out – not with Jackie Woodford keeping watch and ward!' And he tapped his pocket, where, I presumed, lay his pistol. And not for the first time in our acquaintance, I decided that he had been at the bottle.

Our progress through the canal was carried out at a very slow speed so that, I was informed by Lt Conigsby (who upon closer acquaintance turned out to be nothing like Giles Launey at all, save in superficial appearance), the wake of our passing would not destroy the banks on either side, for the great waterway was quite disconcertingly narrow and for the most part rendered the passing of two ships quite out of the question. On the right hand, where lay Egypt and all Africa, a railway line ran quite close, and also a smaller canal – a sweet-water canal that irrigated the fields and villages of the delta, so I was told. Along the latter sailed tall boats called dhows, all ladened down with bundles of hay and other crops, enormous green water melons, coconuts and hands of bananas. For most of the way to Ismailia a chugging, long train followed us along the railway line, and I never saw so many people packed so tightly, nor any train that carried so many; they clung to the outsides of the carriages, they hung out of the windows, they stood on the roofs – and they waved and cheered at the fleet every yard of the way.

Towards evening, with the white buildings and lush greenery

of distant Ismailia standing out in marked contrast to the desert
about it, there appeared on the left-hand bank, on the Asiatic
shore, a small army of camel-men, desert warriors dressed in
the manner of Bedouin, with flowing headdresses and dramatic
cloaks. They galloped their camels abreast of the *Mahroussa*,
over the crests of white dunes, strung out in a single column, a
hundred or more, shouting wild war cries and firing their long
guns in the air. In my opinion, this was the most exhilarating
spectacle of the whole day.

And so, an hour or so later, we made history by completing
the first half of the journey, and came to Ismailia.

THE INAUGURAL OPENING
OF THE SUEZ CANAL
November 17, 1869

PROGRAMME FOR THE EVENING:
8 pm to Midnight: Reception and Gala Ball
in Honour of Her Imperial Majesty the
Empress Eugénie aboard *L'Aigle*.

Midnight: Supper aboard the *Mahroussa*.

Afterwards, light music, dancing and
entertainment will continue on both
yachts.

4 am onwards: English and Continental breakfasts
will be served on both yachts.

(signed)
Mansour el Abbes
Master-of-Ceremonies
at Ismailia 17/11/69

The printed card, which still remains among my souvenirs of
that most memorable of times, was brought to my cabin as soon
as the yacht was moored alongside a quay in Ismailia that
fronted a most handsome street of delightful white villas with
gardens set with flowering shrubs of oriental opulence and tall
palms. I had not seen Mansour since Cairo, and had learned

that he had gone on ahead to Ismailia to make arrangements for the fleet's overnight stay there. He had obviously been very busy. As soon as we were alongside, the imperial French yacht made fast on the outside of us and gangplanks were thrown between the two vessels, making them virtually as one.

Studying the programme, I decided that yet another reception would be a reception too many for me, so I resolved to arrive next door at about nine o'clock. The next question was – what about Rupert? Already, overtired from his most exacting and exciting day, he was pleading to be allowed to stay up and watch the festivities, this with a trembling of the nether lip and that tone of voice which is nearly a whine and well on the way to being a snivel. I took counsel with Mrs Stittle and we came to a compromise: no, Rupert could not stay up and see the whole thing through till they served breakfast in the small hours; but provided he went to bed for a nap immediately, he could get up at half-past eight, have supper in his quarters, go across to *L'Aigle* at nine o'clock and stay to watch till midnight. More than that, we were not prepared to concede. And this he accepted with a fair show of grace.

My white taffeta being obliged to serve me yet again, I made what shift I could to alter the general appearance as much as possible by tying a pale blue silk sash about the waist and putting up my hair in a chignon with a bow of the same material. My dressing, preceded by a leisurely hot bath and a glass of champagne, brought me well past the hour of eight-thirty, and I heard the music of the various National Anthems of the distinguished guests coming from the next-door yacht, and a fine number of tunes there were, too – and all but about three completely foreign to me.

At nine, Mrs Stittle brought Rupert to me, well-brushed and scrubbed, wearing his white sailor suit with blue collar. He looked a delight, but a mite tired around the eyes. I privately determined to amend his schedule if the need came.

We crossed over to the French yacht together, hand in hand, the three of us. The upper decks of both vessels were hung with large-sized flags of the nations, forming walls of colour and greatly contributing to the atmosphere of nautical festivity. The night having turned chill with the going down of the sun, the

Reception and Gala Ball were being held in the great state salon on the main covered deck, down an exceedingly ornate staircase of carved and gilded wood with nude figurines of ebony holding lanterns at every few steps, down which we were guided by an extremely young French midshipman who had greeted us upon our arrival aboard.

The music of a lively schottische resounded loudly in the vast space below, and the dance floor was packed with circling dancers, swaying skirts, white shirt fronts, brilliant uniforms. There was a balcony looking down on to the floor, and it was here that I established Rupert and Mrs Stittle on two gilded chairs. I waited till the schottische was finished, searching the faces below for folk I recognised, but seeing none in all that throng.

At the close of the tune, I nodded to Mrs Stittle, smiled at Rupert and taking a deep breath walked slowly and as gracefully as I was able down the remaining flight of steps to the ballroom. As I reached the bottom, the pattering of applause ceased, and the dancers were bowing and curtseying to each other and returning to their tables set round the floor.

'Who is that most striking gel, I wonder?' said a woman's voice close at hand.

'Don't know, m'dear. Deucedly attractive, what?'

A most distinguished middle-aged couple, she in silver and black, he in a diplomatic uniform, and both of them very English, were looking my way, and the woman's *lorgnette* was directed straight at *me*!

I had scarcely recovered from this experience of mingled surprise, embarrassment and delight when Hal Marius came up behind me and touched my elbow.

'I heard every word of that exchange,' he murmured, 'and I concur with every word. You are everything that they said you are. In fact, I would go so far as to say that you make every other woman in this place look like she's up from the country selling eggs.'

'You are a shameless flatterer,' I said, tartly, but with no displeasure.

'Do you have a *carnet du bal*, a dance programme?' he asked.

'No, I do not.'

'You have one now,' he said, putting one in my hand. 'You will notice that I have written myself in for every dance except the waltzes. You will have to find some other fellows to waltz with you, for I have never got the hang of spinning round like a top without falling over.'

'I will strive to find other partners,' I said. 'It may be difficult, but I will nevertheless strive.'

He nodded. 'I'm sure you will. I'll go and get us some champagne. There are waiters about, but the standard of service on this vessel is not what we've come to expect from the Egyptians. Have you seen Sheikh Mansour tonight?'

'No, I have not,' I replied.

'He turned up for the reception in his full desert sheikh outfit instead of that courtier's rig that makes him look like a shop-walker or a stuffed dummy. You could see that the khedive was furious and took it as a studied insult. The empress, on the other hand, hasn't been able to take her eyes off Mansour and has been monopolising him ever since the end of the reception. I'll go get the champagne. Don't go far away.' He departed into the throng.

'Miss Copley, ma'am. If you are not bespoke, may I please have the next dance?' It was Major Woodford, dressed in yet another military confection of the formal evening sort. An excuse was framing on my lips, till I perceived from his steady, not to say steely gaze, that notwithstanding the state he may or may not have been in at our last encounter, he was as sober as a judge now.

'I . . .' I faltered.

'It is a waltz, ma'am,' he said.

'I should like that very much, sir,' I responded. Then let Hal Marius return with the champagne and find that I had taken no time at all in finding another partner to fill in my dance programme.

Surprisingly, the major waltzed exceedingly well, and the waltz is my favourite. It was taught to me, along with so many other dances and so much about the ways of life beyond my narrow upbringing on Dartmoor, by dear Sarah Ilminster during our off-duty periods at St Thomas's, when we scandalised the other students by waltzing madly around the common room.

The tune to which the major and I danced was one of those wonderful Viennese waltzes so popularised by the Queen and the Prince Consort, and danced in a like manner, that is with an almost continuous circling (what Mr Hal Marius had described as 'Spinning round like a top').

Flushed and breathless, I was glad when the major paused at a corner and said: 'I am of the opinion that I may have been mistaken about Kiprenski. Not as to being a Russkie and wishing to drive the British out of India and set up a Tsarist empire there, but as to contemplating the blockage of the canal to further that end.'

'I am relieved to hear you say it, sir,' I responded.

'Indeed, my observations leave me puzzled, ma'am,' he said. 'The feller's whole attention seems to be directed towards Miss Marchcombe. He has dogged the gel's footsteps all this day, as I have his. Do you suppose he means her – how to put it? – do you suppose he means her some – er – *mischief*?'

I smothered a smile as the lady in question came sailing past on the arm of the Prussian Ambassador, with whom she had made such a signal success in Cairo. She smiled and nodded to me cheerfully, a great change in her demeanour from the morose companion on the train back to Alexandria. Presumably her many and varied conquests were progressing better.

'I think one should have no fears for Miss Marchcombe,' I informed my partner. 'She is a lady who is well able to dispose her own affairs in the manner of her own choosing.'

'I take your word for it, Miss Copley, ma'am,' he replied.

Two more tunes, and the orchestra ceased playing. The major escorted me from the floor. It was then, near the foot of the great staircase, that a most remarkable encounter took place, an encounter which in its dramatic collision I think I shall never forget. And yet it was all over in a matter of minutes.

Just ahead of us, leaving the floor, were Petronella and her Prussian. Crossing in front of them were the couple who had complimented me upon my entrace: the distinguished English couple. So close were we that we heard every word of the exchange that followed.

'Ah, Sir Arthur, Lady Chamberton,' said the Prussian. 'How are you tonight? Permit me to introduce Miss Marchcombe.'

'How do you do,' said Petronella.

'Marchcombe?' said Lady Chamberton, treating the younger woman to the full benefit of her *lorgnette*. '*Which* Marchcombe, pray?'

'I should explain,' said the Prussian, with the air of someone who has just remembered his manners. 'My deepest apologies to all parties. I should have said that this is the Honourable Petronella Marchcombe, only daughter of Lord Marchcombe.'

Silence – and then:

'Oh no, she ain't!' grated Lady Chamberton. 'Right, Arthur?'

Sir Arthur inspected Petronella through his monocle.

'No, m'dear, that she ain't,' he confirmed. 'Not by a blessed mile she ain't!'

'Pet Marchcombe is my god-daughter,' declared Lady Chamberton, 'and I dandled her on my knee . . .

'This creature' – pointing – 'is an *imposter!*'

All this had been carried out in succeeding waves of increasing silence, as when a tide goes out, leaving only the empty rippled sand and the memories of past sound and movement. All eyes in the salon were upon she whom I had known as the Hon. Petronella.

('And what are you going to do now, my dear!' was my silent question.)

What she did was brilliant. With a slight kick of her foot, she brought up the train of her gold lamé ball gown and caught the end of it with her white-gloved right hand. A nod to her former partner, no glance in the direction of the Chambertons, and she stalked, upright and pantherine, to the staircase. The rows of staring people standing there parted to let her pass.

Slowly, with impeccable dignity, she mounted the stair.

Like a queen.

On an impulse that informs so much of my life, I went after her, back aboard the *Mahroussa*. I knocked upon her cabin door, and receiving no answer, went inside. She was packing a suitcase, her back to me.

263

She turned. 'Oh, it's you,' she said.

'Are you all right?' I asked.

Her tight expression – the one she had put on to extricate herself from the salon – softened. 'Only you would bother to come after me and ask that, dearie,' she said. 'I bet I looked a right fool back there.'

'You were splendid,' I said.

'The Chambertons caught me out a treat, didn't they?' She laughed. 'So did poor old Dean Sommerson. I made some stupid slip and he rumbled me.'

'So it was *you* whom the dean suspected!' I exclaimed.

She shrugged. 'Yes, he had some daft idea that I was mixed up in all the trouble on the ship, till I convinced him of my real reason for posing as the little minx I used to work for. He prayed for me. Said he hoped I'd find happiness. The same day, he went and died, poor old feller.'

'So you worked for the real Petronella?' I asked.

'Yes, I was kitchen maid at Mountcarey till Petronella took a fancy to me and had me as her lady's maid. That's where I learned all the tricks and all the patter. I didn't do too badly, did I – considering?'

'You had me fooled,' I admitted. 'Miss – er . . .'

'Amy,' she said, holding out her hand. 'Amy Biggs.'

I took her hand and smiled in grudging admiration. After all, her deception had, so far as I knew, done no one any harm and had caused a certain amount of incidental amusement. And I greatly admired her pluck in adversity. I suppose it was the nurse in me.

'Here, let's have a drop of bubbly to celebrate my downfall,' she said, and producing two glasses poured for both of us. 'Cheers and chin-chin,' she said. 'Here's to deception.'

'You are a mistress of deception,' I said, indulging her.

'Mind you,' she said, taking a deep sip of the wine, 'I nearly gave myself away on the train to Cairo when you woke me up and I thought I was back there at Mountcarey, in the attic room under the eaves with a dozen other half-starved skivvies, woken up at five in the morning to black lead the grates and scrub all the outside steps.'

264

'Life with the Marchcombes must have been very hard,' I ventured.

'The worst part of it was coping with his lordship!' she declared. 'There was no stopping him. Old or young, rich or poor, black or white – he couldn't leave any woman alone.'

'I heard something of this from Mrs Wayne Barlowe,' I said. 'The incident in the royal bedchamber at Windsor.'

'Well, I don't know where *she* got the story, but she doesn't know the half of it,' responded my confidante. 'The story put about was that he chased a lady of the bedchamber and then the Queen came in.'

'That's how I heard it,' I said.

'Well, there's more to it than that, dearie . . .' She leaned and whispered in my ear.

'Not – not Her Majesty *also*?' I cried, appalled.

'That's right,' she nodded. 'Have another champers, dearie.' She refilled my glass.

'If it isn't prying too much, why did you come on this trip – er – Amy?' I asked.

'To find myself a nice comfortable feller to look after me,' she replied.

'A rich husband?' I ventured.

'Rich – yes. Husband? Oh dear, no! No marriage for little Amy. Why a married woman's no more than a chattel, with no rights in law. I might come upon a feller who's on the same game as me. And me with a nice little property in Islington and another in Bow. As soon as the ring's on my finger, they're his in the eyes of the law. Oh, no, I'm not for marrying, dearie.'

'Then what are you going to do, Amy?' I asked her, glancing at the part-packed suitcase.

'I'm off back to Cairo with Mr Kiprenski,' was her astonishing reply. 'That is – if his offer still holds that he made me this afternoon on the way down the canal.'

'Mr Kiprenski?' I stared at her. 'But – I don't understand. He . . .'

'Offered to set me up in a nice villa in the best part of Cairo, he did. He likes Cairo, does Mr Kiprenski, 'cos it's far away from Russia and from England. And it'll suit little Amy a treat.'

'But Major Woodford thought he was a Russian spy and worse!' I said.

She laughed, throwing back her fine head and showing her splendidly sculptured throat.

'That's a good one,' she said. 'He does nothing except wander through life trying to find ways to spend the millions that his grandfather settled on him. His trouble's his mother, who's Ambassadress to St James's. She's a dragon, forever trying to get him to work. Finally, the poor pet could stand it no longer, so he fled England in the first boat he could get – which was the *Hindustan*.'

'Good heavens!' I exclaimed.

'A spy, eh?' she giggled. That's a good one. But I tell you what, dearie . . .'

'What?'

'He spied me out, didn't he?'

I parted company with the irrepressible Amy on exceedingly good terms and went back to *L'Aigle* to see how Rupert was faring: Rupert was faring very badly. As someone who had nursed children as a speciality, I could see all the symptoms of fractious tiredness that are indicative of the overwrought, over-excited young. Furthermore, he was beginning to cough slightly.

'Bed for you, my boy,' I said, gently but firmly.

He began to snivel. 'Don't want to go to bed. There's another boy over there, look – down there, with his mama and papa – *he* isn't being sent to bed.'

I looked in the direction in which he was pointing. 'That boy,' I informed him, 'is at least eight, probably more. And he possibly had a nap this afternoon instead of running round the deck all day, getting excited over the Bedouin warriors and so forth.' I nodded to Mrs Stittle. 'We'll take him to bed.' She nodded back.

'I'll go,' said Rupert, making his last stand, 'if you'll come and read me to sleep, Miss Copley.'

'Oh, very well,' I replied, resigning myself to at least half an hour's reading; an hour if he could force himself to stay awake long enough. I took his hand. 'Come on, Rupert.'

266

On the way to the stairs we met Mrs Wayne Barlowe. 'Hello, my dear,' she said. 'You are undoubtedly the belle of the ball tonight. So beautiful, so beautiful. Oh, to be young – *really* young again!' She was dressed in scarlet and white, and made me feel like a scarecrow.

'The belle will not be seeing much of this ball before supper,' I murmured to her, indicating Rupert, 'for she has promised to read Young England to sleep.'

'Give the little darling a sleeping powder,' she advised. 'Do you have some?'

'Yes, and I might do that,' I said.

'Half a powder will be quite sufficient. In a glass of mineral water.'

'Yes.'

She squeezed my arm. 'Then I shall hope to see you back here before supper, my dear,' she said. 'Your *carnet du bal* is quite filled, I suppose?'

I nodded. 'Mostly with Mr Marius,' I said. 'Except for the waltzes. He doesn't waltz.'

She spread her hands. 'What did I tell you, my dear?' she said. 'Before this trip is over, you will add him to your considerable list of social successes. Ah! – speaking of social success, you have heard of the débâcle of the self-styled Miss Petronella no doubt?'

'I've just come from her,' I said. 'In a way I feel sorry for her, yet in a way I admire her courage.'

Again she squeezed my arm. 'Oh, your heart is so tender, so true,' she declared. 'When you return, you must tell me all about her, for I, too, was drawn towards her for the way she did not reply to her accusers, but departed with dignity. *Au revoir*, my dear.'

'*Au revoir*, Mrs Wayne Barlowe.'

For his bedtime reading, Rupert chose a collection of short stories of the adventurous sort, concerning the exploits of divers fictional characters in the far-flung corners of the world. So interesting did he find the various narratives, so brief, so free of boredom, that I was halfway through the book – a quite slim book, let it be said – before it dawned upon me that the little rascal had no intention of resigning himself to sleep till the last tale was told.

And then: 'I'm thirsty,' he announced.

'A glass of mineral water?' I proposed.

'Yes, please, Miss Copley.'

Into the foaming glass of mineral water I tipped half a packet of a mild but quite efficacious sleeping powder that was a commonplace in the children's wards at St Thomas's in my day. He drank it up as bright as you please, and relaxed back against the pillow to hear the rest of that eminent collection entitled: TRUE AS STEEL – or *Tales of Valour from Kabul to the Klondike*. I had entered upon the adventures of a certain Klondike Kim and his exploits with a gang of claim-jumpers when I saw Rupert's eyelids grow heavy, his head loll sideways against the pillow. I looked across to Mrs Stittle, who was knitting in an armchair, and nodded.

A minute later, he was fast asleep. Closing the book, I left the cabin with a last admonition to the good woman:

'Don't forget to keep the door locked – and let no one in.'

Folks were already beginning to drift across to the *Mahroussa* for supper by the time I got on deck. I saw Hal Marius: he reached out and claimed me.

'Come and have a bite to eat,' he said. 'Where've you been all this time? I've seen nothing of you since you ducked out after the scene with *la belle* Petronella – and, by the way, that's a subject for Grand Opera. We should send the libretto to Signor Verdi.'

'I've been reading Rupert to sleep,' I told him, 'and talking to – Petronella.'

'I must hear more of the latter,' he said, taking my arm in his. 'Meanwhile, let's get something to eat.'

The great salon of the *Mahroussa*, equally lavishly appointed as that aboard her present consort and very much larger, had space for a full orchestra and a dance floor in addition to a buffet table the length and breadth and richness of which I had never dreamed. Every viand, every concoction of a self-indulgent age was there: caviar and lobster in bowls of ice, Scotch salmon, whole turkeys, pheasant, partridge, chicken, pigeon, swan and peacock in their plumage, as well as oriental sweetmeats uncountable.

'We will start,' said Hal Marius, 'with caviar, which is undoubtedly Beluga. Ah, I see that Mrs Wayne Barlowe has attached herself to the empress, and will no doubt be advising Her Imperial Majesty on how to run her husband's country.'

The empress, the khedive and their immediate entourage had seated themselves at a table apart from everyone else and were being served from the buffet by flunkeys. Mrs Wayne Barlowe was certainly with them, but it seemed to me that Her Imperial Majesty was more attentive to the tall figure in the dress of a Bedouin warrior who stood attentively at her elbow. Mrs Wayne Barlow caught my eye and mimed: 'Is he asleep?' I nodded in reply.

'Tell me about *la belle* Petronella,' said my escort. 'But first try your caviar. It's excellent.'

I did not confide in him about Amy Biggs, lately Petronella, for at that moment the twelve-piece orchestra struck up the new and wildly popular 'Blue Danube' waltz, so that many were constrained to lay aside their supper plates and take the floor. Hal Marius merely shook his head, sniffed, and went on with his caviar. Waltzes were followed by pieces from *La Vie Parisien-ne*, which, though not all accommodating themselves to the art of the ballroom dance, were nevertheless most entertaining – and noisy.

A cabaret entertainment followed soon after, in the form of Egyptian dancers, a gentleman who took fire into his mouth, another who balanced spinning plates upon sticks, yet another who lifted a small boy upon his upturned feet (he at the time was lying on his back with his feet in the air) and twirled the boy around in a most remarkable manner. After a little while, I whispered in Hal Marius's ear: 'I'm just going to see if all's well with Rupert. I'll be back.'

'Fine,' he responded. 'Don't hurry yourself. This is not going to be the great vaudeville show of the decade, I promise you.'

I picked my way through the crowd and up and out on deck. After the closeness of the salon, the amalgam of stale scents, it was heaven to be out and in the clean fresh air. The stars of the Milky Way spread in the same lovely confusion that they spread back on Dartmoor; the night air, coming no doubt as it did from Mansour's desert, the Garden of Allah, smelt of sage and pine, of a million blossoms. I stayed there at the top of the steps for a little while, drinking in the night, the scents and the stars, and then I went up to the boat deck.

It was silent on the boat deck. No one in sight. I went into the corridor that led to our trio of cabins. From under a door, only, shone a chink of light: from Rupert's door.

He has woken up, I told myself. He is going to demand that I read him the rest of 'Klondike Kim'. But he is much mistaken.

I tried the door handle and it yielded. On the threshold I almost stumbled over the form of Mrs Stittle, who was lying with arms outflung, and gash of blood across her brow.

And there was more . . .

Shocked, it was another instant before my gaze was directed to the far end of the cabin. There by the child's bunk stood the figure of a man. Naked to the waist he was, barefoot, wearing only native pantaloons. His hair was close-cropped, dark, slightly grey at the temples and above the ears. He was stooping over the sleeping boy with a pillow in his hands.

I screamed.

He turned, and I saw his face plain. It was a face I knew well: and still bland, uncreased, unemotional, bucolic, unsullied by the evil within. A Janus face.

'*You!*' I breathed.

He smiled. 'But not in my persona of Major Woodford,' he said. 'Permit me to introduce myself – Marcel Mayol, at your service.'

THIRTEEN

Away in the distance, they were playing another Viennese waltz. Life was continuing as if nothing had happened to me, or to Mrs Stittle. Rooted to the spot, I made no attempt to escape. In a swift movement, he stole behind me and locked the door. He had left the pillow lying beside the bunk.

I shrank back against the panelled wall, eyeing him. Oddly, there was very little difference in his appearance; save that now he was unequivocally evil. And the transition was shocking.

'I'm sorry you had to be present at the last act,' he said. 'It has to be done now, and then I must go. You see, I think that very soon someone – possibly your clever friend Mr Marius – is going to see through my disguise. And, by the way, your Mrs Stittle is not greatly harmed. I rendered her unconscious – having gained admission simply by being the jolly major – with chloroform. The little abrasion was caused by her hitting her head on the wainscotting when she fell.'

'Why?' I breathed. *'Why . . . ?'*

'Why do I pursue Ormerod with such diligence?' he said. 'It is quite simple. In the half-world of the criminal classes with whom I have consorted since childhood, along with my sister, after our mother and father – who were vaudeville stars in Paris and London – were killed together in a railway crash, the inexorable principle of an eye for an eye and a tooth for a tooth reigns supreme. I believe that Ormerod killed my beloved sister to win a new wife and a fortune. I may be wrong. But the harsh code by which I have been reared admits of no half-measures. I will have nine-tenths of Ormerod's fortune if I have to kill his son to jolt him into the realisation that I mean business. I don't think that he is a very strong man. I don't think that he will wish to die, and that the death of the son will – in the phrase of the admirable Dr Johnson – concentrate his mind wonderfully. I think I show great restraint, do you not, to leave him with his tenth? Of course, I had to kill Lavache because he was an encumbrance.'

'You are – a monster!' I breathed.

That bland, assured, smooth face expressed a trifle of consternation. 'You think that?' he asked.

'And you also killed Dean Sommerson, by some means or other!'

He shook his head. 'No, my dear. Be assured that that worthy divine was gathered in by the Great Reaper by a natural cause. If I had needed him out of the way, I would have killed him with as little compunction as you would swat a fly. But what did he ever do to thwart my plans but take a rather bad photograph of me?'

I measured the distance to the bunk, where Rupert lay in deep sleep from the potency of the powder, and then to the door, now locked. It would scarcely profit me to scream, since he would instantly choke me, and then Rupert would be at his mercy.

What I needed to do was talk. To let some time go by. Above all, to say alive.

'Why did you follow me to the *suq* that afternoon?' I asked.

His eyes, which were of a curious darkness, so that both irises and pupils were of the same sable hue, wavered for the first time and avoided my gaze. 'Why do you ask?' he said.

'Why should I not?' I responded.

He turned away, walked over to the door and leaned back against it.

'I will speak to you of islands, little Suzanna,' he said softly. 'First, I will tell you of a Hell on earth that men call Devil's Island. The island of the living dead. Known to its wretched inhabitants as the "Dry Guillotine", from which, because of the guards, the savage currents, the sharks, there is said to be no escape. Well, I, little Suzanna, made my escape, and Lavache with me. It took money – but we had money, the proceeds of our last great *coup*. On the night we left, in the cockleshell of a boat that we had bought through a double-dealing guard, they buried three other men who had attempted to escape the previous night. The bell above the rickety church rang out, and the sharks congregated in the bay. To await their feast. For the prisoners of Devil's Island are buried at sea.

'You ask me why I followed you that evening. I will tell you in due course. First, let me speak to you of another island that is as different from Devil's Island as Heaven is from Hell. It lies a thousand miles out into the Pacific Ocean. Upon it there falls just a little rain, just enough. For the rest of the year, there is nothing but sun and clear sky, the roar of the breakers on the white shore, and the cry of seabirds.

'There is a house on this island, Suzanna, built by an English eccentric in the eighteenth century: a fine stone mansion with shady courtyards and sunken gardens where lizards sit and blink in the warmth. The house is empty and in need of repair, but not much.

'There is no one living on this island, Suzanna. No living thing but the gentle lizards, coloured birds and the gulls. It is owned by a Dutchman in Surabaja: a fat, rich, stupid, grasping creature who will sell it to me for the equivalent of a quarter of a million English pounds.'

He looked at me straight. The intense eyes bored into mine and I felt afraid.

'Why are you telling me all this,' I said, 'when all I asked was why you followed me that evening?'

'Come with me, Suzanna,' he replied.

'Come with – *you*?'

'To the island – the magic island.'

He was at my side then, and taking my hands in his. 'You did not know – how could you know – that while I was embarrassing you with my inarticulate rendition of a stiff-upper-lip Indian Army *sahib* proposing to a lady (a role which I learned from my father, who earned a great éclat with it in both Paris and London), I was basking in the enchantment of your looks, your smile, the way you bite your nether lip when you are annoyed, the brief touch of your hand, the bitterness of seeing

273

you in tears.' His arm was about my waist, drawing me to his bare, muscled chest. 'Come with me, Suzanna,' he said. 'With Ormerod's fortune – which is rightly mine – we can buy a tall ship and sail her to my island in the far, peaceful sea, where no one will ever find us, and I can slough off my sins the way a snake sheds its skin.'

His lips sought mine. I avoided their touch; as lief be touched by the flickering tongue of a venomous reptile, whose image he had just implanted in my mind.

And there was a knock at the door.

'Are you in there, Suzanna?' It was Hal Marius. 'Are you all right?'

As I opened my mouth to respond, a hand closed savagely over my lower face. I bit upon that hand with all the loathing I felt, all the humiliation, the utter detestation. I tasted blood as my teeth went deeply into the flesh of his palm. He screamed with pain.

Hal Marius heard the cry. Next instant, his booted foot was hammering on the door panels, and I was being tossed aside like a gunny sack.

The half-naked monster with the Janus countenance unlocked the door and threw it open. I screamed some sort of warning to Hal, but his gaze, his whole attention, was directed to the man with whom he was suddenly confronted.

'I've got it now,' said Hal. 'You jumped overboard and swam ashore that night in order to divert suspicion from yourself. I remember you telling me in Malta that the ambition of your youth had been to be the first to swim the English Channel, and that you had attempted it several times.'

Hal said no more, for the monster took him with one hand to the shoulder, and with the palm of the other smote him across the throat; next, stooping, and with no discernible effort (and he was a considerably smaller man than Hal), he hurled him across the cabin, to land in an inert heap against the wall.

'He was quite right,' said Marcel Mayol. 'The night before we were to arrive in Alexandria, I saw the lights of a village ashore and a light on a fishing boat between, and it occurred to me that a little wetting would be to my advantage. I am going now, Suzanna. No power on earth is going to return me to Devil's Island. One day, I shall come to my private island in the uncharted heart of the Pacific. Can I hope that you will join me there?' The dark eyes blazed. 'No? Ah, well. I would not wish to force you. As regards yourself, little Suzanna, what I cannot freely have, I would not take by coercion.

'And now – the last act of the play, and I will be gone as the curtain falls.' He took up the fallen pillow and advanced towards the sleeping, drugged Rupert.

'No!' I screamed. 'No! Don't hurt him. Anything but that! Spare him! I'll go with you! I'll do anything! But don't hurt him!'

We met eye to eye, the murderer and I.

He smiled. It was more of a grin: a rictus grin that I had seen many times upon the faces of those who had died in a mortal agony.

'You little fool,' he said. 'Have I not made it clear that there is nothing for me unless I get Ormerod to unburden himself of nine-tenths of the fortune that he won at the expense of my beloved sister's life? No island in the South Seas. No eternal freedom. Nothing. My plan must run its course. The brat must die. Stand aside. I have no wish to harm *you*. You least of all.'

'Kill him, but you'll have to kill me first,' I breathed.

'That will not be necessary,' he said. And so saying, he struck me across the throat in the like manner with which he had felled Hal Marius. And I knew no more.

I was drifting up through the sea-wrack, my hair floating like wings, arms and legs limp and wavering in the ocean's swell.

I opened my eyes and saw the face of Hal Marius looking down at me.

'Thank God you're all right,' he said.

'Rupert!' I cried, raising myself up.

He restrained me. Gently, but firmly.

'No,' he said. 'It's too late, my dear.'

'Oh, no! No-o-o-o!'

Thrusting aside his restraining arm, I leapt to my feet and

rushed over to the bunk, where lay the pale, still form of the little boy. His mouth was open, his eyes staring. There were the tell-tale signs of manual suffocation: blueness around the mouth, a trickle of vomit, contused limbs.

I felt the pulse. Put my ear against the skinny chest.

Hal Marius's hand was on my arm. 'It's no use,' he said. 'It's too late. That devil has done for the kid.'

'Shut up!' I snapped. 'Bring me a mirror!'

'A – *what*?'

'A mirror, you fool!'

He found one from somewhere. I snatched it from him and placed the cold glass against the open mouth. Closed my eyes and prayed for a moment. When I took it away, I saw to my unbounded relief that there was a small patch of mist in the centre of the mirror.

'He's alive!' I whispered.

'Thank God!'

'Don't stand there gawping,' I cried. 'Bring some vinegar and some water. Plenty of both. And a brush. A hard brush. And a pair of bellows.'

'Bellows?'

'Bellows! There's a pair beside the fireplace in the main cabin. Hurry! Hurry! And bring some smelling salts.'

'Smelling salts. Yes.' He was already halfway out of the door.

I lifted the limp form and laid the child upon his back, with the head slightly raised. This done, I peeled off his nightgown, rendering him nude. There was then little else I could do but await the return of Hal Marius. This I did with as much patience as I could muster. Mrs Stittle still lay where she had fallen; she was still unconscious but breathing easily.

Hal Marius returned quickly, and others came with him.

'Keep them out!' I cried. 'Let them take Mrs Stittle and tend to her. Then shut and lock the door.'

This was done.

'What now?' asked Hal.

'We proceed to revive the patient,' I said. 'Praying all the time. Give me the bellows.'

How often, in the old days at St Thomas's, had I taken part in the grim ritual of trying to snatch back a soul from the edge of

276

oblivion, and so often to no avail? The nozzle of the bellows I placed into one of the nostrils, and proceeded in the following order: first I depressed the throat and released it; next, I raised the chest, and then gently blew air from the bellows into the nostril. This I repeated eighteen times a minute, and was assisted by Hal Marius when he had sized up the procedure: he on the bellows, I promoting the artificial breathing.

An eternity went past: surely an hour, but the longest I have ever known. Had that small life slipped from under my hands, as had so many more?

And then, the little boy stirred and gave a whimper!

'You've done it, Suzanna!' cried Hal Marius. 'You've brought him back to life!'

'Take that brush,' I said, 'and rub the soles of his feet. Hard!'

'Yes!'

Whilst my assistant was addressing himself to his task, I dashed vinegar-and-water over the whole of the small body, then proceeded to rub it hard. By this time, Rupert was threshing his head from side to side and moaning with discomfort. And his eyes were now closed.

I took the bottle of smelling salts and placed them against his nostrils. He flinched away. Sneezed. Opened his eyes and looked up at me.

'Miss Copley!' he murmured. 'It's *you* . . .'

I embraced him, hugging that small life to my breast and weeping for joy and deliverance.

'And what about – him? What happened to *him*?' I asked, and yet with no real concern. A man who might love me after his own twisted fashion but would attempt to slaughter a child, was of no real concern. 'Did his luck hold out? Did he get away?'

Hal Marius and I were together on the upper deck, alone in the soft darkness under the stars. Scarcely anyone, save those who had become immediately concerned in the drama, knew what had taken place that night. The orchestra played on.

'He was trapped,' said Hal. 'The Egyptian sentries barred his path of escape. His only way was upwards, up into the shrouds and ratlines of the yacht's mainmast. They say – they told me – that he went with the agility of a monkey, and no one dared to follow him.'

'They would never catch him alive,' I breathed. And thought of the 'Dry Guillotine' of Devil's Island and all that that wild, evil, wayward spirit would never accept again. 'He'd much rather die.'

'He reached the yard-arm, see,' said Hal. 'What he figured to do then was to leap from the *Mahroussa's* yard-arm to *L'Aigle's* and then dive into the lake and make away.'

'But he didn't – as you put it – make away?' I said.

'The sailors opened fire on him,' said Hal. 'It was like shooting at a sitting pheasant – but they all missed. I'm told that he edged his way to the very end of the yard-arm, till he was at a distance of maybe six feet from the tip of *L'Aigle's* yard-arm.

'And then he jumped,' I supplied.

'There was no hand-hold for him, you see,' said Hal. 'He made the attempt to grab hold of the end of the yard-arm, but missed by one hand. They say he hung there for quite a while, one-handed.'

Hal Marius held me tightly, as I buried my face against his shoulder and keened for the death of a monster who had loved me after his fashion.

'Then he fell,' said Hal. 'And hit the casing of the *Mahroussa's* paddle-wheel.'

The orchestra played on.

The events of the night may have passed without the knowledge of the khedive's illustrious guests; they did not escape the notice of the khedive, to whom the captain of the *Mahroussa* reported without delay. I was tending Mrs Stittle – who had recovered from an overdose of chloroform with no worse effect than a severe vomiting – when the summons came to attend the khedive in his cabin. It was a summons that invited no delay: an officer and two armed sailors enforced it.

The ruler's suite in the stern of the great yacht was like a palace in *One Thousand and One Nights*, and the khedive fitted it as a sword fits a sheath; he sat there upon a divan, a hookah pipe between his beautifully manicured fingers, and extracted the

278

truth from us without even referring to the instruments of torture that undoubtedly lay within his gift. 'We' comprised Hal Marius, Justin Ormerod and myself. We were not bidden to be seated, but were taken through our separate accounts of the night's events – and the sources that had led up to the hideous death of a man aboard the khedive's yacht an hour since.

I have to say that he listened in patience, with only the tapping of his polished fingernails upon the hookah to betray the nervousness that lay within him – and I quickly reasoned he had much to be nervous about. As our tale unfolded, it became clear to him that he had entertained at his table, often by his side, an international criminal of the most lurid hue: a murderer, thief, cheat, extortionist.

One saw it quite clearly, then: the fingernail tapping was that of a man who now saw himself about to be the laughing-stock of the world!

At the end of our evidence, he addressed Hal in his halting English:

'Mr Marius,' he said. 'You will realise that the opening of Suez canal has been a dream come true for me. You are newspaperman, and hold means in your hand to destroy that dream . . .'

'If I may intervene, Your Excellency,' said Hal, 'you may have my word that tonight's events will never be reported by me. I promise this as much for your sake as for the feelings of my friends here . . .' He indicated Justin Ormerod and me.

'Aaaaah!' murmured the Khedive Ismael. I would not say that he wept then, but his dark eyes became mirrors of moistness. 'You are so kind, Mr Marius. In return – as is the custom of the East – I should like to offer you a favour, also. A gift, perhaps? Some trifling honour that you would wish for yourself, or for a friend, perhaps?' He looked hopeful.

'This is on me, Your Excellency,' declared Hal. 'There are no strings attached to my declaration, and . . .'

'Oh, yes there are!' I interrupted.

'Huh?' Hal stared at me. The khedive stared at me. Justin Ormerod stared at me.

I held my ground; fixed the Khedive Ismael with the sort of look that I had learned from Miss Nightingale.

'What Mr Marius *meant* to say,' I declared, 'is that his pledge of silence is conditional upon your releasing the Sheikh Mansour el Abbes from his parole, so that he may return in peace to his people.'

I seem to recall that no one said anything for a while, and then suddenly everyone was shaking hands and congratulating each other on a successful outcome of the discussion. And the Khedive Ismael regarded me with a distinct look of appraisal.

The inauguration ceremonies of the Suez Canal, which had included the completion of the passage to the Red Sea, a week of junketing in Cairo and a lot else, were over.

Mansour and I rode together to the outskirts of Cairo with a pair of the khedive's Turkish guards riding escort – escort, not gaolers any longer. I rode the little grey mare Bit-o-Musk as before; Mansour was mounted on a jet black stallion, reputedly the finest in the khedive's stables; he had confided to me that his people had moved on far into the desert, part of the pattern of their eternally nomadic life, and it might take weeks before he met up with them.

'But you have nothing with you,' I remonstrated. 'How will you live and eat?'

He smiled sidelong at me. 'There is nothing that I would have taken from Cairo,' he said. 'I gave my diplomatic uniform to a naked beggar. All I have with me is a goatskin full of water, which will serve me and the horse till we reach the next waterhole. Beyond that there is all the wide hospitality of the desert. I have only to ride into a small encampment, a caravan camped for the night, a tiny village in an oasis, and I shall be treated as a guest. That is the way of the Bedouin. I know every oasis and waterhole between here and Tripoli, and I journey without maps. Do not fear for me, Miss Suzanna. You have set my foot along the path and I shall follow it safely to the end.'

We had taken the same track that we had taken before. As before, we galloped up the hillock and looked out across the desert to the stark shapes of the greatest man-made objects on earth.

'We will part now, Miss Suzanna,' he said, 'for I have to ride through the night to make the next waterhole before dawn.'

I could not see his face very clearly in the twilight as I gave him both of my hands and he took them, transferred them both to his lips and kissed them gently.

'You will know great happiness,' he murmured. And soon. And as I have predicted – I the seventh child of a seventh child – you will find this happiness with a man who is a properly-tempered sword that will never break.'

'And I will live in a place on a corner?' I asked, with some anxiety.

'That is so. On a corner. With my third eye, I saw it very clearly.'

His black stallion snickered, eager to be off. The darkness was falling over the Garden of Allah and the evening stars were glittering in the illimitable dark blueness – his guardians and guides for the long night's ride.

'Go with God,' he said. *'Bismillah!'*

'Bismillah!' I whispered.

I watched him go till tall horse and tall rider were lost against the scrub and the sand, and there was nothing on the horizon save for the great pyramids etched against the dying edge of sunset.

And then I rode back to Cairo with my escorts following after.

'It is the perfect day for it, Suzanna. Regard! Not a breath of wind. At the Press Club in Boston, they will not be able to accuse me of taking an unfair advantage and driving off with the wind behind me.'

'I think it's going to rain,' I said.

We had driven to the pyramids in a pretty phaeton, Hal with his golf clubs, I in my warm tweed travelling outfit, with my bonnet well anchored by a headscarf tied firmly under my chin.

The great edifice soared above us. Close up, it was awesome, like a staircase to heaven. And, indeed, a staircase it was, a giant's staircase of massive stone blocks.

'I shall never be able to get up there,' I declared.

'Oh, you'll manage it fine,' he responded cheerfully. 'Take your shoes off, that'll make the scrambling easier.'

'But – I might tread on a snake, or something.'

'They don't have snakes up the Great Pyramid, you silly goose.'

There was a small girl standing by the lower, massive step of the monolith: a sweet-faced chit of a thing in a ragged gown. She held out her hand.

'Baksheesh, baksheesh,' she said.

'Hal, give her a penny,' I said. 'She's so pretty.'

The child took the penny and ran off to tell her friends, who were importuning a group of obviously English tourists who had arrived on camels.

'Let's go!' said Hal.

'Can I not watch you from down here?' I suggested.

He seized my hand. 'UP!' he said.

There were grinning touts who would show a tourist the quickest and easiest paths up the pyramid. Each of the massive sandstone blocks would have defeated me; but there were easy patches where people had cut shallow steps in the great blocks. In my stocking feet, as Hall had advised, I found it not too difficult.

We halted for a rest about halfway up, and I saw the glory of the ancient creation, with the dark rain clouds scudding over the triple peaks and the sigh of the wind.

'There is a wind, after all,' I said.

'I will drive against it,' he declared. 'And you will so attest in writing, as evidence to the Boston Press Club when I make my claim.'

A crane – my favourite bird – flew past, between us and the nearest, smaller pyramid.

'The khedive was tremendously pleased with the studies that Justin did for his state portrait,' I said. 'And he's made Justin a bey. I suppose a bey is some kind of knight.'

'Bully for him,' said Hal. 'And, of course, he'll be made a knight by Queen Victoria herself one day. Sir Justin Ormerod, Royal Academician. That'll make you Lady Ormerod, and that'll be nice.'

We outstared each other for quite a while, while the crane gently circled the largest man-made objects on earth, and our guides muttered together in their incomprehensible language, covertly eyeing the two foreigners who were insane enough to waste energy and money on climbing the pyramid. And some time went by.

'I am not marrying Justin Ormerod,' I said. 'I refused him this morning.'

'I see,' he said, tapping his golf clubs, each head, one by one. 'Well, let's get this thing over and we can go back to Cairo for a slap-up tea with sticky cakes and thin cucumber sandwiches.'

The last part was the hardest, for there remains still a lot of the marble casing that once smoothly covered the entire pyramid like a sheet of glass; but there was a single path up to the summit, and our guides led us there.

Hal Marius took a club from out of his bag, and a little white ball, which he proceeded to perch upon a small stick-like object that he stuck in a crevice of the fabric.

'The base of this here pyramid is two hundred and thirty metres long and covers thirteen acres,' he said. 'And that isn't all – because I'm going to tell you this, Miss Copley, ma'am. If I can drive this goddamned ball clear of this goddamned pyramid's base, I'm going to ask you to marry me. What do you think of that?' He eyed me narrowly. One of our guides lit a cigar. The crane continued to circle around: I think he was worrying for me.

'How many of those stupid little balls do you have, Mr Marius, Sir?' I asked.

'Oh, around a dozen, I guess, ma'am,' he replied.

'Then, sir,' I said, 'if your first drive does not clear the base of the goddamned pyramid, you will continue to drive till you do so. And when you have cleared the base, you can propose marriage to me. And I shall probably accept you!

'On the other hand, if you fail in all your attempts, I shall invoke the ancient prerogative of women in a Leap Year – though this isn't a Leap Year – and propose marriage to *you*. Now – get about your business!'

He grinned that lop-sided, guileless grin that had first

attracted me to him – and addressed himself to his task. I uttered a short prayer that he might succeed first time.

THUN-KKK!

The tiny ball rose in the air, high above the Great Pyramid, higher, one supposes, that any other thing (apart from birds) had ever risen in four thousand years. It reached its apogee and began a slanting descent. I prayed harder, and harder still. Our guides were calling out with excitement.

'It isn't going to make it!' cried Hal. 'No – goddamit, I think it will.

'Look – look Suzanna! Just look at that!'

'I can't look,' I said. 'I've closed my eyes.'

'Look, Suzanna – look! There's your whole life ahead coming down to earth!'

I opened my eyes and saw the tiny white speck drift against the opposing wind, and my heart went with it. It seemed to hover at the end, but this must have been because of our astonishing viewpoint.

And then it struck the ground – surely no more than a handsbreath from the base of the greatest man-made object on earth, kicking up a plume of sand.

I took from my reticule the dog-eared relics of the love that I had never really known: the newspaper cutting, the letter that had really been written to someone else, and I tore them up into small pieces and scattered them from the crest of the pharaoh's massive monolith. The wind, freshening from the warm south, carried them like white butterflies into the cloudy abyss.

'What was that?' asked Hal.

'My wedding confetti.' I said. 'And now, I think I should like you to kiss me.'

The pretty little girl in the tattered shift was waiting for us when we reached the base of the great pyramid. Whilst Hal was paying off our guides, I took from about my neck the pearl and garnet ring that a wayward, charming and gallant officer had given me long before and presented it to the child.

'What did you give her just then, Suzanna?' asked the man who, half-known, only part-understood, had filled my life from heaven knows when – possibly from the first moment I set eyes on him.

'It was nothing,' I said. 'Nothing of importance, that is. Just a souvenir of today, so that she'd remember us.'

ENVOI

All that was long ago.

I married my Hal and followed him round the world on his journalistic assignments, mostly carrying his golf clubs. When his father died, we decided to take over the old family farm in Indiana, out in the middle of nowhere, at the foot of a low hill, by a meandering stream. So it was that I returned to my roots in the land, as was proper for a farmer's daughter.

The remainder of the gipsy's prophecies have come true with an uncanny accuracy. I have been blessed with three sons and a daughter, though my youngest, Mark, died when he was only three and has left a great empty space in my heart.

Most remarkably of all, it happened that, some ten years or so after we took over the farm, we chanced to have a small land dispute with a neighbour – nothing much, a matter of who owned the right of way through a wood. There being no maps or plans attached to the ancient deeds of the farm, it was necessary to go to Indianapolis and buy a reliable map to establish our boundaries. In fact, we had to buy *four* maps. The survey of the county, which had been carried out in the mid-fifties, had established the Marius farmhouse at the common meeting point of the four maps of the area, and that point is smack on our front door.

So Sheikh Mansour and the gipsy were right: I came to live in a house on the corner – of four enormous maps covering half the county!

My parents have both passed away. This year, Hal and I and our oldest boy Sammy came to England to visit the old home at

286

Hickleydoek and also to call and see the Ormerods at Castle Delamere. The former I found hauntingly nostalgic, yet curiously bland and benign: Mother and Father share their eternal rest by the cobbled path were Lieutenant Giles Launey and I danced to the tune of fiddle, fife and drum all those many, many years ago on a summer's eve. And I had not the slightest sense of repining, for thoughts of the wise words that my dear friend – still happily with us – the charming, outrageous Mrs Wayne Barlow (oddly, I have never addressed her as any other) came back to me:

> *The world opens up before you. Grief is not sufficient.*
> *One must count the memories . . . make your future life a rock founded upon a rock.*

My return to Castle Delamere was a joy unalloyed, for the occasion coincided with a singular triumph for Rupert Ormerod, now a rising Barrister-at-Law. On the day preceding our arrival, he had been elected as a Member of Parliament for East Suffolk. And so, in a way, a convoluted sort of way, the last of the gipsy's predictions has come true – since there are many who may in truth regard the British House of Commons as 'a place of fools who gabble like apes and think they are gods, kings, lords of creation'.

Mrs Stittle, scarcely changed at all, was the first to greet me when we arrived in the castle courtyard. The Master, she told me, had many times suggested that she retire to one of his tidy little cottages on the mainland estate; but, as she said, 'I shall be carried away from Castle Delamere feet first, ma'am.'

Clovis, the much-travelled pug-dog, long departed, lies in the small, peaceful garden within the castle confines, under a spreading rhododendron bush. His curly-tailed progeny, they say, abound in East Suffolk.

Of Justin Ormerod – now Sir Justin Ormerod and tipped to be the next President of the Royal Academy – I find it difficult to write. Splendid looking as ever, with a shock of prematurely white hair, straight as a ramrod, bright of eye, yet he seems to me like a man for whom worldly success has been no consolation. The melancholy that I had been aware of in the old days is now even more strongly marked. It is only when he gazes upon Rupert, when he speaks of Rupert's success and the certainty of his son's future distinction, that a lightness comes into his voice and into his countenance. I have confirmed the opinion that grew in my mind during those last days in Egypt: that despite his love for Rupert's mother, he has never forgotten the first love of his life – the dark-haired temptress whose portrait, for all I know, still stands in the untended room of the castle, never to be seen by any other human eye; she who, paraphrasing Sheikh Mansour, provided the means to flaw the over-tempered blade of the man.

Today, I stood on the uppermost tower of the castle and looked out over, firstly, the land of my birth, and then to the always restless sea that skirts her peaceful shores: the sea that will carry any wayward soul who chooses to seek out the farthest corners of the earth; that carried me to a land of sage-scented desert and monuments older than history. And to a love and contentment that will never know an end.